Also by David L. Golemon

ANCIENTS
An Event Group Thriller

DAVID LYNN GOLEMON

St. Martin's Paperbacks

This is a work of fiction. All of the characters, organizations, and events portrayed in this novel are either products of the author's imagination or are used fictitiously.

ANCIENTS

Copyright © 2008 by David Lynn Golemon.
Excerpt from *Leviathan* copyright © 2009 by David Lynn Golemon.

Maps by Paul J. Pugliese

All rights reserved.

For information address St. Martin's Press, 175 Fifth Avenue, New York, NY 10010.

Library of Congress Catalog Card Number: 2008012927

ISBN: 0-312-94286-9
EAN: 978-0-312-94286-1

Printed in the United States of America

St. Martin's Press hardcover edition / August 2008
St. Martin's Paperbacks edition / May 2009

St. Martin's Paperbacks are published by St. Martin's Press, 175 Fifth Avenue, New York, NY 10010.

10 9 8 7 6 5

ACKNOWLEDGMENTS

To the United States Navy, Marines, Air Force, and Army; for the assistance in the writing of this novel, you have my deepest thanks.

To the United States Geological Service and the help that was given on theory and science. The assistance rendered was far beyond anything and I am grateful.

For Pete Wolverton, who always reminds me I can be better than the first draft (and sometimes better than even the second).

EGYPT

The Great Posideon Sea

MACEDONIA

The Isles
of Sparta

ATLANTIS

Great Atlatian-Africanus Plain

Pillars of
Heracles

N
W   E
S

200 MILES

0
300 KILOMETERS
0

PROLOGUE
The Fall of Olympus

13,000 BCE

The council elder sat alone in the darkened chamber. His mind focused on the empire's dire situation and the harsh judgment that history would render upon his great civilization. The cruelty they had shown against the lesser peoples of the world was now coming back a thousandfold to haunt the ringed continent. This judgment, this disaster, had begun three years earlier, with the rebellion of the barbarian nations in the outer empire, north and south.

When the elder closed his eyes, he thought he could actually hear the far-off cries of citizens and soldiers alike as they prepared for the final defense of what the barbarians thought of as Olympus and the very gods they once worshiped. While he sat secure inside the Empirium Dome, safe behind the eight-foot-thick triangles of crystal that made up the geodesic bubble, the rest of his world stood unprotected against the onslaught of the allied barbarian nations assaulting the empire.

He opened his aged, half-blind eyes and looked at the order that the Empirium Council had written out only an hour before condemning not only the barbarians but *themselves* as well. Thinking this, his attention turned to one of the duplicate Keys for the weapon.

Androlicus reached out and with a shaking and age-spotted

hand removed the silk wrap that covered the huge diamond before him. He stared deep into the immense blue gemstone for a moment and then allowed his fingers to touch the deep and swirling tone grooves etched into its surface by their finest scientists. There were two more Keys such as the one before him—precious stones that had taken fifty lifetimes to find and half as much to engineer, and were the secret at the heart of the Great Sound Wave.

One Key was being prepared even now, far below the earth. The second was hidden in the land of the hostile Nubians, many hundreds of kilometers to the south in the farthest reaches of the empire. The third sat before him, identical in shape and design and meant to control the uncontrollable.

The great doors of the Empirium Chamber swung open, bathing the room in bright sunlight, dispelling the long shadows that had so long held the elder prisoner. The old man closed his eyes against the brilliance of the day as he heard the general march quickly into the chamber and directly to the council table.

"By your leave, Great Androlicus."

The old man finally opened his eyes to give the general a sad, knowing look before throwing the silk over the three-foot-diameter blue diamond on the chamber table.

"General Talos, I have called you away from the empire's defenses for this." The old man tapped the document with his aged hand. "It is here with my mark upon it as the Empirium Council has demanded, thus completing my culpability in the extinction of our empire."

Talos's eyes darted to the marble tabletop. He slowly reached for the handwritten document, but Androlicus gently laid the full weight of his hand and arm down upon the scroll. He pulled it back as if to withhold it, stopping the general short.

"Our time is at its zenith, My Lord," Talos said. "Our forces on the western and northern peninsulas are close to being overwhelmed, our defenses breached by the combined might of the Macedonians, Athenians, and Spartans. We must act soon or all will be lost. Even now, the Thracians and Athenians are loading the allied states' full invasion force on the Greek mainland. They have drained citizens from as far away as Mesopotamia."

"With my sign upon this order our demise has already come to pass even as we stand here," Androlicus replied. His eyes went from the general to the silk-covered diamond.

"My Lord?" asked Talos, confused.

Androlicus smiled sadly and nodded his head, his long white hair and thinning beard shimmering as the sunlight played on his face.

"We are set upon a course that is far more deadly than those hordes of barbarians we fear so."

"The Science Elders and Earth Council have assured—"

"Yes, yes, yes," the old man said, cutting short the general's response. "We have all been assured the technology is foolproof." He pulled the document back to him and looked at it. "*Foolproof.* This word seems to have more meaning these days."

"My Lord, to delay—"

Androlicus suddenly stood, the action so fast that it belied his 107 years.

"To delay is to continue thinking! To delay is to devise another way of ending this! To delay is to stop fools who think more violence delivered from untested theory is the answer to our woes!"

General Talos straightened, standing at attention and staring straight ahead as if suddenly transported to the parade ground. His bronze helmet was crooked under his left arm and his right hand stayed at his ivory-handled sword.

"You have my apologies, old friend." The elder knew that with his words he had wounded the general, the very last of the great Titans.

The general blinked and then looked at Androlicus. He slowly placed his helmet with its long plume of blue feathers and trailing horsehair on the long, curved marble table before him, then allowed his bearded face to soften.

"You are tired. How long has it been since you slept?"

The old man turned and looked at the large tapestry on the council-chamber wall. The weaving of threads showed the great plain and deserts surrounding their tiny inland sea. Their small continent was at its exact center situated between the four great landmasses to the north, south, west, and east. It also depicted the almost endless western sea beyond the Pillars of Heracles, named after the barbarian Greek hero to the north who was even now leading his monkey-people to the very gates of Androlicus's home city.

"My lack of sleep is but the least of what ails me. Besides, I foresee my long-needed rest is very close at hand."

"Don't say this thing. We will prevail. We must!"

Androlicus uncovered the third Key. "This will fail. The tone grooves mean nothing. The pitch is all wrong and the weapon will be uncontrollable. The Key and its tones will only enhance the Wave to a level that is far beyond the science to keep it caged."

He saw the look of confusion upon the face of this simple but brave Titan.

"The illusion has been perpetrated by testing on plates that are weak and old. Ah, but the crust beneath our own feet?" He wagged his finger at Talos. "Well, they are new, deep, and strong. It will surely end our world. This diamond has the ability to store and increase power; and coupled with that fact, the plate diagram is wrong and will assuredly destroy everything and everyone."

"You are a great scholar, but the sciences, they—"

"*They* are wrong. I have studied the Tone Key and the plate diagram and have discovered it will only work on the smallest of scales. Once the realignment of active plates begins, nothing in our science can control the result. If I am right and the diagram lies—if the fault lines and plates are all interconnected—this Key and her sisters will not control the earth's rage, but put a sword point to an already wounded beast. There is a reason why the gods have made the blue diamond so hard to find—it may generate more power to the Wave from the stored energy of light, heat, and the very electricity generated by our very own bodies. As I said, it's uncontrollable."

"Then why do you sign the order for the weapons use, My Lord?"

The look on the old man's face told the general everything. He knew then that the fate of their civilization was sealed. This great man was going to allow the world to have its way. The barbarians' freedom from their grip was at hand and Androlicus was going to allow it to happen because it was their time. From many nights of talk by warm fires, he knew Androlicus to be an advocate of the barbarians. He philosophized that they just needed a start to become as themselves, an advanced, thinking people.

Talos saw the old man relax.

"Tell me, what of your defense, or should I say preemptive strike to the south?" Androlicus asked while turning once again to look at the tapestry map of the north of Africanus.

"The Gypos prepare their voyage across the inland sea, possibly on the morrow," he said and then lowered his head.

The old man caught his friend's awkward silence after the brief report and turned to look at him.

"Your armies were defeated in the Egyptian Delta?"

"They were slaughtered to a man. We were no match for the combined force sent against us. There were not only barbarians from the west; our former allies, the Nubians Africanus, allied with the Gypos."

"How many are dead?" Androlicus asked, closing his eyes before he heard the answer.

"Six thousand citizens we sent into Egypt will not be joining us for the final defense of the inner circle. That, coupled with the defeat of General Archimedes by the barbarian Heracles on the northern outer ring and that damnable Jason upon the sea . . . five thousand more of our men will not be defending the second ring. The Gypos have also poisoned the Nile, so I have ordered the destruction of the great aqueduct; it has already fallen into the sea. There will be no more fresh water to our shores."

"We have lost eleven thousand soldiers in this one day alone?" The elder turned, as if by looking the general in his eyes the statement would not—just could not—be true.

"It seems our ancient enemies have learned the ways of war well from us."

Talos's face betrayed his sadness as he told the rest of the story. "Arrayed against us are Heracles, who is barely above the mentality of a cave dweller, and also Jason of Thessaly, who is but a thief of the ship and oar designs of our science. The allied armies still bear mostly stone axes, wooden swords, and sharpened sticks, but they have defeated the greatest nation the world has ever known."

"I would say the gods have turned on us, wouldn't you, my great Titan?" murmured the old man in reply.

"The past will always find a way to punish the present." Talos smiled sadly. "The sins of the fathers will always curse the young."

Androlicus nodded in agreement.

"Our greatest treasures, they have been hidden well?" he asked.

Talos had the slightest trace of a smirk etching his hard mouth. "It was difficult, as we lost thirty-two screening ships to Jason in the Poseidon Sea, but yes, old friend, the greatest of treasures is safe along with the histories, our heritage, science, and the libraries. Shipped to the farthest reaches of the western empire, not even our followers will know where they are buried."

"Good, good. Now I am as weary as I have never been before."

"You are sure the weapon will fail?" Talos asked, wanting just a glimmer of hope, not for himself but for the very people he was sworn to protect.

"It is as uncontrollable as we are arrogant. Who are we to believe we can manipulate the very planet we walk upon? We can only hope that the secret of its use will never be found. The bronze maps, the plates, the disks, they are all destroyed?"

"Except for the single plate map and dimensional disk sent with the treasure ships."

"The plate map should have been destroyed," said Androlicus angrily.

"Lord Pythos loaded the plate map himself as a safeguard in case we needed the second Key."

Androlicus placed his hand on the cool surface of the large blue diamond. "No, he won't need a second *or* third Key. It ends here. It ends today."

Androlicus slowly pushed the order forward without removing his eyes from the Titan.

"Give this to that madman below the earth and may the gods have mercy on us. I am sorry you will die by the side of that fool."

"I am also. What of you, My Lord?"

"I have my devices." He lowered his head, a move that made the general feel desperate for his old friend. "These old eyes have beheld too much. I have seen that which I was not meant to see. I choose not to witness our arrogance of science at work." His voice broke. "We could have been such a great people. We wanted to be, at one time ages ago."

The elder looked around the great chamber within the safety of the Crystal Dome; the wonder of the ages.

General Talos took the order and, with one last glance at the covered third diamond, turned away, feeling as if he were leaving a dying father behind. He slowly walked through the great bronze doors of the chamber, closing them behind him, leaving the chamber once again in darkness, as well as the great Empire of Atlantis.

The great tectonic-plate chart was carved directly into the stone walls of the giant and ancient volcanic cavern one mile beneath the city of Lygos, the centermost island in the rings of Atlantis, a mountainous plateau the barbarians thought of as Olympus. To the ordinary citizen the wavy lines and circles of the chart were but a meaningless jumble of scribbles. The only recognizable feature on this strangest of maps were the three great circles of Atlantis.

The diagram was five thousand years in the making and was the great achievement of their time. The Great Poseidon Sea was mapped in intricate detail, but the lines did not stop there. They also coursed through the entire known world, even unto Europa. Hinduss and the vast, barbaric Asiatic nations of the Far East world of the Dragon Men, the Chi, were also depicted. The lines on the diagram diminished as they crossed the vast western Sea of Atlantia and west toward the two giant and mostly unexplored continents of the Far West. Their vast explorations for the past five thousand years were designed toward mapping the faults and continental plates of as much of the world as possible, because only the gods knew from where their next enemies would arise.

The giant chart was engineered by the science of their time. The strange lines actually mapped the minute fault lines of most of the known world, active and extinct, discovered using divining apparatuses. The thicker lines were the actual plates that moved whole continents like slow-moving glaciers throughout the history of the planet.

"Are the warships fully aware of the extreme nature of their mission?"

General Talos glared at the old and slight man before him. The elder, Lord Pythos, had once been an Empirium Council member but had resigned over thirty years before to conclude his work on the science of the Wave. A maniacal passion had consumed the ancient earth scientist for the latter part of his eighty-five years of life.

"The admiral knows his duty and need not be reminded. His destruction is assured, so you may receive your signal, Pythos."

"Excellent," he said as he looked knowingly at the general. "Think not that I am fooled by your being here at this time. I am fully aware that the traitor Androlicus has sent you to dispatch me if the plan fails. I am only surprised he has not chosen to do this foul deed himself."

"To that great man you are not that important; the lesser the task, the lesser the messenger. Your station is far too low for him to be here. And if you once more refer to him as a traitor, that will be the last word you ever utter from your foul mouth."

Unfazed, the old man continued. "Shame; he would have seen the miracle our people so crave. One that will destroy our enemies and shake their homelands with their mud-and-stick huts to dust."

Talos scowled at the crazy old man and then angrily raised his sword for the chain of flags to be readied for the signal. Five hundred of his more severely wounded soldiers had been pulled from the defense of the second circle of Atlantis against the probing invaders. Their duty here would be to relay the signal to the last two warships of the Grand Fleet.

Pythos walked over to a large bronze-and-iron box. He ruthlessly shoved a Nubian slave out of his way and gestured for two guards to lift it. Then Pythos became agitated as the men did his bidding, almost crying out when one of the soldiers let his end slip his grasp. Once steadied, Pythos approached and lifted the wooden lid. His gaze locked on the object inside. He reverently reached in and brought out the Tone Key. He swallowed as he did so. He held the large, perfectly round diamond up to a flaming torch and laughed as he felt its heat rise as it absorbed the flames' light.

Talos could see deep etchings upon its surface. Strange lines like impressions or gouges that were not natural flaws spiraled around the entire round diamond. The general did not understand how the diamond produced the unheard sounds that activated the great bells on the seafloor, as its science was far beyond the mind of a soldier.

Pythos turned and walked over to a large cylinder. He ordered one of the guards to lift a large lid on what looked like a bronze barrel lying on its side. Once opened, Pythos laid the blue-tinted diamond inside with the care of a mother bedding a newborn child. Then he reached up and brought down a large spike tipped with a much smaller blue diamond, only ten centimeters in diameter. This strange spike had a thick copper wire running from its top. The other end disappeared into the large barrellike device. He placed the spike into one of the diamond's deep grooves specially chosen for the targeted stratum of seabed, then he gently closed the lid.

Talos allowed his eyes to follow the copper line to a large wheel. The teeth on that wheel disappeared into the teeth of a larger one and that into an even larger cog. There looked to be thirty such wheels aligned side by side, reduction gearing for a device the general would never be able to fathom.

"Start the paddlewheel!" the old man shouted.

Sixteen hundred naked barbarian slaves, captured Greek, Egyptian, and Nubians, began pulling the thick ropes. As they strained as one mass of humanity, the giant floor gate began to slide back on its iron tracks. Steam and heat shot out like a caged animal and assaulted those in the great cavern. The slaves closest to the gate immediately burst into flame. Their very flesh caught fire as they screamed and ran, and archers who lined the upper tiers of the cavern quickly and mercifully brought them down.

As the gate slowly continued to slide open, whips cracked and men screamed. Muscles bunched and feet dug harshly into the grooved stone floor. More flame sprang from the lava well as the flowing river of magma passed by the opening at over sixty kilometers per hour. Still the gate to the volcanic vent needed to be wider and the taskmasters' whips sang their agonizing song.

"Yes, yes!" the old man moaned under his breath. "That is wide enough!"

The slaves, many burned through to the bone, fell to the floor as women ran to them with water and cooling salve.

Pythos watched and grinned as his plan of action began to take shape. He signaled for the next phase. Five thousand slaves, these bigger and far stronger than the gate slaves, stood as one. Women threw water on their scarred backs in preparation for the great heat that would slam them like the very Wave they would soon produce. Far above them, the great paddlewheel hung motionless in its cradle. The words and hieroglyphs extolling the assistance of the gods etched deeply into the engineered metal made up of the new, hardened steel. The one million copper spikes placed in bundles of a thousand prickled around the great machine. Above the wheel was a three-meter-thick copper plate, held in place by a spun steel cable that bore its massive weight.

"Lower the lightning wheel to the midpoint marker."

The slaves moved in unison not by ordered word but by the crack and scream of the whip. They started pulling the six-hundred-foot-long ropes connected to the wheel. With feet slipping and trying to find purchase on the stone floor, the wheel at first refused to move. Old women threw sand beneath the feet of the slaves to soak up the water from the steam and pouring sweat of the thousands. Now finding purchase with the help of the grooved stone beneath their feet as they strained against the ropes, the cavern echoed with the rumble and creak of the giant wheel as it started to move. With a loud roar, it became free of its iron cradle far above the straining mass of men.

A signal command echoed and the five thousand slaves dropped the ropes and ran to the far side of the open lava gate. Some overflow of the four-thousand-degree magma caught several hundred of the sweating and burned slaves as they ran by. It rendered their flesh and bone to ash so quickly that not one of their screams escaped their lips.

Taskmasters' whips cracked, and once again sand was thrown by the slave women for purchase as the slaves gained the opposite side of the running river of flame and melted stone. They picked up the identical ropes in a desperate hurry as far above their heads the great wheel had started to roll down its elongated track toward the open gate.

"Arrest the wheel before its momentum carries it too far. Hurry or all will be lost!" the old man screamed as he pulled a whip from one of the guards and pushed him aside. His eyes were aflame as he whipped the nearest slaves mercilessly.

The five thousand slaves worked as one as they pulled against the gathering momentum of the sliding wheel as gravity fought to push it down its track. The front ranks, seventy-five slaves in all, were pulled into the open magma gate by the momentum of the wheel. The giant paddlewheel finally started to slow as it reached the halfway point. It hit a twenty-foot-wide downward-angled notch and came to a grinding, ear-splitting halt as it finally arrested. The slaves fell to the floor as one just as a loud cheer went up from the armor-sheathed guards lining the walls.

Talos observed that the slaves still alive and nearest the old man were bloodied and burned. Many more were lying dead at the feet of Pythos. The old scientist slowly turned and looked at the general.

"Now, we wait for the signal from the sea."

Two massive warships waited at anchor four kilometers from the northern shores of Atlantis. Admiral Plius, cousin and trusted naval adviser to Talos, held hand to brow, shielding the blazing sun from his eyes as he scanned the green sea before him. He was beginning to think that the people of his nation had received a reprieve from the barbarians and the expected invasion and the bulk of the Greek alliance would not come. That brief thought and hope died in his mind as the first flash of metal against the rays of the sun twinkled in the distance, just above the horizon of the sea. The admiral removed his helmet, the long blue plume of dyed horsehair gathering at his feet as he stepped down from the prow of the ship.

"The Spartans, Thracians, and Macedonians have been sighted," he said as he took the shoulder of his sailing master.

As the rest of the gallant crew looked out over the gunwales, they saw ten thousand flashes of brightness, as many as the stars in the night sky starting to twinkle off the surface of the sea. The dreaded battle fleet of the alliance would soon to be upon them.

As the admiral watched, the lead ship started to take a wavering, almost dreamlike shape in front of one thousand allied Greek ships of all shapes and design.

The lookout from above called out, "The lead ship has a black hull, black as death, and scarlet sails!"

The admiral knew the legend of the man on the lead ship with the black hull and scarlet sail.

"My Lord, should we signal the mainland?" his ship's captain asked. "The Thracian king Jason and his fleet will soon be upon us!"

"Loose the signal," he ordered with no enthusiasm.

"Loose the signal!" the captain called out.

At the stern of the massive warship was a catapult, its rear stocks removed and the front reinforced to give it the proper angle of trajectory. A sword severed the restraining rope and sent the flaming signal missile high into the blue, cloudless sky. The admiral watched it and prayed that it would be seen through the screening smoke of his burning homeland—the home soil, on which neither he nor his men would ever trod again.

Green signal flags were lowered quickly after the signal was seen from the sea. They coursed down the five-mile-long tunnel as a green wave roaring against stone. In all, the signal took only one minute from the time of the catapult signal to reach its goal.

The slaves again strained and pulled. Whips cracked and captured men from the northern and southern regions grimaced as leather slapped backs already bloody. Slowly the giant paddlewheel started to ease up out of the notch that held it.

More slaves were added as the wheel started down the last hundred meters of iron track. The great machine picked up speed and the slaves started to panic as the wheel gained momentum. The whips cracked, but this time the slaves cowered not from the pain of the lash but from fear of the great paddlewheel as it rolled down the tracks toward the flowing lava. Finally, the taskmasters lost control as the men dropped their ropes and arrows started to cut them down for their cowardice.

Pythos watched intently because he knew that there would be no stopping the giant apparatus now as it carried the full weight of its bulk down the guiding track. One and a half million tons taxed the bending and wrenching thirty-meter-thick iron rail. The great wheel finally slammed home at the bottom, again notching itself in a loop of iron that would hold it in place.

Thousands of tons of molten rock shot into the air as the wheel's massive weight struck the open vent, incinerating slaves and their masters when lava splashed upon them.

"You fool, you'll kill us all," Talos said as he grabbed the arm of Pythos.

The old man looked at the general and laughed. "Yes, maybe, maybe, but look, my large friend!" he screamed, pointing upward.

Talos pushed the old earth scientist from him but froze as he saw the great paddlewheel start to turn from the force of flowing lava. Ever so slowly at first, it quickly started to gain momentum. As the wheel turned, its long steel spikes arrayed along the outer side of the paddles were dripping great drops of molten rock as it exited the lava flow. "Release the cooling water, now!"

Above the giant wheel, another gate opened and seawater came forth, striking the steel brushes and cooling them to prevent their melting. Steam shot into the air and soon the environment was nearing intolerable. The interior heat of the great cave had risen to 140 degrees. The paddlewheel moved faster and faster. The spikes were now connecting with the thick copper plate above and generating an electrical field.

No river or water flow in the world could equal the power of the flowing lava vent. As the great Titan watched, another gate opened and fresh water from the city cascaded onto the paddles and the water was trapped when a door sealed them shut. The live steam was shot through a pipe connected to the wheel's center and that pipe led to the tremendously spinning diamond in its case. Once the steam was released from the paddle, the door would spring free and start all over again as it was dipped into the fast-flowing lava.

The toned grooves whistled their result through the large conducting needle and out into the bronze wire, where not only the tone was carried but the electrical lightning that was needed to power the great bells on the seafloor.

"Red flags—strike!" Pythos ordered.

Talos swung his sword hand down and the long line of signalmen brought large red pendants down to strike the cavern floor.

At sea, the admiral saw three large catapult launches as the missiles streaked from the inner peninsula of the city of Lygos. He quickly nodded his bearded face, giving the signal to connect the line. As he turned away, he saw that Jason's lead ships were but three thousand yards from his lone vessel as the second ship in his line began connecting the thick line of copper.

Flaming catapults shot from the barbarian ships started striking the waters around the admiral's vessel as a mile to his rear the second Atlantean warship struggled with the giant grease-covered line of bending copper.

Onboard the second ship, the great cable had been pulled from drums of wood that had been brought to the shoreline and protected with the remaining soldiers of the army of Talos. Thousands were dying on shore so that this vessel could have the time to make the connection of the thick wire to the strange-looking stanchion protruding from the surface of the Poseidon Sea. The floating connection was held in place by a buoy through which another, even thicker copper wire ran to the bottom of the sea, where the great sound inducers had been placed against the sea bottom. They sat directly over the hidden fault line that the Ancients had mapped with their divining skills hundreds of years before.

Sailors struggled with the giant looped end of the line as the first of the Greek's catapult missiles started to strike the admiral's ship. Some were aware that the large warship had started to burn; others were fighting madly with the weight of the cable. As they fought, they started to feel the vibrations that signaled that the power of the giant machine was ramping up, that only seconds remained before the Wave that started belowground sent the killing force through the line.

"Hurry, loop the line over the buoy!" the captain called out.

Finally, as he watched, the giant copper ball on the tip of the floating marker accepted the wire, and just as a hundred men started to let go of the line the electrical charge coursed through, immediately killing sixty of his seamen as they started to shake and jump. The stench of burning hair and flesh drove the others back in fear and horror.

As the great paddlewheel moved faster far below the main city, the giant two-foot-thick brushes scraped against the copper plate at an ever-increasing rate of speed as the magma current hit its peak. The wire running from the city to the sea and up onto the deck of the second ship finally glowed red and softened as the wood railing and then the deck itself burst into flame. The flames lasted only seconds before the ship itself convulsed, and vanished in a great explosion.

On the sea bottom, arrayed along the mapped fault line above the very crust of the earth, were two hundred giant copper bells that had sound-inducing forks installed inside. Electrical current running through the mysterious blue diamond and the thick spike that was spinning around the grooved surface produced a high-pitched sound that could not be heard by the human ear, but could be felt by all through their teeth and bones. The diamond created the invisible wave sent through the copper line to the submerged bells, where its minute vibrations ran into the forks inside the submerged bells. There, the sound, the vibration, the wave grew and expanded outward into the seabed that covered the great fault line. As the sound wave from the great inductors slammed into the seafloor, some of it escaped—a minuscule fraction of the din—and every fish in the sea for three hundred miles died. The now-powerful sound wave was sent on its course through to the fault and through to the very tectonic plates that wedged against each other with over a trillion metric tons of force that held the great halves in place.

The sound wave struck and the edges started to crumble along a two-hundred-kilometer stretch of plating, the force of which would be felt on the surface of the sea as a directionless wave. The ships of Jason's fleet were tossed about like children's toys as the sound and the swells grew in size and violence. Finally, the two great halves could not withstand the attack and started to crumble in earnest. In addition, the cascading effect cracked the very surface of the great sea bottom. The two plate edges crumbled and collapsed and two miles of the restraining edges fell apart, and the two plates, having nothing to hold them back, whip-cracked and slammed into each other at over a hundred kilometers per hour, creating a ripple effect that was broadcast to the seabed the plates held above them.

The first devastating effect after the two halves collided created a great chasm in the seafloor, not the effect the Atlantean scientist had anticipated. Instead of the force being pushed up and out, it went down. The madman had been seeking a tidal wave of immense proportions that would swallow up the invading fleet of Greek warships, a wave that would eventually wash up on the northern coast of the barbarians' homeland. With Atlantis sitting high against the mainland to the north and south, they themselves would be protected against the tidal surge. But instead the seabed lurched upward and the supporting volcanic lava lake beneath cascaded into a void of a great, widening chasm, taking the sandy bottom of the Mediterranean with it, and that was followed quickly by the sea itself.

Lookouts perched on the tallest structures and Crystal Dome of the main city of Lygos watched as a giant eruption of water rose into the northern sky. At first it rose a quarter of a kilometer into the air, carrying Jason's armada toward the clouds as it went. The lookouts started cheering from every defensive wall of the land as they watched the complete and utter destruction of the barbarians. As the sea started its downward plunge, drowning and crushing twenty thousand Greeks as it did, they watched in awe as the waters started to spin in a whirlpool of enormous magnitude. It spread outward as the seafloor opened beneath, taking the remains of smashed ships and men down into a crazily spinning vortex of death.

The cheers stopped as the walls and parapets started to shake beneath their sandaled feet. An earthquake unlike anything they had ever felt before started to gain in intensity and the very air became a warbled wave of displacement.

The great invisible sound wave had ceased; its crushing effect had done its job as the great sound bells cascaded into the void where the seafloor had been. However, the sand and rock continued to slide into the immense fabricated cavern until it struck the lava that flowed beneath the two great plates two miles below the surface of the sea.

Talos knew that something had gone wrong as the look on the face of Pythos went from one of ecstasy to one of sheer terror when the floor beneath them began to tremble. In the giant chamber a mile beneath Atlantis, the general heard a great crack as if the earth's back had been shattered. It was the sound of the colliding plates sending their killing force back to the source.

The look on the old man's face was frightening as he turned

and ran for the copper barrel. He hurriedly threw the top up and reached inside just as a tremendous shaking started in the subterranean cavern. He ripped out the copper line and spike even as flames erupted on his hands, melting the flesh upon them. He screamed in agony and then lifted the glowing-hot diamond from its cradle. His eyes were maniacal as he turned to Talos.

"We must get to the surface!" the old man screamed as the glowing diamond fell to the stone floor. He stared around him in shock at the failure of his life's dream, and then he slowly started to stumble forward toward the tunnel that led to the shelter far beneath the cavern.

Talos calmly reached out and grabbed the old man by the arm as he tried to run past the last of the great Titans.

"You will stay to see the end result of your witchery, old one!"

As he spoke, the floor beneath them opened and lava spewed forth to cover the running slaves and cowering guards. Then, a rush of seawater swallowed even the eruption as portions of the giant cavern disappeared into the void that had opened beneath them. The last to fall was the great paddle-wheel.

A mile above the cavern, Androlicus watched as the great columns started to tumble inside the Empirium Chamber, but the immense crystals that made up the geodesic dome held firm against the natural forces arrayed against it.

As the old man watched the end of the world start to unfold around him, he quickly reached for the knife he had saved for the inevitable conclusion of his civilization. He raised the sharp blade high, but just as he started to strike his chest over his beating heart, the city started to slip and rise. His last thoughts as the ceiling of marble crushed the life from him: *The treasure is our salvation, and we will live on.*

As panicked citizens ran from the crumbling walls, they had no sense of the cataclysm that was literally sucking their great island from beneath their feet. At first it was just the outer edges that vanished in an eruption of lava and seawater, then more and more went as trees would in a strong wind; first a wave of earth rose thirty feet as it smashed toward the main city, then the very ground broke in and fell.

All at once, with nothing below the island to hold its weight, it simply folded up like a book closing, and the great three rings of Atlantis, a thousand kilometers in diameter, slammed together, burying the intact Crystal Dome in its center as the main island slid beneath the waves. Atlantis vanished into fire and water. And as the earth settled and a terrifying silence grew, the two tectonic plates beneath the island started to settle into their new homes, fifteen kilometers from their original position.

Ten thousand years of civilization disappeared in less than three minutes, the seafloor swallowing it whole. The earthquake—the largest in the history of the planet—had other effects as the great shaking coursed along the fault lines that had been so meticulously and wrongly mapped for hundreds of centuries. The twig-and-mud huts of Egypt and Greece were vaporized as the earth jumped and settled. The sea emptied around the isles of Sparta, creating a large barren spot that would five thousand years later become the Sparta plain. The sea rushed from the shores of Africa and drained into the gaping maw of the wounded earth. The sea retreated as the coastline of modern northern Egypt saw the light of day for the first time, and then the earthquake swallowed whole the barbarian slaves that had come so near to freedom. A population of nearly a million souls was cut down to twenty thousand.

The wave of power continued through the large mountains to the north, crumbling and crushing the barbarians beneath tons of rock, to set their own civilizations back four thousand years. The full length and breadth of Italy made its first appearance as its leading edges fell into the void, but would soon be covered by the retreating waters, until again it rose from the unsettled sea a month later.

The fault line continued to crumble all the way to the Pillars of Heracles. The wave of earth actually made the small mountain range of the pillars jump and then quickly collapse back, creating a difference in height of one-quarter mile in its features and separating the future land of Spain from its African neighbor. The great western ocean started its run into the Atlantean-Africanus Plain, washing away all the features of ten million years. The great sea filled the void left by the Atlantean science, coming together with tidal force that sent water and earth a kilometer into the air, creating, through rain and smoke, a new ice age.

The waters vented their murderous rage into the lands of barbaric Troy and Mesopotamia, creating a great new sea where only a freshwater lake had been before, and would become the great Black Sea. Still the waters roared forth, creating their own weather system, which, on their march east, created the rains and the great flood that would eventually lead to the legends of Gilgamesh and Noah.

The sea took forty days to recede into the basin where the continent of Atlantis once sat. The rush of seawater crushed the lives of almost everything living north and south of the Mediterranean. In the south, the flood still followed the jagged line of the Nile River into Ethiopia, where the remains of a once-great civilization would be buried for thousands of years in a bleak landscape of desert.

The earth would rumble and shift for five years as the world of the West and Middle East settled into the vast area the modern world would come to be known as the Mediterranean Basin.

The Age of Enlightenment was over and the battle of man was just beginning. The last act of a surviving boat crew and citizens of Atlantis, the last of the great Greek gods as they were once thought of, was to bury, on behalf of a forward-thinking Androlicus, the great secrets of science and technology, the very history of a vanished world, and a dire warning of consequence of mind and arrogance. But most of all, the great treasure of Atlantis was safe, and the very means to end the world were hidden a thousand miles from where the Ancients had invented it, where Androlicus hoped that the great chart could never be matched with the weapon again.

However, the arrogance and the desire of some men to hold sway over their brothers would arise repeatedly, as sure as the sun had risen on that last day of the Ancients.

GREECE
46 BCE

The ancient temple lay in ruins. Built by the Greeks who had perished fighting the Atlanteans over thirteen thousand years before, it had seen the soldierly faces of Achilles, Agamemnon, and Odysseus and heard the scholarly voices and teachings of Socrates, Aristotle, and Plato, who had never known of the Greek civilization before theirs. Now the trampled and timeworn marble floor was crossed by the leather-clad feet of Gaius Julius Caesar and Gnaeus Pompeius Magnus.

Pompey hugged his friend in a powerful embrace. The gold-embossed eagles on their chest armor came together with a soft sound, almost as comforting to the old soldiers as a mother's soothing voice had once been in their young ears.

"So, old friend, why have you asked to see me in this place where our ancient ancestors plotted and dreamed so much? I thought you would have been more comfortable meeting at one of the villas of your wife's family, and maybe a just a little closer to home."

Julius Caesar broke the embrace and smiled at his friend as he turned away and removed his scarlet cloak. He walked over to a fallen pillar and slowly sat, placing his cloak beside him. His hair was askew, and Pompey could see that he was perplexed about some matter.

"I have news, brother. News that will astound even you, the down-to-earth Pompey, sensible Pompey, wise and wonderful—"

"Okay, old friend, you have my attention. No need to spread the olive oil on the bread further," Pompey said as he removed his helmet and sat next to Caesar.

Gaius looked at the older man and smiled. It was an honest

look that Pompey had seen many times before in child and man. It foretold an idea, of which his old friend always had an abundance.

"The old stories told to us about the Ancients, our forefathers—remember listening to them as children?" He looked at Pompey and grinned. "Not that you ever were a child."

"True, true. I remember listening to the stories with you upon my knee, but please, continue," he said, looking at the rising moon.

"One particular story from the Ancients intrigued us as boys more than most. You know of which story I speak?"

"Of course: we used to dream about the great power. You speak of the Wave?" He looked from the moon to his friend.

Caesar nodded and then slapped his friend on the leg.

"Your mind isn't as addled as rumor would have it. Yes, the Wave." His gaze went from Pompey to the worn marble floor. "What would you say if I told you I have been searching for the forbidden hiding place of the library of our ancestors?"

Pompey stood so suddenly that his helmet fell from his grasp and hit the hard floor of the temple. The noise was so loud in that revered place that both sets of personal body-guards turned their way. Pompey looked back at the soldiers until they looked away. Then he returned his fatherly stare to Gaius until the younger man looked up.

"You know searching for the scrolls is forbidden. Have you gone mad? If the rest of our brothers and sisters find out, they will have you banished and shunned. Brother, tell me you jest."

Caesar stood slowly and took Pompey by the shoulders and held him in place.

"For you and the others it is easy, your families are like stone, while mine was weak and always without the funds to make the family Juliai as powerful as the rest of you."

Pompey shook off the embrace and turned away.

"Because the family Juliai," he turned back to face his friend with a sad look about his features, "has always been dreamers,

Gaius old friend. You and your fathers have always sought the easy way to power. The rest of the children of Atlantis have always been there for support, but we cannot continue to throw money at your dreams. We share the consulship, isn't that enough?"

"Mere money is no longer a problem."

"Yes, we know you married into wealth, and I hear you are doing wonderfully in Gaul and Britannia, and that alone should be enough—but not with you, Gaius, wealth isn't what you seek. Do not look so shocked. You may fool the rest of our brothers and sisters, but this is me, old friend, I know what it is you seek, and this quest will lead to your destruction."

"I have many soldiers seeking out the scrolls of our people, and now I have knowledge of where they were hidden." Caesar walked a few paces and then turned. "We are allied not only by marriage and blood but by power. With the tales that were told about the power of the Wave we could rule all the earth, bring all mankind together for—"

"The first family of man will not abide this, Gaius," Pompey stated sternly. "Remember the last renegade of the Ancients, our brother and my joint consul Licinius Crassus? He too dreamed of the power of the old story. The families of the Ancients made him pay for his adultery to our new faith by never returning to the old way, and now you, Brother Gaius, now you. My friend, you are diving blindly into black waters I and the others cannot allow you to swim."

Caesar faced his friend, the man who had married his daughter, Julia, and frowned.

"You will not stand by me, brother?"

The light of knowledge suddenly filled the eyes of Pompey. "Spain! I had heard that you sent that little monster Antony there on some sort of mysterious mission. It was he who found the trail of our ancestors, is this not so?"

"My time spent in that horrible place had its merits. Spain is the hiding place and we *will* find the scrolls."

Pompey shook his head in shame. "If you continue this madness, I will have no choice but to inform the rest of the society of your actions to discover the old ways. That will end you, Gaius; it will end *us*."

Caesar looked at his friend and then reached down and removed his cloak from the fallen pillar and swung it so that it barely missed Pompey as he clipped it around his shoulders.

"I must return to Gaul, there is an uprising there."

"Gaius, please do not do this thing. The family of man will send troops to Spain to thwart any effort you may make to recover the old scrolls. You will be banished from the brotherhood of Ancients!"

"I have more than just a few of our brothers and sisters on my side; they are not afraid to rise again as many of you are. I ask you one more time, Pompey, join us in the quest," he placed the golden helmet on his head and then his right hand went to his sword, not hiding the threat the action well conveyed, "or there will be war among us, and that will destroy the family of the Ancients forever. Is that what you want?"

Pompey's eyes were on the ivory handle of Caesar's sword, and then they moved upward to his determined eyes.

"I see far more than you know, Gaius. I see ambition that would allow no interference from the family, even from me." Pompey slowly picked up his fallen helmet and placed it on his head. "I will thwart you, Gaius, even unto the destruction of our ancestral heritage. Even unto splitting us into two factions, one against the other. Leave the Key and the scrolls in their place, I beg you one last time!"

"Return to Rome, old man, and from here on out, stay out of our way. I came to this sacred place to convince you of our true calling, that our race must—must, I say—be the dominate force on this planet. But alas, you have become a timid old man, not deserving of being an Ancient."

Pompey watched Caesar turn away, his scarlet cape blotting out the rising moon as it fanned out in his haste. The old shoulders of the Roman co-consul slumped as he watched his friend leave. The younger Gaius was right about his age, he *was* tired, but he knew that he would have to invigorate not only himself but other brothers and sisters of the Ancients in an attempt to stop Gaius from finding the scrolls.

Gaius Julius Caesar turned back one last time and saw his friend among the ruins. The face he could not see, but the determined stance of Pompey in the moon's glow told Caesar that they would meet on the field of disharmony, and the Ancient family of man would divide forever.

VIENNA, AUSTRIA
JUNE 1875

Karl Von Heinemann cursed his colleague and best friend Peter Rothman. The argument had gone on for days and he was tired of it. He paced in the study of his large home and turned on him once again.

"Yes, the artifacts were found by you. But you are being shortsighted in thinking this is but an archaeological find. It is much more than that, can't you see? Give me two years, that is all I ask, then you may go public with what you found in Spain. After all, it was I who led you to the papers of Caesar, without which you never would have narrowed the search enough to find the treasures."

The younger man sat in the overstuffed chair and packed his pipe. He, too, was frustrated from days of arguing. Heinemann was not only his friend and mentor but his financial benefactor, without whose generous funding this very argument would have been moot.

"The site is still open and we are not sure if all the artifacts have been recovered. What if," he turned in his chair and looked at the older man, "and I say this knowing how tenacious my colleagues around the world can be, the site is found and one of them announces the news of this discovery? I, and I daresay you, will be the loser in that event, and all for the sake of charts and graphs and a device? One that, if constructed, could only be used as a weapon? I daresay the idea is sheer madness."

"Delaying the announcement and results of your dig a few years is not that much to ask. After all, the twenty thousand marks released to you financed this great discovery. Hard and real science must take the lead here, not the fanciful dreams of a dead civilization!"

Peter stood so suddenly that his tobacco pouch slipped from his lap and fell to the Persian rug.

"How dare you—how dare you even suggest your work is the only real science! We piece together history from what we dig up out of the earth, and this discovery we have made is a complete and utter alteration of everything we have come to learn about the past, and you dare say yours is the only real science! The art of war, sir, is no science; it is an evil that must be stopped before we discover a quick and sure method of self-destruction. We keep the secret of the Key and the Wave from the rest of the world, and bring them together with the magic that is our history."

The old professor's eyes widened and his lips were set in a grimace of outrage.

Peter let his shoulders sag. He regretted the words as they passed his lips and now he feared he had caused irrevocable damage to the most important man in his life. If not for Karl's work with the armaments industries, he would never have had the funds to find the treasure trove of artifacts in Spain in the first place. He knew himself to be a hypocrite in accepting the very money he was now ridiculing; after all, it was Von Heinemann who had reached out to the other side of the family of Ancients in an attempt to heal the old wounds between the Juliai and themselves.

"Perhaps you are right, even though your words are disrespectful."

Karl's words caught Peter off guard. Had the argument come down to showing this brilliant man what it was he was asking of him? Had he seen the light of this phenomenal find for what it was?

"My words were foolish and said in anger, my old friend. I respect you and your work more than any man in the world, and I say that not because you are my financier for my research but because you are truly honorable and a brother that few of the Ancients, on either side, understand. We need this disharmony between us to stop, but in order to do that, it's not knowledge of the weapon we need, just the words of our people that have long been silenced."

"When do you plan on announcing your discovery to the world?"

Peter smiled, thinking that he had finally won over the old man. He felt nothing but relief as he once again sat down and looked at his mentor.

"The question should be stated correctly as: When will *we* make the announcement? You must be by my side. It was your grant and your foresight that saw the potential and it was you who came across the trail of Julius Caesar's attempts in Spain to find the treasure trove that led me to the find. Your scholars have deciphered our ancient tongue, so I insist you be there for the accolades. This can only help bring your Juliai Coalition and my side of the family back together to live in harmony with the rest of the world. The old ones of your side, as you said, no longer desire control of the world the way some of our ancestors did. The purification of the races, I hope, is a thing that will continue, but at a more reasonable pace."

Karl nodded, gracefully accepting the invitation to join the young archaeologist in his press release about the results of his dig in Spain.

"If I may ask, all is secured at the site in Spain and at the warehouse where the items have been moved?"

"Yes; the men you sent to Spain have the site under complete guard twenty-four hours a day. It helped immensely, actually buying the barren property under a false corporate name, and what could be more secure than one of your munitions depots for the storage of the artifacts and scrolls? My side of the family will of course be notified of our joint operation, and they will undoubtedly be pleased the rift has been sealed between us. I daresay they will insist joyfully on joint control of the find."

Von Heinemann actually had trouble keeping a straight face. The naïveté of this young fool and the rest of his once-upon-a-time family of Ancients were beyond his grasp.

"Now, as I think about security before your meeting with the press next week, we must have a complete accounting of all on the continent who have knowledge of the find."

"That's simple. I have a list here of everyone who had any knowledge of what we have been up to—it's a short list, but full of the very influential. Since some are from your side of the family of man and few from mine, I suspect they will stay quiet until the announcement; they are all good chaps, at least on our side of the fence." Peter smiled at his small joke and then reached into his coat pocket and brought out the list and passed it to the older man.

"Yes, this will be very helpful, and of course, as you know, the Juliai side has always been able to maintain their secrets well," he said as he pulled out his top desk drawer.

Peter nodded. "Again, my hope is that I didn't hurt you too much with my unthinking and very harsh words. You are a patriot for all the family, all Aryans, to emulate and I—"

His words froze in his mouth as he watched Karl raise a small pistol and point it at him.

"I have no animosity toward you for the things you said; I am only sorry you didn't listen to reason, Peter. Your side of the family has always been so weak when it comes to controlling the proliferation of the weaker and fouler races, and the sheer disrespect for world power—it really is quite boring."

"You are willing to murder me for those ancient designs and even more outdated dreams of the Juliai?"

"Yes, I believe I am. I find my arguments have outweighed your own; the need for science, race control, and the protection of the West is a far more noble cause than the propagation of fairy tales, don't you think?"

"You're absolutely mad! A fairy tale is a make-believe story, but I now have the proof that our kind really existed, that our severed factions can bring about change peacefully, slowly, and with forethought. If you kill me, I will take the secret of the Atlantean Wave with me to my grave, and furthermore I—"

The bullet struck him in the heart. His eyes widened at the suddenness of his death, and all he could do was mouth the word, *Why?*

Heinemann laid the still-smoking pistol upon his desktop and turned his swivel chair around to blot out the view of his dying friend. He saw that the gardeners had looked up at the gun's sharp report. Then he watched as they slowly went back to their work. He was content to look at the garden until he heard footsteps rushing down the hallway. The door opened but Heinemann did not turn around.

"God in heaven, what have you done?"

Karl closed his eyes in thought. He heard his assistant lean over the stricken Peter.

"You need not concern yourself with Professor Rothman; he has gone to a place he is most comfortable with. He has joined our ancestors."

The large assistant removed his bloody hands from the chest of Rothman and looked into his eyes. He blinked once and then his eyes slowly dilated in death.

"You have murdered a man who adored you. Have you gone insane? This can only cause more trouble between the Juliai and the other Ancients. You do realize that, don't you?"

Karl turned slowly in his chair and looked at his tall German assistant. "Humorous, he said the same exact thing to me only a moment ago. I have answered him; do I need to answer *your* concern also?"

The assistant got the clear meaning of what his employer was hinting at and immediately stood up straight and clicked his heels together. "My meaning is only that . . . this . . . was unexpected."

"Yes, I would have preferred to go another route myself, but things are much too important to leave to chance." He looked from Peter's body to the large German. "Do you agree?"

"Yes, Herr Von Heinemann, I—"

"Has the equipment I ordered been received?"

The question took the man by surprise. This monster had one of his best friends and a member of the Ancients sitting dead right before him and he had the gall to ask about scientific equipment? He truly was mad.

"We received a cable from our offices in Singapore; sixteen tons of material was received two days ago."

"Good. Of course you have contracted for shipment of the material to the island?"

"Yes. I thought you would want it delivered as soon as possible because I assumed you would sway—"

"As you can see, I swayed the argument to my side. Now

get a hold of yourself, man. He was my friend and my student, and what had to be done *was* done. We cannot go back, so stop acting like a schoolchild. Get his body removed and don't get any more blood on my Persian rug than is already there."

"Yes, Herr Von Heinemann."

"The archaeological site?" he asked.

"Yes?"

"Destroy it. Leave no trace Peter was ever there."

"And the warehouse full of artifacts?"

The older man looked him in the eye. "They cannot remain in Austria. Contact Joseph Krueger in America. Tell him we are sending crated material for study at a highly secured location. I will have copies made of the material I need, so the originals can stay with the rest of the scrolls. Now, since the main component that the diagram scrolls call for will be missing, have you started a search for the crystals needed to replace them?"

"Yes, but we may also have diamond replacements from Rhodesia."

"Excellent. Now please remove Peter's body, he will be a deterrent to my lunch. And make arrangements for my passage to the island within the day, fastest possible route."

"Yes, I understand," the manservant answered. He started to turn away and then stopped, hesitating to give this cold-blooded man another reason for showing his infamous temper.

"Do you have something to add?"

"Before your meeting this morning, Professor Rothman imparted to me a parcel he wanted placed into the morning's outgoing post."

"Yes?" Von Heinemann asked, becoming agitated.

"It's just that he mentioned it was from the site in Spain, and very valuable."

The color drained from the industrialist's face. Then he sniffed. "Unless it was the size of the Key, it has no value to our design and is of no concern to us." He turned away from the servant to watch the activities of the gardeners. "But, out of curiosity, where was this package being sent?"

"Boston, Massachusetts."

Von Heinemann swiveled back to face his assistant. "America." It was not a question but a statement. His gaze was that of a man deep in thought. Then he waved the manservant away.

Karl Von Heinemann watched as the German struggled with the weight of the dead professor as he handled the body carefully through the ornate library doors. Von Heinemann wasn't in the least bit saddened by the fact that he had killed for what he believed would be the alteration of world power. The situation dictated harshness. He could never allow the fools outside the Juliai to know that at least one of the old tales was fact.

Karl stood and made his way to the large world map hanging in a magnificent gilded frame on the wall. He placed his hands behind his back, then rocked on his heels and back again. He couldn't help but wonder if the parcel Peter had sent to the United States happened to be the source of where the Atlantean Keys were buried. Then he shook his head to clear it of his paranoia as his eyes fell on the lone red-topped pin stuck in the map by a small group of Pacific islands where his and the Coalition's work would take place in the coming years. He smiled at the name indicated, a small island known only for its export of pepper seeds in the East Java Sea.

He spoke the name written in English on the world map, letting it roll off his tongue repeatedly until he thought he had the pronunciation correct: "Krakatau."

In just eight short years, in 1883, the island's name would be synonymous with complete and utter destruction to any person saying it: *Krakatoa*.

HONOLULU, HAWAII, 1941

Lieutenant JG Charles Keeler knew that the men standing in front of him were not the real menace. The antagonist, or the *real* bad guy, as the movie serials would say, was in the chair in the far corner, bathed in shadow. The man had not moved since he had been brought into the small store in downtown Oahu. The tape holding his mouth closed was making him sweat even more than were the serious-looking men before him. It was as if he could not breathe adequately through his nose to maintain his hold on consciousness.

He heard the man in the shadows clear his throat. In the dimly lit room the young lieutenant couldn't see the nod of the man's head toward one of the brutes standing in front of him. Then one of the men reached out and pulled the tape from his mouth. The pain was sudden but was something the lieutenant could handle. He had expected it. He did his best to give the giant of a man the appropriate glare of rage. The brute only smiled and nodded, as if he understood.

"Your father, he sent you a package three weeks ago, yes?"

The naval officer tried his best to penetrate the shadow where the voice had escaped. He shook his head and tried to clear it. The chloroform used to subdue him earlier was still clouding his mind, but not as much as these men might have believed. He knew he had to fight for time to understand what this was all about.

"I will inquire only once more. Your father sent you a package three weeks ago, yes?"

The man in the shadows crossed his legs, the only part of him to emerge from the darkness since the lieutenant had regained consciousness. The young man wanted to smile. The mysterious man was actually wearing spats on his shoes. Who wore spats anymore? He cleared his throat instead of allowing the smile to cross his face.

"My father lives in Boston. . . . I . . . I haven't received anything from him in five months."

Silence.

The man who had ripped the tape from his mouth took two steps behind the chair, and without warning a flare of excruciating pain shot from the ring finger of his right hand to his elbow.

The young lieutenant let out a scream. Then, as he managed to open his eyes, he saw that the large man was holding something up for him to see. It was his finger, and on the finger was his Annapolis ring, class of 1938. The ring was removed, the finger thrown unceremoniously into his lap. The man who had so deftly cut his finger off placed the ring on the little finger of his own left hand, then he held it up to the dim overhead light and admired it.

"Now, Lieutenant, I will go through the bother of asking again. Your father sent you a package three weeks ago. Yes?"

"My father and I don't speak."

"Yes, we know the family history, young man. He was not too pleased with your choice of careers. Nonetheless, he entrusted to you a package. Now, are going to confirm to us you received this package?"

Keeler lowered his face to stare at the bare concrete floor. He heard the honking of horns and curses of servicemen as they passed on the street above. How he wished he were among them right at this moment.

"Mr. Weiss, please remove his thumb. That should effectively end Mr. Keeler's naval career."

The white class-A navy uniform jacket seemed to close around him like an anaconda. It grew tighter as the large man moved toward him.

"Yes . . . *Yes!* He sent the package to me!"

"There, that wasn't at all difficult, now was it, Lieutenant."

The boy lowered his chin to his chest. He had failed his father and the family once again.

He heard the man stand up and then finally step from the dark shadow in the corner.

The man was small. He wore a dark suit with very expensive lines. His dark, oiled hair was impeccably combed straight back with the part slightly left of center.

"If it will ease your mind, Lieutenant, your father will never learn of your failure here tonight. He is dead. Your younger brother would have joined him for his journey, but he was off at school. His death will wait."

He heard the words said in their German accent, but they failed to hit home for a moment. He looked up at the approaching man and narrowed his eyes to mere slits, forcing away his tears of frustration and physical pain.

"What?"

The small man stopped and looked down at him, his features very serious. "I said he is dead. Tortured until he admitted sending to you the item we have sought for sixty years."

"What . . . what are you talking about—what item?" the boy hissed.

"Oh, that's right, you were a wayward boy and not privy to certain aspects of your father's more . . . secretive activities. However, that is unimportant. What he has sent to you will be in our hands momentarily, and his death will be but a footnote in the history books."

The man walked over, poured a glass of water, then turned to his captive. The boy looked at the clear glass and tried to swallow. He was thirsty, had been since he had been snatched off the street hours before. The small well-dressed man nodded to the two thugs, and then he felt his hands being untied; but instead of relief at his sudden freedom another bolt of pain shot through his hand as blood rushed to the open wound. He pulled his arm forward and clutched his hand.

"Mr. Krueger, assist the lieutenant."

His right hand was roughly pulled away from his body and a white cloth was wrapped around the stub where his ring finger had been.

"There you go. Now drink this." The water glass was held out before him and he took it and swallowed the cool liquid in three large gulps.

"Now, one more question and Mr. Wagoner and Mr. Krueger will show you to the door, Lieutenant. Where is the package that contains the bronze plate map? It has hieroglyphs you most assuredly could not understand."

Keeler knew he was a dead man. However, he *did* know something that was going to give him one last defiant punch. His father had trusted him far more than people knew.

"It's in a safe aboard my ship." The boy smiled, this time wide and knowing. Then he grew serious and looked at the small man. "I don't know about fashion in Hitler-land, pal, but no one wears spats anymore—kraut!"

"One more time, you grinning fool: where is the plate map?"

"Somewhere you'll never get to it," the boy said, his smile growing.

The small man nodded and the lieutenant was pulled to his feet.

"You'll take us to the harbor and point out which vessel it is, and then we'll see if the map is out of our reach."

"Fuck off, Nazi. I'm not telling you a damn thing."

"Young man, this may surprise you, but I am not in the employ of the Nazi regime. I am German, as you know. However, nationality has nothing to do with us. Our goals, while similar to Herr Hitler's, are far grander."

"To me, you're just one step removed from my father; you both share the arrogance of class."

The man smiled and then looked as if he had decided something.

"My organization has many members, the likes of which may even be high up in your own government. Even your father's people share some of our ancient ideologies. To compare Hitler to us or even to your father's people? My dear boy, don't make me laugh." He leaned closer to the American. "Without us, that fool in Berlin would never have made it to power." He straightened. "I am through being gentle. What ship?"

This time the large man enthusiastically went to work on Keeler.

An hour later, a large car pulled into a secluded area across from Ford Island inside Pearl Harbor Naval Base.

There were two ships anchored at the end of the very long line of warships at battleship row. A smaller vessel was silhouetted in the starlight next to a second, much larger ship, whose graceful lines and majestic towers silhouetted against the setting moon made her glimmer in the darkness.

Krüeger examined several photos of American warships. "Is that it?" he asked.

"No, that's the repair ship, *Vestal*. The vessel we seek is the larger one to her starboard beam," said the man known as Weiss.

"That foolish American attorney was far wiser than we anticipated, sending the plate map here to his wayward son, and then that smart bastard placing it in his captain's custody, very resourceful indeed."

The German closed his eyes for a second and then opened them and looked into the harbor. He was looking at one of the most famous ships in the world, many times serving as the flagship of the Pacific Fleet. He continued to watch as more laughing and joking American sailors rounded her stern in a whaleboat to board after a night of drinking. His jaw muscles clenched as the last words of the American naval officer echoed in his head:

"It was sent to me, but I was directed to give it to my captain, so good luck getting to it, asshole," the tough American lieutenant had said through his toothless and bloody mouth, and the words had mocked the German to no end, *"because it's in the captain's safe."*

The small man angrily looked at his watch. It was close to four thirty in the morning; the date was now December 7, 1941. As he looked up at the large ship with her graceful lines, he knew he had a difficult job ahead of him in order to recover the plate map, which described the hiding place of the control Key to the weapon.

He had to find a way to board that ship and get what was in the captain's safe. He watched the drunken sailors laughing and talking loudly that Sunday morning, their voices bouncing lazily along the quiet harbor over the one-mile distance.

As he watched the sailors, he hit on a plan to board the USS *Arizona.* The sun had been up for two hours, and it took the three men every bit of those frustrating hours to secure a uniform with the correct rank. The German-born ex-commando Krueger was wearing the uniform of a lieutenant and had successfully boarded a whaleboat that was making its rounds of battleship row. Krueger disembarked with the *Arizona* crew.

"Hey, Lieutenant!"

The German froze just three steps onto the teak deck of the *Arizona.*

"Forget something?"

The German felt the weight of the Luger tucked into his

pants and under his tunic, and with a deep breath he turned to the man who had spoken.

The officer of the deck was eyeing him, hands on his hips. The German knew that he had somehow erred as he was looking at a lieutenant junior grade, a full rank below his own stolen status. He looked around as other sailors clambered up the gangway. He watched as they saluted toward the back of the great ship and then turned and saluted the officer of the deck. Krueger quickly deduced where he had gone wrong.

He swallowed and with a determined stagger, feigning drunkenness, turned to the stern of *Arizona* and sloppily saluted the flag, then turned to the officer of the deck and saluted him.

The salute was returned.

"Now I advise you to get below, sir, before someone that outranks us both sees your condition." The officer looked at his watch. "Ten minutes until reveille, Lieutenant. I'd move it if I were you."

Krueger looked at his watch as if he cared and saw that it was ten minutes until eight. Then he nodded and ducked into the nearest hatchway.

The officer of the deck didn't think it strange that he hadn't recognized the drunken lieutenant; after all, he had been onboard for only a week before he'd drawn OD duty. Still, he turned and looked after the figure as he disappeared.

Krueger had asked two passing sailors the way to officer's country. After looking at him strangely, they sent him in the right direction. When he found the right deck and the right cabin, he was not shocked to see a U.S. Marine guard standing at parade rest to the right of the door. He swallowed and made his way forward just as the bugle sounded for reveille up on deck. He walked toward the marine, who chanced a look down at his watch and didn't see the German reach for his Luger.

"Silence will see you through this morning, Corporal. Now, hands away from your weapon, please."

"Listen, mac, this ain't too goddamn funny. The captain's liable to—"

"Open the door, please."

"Isn't happening, lieutenant. Now quit being a wise guy and put that German peashooter away before you get us both in hot water."

Krueger had had enough. He reached out and slammed the Luger into the corporal's head, and before the stunned marine could fall he reached out, twisted the knob, and let the door fly open, using the weight of the slumping man.

As he stepped over the fallen marine, he was stunned to see the occupant of the cabin sitting at his small desk, fully dressed. What was worse was the fact that he had a Colt .45 pointed right at his chest.

The German slowly brought up his weapon, but the captain of the *Arizona* raised an eyebrow, indicating that it would be the last move he would ever make.

"You knew?"

The man sitting at the desk in his sparkling white uniform waved the German farther into the cabin, his eyes moving only when the young marine moaned on the floor. Then his eyes darted back to the intruder.

"Franklin Van Valkenburg, Captain, BB-39, USS *Arizona*. That package was addressed to me, and the boy's father used his son to deliver it."

"You're one of them?"

"Where is young Lieutenant Keeler?"

The German said nothing.

"I assume you killed him."

Still the German commando said nothing. Van Valkenburg cocked the .45.

"If I may explain, Captain?" the German stammered.

"No need. Your group tracked the plate map to Massachusetts and then through the torture of the boy's father you traced the package to this very ship."

"You must let me—"

"Explain? Let me take a stab at it to see if my brothers and sisters have informed me correctly. You are about to say you're here to make sure Herr Hitler and his cronies don't get the plate map and then the Atlantean Key. That your Coalition is pulling out of this mess started by the man you placed into power." Van Valkenburg smiled. "Am I warm?"

The large commando allowed his jaw to fall open.

"Who are you?"

Van Valkenburg smiled.

He tapped the chart and maps on the table with his free hand. "I have a passion for old maps and such. It took me a long while to figure out the plate map and its extraordinary features. It is far beyond any technology we have today." Again he smiled. "I have the very location of the Key your people are seeking and my former associates are trying to hide, right here on this map and chart. Navigation and maps are my hobby and I just couldn't resist. Too bad; you could have delivered this on a silver platter to your masters."

Suddenly loud sirens started to wail across the harbor and the ship came to life with battle stations called over the loudspeakers. The battleship was rocked violently just as the German commando brought up his weapon. Captain Van Valkenburg was faster and steadier. His shot caught the man squarely between the eyes and he fell across the marine guard. Just as he fired, the captain heard loud explosions out in the bay. Then, without warning, the *Arizona* was rocked by an explosion.

The captain quickly pulled the map and charts from his desk and made his way to the bulkhead. He folded them and placed them in a waterproof case, then quickly dialed the combination and opened his personal safe. He made sure the oil-cloth wrapping the plate map was secure before he placed the map case in beside it. He was sorely tempted to remove it and keep it on his person and then tear to pieces his map and charts of Ethiopia, but decided against it. He quickly closed the thick steel door and then made his way up to the bridge.

Ten minutes later, a group of high-altitude Nakajima "Kate" bombers made their way over Pearl Harbor. The Japanese pilots had been practicing for months on silhouettes of ships just like the *Arizona*. By the time Van Valkenburg made it to the bridge and started to give orders for the defense of his ship, several torpedoes had already struck her, along with three bombs.

However, the killing blow came from a redesigned naval artillery shell. A 1,760-pound bomb made its way from the third "Kate" in line and traveled three thousand feet down. The bomb penetrated the deck just to the right of the number-two gun turret. The armor-piercing bomb traveled through several decks, finally lodging in the companionway just outside the *Arizona*'s forward powder magazine.

The resulting detonation lifted the great ship's bow into the air, completely separating her teak deck from her armor. The internal explosion ripped through her as if she were made of tin, taking nearly her entire compliment of crew with her in a death that would rock the world and incite American passions for years to come.

Captain Van Valkenburg never made it back to his cabin and the safe that contained the whereabouts of the Key. He died on the bridge of his ship, knowing that the secret of the Ancients would go down with the *Arizona*. Of the 1,177 men of the great warship, fewer than 200 survived, and not one of them knew of the great secret taken with her to the muddy bottom of Pearl Harbor, on December 7, 1941.

BERLIN, GERMANY
APRIL 28, 1945

The Brit and the American, wearing the uniforms of Waffen-SS colonels, waited beside a bombed out building three hundred yards away from the German chancellery. The artillery barrage was relentless. The Russian army had just closed the circle of death that very morning. Berlin was now surrounded by the whole of the Red Army, and the order of the day was to smash the German capital until no stone stood upright.

"Maybe Moeller and Ivan got the hell blown out of them," said the American as he ducked back behind a wall of fallen masonry just as a shell burst in the road a hundred yards away.

"We'll know in about thirty seconds. The barrage should lift to our right. That's when they should show," the Londoner said as he looked at his wristwatch.

"This is a lot of risk just to deliver a message to a dead man, if you ask me."

The Englishman smirked as he looked from his watch to Harold Tomlinson, his American counterpart in this madness. "Ours is not to wonder why . . ."

"Don't hand me that 'do or die' crap. Our part in this little war ended when we pulled out in 1941."

Suddenly the shelling lessened enough that they heard the sound of a motorcycle winding its way toward them.

"Right on time. Bloody amazing coordination if I do say so myself," Gregory Smythe said as he spied the motorcycle with a sidecar attached approaching them erratically.

As the driver and rider stopped and ran for cover, the artillery barrage started up again, shattering buildings and tearing into the last of the German home guard.

"Someday I hope someone explains to us how the Coalition Council pulled off this little stunt," the American said as he hurriedly waved the Russian and German to the protective side of the broken wall.

"Friends in high places, I imagine, even in the Soviet army," Paul Moeller said as he slumped against the wall. "But that didn't stop those German children and old men from shooting at us."

"Viktor Dolyevski, when we enter the bunker, may I suggest that you not utter a word. I think even the slightest Russian accent may set these fools off. Our masters may think we are expendable, but I do not."

The big Russian just nodded at Smythe as he placed his black helmet on his head and slapped at some of the dust he had gathered on the ride through the lines.

"Well, gentlemen, this way to the chancellery," Smythe said as he gestured to his left.

The four counterfeit officers were led into the alcove 130 feet below the chancellery building. A sour smell permeated the inducted air and a mildewed presence hung in front of the men like an angry ghost.

A colonel who had a decidedly skeletal look about him had taken the wax-sealed envelope from Smythe and arched his brow, and then had quickly ordered the Coalition visitors to be disarmed. As they were unceremoniously searched and prodded by the overly large SS guards, the four men could hear the sound of drunken laughter coming from somewhere in the back of the cavernous bunker.

"What could have been, reduced to this," Smythe said sadly, as he looked around the sparsely appointed waiting room.

Before anyone could answer the Englishman's comment, the SS colonel returned and smartly clicked his polished heels together and half bowed. Behind him stood a short man in a gray, very plain uniform. He was hatless and his hair had been oiled so heavily that it shone brightly under the harsh bulbs hanging from the cement ceiling. Behind him was a skinny soul who had the face of a ferret. This man was of course recognizable not only to the visitors in the room but to most people the world over. Joseph Goebbels, Hitler's Minister of Propaganda, was sneering at the men before him.

"I must know what it is you are here to see the führer about," he demanded, looking from one face to the other. His eyes lingered upon the countenance of Dolyevski a moment longer than on the American, the Brit, or the German.

The smell of cologne was thick in the air and radiated from Goebbels, but it was the underlying smell of sweat and fear that was sickening above all else.

"We are not here to talk with the likes of you, Herr Minister, but must speak with that fool you call—"

The Englishman held a hand up to the American's face to silence him.

"Our business is with your führer, no one else," Smythe said, shooting Tomlinson a withering look.

Goebbels looked at the American with disdain.

"This man will take you to him," he said as he stepped aside, the movement hampered by his clubfoot. "But make no mistake: your business here will change nothing."

The four representatives of the Coalition exchanged amused looks.

"My name is Boorman. Will you gentlemen follow me, please." He gestured for the men to follow him.

The two secretaries outside the single door looked as if it were a normal workday. They did not flinch when a woman located somewhere in the labyrinthe depths of the bunker screamed. Both secretaries looked up, not with smiles but with nods at Boorman.

"You may go right in. He is very pleased the representatives of the Coalition have arrived," said Traudle Junge, the younger of the two secretaries.

The American looked at the not-too-bad-looking woman for a moment and smiled. She just stared at him until he became self-conscious and followed the others.

Before Boorman had a chance to open the thick door, another woman opened it, hurried out, and smiled as she passed the five men. Her blond hair was perfectly coiffed and her makeup was impeccable.

"Excuse me, gentlemen," she said as she fluttered her thick lashes and moved off to confer with Hitler's secretaries. Eva Braun did not give the visitors so much as a curious second look.

The four men entered the antechamber of Hitler's personal quarters. They smelled fresh flowers and the ghostly remains of Ms. Braun's perfume as they stood rigidly before a man who was ghostly white and as frail as a man twenty years beyond his age.

"You gentlemen have five minutes to state your business. The führer has a defense meeting with his generals at that time," Boorman stated flatly.

Smythe almost laughed at the statement. He felt as if he had stepped into the antechamber of the Mad Hatter instead of the leader of the Third Reich.

Hitler was using his right hand to write something; he kept his left hand out of sight. The glasses he wore looked bent and out of shape. Finally, he looked up with medicinally dilated eyes, dead eyes, the eyes of the insane.

"Why would traitors to my Reich show themselves here?" he asked quietly as he removed his glasses, but refused to look at the four men.

"The Coalition Council is aware of your plans to escape this bunker; we have also come into intelligence that you and your people plan to make for the Argentine coast. We are here to tell you that this thing *will not* happen."

Hitler closed his eyes and allowed his right hand to disappear under his desk to still the left hand and arm, which shook uncontrollably.

The German guest spoke up. "The Coalition has ordered that you remain here." He reached into his pocket, pulled out a large box, and placed it on Hitler's desk. "The contents of this box are far more lethal and will end this fiasco with more assurance than anything that quack doctor of yours may prescribe. Since you will not be taking your U-boat cruise to the Americas, you are to take your life within twenty-four hours of this meeting, or the Soviet army will take you as prisoner, a sentence that many in the Coalition insist upon anyway. Some believe these pills are too easy."

"You failed me in not . . . not—"

"What the führer is trying to say is, if you had delivered upon your promise of the Atlantean Key and the bulk of the tectonic sciences, the Reich would still be intact," Boorman said as he stood angrily.

Smythe ignored the man behind him.

"Herr Hitler, you failed the Coalition five years ago when you disobeyed your orders and attacked Poland, bringing about war with the western powers, thus ending the subtleties of the Coalition plan. Did you think this deed would deserve the reward of the Atlantean sciences? We will just wait for another opportunity; maybe one will arise a little west of Germany next time." Smythe lightly slid the box toward Hitler. "After all, we have all the time in the world. Now, it's either this," he tapped the box, "or you will take the risk of being placed on display in Red Square like the animal you are. It's your choice."

With those final words, the four men turned and left.

As the door closed behind the representatives of the Juliai Coalition, little did Adolph Hitler know that planning was already under way for another attempt to consolidate Juliai power and race policies throughout the world. Only this time the Coalition would eliminate the need for a host country altogether to achieve their aims, and soon an all-out attempt would be made to secure the final piece of their plans by having the weapon of the Ancients at its disposal.

The darkness Germany experienced in 1945 was nothing compared to the utter blackness that was about to set in almost seventy years later.

The red banner with the golden eagle minus the swastika would be unfurled in a new world.

PART I
Thor's Hammer

As Thor raised his hammer with a mighty bellow for Germanic sake, he brought it down with a curse and roar and the world did but shake.

—Germanic Tome from
the Early Days of the Third Reich

CHAPTER ONE

CNBC NIGHTLY NEWS

"Tensions between the United States and the Russian Republic grew today when the U.S. State Department said that the withholding of grain shipments was directly linked to the Russian aggression in the former Republic of Georgia. This policy is a dramatic shift for the outgoing president of the United States as he strives to rein in the Russian aggression toward its breakaway former republic."

The scene shifted to a stock shot of the empty and barren wheat fields of the Ukraine.

"Since Russian crop failures of the past four years struck the former communist nation, tensions over the slowing of grain and other essential shipments from the United States have become a major roadblock in East-West relations. The inflammatory declaration from the Russian president stating that his counterpart in the U.S. was using food as a weapon against his nation was deplorable."

NEW YORK TIMES (AP)
WASHINGTON, D.C.

As the newly elected president of the United States was sworn in, his dramatic statement that he would remove all barriers to shipments of grain to the Russian republic was seen as a conciliatory move to jump-start negotiations for the removal of Russian troops from the former Russian Republic of Georgia. Although the Russian president hailed the announcement as "promising," he was still adamant about his statement that "the damage has already been done."

In a related story, the three-year drought in the People's Republic of China has again wiped out over 50 percent of that nation's exportable rice harvest, affecting unstable North Korea. With food shortages in the United States curtailing any extra shipments to Korea, the leader of that nation, Kim Jong Il, has been quoted as saying, "This is just another example of how the United States and Japan view the relations between Korea and the West. The rhetoric could not come at a worse time for the new president as he seeks to quell a growing concern over recent allegations by Russia and China over the unfriendly way they have been treated by the U.S."

PYONGYANG, NORTH KOREA
PRESENT DAY

The military parade was for the sake of the visiting diplomats. They had come to Pyongyang to negotiate the food shipments that had been curtailed by North Korea's neighbor to the south. The real hope was that they could convince the northerners that the shipments had been stopped because of bad harvests. The proof they offered was that not only the two Koreas were suffering but Japan and most other Asian nations as well. Clearly, this parade was Kim Jong Il's way of announcing that he was continuing on a warlike path. Begun three years before with a series of nuclear tests, Kim Jong Il's animus toward

South Korea and the rest of the Western world seemed as strong as ever. The German, Japanese, and American delegations had left, refusing to play North Korea's game.

As the remaining diplomatic teams sat in the viewing stand, bored beyond measure, they felt the first light tremor through the soles of their feet. They assumed that it was the brigade of T-80 tanks rumbling by in the square below.

"This is the most blatant display of brutishness I have ever seen," the delegate from Great Britain declared.

He and several others was about to stand up and leave, but another light tremor coursed up through the stone balcony and made him hesitate. He looked out over the parade and saw that the T-80 tanks had passed by and there was nothing but spit-and-polish troops marching below, surely not enough to shake the very earth.

"Did you feel that?" he asked the Chinese delegate.

"Yes, I—"

The first real tremor struck. The British negotiator was thrown from his feet as the crowd below screamed in fear. The marching soldiers stopped and braced themselves against the heavy shaking. Suddenly a large building façade across the square broke free and fell into the mass of onlookers, crushing at least a hundred people. The Chinese delegate managed to get the Englishman to his feet, but as he did so the stone railing that surrounded the large balcony broke away and fell to the street. The men recoiled as screams of those crushed below rose from the street. As quickly as it had started the quake ended. The diplomats were shaken but unhurt as guards rushed forward to assist those who had fallen.

The earth suddenly rolled and shook again. The balcony, with more than a hundred of the world's representatives, cracked and broke away, sending them all a hundred feet to the street below. Several buildings swayed and then collapsed. Panic started first from the lingering crowd and then from the soldiers marching in the parade. As one, they broke ranks and ran for cover. As they did, the cobbled roadway split open beneath their feet and the gaping wound spewed high-pressure water from a hundred broken mains. Fifty or sixty of the smartly dressed soldiers fell into the widening crevasse and disappeared.

Across the city, buildings toppled and roadways collapsed. The very air around the city wavered as wave after wave pummeled the dilapidated and poorly constructed buildings. As the world cracked beneath them, the brigade of tanks vanished in a millisecond. Soldiers followed quickly afterward. At the airport, several of the MIG 29s that had taken part in the parade's flyover crashed as they attempted to land, the runway splitting and sliding thirty feet from its original position.

Three miles offshore, the seabed flew up like a bedspread being depressed and then quickly released, and the resulting tidal wave took two warships—a British and a United States destroyer—with it. Then the tidal surge wiped out thirty small towns and villages along the coast, the ocean washing up ten miles inland. It would be discovered in the days and weeks ahead that eighty thousand people had died. The earthquake continued for an unprecedented ten full minutes, sending a half a million North Koreans to horrible deaths from being crushed, burned alive, or drowned.

Across the border, barely a whisper of the earth's movements were felt as the South Korean military, along with the twenty-eight thousand American troops stationed at the border, went on full alert as a precaution against the North.

Across the Sea of Japan, seismographs measured tremors that went off the charts. Within minutes, word spread over the newswires that an 11.8 earthquake had rocked North Korea, the largest earth movement ever recorded. Immediately calls were sent into North Korea requesting that humanitarian forces be allowed to cross the border and land in ports for assistance to their people. However, the requests from frantic neighbors and other nations of the world went unanswered. They were informed, however, that the Communist military of Kim Jong Il had gone on full alert and division upon division had started to assemble at rallying points near the border.

The first strike of Thor's Hammer had sounded, and the world was stunned by its power.

THE IRAQ–IRAN BORDER
THE NEXT DAY

In the haze of the evening, when the sun was at its lowest point before disappearing into the flat wastelands of his country, the Iraqi general who had supervised the rebuilding of his nation's tank divisions after the devastating war with the UN used his binoculars to scan the miles directly to his front. The newly elected government of Iraq was using the American and British equipment that had been gifted to demonstrate a show of strength for his Iranian neighbors. Two full combat-equipped divisions were in place along a 170-mile front of the common border. It was indeed impressive, and the general knew that he could crush the Iranians in less than a day if it came to that.

"General, our radar has picked up a large aircraft in Iraqi air-space that has strayed from the designated commercial route. It is at thirty thousand feet and holding steady on a northerly heading. We have deduced it is a French-built Airbus commercial heavy."

"Very well, keep me informed. Also bring the air-defense batteries to full alert."

The Iraqi colonel nodded and moved off.

The general could not be concerned with a pilot who did not know his own routes. His concern was the five thousand Iranian T-90 tanks that faced him less than four miles away.

His priorities would soon shift.

The ranking Iranian general was just starting his evening prayers, when a tremendous headache suddenly struck him. It seemed to resonate from his inner ear and travel to the center of his brain. He became dizzy and almost fell over on his prayer rug. He steadied himself, feeling nauseated and shaky. Then the headache passed as suddenly as it had come. He straightened, using both hands to right himself, and that was when he felt the first tremors through the palms of his hands.

Outside, a thousand tank men had experienced the same effects as the general, some worse, others less, but they all had felt it as a wave that passed through them. Then they became disoriented as the earth started to move in earnest.

A hundred miles to the west, the same devastating headaches and earth movement were felt by the Iraqi military as they, too, were preparing for evening prayers.

Suddenly and without much more warning than a slight tremor, the earth became a liquid wave. On both sides of the border, tanks and men were tossed about as if they were walking upon a liquid surface. The movement increased as the very air became a wavy, disorienting wall of displacement. The earth cracked along a line that almost mirrored the border between the two nations. On both sides, artillery batteries were knocked over and explosions were heard and felt as air-defense batteries were tipped and knocked from their launchers.

The first of the Iranian tanks disappeared into a giant void hundreds of yards across that opened up as if the very earth had disappeared. Thirty-five tanks and their crews vanished in a split second. The devastation did not stop there. The fault opened even farther, faster than any of the men or their machines could respond to. In less than a minute, 90 percent of the Iranian divisions had disappeared. It was as if they had never existed.

On the Iraqi side of the border, the ground split and rushed toward the newly installed corps commander's HQ. The entire reinforced camp exploded upward and outward as if it had been sprayed off the desert floor by a giant fire hose. The land situated between the Tigris and Euphrates rivers rose to a height of 170 feet before it started its plunge back to the rivers. Then the rivers rippled violently, emptying their waters into the sky and surrounding desert. Entire villages and towns collapsed and were shaken into the desert sands. The fault ripped north into Baghdad and south into the Persian Gulf. The quake was causing the newly repaired capital city of Baghdad to moan as if it were a tired animal caught by the throat and shaken by a powerful beast. Towering buildings fell into their smaller neighbors, immediately killing hundreds of thousands.

Out at sea, three commercial oil tankers being escorted by two British destroyers through the Strait of Hormuz were suddenly pushed a mile from the shores of the United Arab Emirates as the gulf waters retreated from a conjoining undersea quake. Then the giant swell of water rushed back toward the land that it had only moments before vacated. The sea rose one hundred feet before the watery tumult crushed the two warships and capsized the three supertankers. The tsunami continued into Kuwait and the United Arab Emirates, destroying the coastal cities and dragging back into the gulf more than 130,000 souls.

Finally, the earth became still.

Above, the supposed off-course commercial jetliner turned away after overflying a fifty-mile-long line of recent oil-well excavations that had gone unnoticed in the previous weeks just inside the Iraqi border.

The second strike of Thor's Hammer was complete, and the chess game had begun in earnest.

CHAPTER TWO

THE BLUE NILE RIVER, THREE HUNDRED MILES NORTH OF ADDIS ABBA, ETHIOPIA

On the quiet river, a fishing boat bobbed gently at anchor. A red and blue striped awning was spread out over the length of the boat and its occupants were unseen. Several fishing poles were lazily bending over the gentle current.

The quiet of the late afternoon was harshly broken by the sound of a boat motor as it approached the anchored fishing vessel in the center of the laziest part of the river. This second boat was painted dull green and there were several men standing at its gunwales. As they approached the center of the Nile, they scrutinized the anchored boat with suspicious eyes. They saw a small American flag near the stern, next to the powerful outboard motor. The stars and stripes caught the gentle evening breeze and then relaxed as the brief respite against the heat dwindled to nothing.

The men watched as a lone head popped up from the interior of the boat and looked their way. One hand plopped over the side and struck the water and then the man gently rubbed water on his face. The men in the approaching boat sneered and the tall black man at the stern said only one word: "Americans."

They watched as the dark-haired man slid slowly into the

boat as they moved on toward their destination. All twelve men were armed with lethal-looking machetes and four of them had Russian-made AK-47 assault rifles. The African leader kept his eyes on the American boat but relaxed when the American didn't reappear. Then he looked at the American camp across the way and saw that they were being watched from there also. He thought that after he was finished he just might as well see what the American archaeological dig had in the way of ransom. He smiled and hefted his automatic rifle and its weight felt good to him, offering up that surge of power he always received when he was about to take human life.

"Who in the hell is running an aircraft engine on the river?"

Lieutenant Jason Ryan moved his head again and felt the explosion of pain as he attempted to open his eyes.

"Boat," he managed to say through a mouth that felt as if a herd of wildebeests had crapped in it.

"What?" another man asked from his prone position.

"It looked like a boat full of Bloods or Crips, or both. Some kind of nasty-looking gang anyway," answered Ryan.

At the stern, Colonel Jack Collins attempted to raise his aching head and look around. He saw the stern of the offending boat as it was now about fifty yards past their anchored position.

"I don't think Ethiopia has a gang problem, at least not yet," he said as he lay back down. "All I want is for that noise to stop."

Another irritating sound entered the air as another boat shoved off from shore and headed their way.

"What in the hell is all that noise? Is the Ethiopian navy conducting drills out here or what?" asked a large blond man in the front of the boat. He sat up and immediately regretted it. He pushed his way out from under ten beer cans and looked around.

Jack Collins looked from Jason Ryan to Captain Carl Everett and then nudged the black man passed out at his feet with dirty bilge water lapping at his face.

"Hey, Lieutenant, this was your party, so get up and get to the bottom of this, will you?"

"This was not my idea, Colonel. I was bushwhacked," the newly commissioned officer said, not even attempting to rise from the filthy bottom of the boat. "I don't feel so good," Will Mendenhall said as a follow-up.

"That new second lieutenant drunk and disorderly already, Jack?" Everett asked as he leaned over the side and splashed water onto his face and over his short hair.

"I think it was the combination of sun, rotgut whiskey, beer, and those old CDs the colonel brought," Ryan said as he leaned over the side of the boat, wondering if he was going to keep his dinner down or feed it to the fishes.

Collins squinted into the setting sun and shaded his eyes to spy the boat from camp as it moved toward them at a good clip. "Leave my music out of it, Lieutenant; you junior officers just can't handle your liquor," he said as he gently shook his head, trying to clear it of the effects of the alcohol they had consumed early that morning.

A man and a woman slowed and brought their rubber Zodiac next to the larger boat. The woman, who knew Colonel Collins only from hearsay, was shocked to see the state of the man and his security team. Vacation or not, this was not what she expected from the man who had become a legend in his two short years at the Event Group.

"Colonel, did you see those men just pass you?"

Collins looked into the young face of Lance Corporal Sanchez, who had taken over for Mendenhall so that he could join them to celebrate the former staff sergeant's commissioning as a new officer in the U.S. Army.

"Ryan did; he said they looked kind of salty."

"Well, we just received orders to take the dig team out of here. Seems something is going on farther north of here. Major earthquakes, the Group said. There's something else: the Ethiopian government issued a warning about groups of raiders plying the river. Those salty-looking guys just may be some of them," Doctor of Archaeology Sandra Leekie said as she tied the Zodiac to the larger boat. "And it's a shame, too, Colonel; we're starting to find some very strange stuff in these sands, things that really have no right to be here."

"Well, officially, Mr. Everett, Lieutenant Ryan and I aren't even supposed to be in this country. Will here"—he nudged Mendenhall with his shoe again—"is officially the security leader on this dig."

"The director radioed and warned us that there have been several raids on Ethiopian and Sudanese national and private dig sites all along the Blue Nile. He ordered us out," Leekie said as she spied the liquor bottles and beer cans strewn about the boat.

Collins looked downriver, where the first boat had disappeared. "Do you know who's down that way?" he asked.

"As far as we know, there's a minor dig site managed by some students and professors from Addis Abba, about a thousand yards upriver."

"Well, Doctor, get your ground team ready to move and—"

A distant gunshot sounded and echoed along the river. A scream was heard, followed by another crack of weapon fire. Mendenhall sat bolt upright at the sound and Everett and Ryan did the same.

"Sanchez, you and the good doctor get back and get our team to start packing up. I assume we have helicopters coming in to remove the dig team?"

"Yes, sir," the lance corporal answered.

"Okay, move. We'll check out what evil deeds our guests upriver are doing."

"Colonel Collins, may I remind you of what you just told me? You guys aren't even supposed to be here. Corporal Sanchez said you told Niles you were going fishing in Canada, so why don't you just come with us?" Leekie asked nervously.

Collins just looked at her and started pulling up the anchor. "I'm not responsible for my junior officer Mr. Ryan not knowing the difference between east and west when he flies. Besides, what Director Compton doesn't know won't hurt him."

When silence greeted his remark about the director of the Event Group, Collins, in between pulls to get the anchor aboard, looked at the pony-tailed Leekie.

"I kinda let it slip that you guys were here to celebrate Will's commissioning. I'm sorry," she said, biting her lower lip.

Everett stumbled back toward the stern. "Well, that cat's out of the bag. I guess we're in trouble again, Colonel," he joked, but then he turned seriously to the Zodiac. "Sanchez, you still have an Ingram in camp?"

"Yes, sir," the lance corporal answered the question about the rapid-fire automatic machine gun hidden in a box of tools.

"Good, toss me that 9-millimeter, we may need it. Will, are you still armed?"

Mendenhall, not looking hung over at all, reached under a seat and brought out his own Beretta.

"Good. It's not much against what sounded like an AK-47, but it'll have to do."

"You guys are nuts. Director Compton's going to hang us all," the professor said as she untied the Zodiac just as Collins fired up the boat's motor.

"Hang on, Will; don't want to lose my new officer overboard. And grab that boom box and my CDs before they fall in the river."

"If these oldies went into the water it would be no great loss," Mendenhall mumbled as the boat shot forward.

"What was that?"

"I said I wouldn't want to lose this great music."

"That's what I thought you said."

Jack cut the large motor and let the boat's momentum carry them to the far riverbank, where it slid onto the soft brown sand with a hiss.

"Ryan, you and Will wait here while Everett and I check this thing out first."

"Oh, come on, Colonel, you always leave us be—"

Ryan's complaint about always being left behind was cut short when another scream erupted from somewhere in the bush ahead of them. It was definitely from a young woman.

Jack and Carl jumped from the boat and quickly and silently made their way into the scrub that lined the river.

Ryan watched them disappear and had to remind himself that those two men were probably the most formidable and deadly military officers he had ever met. Colonel Collins was a former Special Ops genius and Captain Everett a highly decorated SEAL, but still, heading into an unknown situation blindly with only one 9-millimeter handgun was madness.

The African leader held a small young black woman by the back of the neck. He shook her and threatened her with a machete. Her professor lay dead at her feet. His blood had already disappeared into the hot sand of the riverbank. Another woman was dead; her body lay across a large equipment trunk, and her head was five feet away. Nearby, boy was having his wounds tended to by two Ethiopian students in one of the ten tents that had been placed around the center of their dig. Six of the mercenaries were tearing through marked and tagged objects, reading the tags hastily and then throwing them away. They were obviously looking for something in particular.

The other five men were standing in a loose circle around the Ethiopian camp. Again, the large leader shook the young black student and shouted a question. Her tearful eyes never left the hovering machete as she cringed at the pressure on her neck. As the man lifted the machete above her head, she suddenly screamed out an answer. The other students, made up of half male and half female, shouted out and cried in support of the girl. As the leader let off the pressure on the girl's neck, she straightened and spit blood in the man's face. The man spit back as the girl screamed out a long blast of profanities at him.

"Dammit, they're going to kill those kids, Jack," Everett said from a small knoll where he and Collins had stationed themselves. "Who are these bastards?"

"I think they're Sudanese. It sounds like they're speaking Dinka."

"Dinka or pig latin, doesn't matter, Jack—we have to move. That girl's just about the bravest kid I've ever seen."

"Easy, Carl. This asshole has a purpose in mind. This isn't a normal crash and raid," Jack answered softly. "Look at those men: they're looking for something specific," he said as he pushed back from the rim of the knoll and lay on his back in the cooling evening.

"Our own team is here for, what, some speculation about an ancient flood washing up artifacts in the Nile basin?"

"Yeah, that's what the predig report stated. Why, what are you thinking?"

"It's just strange that these ass-bites don't look like they would know the difference between Tupperware and a Ming vase. They want something they know could possibly be here . . . or maybe in the American camp. Either way, you're right, we have to do something about this. Our people won't be ready to go soon enough, so it's deal with them here or deal with them with our people on the line."

Everett nodded as Jack slid back down the knoll, and he followed. He knew that Collins was just using the American field team as an excuse to get these murdering bastards now, and he wasn't about to let those kids get killed down there. That's what he liked about the colonel. When right was right, the "book" went right out of the nearest window.

"And what do I do as you guys risk your life, sit here and mind the boat?" Ryan asked incredulously as Jack finished his hastily planned rescue.

"No, Mr. Ryan, you're the most important part," Jack said as he reached into the boat and brought up the boom box and thrust it at the naval man. "Pick some appropriate music and cause a stir on the river and just get their attention. Without a distraction our little raid will end up like the St. Valentine's Day massacre."

"And when I get their attention?"

"Then you're welcome to improvise, Mr. Ryan," Jack said as he, Mendenhall, and Everett hopped over the side of the boat and made their way stealthily back to the small ridge. Then he held up his right hand with three fingers raised: three minutes until they would need the distraction on the river.

Jason Ryan watched them leave, then shook his head and hoped that he improvised just a little faster than those mercenaries with the automatic rifles did. *Jesus,* he thought, *all this just hours after a celebratory drinking binge.* Ryan loved his job and the men he worked for; besides, where else could you kick ass on bad people before dinnertime?

Once they were in place on the knoll above the Ethiopian encampment, Jack removed a small knife and extended the blade. He looked from Everett to Mendenhall and then nodded.

"Don't be late, guys. When you see me move, take out the fastest-reacting threat elements. I would say the ones shooting at me would be a good start."

"Jack, I don't mind telling you that this plan is a little risky. I mean, depending on two men who have just a tad more alcohol than the legal limit in them to hit moving targets, well—" He let the statement fall off.

"Not up to it, swabby?"

"You know, Jack, since the president promoted me two ranks, I officially outrank you?"

"Read the small print, swabby, me boss, you little man: when you take over, you can take all the risk."

"He's right, Colonel, you're taking a knife into a gunfight—"

The stern look from Collins made Mendenhall close his mouth quickly.

"We don't let children die when we're around. No diplomacy and no red tape, clear?" he said as he looked from man to man. Both nodded.

Down below in the camp, the search continued for whatever it was the mercenaries were looking for. The students were cowering against one another, and the African leader was still holding the small woman by the throat, only by now he had stopped shaking her. Just as Jack was about to move off to the far side of the encampment, from which he would make the initial strike, there was a ringing coming from the vicinity of the leader. As they watched, the large man dropped the woman and she sprawled to the sand and just lay there holding her throat. He reached into his vest and brought out a cell phone. Everett strained, trying to listen.

"Yes?" the man said in English.

Everett slowly brought back the slide of his Beretta and chambered a round as he listened.

"Nothing like you described. I'll take pictures on my phone and send them to you. How am I to know the period of the piece if found?"

Everett turned to Will and whispered, "Whatever happens, we try and get that cell phone, we may just have gotten a break in finding out who's paying this dickhead."

Mendenhall nodded as he clicked off the safety of his 9-millimeter and took aim on the man nearest the students who held an AK-47.

The leader angrily slammed his cell phone shut and pocketed it. Then he screamed a question at the cowering woman at his feet as he slowly raised his machete. Everett had just taken aim but he held his fire, per his orders, and forced himself to lower his weapon.

The leader got a strange look on his face as he looked at the river. He tilted his head, listening, and then gestured for two of his men to move toward a thumping noise coming from the water.

"Oh, shit," Mendenhall said as he looked at the Nile and saw the diversion Ryan was attempting to pull off.

"Un-fucking believable," was all Everett could say.

The loud sound of the motor was nothing compared to the amplified music emanating from the boom box that Ryan had fixed with wire to the tarp support. The 1970s band the Eagles blared out their hit "Take It Easy" as Ryan tied off the steering wheel and placed the boat in a slow circling spin in front of the Ethiopian encampment. All eyes were on the small, shirtless man in Bermuda shorts standing on top of the boat's awning with his arms splayed before him as he balanced himself as if he were surfing the boat. It spun crazily in the river to the sound of the rhythmic song written about hitchhiking through Arizona. The former naval F-14 Tomcat pilot had lost nothing of his sense of the dramatic since joining the Group. He was still just as crazy as the men who had recruited him.

The mercenaries were stunned by the sight. This American fool was obviously drunk and playing games with them.

"Shoot him!" the leader screamed out in Dinka as he brought the machete back up to strike the cowering girl.

Before the man could act on his murderous thrust toward the prone woman, something burst from the brush and slammed into the Sudanese leader. Jack brought down the small pocketknife with tremendous force directly into the man's neck. The blow immediately froze the machete in midair. Once the killer started to fall, Jack turned and threw the knife at the nearest armed man he saw. The knife, though not a lethal blow, struck the merc in the chest just below the collarbone, but it caused enough injury and shock that the man dropped his weapon.

On the river, Ryan heard the first distinctive AK-47 reports coming from shore and had the audacity to continue balancing himself for a moment on the boat's tarpaulin cover. Then, with the better part of the show over—*his* part, anyway—he grabbed the steel frame and flipped over the top and into the boat just as 7.62-millimeter rounds started striking the wooden boat. As Ryan struggled with the knotted line on the steering wheel, a sharp crack severed it and knocked it from his hands. After suddenly discovering that he had control of the boat again, he jammed the throttle to its stops. All the while, the Eagles continued to play loudly, drowning out the shouts and curses of the mercenaries onshore.

Everett sighted the first of his targets. A tall, very thin man was just turning to take aim at Jack and the young woman he was hurriedly helping to her feet. The 9-millimeter round caught the man between the eyes just to the right of his nose. At the same moment, Mendenhall outdid Everett by dropping two men who were already firing on Ryan. Both rounds struck the men in the backs of their heads. Others had turned their attention to their leader and were starting to take aim at Jack.

Carl and Will opened fire in earnest, hoping to drop as many as possible, but they were torn between the men with rifles and those who were starting to turn their attention, and their machetes, on the Ethiopian students.

Jack pushed the small woman away and charged the nearest man threatening the students. As others started to succumb to the withering fire from the knoll, Jack struck the nearest man and drove him into the ground, pounding at him with his fist. One of the young students tried to reach for a fallen machete to assist Collins, but immediately another mercenary got between him and the weapon. Then the assailant was brought down by a round from Everett.

The leader, who had been the first man dropped in the makeshift assault, started crawling away unnoticed. The killing blow that Jack thought he had inflicted guaranteed only a slow death—too slow to stop the man from doing what he needed to do. As he stumbled and tried to stand, he brought out the cell phone and struggled to his knees, just as Mendenhall and Everett shot down the last of his men. He opened the cell phone and, with his wound bleeding nastily, smashed it against a rock. Then he raised his arm to throw the remains into the river; but he hadn't noticed the changing sounds from the river as the angle and loud sounds of "Take It Easy" had changed direction.

Unknown to everyone, a stray bullet had finally found its mark and struck Ryan. The heavy round had only grazed his temple, but it was enough to leave him dazed and to send the large boat straight to the riverbank. The bow struck the small rise of sand and sent the boat full speed into the air. It rose over the scrambling students and the shocked face of Collins, who was pulling a machete out of the hand of the man he had just killed.

"What the hell?" Everett started to cry as the large boat, its motor screaming with exertion and traveling at thirty-five knots, went airborne by thirty feet.

As they all watched, the boat came down with a crash right onto the Sudanese leader, catching him in midthrow. The boat crushed him underneath as it split in two, sending the unconscious Ryan flying into the top of the nearest tent. Just like that, the assault was over, as quickly as it had started.

Collins rushed over to see if Ryan had survived his improvised diversion. Everett came down from the knoll with Mendenhall covering him and started checking the bad guys for life.

In all, the assault by the Event Group security team had taken less than two and a half minutes.

Half an hour later, as the sun was just dipping below the Ethiopian horizon, Jack, Everett, and Will Mendenhall, with the help of the Event Group dig team, assisted the stunned Ethiopian students. In the distance came the gentle thump of helicopters coming from Addis Abba, to the south.

Collins was kneeling beside a bandaged Jason Ryan and was angrily shaking his head.

"When I say 'improvise,' it doesn't mean to stand on top of a boat and have people shoot at you, Ryan."

"Did you like the choice of music? That's all that matters, Colonel."

Jack smirked and shook his head as he stood. "Yeah, as a matter of fact I did."

Ryan then grimaced, as he allowed one of the women of the Event Group to assist him to his feet.

"Jack, the doc says that we have four army Blackhawks inbound to take everyone out, courtesy of the American consulate. The Ethiopian government has been notified about the assault on their university students and the doctor also said that Niles was quoted as saying, 'Leave those idiots in Ethiopia, I have no need for them back in Nevada,'" Carl said.

"The director's not happy with our choice of vacation spots, huh?"

"Not exactly." Everett started to turn away and then stopped. He tossed Jack a small black object. "The head asshole was using this just before you started to play Tarzan with your knife. It's broken, but with a little bit of Event Group magic it may lead us to whoever was running this team of mercs."

"Colonel, I have someone here who would like to say thank you," Professor Leekie said as she placed her hands on the shoulders of the young African student who had put up the brave front against the leader of the mercenaries. "Colonel Collins, Captain Everett, I would like to introduce you to Hallie Salinka, daughter of Ethiopia's vice president, Peter Salinka."

"I . . . would . . . like . . . to—"

That was as far as the young woman could go. She broke down crying as she threw herself into Jack's arms. She sobbed uncontrollably and Collins knew that she was still feeling the shock of the assault. He looked at Everett, not really knowing what to do, but Carl did not offer any advice. He just watched the scene stoically. Leekie placed a hand over her mouth as she imagined the terror this child must have endured. Feeling awkward, Collins finally and very slowly reached up and patted the girl on the back. Slowly her sobs lessened and then Leekie pulled her away.

Jack watched as Leekie slowly led the bloodied girl away. He looked at the cell phone in his hand for a long moment before he pocketed it. *Lord, I know it's too much to hope for, but let me have that number. I want to have a very intimate conversation with the person on the other end of that call.*

CHAPTER
THREE

EVENT GROUP CENTER
NELLIS AIR FORCE BASE, NEVADA

The hidden complex that housed the Event Group sat a half a mile below the desert scrub of Nellis Air Force Base. Its location underneath the northern firing range was not by accident. The mere fact that you could end up setting off one of the experimental missiles deployed by the air force was reason enough not to go snooping in the area. The complex had been finished in late 1944 by the same design team as had built the Pentagon complex. They had used the expansive natural cave system that dwarfed its more famous cousin in Carlsbad, New Mexico.

Housed along with the military and science teams that made up the secretive Event Group were secrets that the world had mostly forgotten or that lived on only in folklore and legend. Behind thousands of banklike vault doors and inches of reinforced steel, the secrets of world history, once buried in time, were studied and cataloged. The charter of Department 5656: to make sure mistakes and civilization-altering moments from the past were never again repeated. The Group had been in existence officially since the time of Teddy Roosevelt, but their roots went far deeper, extending to President Abraham Lincoln.

The president of the United States handled the Group personally. The person who occupied the Oval Office—that person alone was trusted with the secrets studied in the ancient cave system below the sands of the high-desert airbase.

For every sitting president since the time of Woodrow Wilson, the first tour of the magical wonders of the Group, a subdepartment of the National Archives, always amazed and usually won over a new president.

The current director of the Event Group was Professor Niles Compton, recruited from MIT. Compton had been chosen by his predecessor, Senator Garrison Lee, and groomed specially to become the head of the most secret agency in the world outside of the American NSA.

He escorted the newly elected president past the third-vault level of the underground complex.

"Apart from the fact that you have artifacts like the Roswell saucer, something that may or not be Noah's Ark, and several items that include the bodies of historic figures, just where does it say you have achieved your mission, that you have been a deterrent to those who would harm our nation by studying past events?"

Niles Compton studied the newly elected president. The commander in chief was at the very least studious. It was a well-known fact that he came from an intellectual family and his platform of budget restraints and checks and balances had gotten him elected. Niles had his work cut out for him.

"Let us take the Ark as an example. Did it tell us anything about religion other than it fit the dimensions and design as stated in the Bible?" Niles shook his head. "Absolutely not. What it did lead us to is the now well-accepted science that the Middle East was most definitely flooded around thirteen to fifteen thousand years ago, which has led the scientific community to the conclusion that it was caused by a seismic event or a nonterrestrial occurrence like a meteor strike. Thus, we monitor the movement of the earth for patterns like they may have faced thousands of years ago. Our policy of tracking large bodies out in space is another example of what we have learned, just from this one Event."

Niles knew that the president needed this information to make a sound judgment when it came to budgeting hidden money for his department. Thus, he brought out the heavy guns on the initial tour.

The last soldier to be nominated for a fifth star in the nation's history, the new president didn't look at all convinced as he stepped up to a small vault and waited for the director.

"And that's just one artifact from the world's past," Niles said as he waited for his assistant, the eighty-two-year-old Alice Hamilton, to enter her security clearance on the keypad beside the vault. Then he and the president watched as she placed her thumb on a clear glass plate that read the minute swirls and valleys of her print. The vault hissed open.

"Okay, Dr. Compton, please explain the subject of this vault and its direct relationship to our nation's security, if you please."

Niles nodded and Alice opened the eight-inch-thick door of the small vault, and a cool mist rolled out and formed at the feet of the president.

"Very mysterious," was the only comment he made.

"This way, sir," Compton said, gesturing to the open door.

As they entered, the interior lights came to life. The two men stared at a small glass enclosure that had lines running into it, supplying nitrogen in its coldest state. Niles placed his thumb on a small plate just inside the door and allowed the center's Cray computer system to explain the find.

"The item you see before you, Event Group artifact and file # 4578-2019, was discovered in a Swiss bank vault by an undercover operative of Department 5656 in 1991."

The president looked closer at the acrylic enclosure and saw what looked like a small disk and disk player. Both items were worn and very old-looking. The disk itself was cracked and scratched and a third of it was missing.

"The object has been identified as a portable video-recording device manufactured by the Sony Corporation. Market date for this item was discovered to be in 2019 AD. This information was formulated through the serial number located on the video player/recorder and according to company sources the

serial number coincides with a future manufacturing date as indicated by the last four digits of the serial number."

The president looked from the enclosure to the face of Niles Compton. The look told the director that the man was skeptical at the very least.

"Upon study by the Mechanical Forensics Department, the damaged disk, though incomplete, held a visual magnetic resonance of the Battle of Gettysburg, recorded on the evening of July 3, 1863. This has been verified by the alignment of stars recorded at the 1678 reference point of the disk's recording. Department historians authenticating the images recorded of the battle indicated no evidence of staging. The material enclosed was found on August 26, 1961, by Park Ranger August Schliemann one hundred and ten yards from the area known as 'Little Round Top.' This material was stolen from the National Parks Service and stored in The Bank of Switzerland, safe-deposit box number 120989-61. The item has been declared authentic by Group historians."

"What we have here is a device that was used to record the battle of Little Round Top in 1863. While we speculate that the damaged portion of the disk shows the actual battle as recorded at the time, we at Group have come to the realization that coupled with the manufacture time of the recording device, that battle was not only observed by someone from the future but recorded, for what reasons we can only speculate."

The president was speechless. He looked from the director to the acrylic enclosure. He turned and was about to ask a question when Alice, standing by the vault's door, cleared her throat.

"Director, the president has an urgent call from the White House."

"Thank you, Alice," he said as he gestured for the president to take the phone, which was just outside the vault door. As he moved off, Alice stepped in and smiled at the director.

"How's it going?" she whispered.

"I hate this stuff," he said back in a hushed voice. "It could go either way."

She patted Niles on the shoulder. "Well, it may cost us some budget money, but he can't close us down. Just keep that in mind." She smiled and turned toward the president as he spoke in quiet tones on the phone. Then she looked at Niles. "You seem to be taking this rather calmly, Niles. Are you forgetting to tell me something about you and our new commander in chief?"

Niles pushed his glasses back up to their proper resting place on his nose and then looked at Alice curiously.

"Forgetting something? No, I don't believe so."

The president hung up the phone and started to turn to them. Alice was looking at Niles with even more curiosity. She knew him well enough that she thought he wasn't being totally honest with her.

"Mr. Director, I'm afraid I have to cut this meeting short." He looked at the enclosure and then half smiled. "Even though I must say you have indeed piqued my imagination, the real world is intruding on us. The North Koreans are still rattling their sabers and now we have a serious incident at the Iran-Iraq border. It seems an earthquake caused a lot of deaths."

"Sorry to hear that, sir. We can continue when you have more time."

A frown crossed the president's face. "I can tell you're not used to being challenged on budgetary matters, Doctor. I assure you I just don't start axing programs and budgets without due consideration."

"Yes, sir."

"Ms. Hamilton, it's been a rare pleasure to meet a lady of your . . . your—"

"Years, Mr. President?" she finished for him while batting her lovely eyes.

"Well, I was going to say quality. But if Dr. Compton has the smarts to keep someone like you way past mandatory retirement without anyone catching on, well, maybe you folks deserve the benefit of the doubt." The president turned to Niles and held out his hand. "Until we have more time, Mr. Director."

Alice watched their eyes meet and became aware of a momentary softness there that had not been evident before.

Niles watched Alice lead the president to the secure elevator, where he would meet his Secret Service escort, and frowned. He wanted to tell Alice and a few of the others about the president and himself, but he didn't know for sure what the man wanted everyone to know just yet. He decided that since the president hadn't said anything, he would play it close to the vest for now.

The presidential helicopter was waiting just inside the ancient-looking hangar. The staged dilapidation kept prying eyes from paying too much attention to gate number one of the Event Group complex. As the five-bladed rotor started to turn, the president frowned at the folder just given him by his chief of staff, Daniel Harding.

"Do we know just how much armor loss we're looking at?"

"No, sir. With the earthquake damage it's still a mess over there. The Iraqis are claiming to have lost forty percent of their ready divisions in the disaster. CIA reports that Iran has lost a like number. The quake hit at just the right area and the ayatollah is saying it's a divine sign that the end is near and that disarmament is the only option, starting with Iraq of course."

"Well, I wouldn't be crying over that, but how about unilaterally first," the president said as the huge marine helicopter eased out of the mysterious hangar of the Event Group. "Might make the world a sight happier."

"Indeed," the chief of staff said. "Now, that damn Kim Jong Il is a different story. He's claiming he has evidence of offshore tampering by South Korea that caused this earthquake and tsunami against the People's Army. He says it was underwater drilling that sparked the episode."

"Has he completely lost his mind? The South Koreans manipulated a seismic event by drilling for oil?"

"He claims to have evidence that shows naval elements and aircraft in international waters doing the foul deed. Even the Chinese are looking at him like he just fell out of the idiot tree and hit every branch on the way down."

"Well, get UN Ambassador Williams on it and tell him to find out what he can through unofficial channels. I don't want the State Department to officially give this story any credibility, understood?"

"Yes, sir."

"Listen, also get Nathan Samuels to the White House. I want to know from my science adviser just how natural two quakes of this size almost half a world away can be separate natural events. I want an answer to tell the press when this idiot Kim Jong Il's statements hit the newswires."

Alice rode with Niles Compton on the elevator up to level seven. At first, the director was content to stare at the numbers as they rose. Then without turning he said, "I want a detailed report on all the field teams that may or may not have been affected by these quakes. Any team, no matter who they're attached to, gets removed if there's the slightest danger. We don't need anyone getting hurt while the president mulls over our value."

Alice was silent as she wrote his instructions in her small notepad. When she was done, she saw Niles remove his glasses and rub the bridge of his nose in worry.

"Everyone is out and safe."

Niles half turned and replaced his glasses. "Excuse me?"

"The Ethiopian field team—they're safe and should be home in about twelve more hours. Our wandering vacationers are with them."

Alice saw the director relax. He nodded as the real reason for his inquiry into the field teams had been answered.

"Are you angry with Jack?" Alice asked, looking at her notepad.

The elevator stopped and Niles waited for Alice to exit before following. He walked straight to his large office, which had the Group's motto above the door in gold letters: THOSE WHO CHOOSE TO FORGET THE PAST, ARE CONDEMNED TO RELIVE IT. He gestured for Alice to close the large double doors behind her.

The office was spacious and dominated by thirty small-screen monitors that could be tuned to any science department or vault on any of the seventy-five sublevels of the complex. In the center of these monitors that were situated on the wall in the circular office was one large monitor that was currently tuned to the dilapidated hangar designated gate one. It was empty, meaning that the president had safely lifted off. He went to the credenza and poured himself a glass of water, then sat behind his large desk.

"You asked if I was angry at Jack."

"Yes," she said as she sat down in a chair beside the desk.

"Not as much angry as I am worried." He took a sip of his water and rifled through some papers on his desk. He found what he was looking for and pushed the paper to Alice. "I requested that Jack be here for the briefing of the new president; he instead requested leave for himself, Everett, and Ryan."

"You granted the leave."

"How could I say no after what Jack has done for this Group in the past two years?"

"Then why are you worried?" Alice asked as she laid down the memo.

"He takes too many chances sometimes."

Alice smiled and looked at her boss. She knew that Niles from time to time overthought a situation, and she was duty-bound to ease his mind. Jack Collins was the very best at what he did. His army record was unparalleled in achievement. The only mark against him was his battle with the Pentagon over policy, which had eventually led him to be transferred to the Group.

Carl Everett was Jack's equal in many ways, with the exception of his heart. Everett was the one to whom Jack turned for the harder things involved with his new command. Such as how to handle people.

"Jack doesn't have a death wish, Niles, if that's what you're thinking. What he does have is an overwhelming commitment to do what is right. He was restrained for so many years in his duties with the army. The inability to do the right thing instead of what policy dictated he do. You gave him the freedom he needed to act when you brought him here. Bad people were hurting us in the field and Jack stopped that after you gave him a free hand, and I must say it was the smartest order you could ever have given a man like Colonel Collins."

Niles placed the glass down and then looked at Alice and nodded. "Do I always overlook the obvious?"

"Jack's not growing bored. He wanted to be there to give Will Mendenhall his new second-lieutenant's bar. He's proud of Will, you know that. A fishing vacation was only an excuse."

"He goes fishing and thwarts an attack on innocent students. Taking chances is a bad habit I want him to break."

"If he breaks that habit, we go back to losing field personnel. It's still an ugly world out there, Niles, and Jack just happens to know how to deal with it."

Eighteen hours later, Collins stood at semiattention before the desk of his director. He had not taken the seat offered by Niles, preferring to wait until the director got off his chest that which had to be said.

"Bring back any fish, Colonel?" Niles asked as he looked at the debrief folder that Jack and the others had filed.

"All we brought back was a hangover and an Ethiopian field team."

Niles flipped a page in the file and then looked at Collins. He tossed the filed report onto his desk and then gestured for the colonel to sit.

"Take a seat, Jack . . . please."

Collins finally relented and sat. The silver bird on his collar sparkled in the soft light of the office.

"You take too many chances, Jack," Niles stated flatly as he looked straight at Collins.

Collins was about to speak when Niles held his hand up.

"Save it. For people like me who only see science and numbers, we can't even begin to imagine what it's like to have the ability you have. It is a hard thing for us to conceive of risking one's life to save a stranger. Cannot fathom it. I just want you to think before you leap. You are too damn valuable to this Group. *To me*." He mumbled the last words.

Collins watched the director. While he and Niles had never become close, they had a mutual respect for each other that went far beyond the normal working relationship. He may not have expressed himself to the director the way he should have, but Jack knew that the bookish director was the smartest man he had ever had the pleasure of meeting. In addition, the two worked well as a team, always thinking about the safety of their people.

"You and many others sell yourselves too short around here, Niles. My abilities are no greater than any one of the five hundred people assigned to Group. In my time you've made choices I could never imagine making—life-or-death decisions for people out in the field—and I must say you have never come up short. All soldiers ever ask for is a superior to have his back. They all know that you do."

Niles Compton nodded, signaling an end to that discussion. He cleared his throat, undid his top button, and then slid the knot in his tie down. He picked up the file with the field report in it.

"This Addis Abba archaeology team—their dig was similar to our own?"

"As far as we know, it was an information-and-acquisition dig only. No one knew what would be found."

Niles turned in his chair and typed a command on his computer. The main ten-by-fourteen-foot monitor came alive, and he and Jack looked into the clean room on level forty-three of the artifact-sorting room.

A straitlaced technician no older than thirty stepped up to the monitor. Professor Alan Franklin smiled and nodded at Niles.

"Mr. Director, good morning."

"What have you got so far?" Niles asked.

"Well, the team brought back some very rare finds. Artifacts, I may add, that had no business being in the area where they were unearthed. For instance," he turned away and pulled up a shard of pottery, which he held very delicately in glove-encased fingers, "this little item: I can tell you, even before my assistant hands me the carbon-14 test results, that it predates anything we or anyone else in the world has on record. The pottery is almost porcelainlike in looks and made from a material civilizations have never used before in the making of pottery. Initial analysis says it's made from crushed volcanic glass."

"That's interesting, but—"

"Now here's the twilight-zone moment, Mr. Director. The shard itself had no business being in Ethiopia. We suspect that a great and powerful flood event may have carried it *against* the Nile's flow from the Mediterranean. The design is usually associated with a carafe and is a cross between Greek and Egyptian lineage."

"Your point is . . . ?"

"You don't see? It should not exist. A cultural exchange between Egypt and Greece couldn't have happened before 3700 BCE." The professor accepted a handed printout. "Just as I suspected, carbon-14 dating places the aggregate material in the shard between 11,000 BCE and 14,000 BCE, give or take five hundred to a thousand years. This is totally amazing!"

"Have your team run the carbon-14 testing again. Test everything our team came back with."

"Yes, sir, we're on it."

Niles turned off the monitor and faced Collins. "You're steeped in history, Jack; tell me, have you ever heard of anything that old?"

"No."

"You know why?"

Collins knew he was not going to like the answer.

"The Egyptian and Greek civilizations didn't even exist at that time."

"Then who made this little item that was unearthed two thousand miles away from where it was made? And what event could have been powerful enough to make the Nile River reverse its flow?"

"That's what we need to find out. In addition, what artifact could those mercenaries have been looking for that was important enough to kill for?"

"I think maybe I'll bring in our new operatives at the FBI we recruited last year, it's time they earn their keep anyway. They can also find out who was on the other end of that cell-phone conversation in Africa."

Director Compton nodded, agreeing that Jack should contact FBI Special Agent William Monroe in New York to bring him up to speed on Ethiopia.

"This could be a find that changes the face of history. It would predate any known civilization by at least four thousand years."

The Event Group had a mission.

GOSSMANN METAL WERK BUILDING
OSLO, NORWAY

The large conference room was situated 160 feet below street level, under one of the oldest manufacturing firms in Europe. Grouped around this table were men and women from most western nations of the world, plus Japan, India, and Hong Kong.

The flags arrayed along the walls of the conference room were bright red and each carried a symbol handed down since the time of the Caesars, and each one differing only slightly from the others. A large golden eagle was prominent on all of them. Some had sloping lines that resembled a bent swastika clutched in the eagle's powerful talons, while others depicted more bizarre symbols from antiquity. The prevalent theme of all the flags was the golden eagle emblazoned over a scarlet field.

The most recently designed flag, the symbol of the Third Reich, was not present. The episode in the 1930s and '40s had almost dealt the Coalition a deathblow and the flag had become an embarrassment, especially to the younger and far more radical element now sitting among the old guard.

"Gentlemen, gentlemen and ladies, this meeting will come to order," said the small man known as Caretaker. He rapped a gavel on his small desk in the rear of the luxuriously appointed room. "We have many items to discuss this evening."

The twenty-six men and five women who made up the Juliai Coalition, named for the esteemed Roman family that was the precursor to the Caesars, calmed and took their seats. Though many were there for reasons outside that of legacy, they had many things in common. One of these was the fact that they

were the richest private citizens in the world. Not one name
would ever show up on any registry of the world's richest people, and you would never find the likeness or name of any Coalition member in a gossip column or tabloid. They did not
bicker with governments in courts of law over the cornering of
markets or the breakups of conglomerates so large that their
value could not be computed. The Juliai Coalition answered to
no power in the world.

"We will forgo the reading of the last meeting's minutes to
concentrate fully on this first day of initial operational testing."

There were nods and smiles around the conference table.
Then a lone figure at the center stood and chimed a knife
against a water glass.

"The gentleman from Austria, Mr. Zoenfeller, has the floor,"
announced Caretaker.

"Before we have the report read to us from operations, I
would like to bring to the attention of this council that we have
ongoing missions to find the Atlantean Key. Without it, I daresay we will have more episodes like the one this afternoon."

There were a few nods and words of agreement with the
large, gray-haired man, but they were far fewer than the hard
looks coming from the younger majority.

"What was wrong with the initial tests of today?" asked a
tall man with a head of boyish blond hair. "This is why we
have started with nations that have neighbors who will eventually have to be dealt with. We all agreed that pinpoint strikes
were not necessary, so it was effective to start with these locations." He was staring at the Austrian with mild contempt.

"The young gentleman from America has voiced the standard 'toe the line' opinion of the youth in this room. An opinion, I might add, that rings of dictate and not council."

Only a few of the older people rapped their knuckles on the
polished table to indicate their agreement. With a bemused
look, the American Coalitionist took note of those few who
sided with the Austrian.

Nonplussed by the limited agreement, the old man plodded
on.

"I must say, the tests today were reckless and their random

destruction will attract attention to our endeavor. Without the Atlantean Key, we have no pinpoint-strike capability. We can and will harm the economies of friendly nations, and that, ladies and gentlemen, will affect most of us in this room directly."

The aged man from Austria sat down. The tall American watched but remained standing, intent on finishing his statement. Now was the time to hammer home his points against the old guard of the Coalition. As he waited for the murmurings to subside, he decided upon a gentler approach. After all, he really hadn't expected that the circle of destruction would spread so far across the Iranian border in the afternoon strike of Thor's Hammer.

"My friends, I know many of you have expressed your fear of starting before the Key has been recovered. I must again remind you that many of the economies of our own nations cannot afford the luxury of this wait. The elimination of old thorns must begin now so that new growth can begin. These outlaw and backward nations that we have targeted are a drain on everyone and every government represented in this room. Limited strikes with the Keyless Hammer can lessen some of the pressure of defending against such fools. We need these limited strikes for the time being. When our own people are in place at the head of these governments and our loans negotiated for boosting their economies, you will see the benefit of acting now."

The man from Austria stood suddenly, slamming his hand on the tabletop.

"We must limit Thor's Hammer to today's strikes only and curtail operations until the Key is recovered. I am sure all here are thrilled at the power achieved in this first test. But, like most of you, I saw today what *could* happen if we act without knowing the full potential of the weapon, without some form of control."

"May we inquire as to the progress of the Ethiopian venture, Mr. Cromwell?" asked Caretaker from his seat at the small desk.

"The report filed this afternoon describes a disappointing end to one of our scout teams in Ethiopia, who it seems conflicted with a group of Americans that were conducting an unrelated dig nearby and were eliminated. The details are rather sketchy at the moment, but nonetheless cannot help but have the adverse effect of setting us behind in our search for the Atlantean Key, at least until another team can be dispatched from the Sudan." The Englishman sat after giving his brief report.

"I take it these Americans have no idea these mercenaries were working for us?" the Austrian asked, nodding toward the American. "Mr. Tomlinson?"

"I and the two other Americans in this room can hardly control the actions of every agency in our country. The identity of this agency is still unknown. How could the Americans have received any valuable information if the men we sent into Ethiopia had none to offer? However, I promise to use all of our influence and resources to discover who interfered, and those people will be dealt with."

"Even more ruthlessness?" Zoenfeller asked loudly.

"We are ranging far off the subject. The two strikes *were* a success. North Korea is hurt and hurt badly and is liable to strike out at any time. Iran will not soon recover, at least in the near future."

"What we have done, and *all* we have done, on the Korean peninsula is angered an old and weary tiger that is now wounded and fearful for its life. The weapon was weak in Korea and too powerful in Iran, and we ended up hurting Iraq!" Zoenfeller said as he tried to bring his point home. "And now the Middle East ally many of us, including your own country, have created in the past ten years has also been hurt beyond measure, now requiring even more funding from us in the near future, all because the weapon didn't have a particular enemy in mind." Zoenfeller was unhappy to see that only a very small percentage of members were nodding in agreement with his words.

Coalitionists who seemed to be losing their nerve were noted.

"Regardless, the next set of strikes will go forward. The Atlantean Key will be recovered before we start hitting government assets in our own nations and those of our allies. As for old enemies, we must continue to lay the groundwork. The last few years of drought have crippled the Russians, and the flooding in China has weakened an already flagging support base for their leadership. The time to hit them is now, not later," said Tomlinson, with so much calm that it froze the blood of the elder element of the council.

"You are *suggesting* that we advance our carefully planned timetable for the elimination of those two powers by four years? Am I correct?"

"Yes. Most here are so very tired of the Juliai Coalition's timidity when it comes to dealing with these two backward powers. The fear of these toothless tigers in the East has been so greatly exaggerated that it sickens those of us who have had to stand here in this room and hear tales of terror of how dangerous these nations are, when in fact it would take but a single nudge to send them both toppling over. This is not the fifties; it is now."

"And neither nation will react the way Kim Jong Il has? I guarantee you, instead of folding like a shoddy house of cards, they will fight to stay their power over their people. What if nations start believing North Korean claims of the disaster not being a natural occurrence? Silly as he seems to most, what if Kim's wild accusations cause other, more levelheaded people to start investigating your not-very-well-disguised laying of the sound amplifiers in North Korean waters? Russia and China are capable, my young friend, of doing the unexpected."

"That is your opinion of them. They are weak and they will fall. Their economies cannot withstand a natural disaster on the scale we plan. And the intelligence Kim has only shows oil exploration that was cleared far in advance by international treaty," Tomlinson said.

He looked around the room and smiled. A soft gesture coldly calculated to ease the minds of the elders.

"Due to our efforts in America, the grain and other food-stuffs that are needed by these nations just won't be available. They are already looking to the West and the United States in particular with a large degree of mistrust. The new president is having a hard time convincing them that he is not using food as a weapon to alter their national policies against rogue elements, like Georgia and Taiwan. A limited confrontation between East and West is an ally to our cause."

"I agree. The timetable must be adjusted to take advantage of these elements that can only have a positive effect on our plans," said the man from France. "We must accelerate."

More than 80 percent of the people in the room felt the same as they rapped their knuckles on the table before them. However, Tomlinson, ever the politician, felt he needed the support, at least for the moment, of the older members.

"I have assets in Ethiopia that are standing by to find the buried Key. In the States, my best intelligence person is close to tracing its whereabouts by finding the hiding place of the plate map stolen in 1875 by Peter Rothman. She has already learned it was sent to our brothers and sisters of the Ancients. Now is not the time to lose your nerve, ladies and gentlemen—not with your own governments in *your* control as the prize for rising above any timidity."

"The timidity we show, Mr. Tomlinson, is due to the fact that we only agreed to the tests in Iran and Korea. We did this because you guaranteed we could test the weapon without the Key."

"This argument is getting very tiresome. Now if you will excuse us . . ."

The man from Austria shook his head. Events were moving too fast and the elder statesmen of the Juliai were worried. Maybe it was because the memory of another, even more zealous renegade was fresher in their minds than in those of the younger men and women. Adolph Hitler had once defied the Coalition and nearly destroyed them. Now it was happening again, and they were helpless to stop it. Tomlinson was bringing on the Fourth Reich *his* way.

The young lions had taken control of the most influential entity in the history of the world. It had happened once before, in the time of Julius Caesar, and that had ended in the splintering of the first family of man.

The young members of the Coalition were now in a state of

near rebellion and the elders feared that the result could well mean the devastation of the planet itself.

EVENT GROUP CENTER
NELLIS AIR FORCE BASE, NEVADA

Second Lieutenant Sarah McIntire sat with Collins and Everett in the cafeteria. She acted as if she were somewhere else as the two men spoke while eating. Then Collins looked over at the diminutive geology professor and nudged her out of her trance.

"All right, what's up?" he asked.

Sarah looked from Jack to Carl and set her fork onto her plate. "There's a rumor going around that you guys had one hell of a fishing trip."

"Nah, nothing special, didn't catch a thing," Carl said, straight-faced.

"Will had a nice commissioning party, that's all that happened. So, what are you up to?" Jack asked.

"My department's been running a little slow. A lot of people out on leave, like most of the complex. I have what's left of the Geology Department teaming with earth sciences and we're going over these earthquakes just as a training exercise. Everyone seems to be stumped."

"Stumped about what? That Korea was hit with a megaquake? It is on the Pacific Rim, you know. It's the old ring-of-fire thing. In addition, Iraq and Iran aren't exactly on stable terrain either. Shit happens," Carl said as he swallowed some water.

"Yes, they are all unstable. But there hasn't been one aftershock in either location since the main shaking stopped."

"Is that normal?" Jack asked as he tossed his napkin onto his plate.

"Jack—" Sarah caught herself and hoped that no one had heard her address him in the familiar sense. "Colonel, there are always aftershocks. It's just like a long-distance runner cooling down after the main shock of a race. There are always tremors, and this is so unnatural it's raising eyebrows across academic circles. And it's not just because of the wild claims by North Korea."

"Well, I'm sure the eggheads will—"

Will Colonel Collins and Captain Everett please report to the computer center. Colonel Collins and Captain Everett to the comp center, please.

The computerized female voice cut short the academic question of Sarah's point as she watched the two officers reach for their dinner trays and stand. Jack looked at Sarah and she smiled. As she watched the two officers leave, Sarah remembered the very first time Jack had smiled at her and the butterflies she'd gotten in her stomach, making her feel like a schoolgirl. She smiled inwardly at the warming thought. She knew that her love for Jack had become common knowledge among their closest associates like Carl, Mendenhall, and even Director Compton, but the secret had to remain intact because Jack was a stickler for military protocol. Soon a decision would have to be made, and she knew that it would be hers to make.

The main computer center was set up like a theater. Desks were arranged on the upper level, each with a monitor, and they looked down on the main floor, where technicians worked at other stations for direct access into the Cray system known as Europa. This system was the most powerful computing apparatus known in the world and there were only four in existence. However, the Event Group's system was special. It had the ability to "talk" its way into any computer in the world, bypassing security mainframes of most governments, universities, and companies.

Jack and Carl made their way down to the main floor and saw the man who had called them in. Professor Pete Golding, director of operations of the center, greeted the two men.

"Colonel, Captain, good of you to come." He turned to a small monitor attached to the plastic wall of the center and waved a hand across its face. That activated the screen, and as they watched, the face of Niles Compton appeared. "Okay, they're here, Niles. Shall we start?"

Compton nodded and watched on his own monitor in his office.

"Okay, the cell phone you came back from Africa with was damaged beyond repair. But the idiot who thought just disabling it never learned the fact that a cell phone is nothing but a small computer. It has a nonvolatile memory and this is what's used to store information. You know, it's amazing when you think—"

"Pete, listening to you is like having your teeth drilled into. Would you get to the point, please?" Niles said, rubbing his temples.

Pete looked hurt. Red-faced, he shoved his glasses back onto his nose.

"What did you learn, Pete?" Jack asked, to get things back on track.

"Well, the cell was used to call only one number. Europa tracked the owner of this number and we gave it to the Group's contact at the FBI for investigation."

They watched as Pete switched on another monitor and then they were looking into the young face of special Agent William Monroe. He was at his home in Long Island, New York.

"Bill, how are you?" Jack asked.

"Good evening, Colonel and Captain. Pete has passed on to me your information and we have tracked a rather shady individual right here in the U.S. As a matter of fact, he's in my own home state."

"Fortuitous," Niles said.

"As I was saying, our friend is an investment banker and commodities broker who has an estate in Westchester County. A small burg called Katonah. Our friend had over twenty-seven calls into this mercenary's cell phone, and after checking his phone records we've learned that he had numerous other calls to Africa, not only on this cell but many others—thirty-five to be exact."

"Talk about reach out and touch someone," Everett said.

"Also our friend has a black area that falls in line with this whole mess. He's a collector, anything and everything, from Greece to China. Under-the-table dealings mostly, very few are reported, thus he makes for an interesting entry in the books of the FBI *and* the IRS."

"What do you think, Bill—can we get into this man's humble abode without your bosses in D.C. getting wise?" Jack asked.

"Yeah; I have enough to get a search warrant. How you cover yourselves will have to be the key here. No one on my side of the fence can get even a hint I let someone pull a raid in my backyard."

"I think we can manage that. Can you have a few of your boys standing by in the wings for recovery purposes?"

"You got it, Jack. Just let me know and I'll have the warrant ready," Monroe said, then signed off.

"Well, Mr. Director, do we have a 'go' to get out to New York?" Collins asked.

Niles looked into the monitor and nodded. "You have a go, but remember, the main reason for bringing this guy down is the fact that he at the very least ordered the murders of innocent college kids and their professors, and for what, some shards of pottery? Yes, Colonel, you have a go."

Jack nodded.

"But it would be nice to know what it was they were looking for. I mean, if ten- to fifteen-thousand-year-old artifacts didn't interest them, just what does? That's the main reason we're handling this instead of the regular authorities," Niles said before he signed off.

Jack looked from the darkened monitor to the face of a grinning Everett.

"You packed yet?" he asked.

"Been packed. Let's go."

As they turned to leave the computer center, they heard Pete Golding behind them as they climbed the stairs.

"Does my voice grate on people like a dentist drilling teeth?"

"Don't worry, Pete, it only happens when you talk," Everett said as they reached the door and left.

KATONAH
WESTCHESTER COUNTY, NEW YORK

The mansion was surrounded by immense manicured lawns and gardens, which belied the fact that hidden among imported shrubs and trees was the most sophisticated security system ever installed within the confines of a private estate. It had taken Special Agent Monroe only hours, with the help of his Europa link, to track the owner's business expenses, and the discovery of the advanced security system told the agent that the man had something to hide within the walls of the estate. The eight-million-dollar system had drawn scrutiny and been cross-referenced with the owner's identity. From there it had been only a matter of digging a little further to find the truth behind the wealthy world traveler.

The team had decided to travel over a mile overland to reach the outer gate at the rear of the property in lieu of using a helicopter. Nothing would have been more conspicuous than the taletell thump of rotor blades after dark in quiet Westchester County, New York.

The ten-man assault element watched as one of three security trucks negotiated the long driveway from the front of the mansion. They were nearly invisible in the dark, blending in well with the cloudy night in their Nomex clothing and hoods. The team was armed with MP-5s—lightweight, short-barreled automatic weapons.

The dark figure squatting beside a tree raised his hand as the small pickup truck cruised by, its spotlight swinging toward them but missing the ten men. He then held up two fingers and made a scissoring motion.

A large man in the middle of the line came forward after the truck had vanished around a curve. He removed a small black box and held it as close to the steel fence as he could without touching it, then he switched on the power to the box. The soft glow of the gauge was covered by the big man's hand as he studied the LED readout. He nodded and held up his left hand. He splayed his fingers wide, indicating five, then closed his hand again and spread them once more: ten. The man in the lead nodded, easily seeing the signal with his ambient-light-vision goggles, bringing the team into a silhouetted ghostly image of greens, blacks, and grays. The large man lowered his hand and removed the twin electrical leads. He was hearing the soft hum of ten thousand volts of electricity as it passed through the chain-link fence.

Another of the team duck-walked forward and brought out the insulated wire cutters, then he waited while the larger man ran rubber-coated wires from one link of the fence to another. He did this until he had a four-foot circle woven into and connecting the chain links. Then he held out his hand and took the cutters from the second man. Then he started snipping the thick wire of the fence.

The wiring he had woven into the fence was an electric-free corral, designed to isolate an electrical current and keep a connection of the fence to fool any alarm that would sound as the links were severed. With the last of the links cut, the man pulled free the circle of wire, and the team moved in.

Two three-man teams went left and right, hunkering low as they went. The leader took the last three and went straight ahead.

On the left, that team would make first contact, so they lowered themselves to the ground and waited. They were rewarded a moment later when headlights came around the corner from the back of the house. This was the second security truck. As it approached, one of the three men removed a small ball bearing from his armored vest and waited until the truck was ten yards away on the other side of the slope.

The first man in line crawled the last three feet to the top of the rise and pulled a funny-looking pistol from a holster at his side; then he aimed. The other drew back and threw the light-weight ball bearing in a nicely tossed arc. It struck the side of the truck, making a louder-than-expected crack as the vehicle came quickly to a stop, its driver curious as to the cause of impact. As soon as he stepped from the small truck and walked three steps to its hood, and looked to see what had struck the vehicle, the compressed-air dart caught him in the left side of his neck. The security guard yelped and then tried to make it to the driver's-side door, but he made only two steps before his legs refused to cooperate and gave out completely. He fell with a muffled thud. He would be that way for several hours, awakening with the worst headache of his life.

The three other vehicles and the three foot-patrol officers were dispatched just as easily. Only one had given the team a fright, as he had actually had the physical strength to get his hand on the radio clipped to his shoulder before giving up the ghost.

The team spread out into their designated entry points and waited for the signal. The large man who had cut the fence found the telephone and power boxes on the outside of the house near the basement door and placed a small, circular object against the incoming phone and power lines that ran in from the county grid. He set the timer for ten seconds and then backed away. A small electrical charge sent power racing back into both lines, popping the circuit breakers somewhere inside the house. The phone line would be useless until the phone company discovered that the fiber-optic line had been fused and clouded from the electrical charge.

The lights around the compound went out: that was the signal for step three in the structure assault. At that exact same instant, the front and rear doors, along with the center panel of French doors beside the pool, exploded inward with a shower of wood splinters and glass. The black-operations team entered with weapons held high.

On the ground floor, the unseen and invisible assailants roughly pushed several shrieking servants to the ground. They were expertly bound with plastic ties and then the men moved off quickly. The raid took exactly three minutes and twenty-two seconds from the time the first guard had been taken down.

The leader of the team stepped forward after counting heads and looking at each face. He came to a man who was looking up into the hooded face above him arrogantly.

"Your name is Talbot?" the man with the funny goggles asked.

The man only stared up into the darkness, not as arrogant now as he'd been before the man called him by name.

"Are you Talbot, the butler, the man in charge?" the man asked quietly again, this time kneeling down, bringing his science-fiction-looking outfit closer for inspection. For emphasis, he adjusted the MP-5 weapon on its strap menacingly.

"Yes, yes," the man said quickly.

"Where is William Krueger?"

"He . . . he . . . was upstairs when we retired for the night. . . . I swear."

The menacing figure glanced up at another even larger team member coming down the stairs. This man shook his head, negative, and then the man kneeling beside the butler unsafed his weapon, and everyone in the room, even the maids and cooks, knew a menacing click when they heard one.

"I'll ask one more time, and if I don't get the answer I want, you'll be serving your next high-paying master with a limp, because I will shoot you right through the kneecap—understood?" The threat was delivered with a menacingly cool voice.

"You can't do this . . . you're . . . you're police officers!"

The man chuckled and looked at the big man above him. "Who in the world ever said we were police officers? This is what you would call a home invasion, and we're the invaders. I'm also running out of patience."

The calm and sensible demeanor of the man wearing the strange goggles terrified the butler.

"For God's sake, Albert, tell them what they want to know!"

The man calmly looked over at the belly-down servants and saw an arrogant-looking woman trying to peer at him through the darkness. Then he remembered the detailed pictures shown to him by the recon team. She was Anita McMillan, the estate's chef.

"All right, all right. There's a panel in the library behind the desk. It's a false front, there are stairs behind it. Just slide it, it'll open right up. That's the only place Mr. Krueger can be."

The leader nodded toward the larger man and he and three others went to the library.

"Thank you, Albert. Your cooperation has been noted." The man gestured for another of his team and soon all the servants were blinded by black bags that were placed over their heads.

The leader joined the three men inside the library and watched as the paneled wall was probed. Then he heard the panel slide into the wall. He gestured for the middleman, the best rifleman on the team, to take point. As he did, the others waited until he was ten steps down the flight of stairs before they followed.

The men removed their night-vision scopes as there was a soft light coming from below. They were halfway down when the point man held up his hand with splayed fingers, and they stopped. As they watched him take another step, they were surprised by the sound of a pistol shot as it glanced off the stone wall, just missing the man in the lead position. They saw him grimace as stone chips struck the side of his face. Then he took a determined stance, braced himself against the stair-well's railing, and fired a ten-shot burst of 5.56-millimeter rounds into the basement. Then he waited another split second and fired ten more. The men behind him knew his routine and prayed it would work.

"Now, that was a warning! The next burst is going to chew your ass up. You have three seconds to surrender that popgun you have. Oh, hell, forget it. I'm not waiting." The point man fired a three-round burst into the stairwell and the basement be-low. The men behind him on the stairs smiled as he did so.

"Okay, okay, you son of a bitch. You didn't have to do that. Give a man time to think goddammit!"

"You're all out of time, fuckhead! You took a shot at the wrong goddamn black man!"

"Who in the hell are you?"

"That's of no concern to you at the moment!" Another three-round burst was sent into the basement, close to but not near enough to the unseen man below to cause him any harm. "I didn't hear that cap gun hit the floor yet, asshole!"

"Goddamn maniacs!" The whimpering voice answered from below, but that was quickly followed by the clatter of metal hitting concrete.

The point man didn't hesitate. He took the stairs quickly and the others behind him made as much noise as possible to tell the man below that the maniac had a lot of company. They heard the commands before they reached the bottom of the stairs.

"On your belly, Rockefeller. Hands spread out in front. *Now*, dammit! Put those silk pajamas on the cold-ass floor!"

The others arrived and watched as a plastic wire tie was placed on the wrists of a very large, rotund man. The man's breathing seemed distressed, and the leader of the assault team gestured for the point man to get him on his feet.

"Who . . . who . . . who are you? What do you want?" the man rasped in halting words.

The team leader found a large chair behind an even larger desk and pushed it toward him with his black boot.

"You're not going to die on us, are you?"

The fat man took several deep breaths and finally color began to run back into his face. The lighting was sufficient in the spacious basement to see that he was recovering from his initial shock.

"As for who we are, we're the people that have come to take back the things you have stolen over the years and to make you account for the lost lives of innocent archaeology students in Ethiopia. That's who we are."

The owner of the mansion watched from his chair as the black hood was removed. The three other men did the same. The angry black man to his front was staring a hole through him. He shied away, leaning as far back in the chair as possible, when he realized that it was the man he had taken the shot at.

"I don't know what you're talking about. I'm an investment banker and commodities trader," he said, still looking at Mendenhall.

Colonel Jack Collins stepped forward, tossing his hood to Carl Everett, standing at his side.

"Mr. Krueger, do we look like men who have been misinformed? Do you think we came here on a whim, or do you think we may have a purpose?"

Krueger looked from face to face. There was no identifying insignia on their clothing and each man had his face set, and it was a determined look.

"No . . . I mean yes, you look as if you have a purpose."

"We know about your collection, so, if you would like to leave this house in one piece, you'll show it to us right now. I'm sure you don't want the authorities involved here, do you?"

Krueger looked as if he had accepted his fate in one fell

swoop. His head lay to the side and he started to cry. His large frame shook with his sobbing as Will Mendenhall helped him to his feet.

Colonel Collins looked over at Everett, who nodded and then walked over and assisted in getting the overweight Krueger to a standing position. Collins waited while the art-and-antiquities thief, not to say murderer, composed himself. He heard a click in his earpiece. He thumbed a small switch at his throat that activated his transmitter. He turned away from Krueger.

"Recovery One," he said softly into his throat microphone.

"This is Eagle Eye. All palace guards are cooperating and we have Ernie's Fix-it Shop and Recovery Three on property and moving toward your pos, over."

Collins heard the whispered voice from his outside security. Instead of answering, he reached down and manually clicked his mic twice.

Everett also heard the report. All the security guards had been rounded up and placed in a safe location, still out from the tranquilizers, and now the three-man outside security element reported another Event team approaching the house. Carl rolled back his black glove and looked at his watch. *Not bad,* he thought; Ryan and his team were right on schedule. *Not bad for a flyboy.*

"Okay, Krueger, the artifacts," Collins said, stepping toward the man.

"Take me over to my desk, please."

Jack nodded, and Mendenhall and Everett walked him over to a large, ornate desk in the far corner of the basement office. The large man reached out for the top drawer.

"Ah-ah-ah, we'll open it for you," the black man said. Mendenhall leaned forward and gently pulled out the top drawer. He gave Krueger a mock-disappointed look and removed the snub-nosed .38 Police Special and tossed it over to Collins.

"That was not my intent. There's a button just under the lip of the desk. Push it once."

Mendenhall felt around until he found it and then pushed it.

At first, there was nothing. They could hear only the activity upstairs as Ernie's Fix-it Shop, an Event Group maintenance team, went to work with subdued hammering and electric-tool sounds. Then battery-powered floodlights joined those few emergency lights and illuminated the room brightly. In the harsh glare, the team could see nothing but barren walls. There were a few things like diplomas and family pictures, but other than that, they were white and empty.

"Push the button one more time," Krueger said with his chin almost touching his chest in despair.

Mendenhall repeated the process and they heard an electric motor, obviously battery-operated also, start to hum, and then the far eighty-foot-long wall parted in the center and slowly slid back in two sections on hidden tracks.

Instead of watching the false wall divulge its secrets, Collins watched Krueger. He sniffled and wiped a hand across his sweating face, but his eyes weren't concerned about the secret door. Jack watched as the man's eyes quickly darted to the desk once more and then just as quickly looked away. Collins saw that the desk sat in front of one of the basement walls, and beyond that wall one would assume was dirt and rock. As he looked back, Krueger was again sobbing, but once again he saw the man's dark eyes glance at the desk.

"Jesus, you've been a busy little thief, haven't you?" Mendenhall said as spotlights illuminated a treasure trove of ancient and not-so-ancient artifacts.

Collins and Everett stepped forward and looked at the commodity trader's extensive collection. There were special pieces sitting atop pedestals from the third and fifth dynasties of Egypt. Lights shone down on armor dating back to the days of Alexander. There were oil paintings from the Renaissance. Other displayed jewelry had been stolen from collections around the world. Crowns of kings long dead. Collins activated his com link.

"Recovery Three, you can bring the trucks in now."

Jack turned to Krueger, who was still being held by Will. He stepped up to him, raised his double chin, and looked him in his watery eyes.

"Your cooperation will be noted and the prosecuting authorities will be notified."

"But you're thieves! Why . . . what—"

"To further enhance the chances your team of defense attorneys have of getting you acquitted, do wish to tell us about the second room now?"

The man's face drained of blood right before their eyes. His thick lips started to tremble and his eyes widened. All at once, he wasn't timid or frightened any longer; he was mad.

"You bastards, you're dealing with things beyond your concept!"

"Seems you hit a nerve, Jack," Everett said.

"Will, reach in and push the same button again. I think our friend is hiding his real treasure in another location. This room here is nice, but X doesn't mark the right spot, does it, Mr. Krueger?"

As instructed, Mendenhall pushed the button again. This time there was a loud whine of an overgeared motor, and as they watched in amazement, a large circle in the center of the floor separated from the surrounding concrete and started to corkscrew down into the earth. The opening was about sixteen feet in diameter and started spinning faster as they watched. They could see the threads of the giant screw-type elevator as it spun and descended farther and farther. Jack could see that a man would use those threads as a winding staircase to enter the real treasure room.

"Now we know why his security system was so expensive," Jack said as the whine of the large motor stopped.

"Jesus," Everett said, looking from Krueger to Jack. "This guy and his engineers should have been working for us."

"You don't know what you're doing. You've just killed us all."

Everett feigned shock at Krueger. "Now that's a scary statement. Care to expand on it?"

Krueger closed his mouth into a tight line and looked away. His eyes did not follow Jack as he walked to the opening in the floor. Everett caught up with Collins and they both went down into the true light of the ancient past.

When they reached the bottom of the screwlike stairs, they couldn't believe what they were looking at. Row upon row and stack upon stack, layered a hundred thick, were scrolls of every shape and size. They had been neatly placed on specially designed mounts in hermetically sealed glass cabinets. As if they had entered an old library, Jack and Carl took in the most amazing collection of ancient writings they had ever seen.

The room was temperature and humidity controlled and they saw plastic clean-room suits, of the sort they had used on occasion when working with Europa, hanging on pegs in the corner. There were examination tables and viewing stands. In a clean area fifty feet to the rear was what Jack recognized as an electron microscope. There was a rolled-out scroll on the glass top in the process of examination; it was covered in thick plastic to protect it from any dust particles that filtered into the room.

Also lining the walls were a hundred different flags. Some were emblazoned with a symbol reminiscent of the swastika, different only in small and varying ways. The one constant symbol on every flag was the shape of a large golden eagle. Some had straight and unyielding outstretched wings, and others had the wings turned down.

"Holy shit—is this guy Krueger for real?" Everett asked, staring at the strange banners.

Jack shook his head as he moved on. Also arrayed on one of the walls were several large relief maps from ancient times, sealed in the same manner as the scrolls. There were signs beneath each, warning of severe shock if the frame was touched. Jack stepped up to one and examined it more closely. It was an ancient depiction of Africa before the continent of Antarctica had separated from it. The rest of the world's continents had just broken away from one another and were in the process of moving as depicted in the next four wall-mounted maps.

Everett turned to the rear wall and looked at a strange chart that had millions of lines running through a mosaic relief of the African, European, and even North American continents. The strange lines wiggled through the Atlantic and Pacific oceans. Beneath this ancient diagram was a small table with a computer and a stack of research materials laid out upon it. Everett quickly rifled through it and then turned to face Jack.

"It looks like someone was trying to interpret this chart. Just what in the hell is this?"

Collins didn't answer. He was standing at the farthest end of the chamber, looking up at a giant glass-enclosed map that was by far the largest object in the room. A large spotlight shone upon it and illuminated the frame's meticulous construction, which showed specially designed nitrogen and air evacuation hoses built into it.

"Jesus," Carl hissed as he saw the huge map.

Everett walked over to where Jack was standing and staring upward. He saw what looked to be the ancient Mediterranean. The map looked as if it had been painted on some form of exotic paper. He could also see the age-induced crumbling around the edges and corners. While the obvious age of the map was a striking feature, it was not the one that held the colonel's attention. Everett had to take a step back when he saw the ancient depiction. It showed a large island, made up of four distinct circles of land radiating outward from a center island, that was surrounded by the great inland sea that was one day to be known as the Mediterranean Ocean.

"What in the hell?"

"Mr. Everett, contact Group and inform them that we will be bringing some things back to the complex. We cannot let the FBI have these. I will let Agent Monroe know he'll have to prosecute Mr. Krueger with what stolen items he finds upstairs. I'm sure there is enough."

"Right. Uh, by the way, Jack, are you thinking what I'm thinking?" he asked as his eyes centered on the island that should not have been in the middle of the sea that would someday be known as an ocean.

"You don't have to just think it," he said as he reached out and touched the gold plate beneath the twenty-by-fifteen-foot map of a world long gone. "I think this spells it out quite clearly."

Everett stepped closer as Collins moved away so that he could read the plaque. Carl closed his eyes and shook his head.

"Yeah, I don't think the FBI would truly appreciate the value of this room as much as our people would."

The gold plaque glittered in the illuminating spotlight and both men looked at it and felt numb inside.

Engraved on the plaque was only one word: *Atlantis.*

An hour later, the servants were in the process of being moved to a safe house where they would be informed of their possible prosecution for assisting their employer in his theft of stolen antiquities. That should worry them enough to guarantee their cooperation and silence, Jack thought.

Ernie's Fix-it Shop had just replaced the last door and fixed and replaced the fuse box. The Event Group specialists had cleaned up nicely and were just packing up when Special Agent in Charge Bill Monroe was allowed inside the mansion for the first time.

"Bill," Collins said as he stepped toward the man with his hand outstretched.

The FBI agent shook Jack's hand.

"Colonel, I hear you took quite a haul?"

"Enough so that you'll get a nice little commendation in your Bureau file." Jack released the man's hand and then gently pulled him aside. "Look, this Krueger—there's far more to him than meets the eye. You need to find out all you can on him. He has stuff here that's pretty damn spooky and he keeps saying that we're all dead men for finding it."

"Isn't that usually a standard statement tossed about by scared rich men?"

"There's something in his eyes, Bill. I can't touch on what it is, but this guy is not scared of being prosecuted; he's afraid of something else."

"All right, I'll get what I can out of him. But too much might attract attention to who I really work for, Colonel."

"Don't give yourself up to your FBI. Just get what you can and hold him as long as possible until the Group can examine some of the more obscure items he has. Can you get a judge to recognize that he's a flight risk and not allow bail, at least for the time being?"

"Yeah, I think we can pull that off for a while. So, I only get the upper room of artifacts and you get the really good stuff Ryan's loading up—that right?"

"Sorry, Director Compton says this other room's contents are off limits until researched by the Group. Don't worry, you're getting some great stuff, Billy. Hell, there's a crown in there that belonged to Charlemagne."

"You're kidding?"

Jack Collins just smiled and walked into the darkness beyond the lights.

PRIVATE FLIGHT 1782 ZULU OVER THE ATLANTIC OCEAN

William Winthrop Tomlinson came from an old line of wealth that stretched back far before the Revolutionary War in the United States and then even further back in Europe. It would have taken a specialized team of IRS agents approximately a hundred years to unravel the intricate web of hidden properties and ownerships to discover the fact that he was three hundred times wealthier than the public figurehead who led the nation's and world's periodicals on that subject. He had used that family wealth wisely. He was now the most powerful man in the Coalition. Money was never an object to attain; it was a means to gather what he really craved—power, the power of rule.

Tomlinson was watching the dark sky outside his window as his private Boeing 777 streaked across the night sky, heading to New York. The remains of his salad and bottle of wine were still in front of him on the ornate cherry table.

He did not look around when one of his assistants leaned over with a fax. He absently continued to look out the wide window.

"Sir, this is quite important," the young assistant stated quietly.

The expensively attired Tomlinson still watched the night sky. Ignoring the man at his side, he merely held up his left hand and accepted the fax. He waited until the assistant had turned silently away and gone back to the office areas of the large aircraft. Then he reached out, lifted the crystal wineglass, and sipped the two-hundred-year-old vintage that came from his private stock in the belly of the giant plane. After savoring the deep richness of the wine, he finally looked at the paper in his hand.

0023 hours: Silent alarm tripped at storage station JC-6789. Security dispatched from New York City at 0031 hours by air. Observed a US federal agency raid upon property. Artifact examiner Krueger was removed from property in restraints. Artifacts confiscated and removed from secure location. Instruction require. —L.M.

Tomlinson raised the wineglass and drained its contents in one large gulp. His eyes were steady but belied the fact that his insides were crawling. He squeezed the wineglass almost hard enough to break the exquisite crystal, but then used his formidable willpower to calm himself. He pushed a call button beside the window frame.

"Yes, sir?" the assistant asked as he stood beside the large leather-covered chair.

"Signal our main asset in New York and order her to take care of this development in Westchester." Tomlinson looked at the assistant for the first time and his blue eyes were penetrating. "By any means necessary. There will be no expenditure of funds or personnel too extreme to that end. Is that clear?"

"Clear, sir."

"And inform Dahlia that this information is for my eyes only. The rest of the Coalition is *not* to be informed as of yet. In addition, I want her most up-to-date research and information on the Atlantean Key, and the plate map currently ongoing in Massachusetts, to come directly to me. I want all Westchester materials recovered as early as possible and the name of any agency involved in the raid on Coalition property. An extreme effort on this front is required, and I stress once more, *regardless of losses.*"

The man nodded and quickly turned away to fax the instructions to New York.

Whoever was responsible for this action in Westchester was about to be introduced to the wrath of the new chairman of the Juliai Coalition.

SITUATION ROOM
THE WHITE HOUSE

The president stared at the situation report from Korea. As a former general, he understood the dire consequences of an unstable man and his shaky regime that held a nuclear trigger in his hands. The sit-rep said there had been a limited artillery exchange between the Second Infantry Division and Korean shock troops lining the border. Almost a hundred Americans and South Koreans were dead and a like number of Northern troops.

The intelligence reports that had flooded his desk in the last twelve hours were full of long fitness reports of Kim Jong Il, but what was not printed was the fact that no one really knew where the man was coming from, or where he was going, and in international politics that wasn't good.

"How do we stand on getting the Second Infantry Division reinforced?"

The chairman of the Joint Chiefs opened a file folder and read from a report. "We have the 101st Airborne Division on alert for deployment, as well as the 82nd fast-response units. But I'm afraid they were scattered for the July Fourth holiday and will take at least forty-eight hours to recall and deploy."

The president looked at Kenneth Caulfield and grimaced. "That's it, Ken? What about moving more air force units into Kempo from Japan—how are we looking on that front?"

"We have sent elements of the Third Tactical Fighter Squadron in from the Philippines, where they were conducting joint maneuvers with that government. We're also moving the *John F. Kennedy* and *George Washington* carrier groups into position off the coast of North Korea, but that will take more than four days."

"Jesus, can the Second ID hold if the North comes across the border?"

Caulfield lowered his eyes and shook his head. "Six hours' defense is estimated without tactical-weapons authorization."

The president looked stunned.

"We still have hope of the ceasefire holding as we make our case at the UN," said National Security Advisor Nate Clemmons. "But Kim is still claiming that we and the South Koreans were responsible for the seismic activity off their coast."

"What about the ships depicted in this surveillance footage of theirs?"

"CIA traced the ship's registry on each of the three vessels in question. They are registered to the Mid-China Oil Corporation, with exploratory permits issued legally from Seoul."

"Is there any scientific authority in the world that could prove this ridiculous theory he's spouting about these ships or aircraft being responsible for an earthquake? I mean, does Kim have any firm ground to stand on here?"

"In his country's weakened state, Mr. President, does it really matter? We are dealing with a wounded, very paranoid man here. Forget about walking softly; we have to hit this bastard with a heavy stick and do it before he has the advantage of tank divisions on the south side of the thirty-eighth parallel," General Jess Tippet, commandant of the Marine Corps, said, facing the others around the long table.

"As of this moment I want every single entity of our armed forces breaking their asses to get the Second Infantry Division some help. Strip whatever forces you need to strip. I also want our best minds working on this earthquake crap that he's thought up as an excuse to move south. I want a firm and decisive answer if this seismic thing could possibly be a manmade event."

EVENT GROUP WAREHOUSE 3
SEVENTH AVENUE, NEW YORK CITY

The warehouse used for East Coast storage was a temporary-use facility only. Items recovered from digs, or in this case the raid on the Westchester mansion, could be secured and a precursory examination done before the trip out to the Nellis complex and the secure labs and vaults there.

While Jack and his recovery team took a needed rest, five stories below street level, the items recovered in the raid were getting their initial examination by an East Coast Event team of technicians called in from their various universities. These scientists and techs had the highest of security clearances and all worked for the Event Group in one capacity or another. The leader of the forensic effort was Professor Carl Gillman of NYU. He would work the archiving of the scrolls and artifacts until a better-equipped team from Event Group Center could arrive on station.

It was after Jack had received four hours of rest that Gillman tapped him on the foot. His eyes opened and he looked around before sitting up.

"Sorry to wake you, Colonel, but you have an urgent call from the director."

Jack nodded and placed his feet on the floor. He rubbed a hand through his hair and then took the offered phone.

"Collins."

"Jack, Niles here. I just wanted to let you know that the president has just placed the armed forces on full alert."

"The Korean thing getting worse?"

"Yes, to put it mildly. As a department in the federal government, the alert affects us also. I have a C-130 standing by at JFK airport for your team. I also want all written materials, scrolls, and maps you recovered last night to be brought to Nevada. I could only squeeze one plane out of the air force due to the situations in Iraq and Korea, so for now we have to leave the bulk of the artifacts until the next flight. Professor Gillman will remain there and catalog what we don't take now. Clear, Jack?"

"Yes, sir. We'll get the scrolls, maps, and ourselves out now."

"As for the security element for what items stay in New York, are we good on that point?"

"We have building security in place, plus I'll only take Everett and Will Mendenhall back with me. I'll leave Lance Corporal Sanchez here with the rest of the assault team until we get the rest out."

"Whatever you think best, Jack. Sanchez is quite ready for more responsibility; he's a good man."

"A kid really, but a very capable marine."

"I understand we have some interesting stuff. Carl Gillman is in the process of sending us a video feed of some of the more fascinating discoveries. Do you have any idea why he has requested Sarah and a geologic team to stand by here?"

"No idea; I've been out for a while."

"That's fine. I also understand our friend Mr. Krueger is to be charged this morning in federal court. Monroe said they filed fast to keep him in jail while other charges are sought. Good work, Jack. We'll talk soon."

Jack handed the cell phone back to Gillman and then fixed the professor with a tired look.

"Doc, Director Compton said something about you requested a geologic team to stand by for your video feeds?"

Gillman removed his glasses and ran a hand through his thin and graying hair.

"Besides the existence of several pieces of very ancient jewelry, pottery armor, and the treasure trove of ancient scrolls and books, we have something that is baffling the hell out of our team here. It has something to do with the earth's plate movements. Strange stuff. We just want a geologist to look these charts over so we can know how to catalog them. So, nothing earthshaking, just strange."

Jack just nodded his head and yawned, ignoring the pun by Gillman. "Is the complex locked down, Doc?"

"It's buttoned up tight as a drum. Your men are even shutting down the loading dock and lobby areas."

"Good. Listen, a part of my team is taking the scrolls and maps out of here this morning, but I'm leaving a large security contingent here under Lance Corporal Sanchez. So everyone watch out for wolves at the door."

Gillman watched Jack move off, yawning, to wake the others to load the scrolls and maps and leave for Kennedy, then he moved off himself to return to the most wondrous discoveries he had ever seen. The most interesting of which was a large world chart that had thick lines running through the continents and oceans that just so happened to dissect in many areas of the known tectonic plates. How ancient man had known about these was a puzzle that was driving him and his small team mad.

Little did Gillman know that, over a hundred years before, Professor Peter Rothman had dubbed this particular chart the Atlantean Parchment just a day before he was murdered by a man from the Juliai Coalition.

Now, over a century later, that same Coalition was using the Atlantean Parchment in conjunction with an ancient weapon known as Thor's Hammer.

OYSTER BAY
NASSAU COUNTY, NEW YORK

As Special Agent William Monroe sipped his coffee and read the morning paper, he heard the town's garbage truck outside and then frowned as he heard the clatter of his trash-can lids being tossed like Frisbees into his driveway and then the loud crash of the cans themselves onto the ground. He closed his eyes in frustration as he lowered his paper, then he looked toward the stairs, where he heard his wife moving around. The garbagemen must have awakened her, because it was a good two hours before she was due to get up.

Monroe just shook his head. He moved to the front door with coffee cup in hand, preparing to enjoy chewing on someone's ass for waking his wife, and for tossing his garbage cans just as if he could afford to buy new ones every week.

As he opened the door, he was shocked to see two men in casual clothes standing on his porch. His hackles rose immediately as the sense of danger hit him like a Mack truck.

He dropped his coffee cup and tried to slam the door closed but the two men were fast and he was hit and knocked backward into the entrance hall and then before he could recover was wrestled to the floor. One of the large men hit hard him hard on the face just as he saw through the still-open door the garbage truck move slowly down the street. As his head rocked backward from the blow, he was amazed at the normalcy of things just outside the horror that was happening in his home.

Monroe was stunned, but he was determined to get upstairs somehow. He was roughly turned over, and as the front door and the view of that normal world was cut out of his view, he felt a plastic wire tie being zipped to his wrists behind his back. He was frustrated beyond measure but tried to keep his cool. He had to allow his wife, Jenny, time to realize what was happening. He was pulled roughly to his feet as blood dripped from his mouth and stained the white bathrobe he was wearing.

He heard his bedroom door close upstairs and he closed his eyes. He just knew that Jenny was going to walk right into the middle of what was happening to him. But then again, he had the single ray of hope that his wife had the gun that was kept in the nightstand next to their bed.

Monroe was picked up then and led into the living room, where he was pushed to his knees. He raised his head just as he heard the soft padding of feet on the stairs. He looked up and his heart sank as he saw that it was a woman dressed in a nice pantsuit with a black overcoat. Her hair was blond and she walked with an air of confidence into the living room. She looked from the two men to himself and then sat on their couch and leaned forward with her gloved hands resting in her lap, one on top of the other.

The FBI agent lowered his head to try to get some sense of the situation. His hair was pulled roughly upward so that he faced the woman.

"Pay attention to the lady, she has words she wants to say," the larger of the two men said, leaning over Monroe's right ear.

"For you, Special Agent Monroe, this morning will not turn out as well as you're now hoping," the blond, very elegant-looking woman said as she held Monroe with her eyes and slowly removed her gloves, one finger at a time. "But for your wife, Jenny, who is now being detained upstairs, there is still hope that she can live beyond this day. Do you understand what

I am saying? Just nod your head; no need to speak, as there will plenty of time for that later."

Monroe did as she'd instructed, giving a single dip of his chin.

"Good, we are off to a wonderful start. Your little foray into Westchester County last evening was beyond your scope of charter and expertise. I want you to tell my associates here who it is you are working for, and don't bother saying it was an FBI investigation because we have people in your field office that claim they had no knowledge of your actions. Your deceit may pass muster with your superiors, but I assure you it will not with me."

The woman, having stated what she had to state, slowly stood and looked at her wristwatch.

"Be very forthright, Agent Monroe, and your wife will be alive in the coming weeks, months, and years to mourn your passing. If you lead these men falsely, they will not kill your lovely wife without very much pain and humiliation. All we need to know is where the artifacts are and who it was that assisted you in your daring raid. Okay?" She smiled and nodded at the two men and then walked through the living room and disappeared.

The two men pulled him to his feet and led him into the kitchen. They sat him in a chair and then closed the curtains on the sliding glass doorway that looked out into his backyard. Then one of the men went to the kitchen table and moved a chair over to face him, and then sat down. He was smiling.

An hour later, the two men reported to the woman, who had relocated not far away in Islip, New York. They passed on the required information they tortured out of the FBI agent. What they had learned was almost unbelievable. They asked for instructions about the wife and they received them.

The man closed his cell phone, then reached out, and expertly sliced into the throat of Agent William Monroe, severing the jugular vein with ruthless precision. Then he stood slowly from his chair and made his way toward the stairs and the bedroom.

UNITED STATES FEDERAL COURT-HOUSE, CENTRAL ISLIP, NEW YORK

The new federal courthouse was situated in the middle of Long Island. The giant white concrete building had been constructed not for beauty but with security in mind, and all who passed by it had to shake their heads at the ugly monstrosity where federal justice was meted out.

William Krueger was waiting in a holding cell in the lower level of the courthouse. The orange jumpsuit they had issued him was four sizes too small and he could not even unzip the tight-fitting collar due to his handcuffs.

There were two other men waiting with Krueger to see a federal judge. One was a large black man with a shiny bald head who looked about with the soulless eyes of a career criminal. The other was what Krueger would have called normal-looking. His hair combed neatly, he looked as if a tailor had fitted him for his prison jumpsuit.

There were three guards in the holding area. Two sat behind a large desk and another walked a slow path between the three holding cells, of which only theirs was in use. Krueger watched as the guard looked in quickly and then moved off. He could not figure out what he was looking in the cell for: after all, the three of them were handcuffed to a chain that was bolted to the floor in front of them. They couldn't scratch their noses even if they wanted to.

Krueger was watching the large black man when he heard a noise in the corridor leading to the holding area. He figured that it was the courthouse guards coming to take him in to see his lawyer before he was to be arraigned. From what the guard had told him earlier, that was the procedure.

"Good morning," an unseen voice said to the guards.

"Morning," a female voice answered. Krueger figured that it was one of the guards from behind the desk. "Where's Stan?"

"He called in sick, so they got me moppin' in his place."

Krueger heard the sounds of a janitor and he relaxed. He heard the guards go back to an earlier conversation as the janitor went about his work.

The black man with arms the size of tree trunks was squeezed into his jumpsuit almost like Krueger was, only his discomfort was due to being muscle-bound. The man was looking at Krueger as if he were a bug that had just crawled out of his kitchen cabinet. Krueger immediately looked away.

Outside the cell, as the conversation continued between the two guards at the desk, Krueger heard two loud popping noises as if someone had hit a hollow cardboard tube. Then he heard running and then another hollow pop and then a clattering noise. As he looked around, he saw the thin white prisoner, who had a limited view of the area in front of the cell, lean back and then saw his eyes go wide. Krueger now became concerned.

A shadow fell inside the cell as a man stepped up to the bars. The three prisoners looked around wildly as they saw that the man was armed with what looked like a handgun with a long tube attached to the end. He was dressed in a janitor's jumpsuit and even had an ID tag with his picture on it. He looked from face to face and then raised the silenced weapon and fired twice into the small white prisoner.

"Hey, what the—"

The large black prisoner had tried to stand as he spoke but the chain held his cuffed hands and body close to the bench he was sitting on. He was then caught in midquestion by two bullets fired directly into his forehead. His head jerked backward. Then, just for certainty, another round went into his temple. Despite the silencer, the noise was loud enough that it echoed into the hallway and into the rest of the holding area.

William Krueger leaned as far away as his restraints would allow. He could only hope that the loud reports would bring someone running. However, that hope was fleeting because he knew exactly why that man was there. He also knew that the man would not fail at what he'd been sent there to do. He had expertly shot the three guards and then his cellmates. The silencer had worn out its insulation and had become very loud, which meant that the assassin had never intended to get away with his murders. Krueger's eyes were wide as the dark-haired man looked straight at him.

"I was told you would understand the price of failure, Mr. Krueger."

The fat man started shaking uncontrollably. "But . . . but . . . you'll die too," was all he said.

"That was a forgone conclusion long before today. What is better than to send a dead man to kill another?"

There were sounds of many footsteps running down the hallway and shouts of more guards. The assassin did not bother to look away from the cell. He simply raised the handgun and fired four times into the head and face of William Krueger. The Coalition had just made a public statement of their intention to come out of the shadows and protect what was theirs.

The assassin reached through the bars and tossed the smoking weapon into the cell, were it hit the body of William Krueger and then clattered to the floor. Without hesitation, the man turned and left the holding area and made his way to the back door.

Outside the courthouse, the blond woman watched from her expensive car as the federal building was hurriedly evacuated. Once outside, workers and visitors alike were held in an area just to the left of the white-painted fortresslike courthouse for questioning. As she watched, she saw guards and United States marshals swarm the interior of the building.

The woman started her Mercedes and slowly left the large parking area. She did not smile or gloat on how good she was at arranging things like the assassination. She did exactly what she was paid for—to fix problems.

She slowly turned her car out onto the street and made her way to the Southern State Parkway for her trip into New York City, where she had another job to do before she moved to her next location in Boston. This next venture was also to be a public statement by a power that was far beyond American law enforcement to thwart. It was against an entity that was as secret as the Coalition she worked for—the Event Group.

EVENT GROUP WAREHOUSE 3
SEVENTH AVENUE, NEW YORK CITY

Two Mayflower moving vans backed into the large loading
dock just a half hour after a nondescript truck removed the
scrolls and maps—and the three-man security element of Jack,
Carl, and Will—to JFK airport. The back of the Event Group–
owned Freemont Building was deserted, with the exception of
a guard in his shack overlooking the dock area.

A driver stepped from the first moving truck and hopped
up to the dock. He was carrying a clipboard and was wearing
the livery colors of Mayflower Transit. He looked around and
waited.

The guard-shack door opened and a man stepped out wearing a standard security uniform. He placed a cap on his head
and stepped toward the man who was looking at him with a
smile.

"We don't accept deliveries at this address, son," the man
said as he eyed the two trucks.

"Actually, my boss called and said that we had a pickup at
this building." He made a show of looking at his clipboard.
"Yeah, says right here, the Freemont. There isn't another
building with that name on this street, is there?"

"No, but you may want to check back with your—"

A seven-inch knife in between his ribs cut the guard's words
off as effectively as if he had shut off a radio. The man who had
come up behind the guard was the driver of the second truck.
The first man laid his clipboard down and then reached out and
raised the sliding door of the first large moving van. As he did
so, thirty-five men exited quickly. All were dressed in black
Nomex and all had black hoods on their heads. It was exactly
the same uniform that Jack and his men had worn for their raid
the night before in Katonah.

A three-man team ran to the guard shack and another
group to the large sliding doors of the loading dock. The first
group smashed the communications-and-monitoring console
in the guard shack and the second group placed quarter-pound
timed charges against the base of each of the two loading

doors that led into the warehouse. Each thirty-five-man team from the two trucks lined up on either side of the two doors just as two loud pops sounded, freeing the doors from their interior lock slots. As one man from each team slid the doors up, the rest ran into the dark interior.

Lance Corporal Jimmy Sanchez had been part of the Event Group for four years and loved the detached duty. He was moving up fast and the work under Colonel Jack Collins was challenging, to say the least. Being a veteran of the Event in the desert and the expedition down the Amazon the preceding year, he had come to be a trusted member of the security team that Collins had forged since he'd begun work for the Group. He'd even heard from Will Mendenhall that he was to advance in pay-grade to sergeant in the fall.

As Sanchez started to move, the ceiling lights flickered just as the sound of automatic gunfire erupted somewhere below them. He immediately ran to the wall-mounted phone and picked it up. There was no dial tone. He then reached into his pocket for his Group cell phone and punched only one number. It would alert all Event Group personnel that an emergency had arisen, which meant that the security team should come running to their aid. It also sent an automated message via satellite to Nevada, where the emergency alert would be relayed to Group Center.

Sanchez tossed the phone to the nearest wide-eyed technician.

"Dial 911 and tell them we have a break-in and shots have been fired!"

Sanchez withdrew his holstered 9-millimeter automatic and ran to the door. The corporal was on the second floor of the thirty-story Freemont Building, placing him only three levels above the loading dock. As he rounded the corner heading to the large staircase, he heard the volume of gunfire increase. He heard the distinctive reports of his own team's XM-8 automatic assault rifles, which meant that they had responded quickly to whatever was happening. As he gained the balcony overlooking the first floor, he stopped suddenly. Below, just as his men came into the main foyer to meet the attackers, they ran into at least fifty men. They quickly overwhelmed his first-floor team. They were everywhere. Sanchez cursed and ran back the way he had come. He had to get the technicians and professors out of harm's way.

"Corporal, the phones aren't getting a signal. At first we could, and then they all suddenly stopped sending. We couldn't get the police," the field tech said as Sanchez ran by him.

"They are jamming the cell signals with independent microwaves! Get upstairs with the rest of security; this is a kill raid!"

As Sanchez was trying to rally what was left of the Group's security element, the attackers started making their way upstairs.

Waiting below with a five-man protection team, the well-dressed blond woman looked at her watch, impatient for the long morning's work to be finished. She turned to her personal bodyguard.

"I want at least four of these people alive to answer questions. In addition, after we are finished here I want a man stationed outside to take photos of everyone who comes into the building. Police, medical teams—I want everyone documented, with particular interest taken in subjects in civilian attire."

JOHN F. KENNEDY AIRPORT
QUEENS, NEW YORK

As the last of the pallets containing the maps and scrolls were rolled into the vast cargo hold of the giant air force C-130 Hercules, Jack was approached by the aircraft's commander.

"Colonel Collins, a man by the name of Compton is on the radio. He said he couldn't get through to you on your cell phone, there isn't much signal here in the cargo hold. So he's been patched through the tower."

Jack followed the air force captain into the cockpit and took the offered headphones.

"Collins," he said, holding the headpiece to his ear.

"Jack, we have some major problems."

Jack heard the strain in those few words from Niles Compton.

"What've you got, Niles?"

"Jack, listen . . ." Niles hesitated. "Agent Monroe has been murdered."

"What?"

"He was tortured and killed in his house. His wife was . . . well she's dead also, Jack. That's not all I'm afraid of. William Krueger was hit this morning inside his secure holding cell at the federal courthouse out on Long Island."

"Dammit! How in the hell could this have happened?"

"Jack, you and Carl get back to Manhattan. We had an emergency alert from Sanchez. We don't know what's happening at the warehouse and we've been unable to establish contact. We had no choice but to bring in the local authorities. Their cover as a National Archives depot will hold up to scrutiny, so act accordingly when you arrive. Now move, Jack—move!"

Jack didn't comment, as he had already tossed the headphones to the aircraft's pilot.

"Get this bird in the air ASAP and don't stop for anything. You'll be given instructions in flight on your way to Nellis. Clear?"

Again, he didn't wait for an answer. Two minutes later, he, Everett, and Mendenhall were on their way back into Manhattan.

EVENT GROUP WAREHOUSE 3
SEVENTH AVENUE, NEW YORK CITY

Collins, Everett, and Mendenhall were met at the front of the building by a police captain from the NYPD. Jack gave him identification stating that he was a field supervisor for the National Archives in Washington. The captain looked it over and then eyed Jack closely.

"I didn't think the National Archives Security Department carried firearms?" he asked, still holding Jack's ID.

Collins stared at the man and did not blink. Nor did he offer any explanation. All he knew was that this man was stopping him from checking on his team inside the building.

Everett stepped up and offered an explanation: "When you are used to guarding little documents like the Declaration of Independence, firearms are desirable, Captain. Now may we check on our people?"

The captain relaxed and returned Jack's identification.

"It's not good, gentlemen. We have paramedics working on the only survivor. It looks like a straight robbery. If you have information on what was being stored here, my detectives would be interested."

Jack didn't wait, he just brushed by the captain and went through the front doors. What he saw inside was like a scene from a battlefield. He noticed the covered bodies strewn about like so much dropped laundry. He counted thirteen on the first floor alone. He was joined a moment later by Everett and Mendenhall.

"Jesus, who in the hell hit this place?" Everett said as he turned to face the police captain.

"As far as we can tell, it was at least a fifty-man raid. So far, only your people are accounted for. Due to the fact that around each of the bodies are several expended rounds, we must assume that your security put up a fight, and bloodstains show that the suspects must have carried off their wounded and dead."

"You said there was a survivor?" Mendenhall asked, looking ashen, as he knew personally all the men in the security team they had left there. Jimmy Sanchez was a close personal friend.

"Second floor."

The three men left the captain and trotted hurriedly up the stairs. Everywhere they looked, the walls and doors were riddled with bullet holes. Technicians were lying about where they fallen after being hit. A few of the academics had been dispatched execution-style in one of the offices. Four of the scientists and assistants looked as if they had been tortured. The artifacts, as far as they could tell, were all missing.

"Over here, Jack," Everett called out.

Jack looked up and saw three paramedics close to the second-floor elevator. They had a single soul on a stretcher and were fiercely working on him. As they approached, Mendenhall froze as he discovered who it was who was fighting for his life: Lance Corporal Sanchez.

"Oh . . ." was all the stunned Mendenhall could say as he looked on sadly.

Everett placed a hand on Mendenhall's shoulder and watched helplessly as the medics worked furiously.

Jack's eyes never blinked as he watched another one of his men slowly slide away from the living. As Sanchez took his last breath, Collins closed his eyes. When he opened them, he saw the stairwell that still sported the blood where Sanchez had made a stand against the overwhelming odds he had faced.

One of the bodies closest to the corporal was a full-time archaeologist assigned to the main complex in Nevada. The boy was taped into a chair, and Collins could tell by the missing fingernails that he had been tortured in the most brutal manner possible. He closed his eyes, knowing that the poor kid would have given information on the Group. He didn't have to look far to find his proof. His eyes locked on a portion of the wall above just as Everett joined him. They examined the four words written in the blood of Corporal Sanchez, declaring the Event Group fair and open game. They dripped and ran red down the white wall above the stairwell.

NOT SO SECRET ANYMORE!

A man who had been taking pictures most of the morning from across the street changed his position and climbed the stairwell inside the building. He went to the second floor, where he was surprised to find a great location to shoot directly into the Freemont Building. He adjusted the telephoto lens and framed three men standing on the second-floor landing. A large blond man, a black man, and a man who stood ramrod-straight were glaring at the message left on the wall. As he clicked away, the hard-featured man turned to the landing's large window and seemed to look right at the camera's lens. The shooter abruptly stopped snapping pictures, as he could have sworn that the man was looking right at him. He lowered the camera and swallowed. He decided that what he had was enough.

Dahlia would have to make do with what he had learned, because, for some reason, the man on the landing scared the living hell out of him.

RUSSIAN PACIFIC FLEET HQ
VLADIVOSTOK, RUSSIA

With the situation in Korea growing steadily worse, the Russian navy was on deployment alert. Every man in the Pacific Fleet, both surface and subsurface, had been recalled and awaited sailing orders.

Of the serviceable surface combatants, the fleet was in a sorry state, to say the least. Only three of her large battle cruisers were operational, and only one of them could ship a full-crew complement of trained seamen. The rest were out-of-date and undermanned light cruisers and destroyers. Still, the Russian navy was a proud entity and could still draw blood when needed.

The crew of the Russian heavy battle cruiser *Admiral Nakhimov* had been at their stations, ready to put out to sea for the past two hours to shadow the two U.S. carrier task forces. The captain of the *Admiral Nakhimov* was delayed, waiting for the bulk of their task force to form up before putting out to sea.

The surrounding harbor was full of antiquated warships, but the *Nakhimov* was part of the Russian president's massive strive to reclaim some of the old Soviet pride and power. Next to the *Nakhimov* was the heavy cruiser *Petr Velikiy*, commissioned the *Uri Andropov* in 1998. She would sail with the *Nakhimov* to the Sea of Japan.

Seven hundred miles out at sea in the freezing waters of the Pacific, a large aircraft strayed off course just as she had in the Middle East. This time her course would not take her over any appreciable landmass.

The navigator of the large Boeing 747 tracked their marker, an undersea beacon laid down a full year before by a Japanese-flagged fishing trawler.

Tomlinson, with his assistant in the seat next to him, had been silent since the registered charter flight lifted off from a private airstrip in the Philippines. The navigator and the pilot knew who the man was and it showed in their nervousness.

The head of the Thor program stepped out of the protected area and walked to Tomlinson. He cleared his throat.

"The Wave is operational and online. We have return echoes from the amplification modules on the seabed. Radar reports no contact of any air-superiority fighters in our immediate area."

"Then all is well for the strike?" Tomlinson asked, his blue eyes boring into those of Professor Ernest Engvall, former head of the Franz Westverall Institute of Geology and Seismic Study in Norway.

"All is as planned; nothing has changed for the past three years of calculations," he said, but Tomlinson knew that he had stopped short of finishing his report.

"Except?" he asked, holding his penetrating gaze on the world's foremost seismologist.

The thin, bookish man held his tongue for a brief moment but knew that he had to bring up what his entire technical crew was discussing.

"Do I have to ask twice, Professor?"

"We have two wave aircraft at our disposal, both of which could be tracked and attacked at any time. If I may ask, why have you risked your life to be on this particular strike?"

Tomlinson smiled and looked away without answering. His assistant cleared his throat and concluded the conversation.

"You may resume your countdown without further delay. Release Thor's Hammer, Professor."

Engvall's look went from Tomlinson to his impeccably dressed assistant. Then he abruptly turned and entered the protective area of the 747.

Tomlinson was staring at nothing as he thought about his father. He had been integral part of the Coalition in the latter days of the world war. He'd never risen as high in the council as his son would in future years, but he had done his part. The thought of his father being held up against a crumbling wall and shot by Russian shock troops just outside Berlin, after delivering the Coalition's ultimatum to Hitler, didn't anger him like it used to. After all, his father had allowed himself to be used by those higher in the order and thus had reaped that particular harvest. It was the Russian leadership he had always despised and their weak-minded followers. It was not personal, as most on the Coalition Council would believe, but the smart thing to do, with their government weak and their populace uneasy.

He looked up when he heard the soft humming of the Wave equipment. He wanted the strike to be flawless, and that was the real reason why he was here. The old guard of the Coalition would be shown that a limited strike did not need the Atlantean Key for control of the weapon. Now, he was here to prove it. Their race had split once before and it had almost cost them their existence in the time of Julius Caesar. He would see to it that if this demonstration did not have a positive effect on the Coalition members who refused to follow, he would scratch them from the equation in totem.

"Bring the Wave up to full power. Directional beacon is locked and confirmed."

Engvall ran to another panel and watched as the Wave buildup became a steady stream of blue and red on the computer's monitor.

"We have solid tone," one of the techs called out.

Once the stream turned pure red, the audio wave was pulsed to the amplifiers on the seafloor. Once the trigger had penetrated the depths of the sea, the audio signal would be activated and then the three-pronged decibel enhancers set inside the large steel enclosures would chime like a tuning fork, creating the desired tone that the Ancients had calculated thousands of years before for the science of breaking solid stone.

The amplifiers were laid along the Koryak-Kamchatka orogenic belt, which sat above one of the most active continental plates in the world. The wave from the amplifiers would sink to crust depth and hammer at its edges in an assault of sound that would crumble any natural strata in all of known geology.

The duration of the three-second pulse would be short, due to the instability of the Wave of the Ancients. That and the fact that the fault line above the plate ran all the way to Sumatra.

"Initiate trigger, now!"

Located at the bottom of the huge aircraft, a set of doors swung open and the small laser cannon deployed. It was not a cannon in the normal sense of the word; it was a laser-guided sound pulse. A three-second burst at full power shot downward into the sea, where it would actually pick up speed as it was not diminished by one single decibel due to the salinity of the water. Twenty-one miles below the surface of the sea, the wave penetrated the waters of the cold Pacific at the speed of sound. It struck the first amplifier, then relayed down the line of six. More than six hundred miles of fault line and its supporting plate were under attack. The strike would generate enough explosive energy as fifty twenty-megaton nuclear detonations going off in the earth's crust.

As it struck, the audio wave radiated in the only direction it could: straight down through sand and rock.

The Boulder Institute of Seismology in Colorado recorded the eruption underneath the crust as it traveled as far south as Australia and as far east as the United States. The epicenter of the quake originated two hundred miles north of the undersea Siberian Seamount. As the seafloor split, ten trillion gallons of seawater flooded into the void. The smaller seamounts nearest the eruption cascaded into the gap that had instantly gone from a mere fracture to the size of the island of Hawaii. The quake hit the Siberian coast and shook houses to their foundations. The first shocks hit Japan and China only twenty-three seconds later.

As he monitored the reports coming in from prepositioned seismic stations in the Pacific, Engvall knew that they had unleashed a strike accurate to the mile. As he listened to the euphoria in the voices of his technicians, the realization had struck him that he just might have destroyed a great deal of Russia's eastern coast.

RUSSIAN AND NORTH KOREAN
JOINT SEISMIC LISTENING STATION
(JSRCLS) 12

As a listening post at the northern end of the Sea of Japan, the Joint Communications and Seismic Station did not garner much respect from the U.S. Navy. The antiquated equipment failed to measure seismic activity accurately. Japan and the United States had succeeded in doing that in the late 1950s. The communications network was in an even worse state.

As the bored men fought to stay awake, the needle on the antiquated Richter monitor moved once and held steady. The operator failed to see the quick jump of the needle. Instead, the ancient radio monitor told them something was amiss.

The two young Korean and Russian officers listening in on the Japanese and American chatter were using a radio and direction finder that was surplus back in 1959. The constant replacement of its tubes and the limited-frequency channels made finding anyone, anywhere, talking openly as rare as good food on the anchored station. However, the one thing it was good at was picking up low-range high-decibel-burst releases, only because the equipment lacked the necessary filters of modern sets to block it out.

Both radiomen suddenly shouted out and threw the headphones from their ears. The Russian doubled over in pain and the Korean actually felt the trickle of blood flow from his right ear.

"What are you two fools doing?" asked the Korean duty officer.

"It must have been some sort of burst transmission," the soldier said as he grabbed his Russian counterpart for support. "An aircraft directly overhead, that's the only thing it could have been, maybe—"

That was as far as he got as the anchored platform was rocked on its stiltlike legs.

"My God, look at this!"

The officer gained his balance and turned to the Richter

scale. The long needle was swishing back and forth on the graph paper, almost creating a solid wall of red as it moved.

The technician shouted out, "6.5 . . . 7.1 . . . 7.9 . . . 8.0," as he counted the numbers the needle struck. As he did so, the platform—an old oil derrick of Russian design—lifted and then swayed. He continued: "8.7 . . . 9.6 . . ."

"My God, the sea is erupting around us!"

"Track that aircraft!" the officer screamed as he lost his footing.

TARGET AREA 1: VLADIVOSTOK

The men of the battle cruiser *Admiral Nakhimov* were making ready to get under way when the harbor waters started to recede. At the same time, warning sirens sounded throughout the naval base. The above-deck crew ran to the railing and watched in amazement as the sea rolled out from under them and her sister vessel, *Petr Velikiy,* as both giant vessels strained at their many mooring ropes. As the two great warships groaned and creaked, their heavy bulk settled into the dark mud of the harbor. Smaller warships of the fleet were torn from their moorings, kidnaped by the retreating waters of the Pacific.

Onshore the quake hit with devastating power. Buildings constructed to withstand direct bomb hits were knocked flat with no warning. Streets buckled and fell into voids created by ancient riverbeds collapsing underground. Thousands of people were crushed to death as cranes and material in the dry dock area broke and fell. Giant cruisers rolled over and crushed the lives of seamen as they tried in vain to make it over ships railings.

Men aboard the *Admiral Nakhimov* were knocked from their feet as thick, viscous mud erupted like lava from the harbor floor. The giant ship rippled as the mud below waved up like a maddened sea. At that moment, the men heard the most horrible of sounds. It rumbled even above the noise of the quake. It was the return of the sea.

"Abandon ship, all hands abandon ship!" the loud speakers on both vessels bellowed.

The horrible roar grew from the east and the sea beyond. The sun was blotted out as the giant wave built as the ocean rushed back in to fill the land vacated in its backlash. As the sea started to crest, just one mile south of the port of Vladivostok another quake, of greater magnitude, struck. The air itself became a living thing as scared people became disoriented and fell to the undulating ground. Then the water was returning just as if hell itself had opened its gates.

The crew of the *Nakhimov* knew they were about to die as the wall of water was seen taking out the city before them. Entire buildings were knocked free of their foundations, their debris joining the onrush of destruction. The wall of water hit the two great ships. They were smashed and then lifted and flipped over like toys in a tub as they cascaded into the eastern end of the port city.

The *Petr Velikiy* disintegrated like it had been made of wood. The thick steel plates made to withstand a standard torpedo strike caved in and fell apart as easily as if made of the finest crystal. The *Nakhimov* was flipped end over end three times before it struck the roiling waters below, breaking the ship into three pieces. Still the waters rushed inland.

The Wave had created an earthquake with its accompanying tsunami the likes of which the modern world had never seen. The quake struck in Sydney, killing seventeen people when one of her older bridges collapsed. The tsunami, though diminished by that time, struck northern Japan and destroyed two small villages.

The American carrier force sent to help the Second Infantry Division lost one supply ship and two destroyers, as the sudden surge of ocean had caught the smaller ships in a wide turn. The carriers themselves suffered only minor damage.

By far the second-largest devastation and loss of life occurred in China, where it struck as far inland as Beijing. One hundred thousand Chinese lost their lives to Thor's Hammer.

The target city of Vladivostok was destroyed. Not a single human life survived the quake and tsunami that followed Thor's Hammer. The water reached as far inland as Mongolia and wiped out mining operations in Siberia. All told, the death toll in Russia would exceed one million people. The Russian

Pacific Fleet, which was preparing to monitor the American response to North Korea's actions, was gone forever.

Now, the one thing not expected by Tomlinson and the younger Coalition members was the fact that a Russian and Korean monitoring station had picked up the initial trigger broadcast that activated Thor's Hammer. The president of Russia, after finding this out, grew suspicious and suddenly the ravings of Kim Jong Il didn't seem so far-fetched. The Russians and Chinese for precautionary reasons brought their military forces to red alert.

The Doomsday Clock had started.

Police Plaza and that piece shared up with the shooting
contract to keep Koverchenk there, was all he knew.

Now, the one thing that appeared by Danny Wu and one
thing Coughlin did not want. "Oh, hell." As she and
Kevin monitoring radio had picked on me found in cop
treachery picked out that exhaling the president of the
an affair linking this one-gang suspicions and and with the
slaying of Kuo Jong If still safer section TS
state and cabin up and many voices thought a of
many voices urged aloud.

The Diamond Clock Runs Red

PART II
On the Trail of the Ancients

CHAPTER
FOUR

HEMPSTEAD BUILDING
CHICAGO, ILLINOIS

William Tomlinson accepted the drink from his assistant as the other members of his inner circle waited. On the large liquid-crystal screen was a broad view of the conference room in Norway. A test of wills was so palpable that the air was as thick as molasses.

"You have missed the point entirely, sir. The weapon has caused damage to the two American carrier groups en route to the Sea of Japan. This is jeopardizing the American and Korean lines of resistance if the North attacks. They will be overrun, and that, regardless of your bravado, is not now nor ever was the goal of the test strike. And your blatant disregard for the loss of life in Japan and China was never in the Russian plan."

Tomlinson did not even look up from his drink as the Austrian spoke his condemning words.

"We weaken the old enemies, not destroy our own governments. We need them, for the time being!"

"You gentlemen may need them; we, on the other hand, do not." Tomlinson placed his drink on the polished tabletop and stood, knowing that the camera would stay on him. "This organization made the fatal mistake three times in three hundred years of trusting existing governments to bend to our will, only to have these power-mad individuals balk at our orders and deviate from our hard work and intricately detailed plans. This," he turned and faced the camera lens with steady eyes, "will never happen again. The plan has evolved from our original strike plan and *this* executive council has overruled the initial strategy in favor of utilizing the drought and flooding in Russia and China and forging ahead. We will bring down those who would eventually stand in our way, just ahead of the schedule we had deliberated upon."

"Have you all gone completely mad? Who will control these governments when anarchy tears them apart?" Zoenfeller exclaimed, slapping his hand on the conference table. "Russia first, after we have the Atlantean Key. You went against our vote and struck anyway!"

"May I say a word?" A smallish man stood and buttoned his jacket.

Tomlinson had coached him on when to talk and what to say. He gestured to the owner of a large consortium of Japanese electronics firms.

"You are judging our small enclave too harshly. Yes, we have changed small parts of the offensive to take advantage of Russia and China's weaknesses in the present time. The weapon was precise and did no more damage than a natural quake would have caused in the same target area. It was, after all, part of my own nation's coastline that sustained damage by the residual effects of the wave. Yet I am still wholeheartedly onboard this accelerated plan."

"That does not give you the right to—"

"Russia, along with China must be out of our way. Let us do it now. This is the moment to act. As soon as the Atlantean Key is in our possession, we can get back on schedule and deal with the western governments. Then, when countries start crumbling from natural disasters, it will be our corporations and leadership worldwide that step in. We will be hailed as deliverers of new hope and then we will *all* at last have total control. Now is the time for resolve," the Japanese council member waved his hand toward the video screen, "not for timidity. The Juliai and Caesarean Reich will prevail."

The sixteen council members of the inner circle patted their hands on the conference table in total agreement as the Japanese representative bowed and sat down.

The next person was an elegant woman from Great Britain who slowly stood and smiled. She looked at Tomlinson and then spoke.

"Ethnic purification, economic control, and the elimination of formal governments have always been the goal of the Juliai. Regardless of who is struck and when, it cannot help but destabilize the West. As Mr. Tomlinson has stated repeatedly, we have our people ready to step in and take control, but we cannot do so until the destabilization process has begun." Dame Lilith opened her folder and pulled out a sheet of paper. "Germany, Japan, and America must be the first to fall. Therefore, it has been determined that the leadership in these countries must be eliminated, and a timetable within the framework of three weeks is not impossible," she stated in the matter-of-fact way that she would give instructions to one of her servants.

"Again, this is at least four years ahead of schedule. We must—"

"Now, to give you gentlemen and lady a dose of faith in what we have planned, I will now inform you on what is currently happening," Tomlinson said, yet again interrupting Zoenfeller. "As you know, the setback that occurred in New York at our study facility was at first worrisome. However, I am very pleased to announce that the fat fool you gentlemen had placed so much trust in many years ago, has been eliminated before he could cause harm to us by any plea bargain he could have eventually made."

Again, the others on the opposite side of the Atlantic were shocked that death orders had been issued without their conjoined approval.

"The second fact is that the agent in charge of that raid is now dead, along with his entire team. The material from Westchester has been recovered intact," Tomlinson said, smiling, not even flinching when the small lie flowed from his lips.

Again, the younger members gathered in Chicago started slapping the table with the news just delivered.

"Now the good news. Our operative Dahlia has also learned that the location of the plate map that was stolen by Peter Rothman over a hundred years ago has finally been traced to an Ancient in Boston. We will soon have it in our possession."

"Then why not wait for the recovery of the Key before any more strikes?" the Austrian asked as many of the heads nodded agreement on the other side of the Atlantic. "If you're so sure—"

Tomlinson cut the Austrian off brutally.

"The Key is recoverable and will soon be here; that is all you need for the moment. Our efforts are also almost complete in regard to Crete. They broke into the city just hours ago. We will have the location from which we can strike the rest of the world with impunity. After all, how can you trace us to a site that most of the world does not even believe ever existed?"

The elderly members of the Juliai Coalition looked away from the screen on their side of the Atlantic Ocean. Zoenfeller looked around him for support but found that even the elder membership, for the most part, had been swayed by Tomlinson's arguments and by the audacious actions of their once-junior members.

Tomlinson straightened his suit jacket and slowly sat down. He looked at the screen and smiled.

"Our long quest is finally at hand. From the time of the Caesars, through the Templar quest for the burial site of the scrolls while feigning a search for a ridiculous Grail, to our Germanic and Napoleonic attempts, we have learned the hard lesson that the world will not just fall into our hands. Now, with this adjusted plan, the world will actually beg for deliverance. No more foolish ideologies and no more patriotic zeal to stand in the way of an orderly world."

"What of the claims now circulating by that fool in North Korea?" Zoenfeller asked in a last-ditch effort to regain some control.

"There is not one entity in service to *any* government on this planet that can discover what it is we are attempting. There is no hard evidence to back those claims. Just follow our lead and we will soon inherit the earth much sooner than the original plan called for."

THE WHITE HOUSE
WASHINGTON, D.C.

The new president was late for a briefing downstairs in the Situation Room but the last-minute restructuring of departments was of a higher priority, due to North Korea's absurd claims that country's ills had been manmade. He had to start with the very department he had visited just the day before.

"I'm sorry, Director Compton, for your losses, but I can't concern myself with this matter at the moment. Am I clear as to the staffing requirements I have outlined?"

The phone line went quiet for a moment and then Niles Compton said, "Mr. President, giving you my earth-science departments is not a problem. But if you take one hundred percent of our computer sciences, we have no way of tracking who hit my warehouse this morning in New York."

"That matter will be turned over to the FBI and local law-enforcement authority. Is that clear?"

"You're breaking apart the best chance we have at finding out what's happening here. My people are capable of multitasking beyond anything and any entity in the world. They work as a team and separating them is a mistake. It takes away their ability to think together. Something is wrong here and you are condemning my Group to facing the deaths of many of their colleagues without a chance to find out why."

"Mr. Director, I assume you are on a speakerphone?"

Niles looked around his office. Virginia and Alice were the only ones present.

"Yes, sir."

"Please pick up the phone. I wish to speak to you in private."

Niles leaned over and picked up the receiver. Niles listened, his eyes intentionally focused on the top of his desk. The conversation was one-sided as Virginia and Alice exchanged curious looks.

"Yes, sir," Niles answered, and then reached out and punched a button, placing the call back into conference mode.

"Dr. Compton, who is your assistant director?" the president asked.

"Professor Virginia Pollock, Mr. President," Niles answered as he looked at Alice and shrugged.

"Professor, are you listening?"

Niles stood and then sat on the edge of his desk and looked at Virginia and nodded. The tall woman with dark hair and sharp features stood and walked closer to the speakerphone.

"Yes, Mr. President?"

"Professor, I have ordered Dr. Compton to Washington for direct consultations with me. I am placing you in temporary command of Department 5656. I am ordering you to transfer control of your Group's science departments over to my national security adviser. You are also ordered to utilize your agency's superior computing power to help discover if the allegations put forth by the Koreans have any validity. Is this order understood?"

"All but me reporting to your adviser, Mr. President, because according to our agency charter, the national security adviser is not a cabinet posting, therefore he cannot have knowledge of our department, and as we are—"

Niles cleared his throat, interrupting Virginia. She looked up and he shook his head.

"Excuse me, sir. All departments are standing by to assist in any way we can."

Niles nodded and then walked behind his desk and sat down.

"Very well. Dr. Compton is hereby ordered to stand down and to report to Washington for consultation with my science adviser, and to act as liaison between myself and your Group. He is to be on a plane in the next half an hour. Is this order clear?"

"Yes—"

Virginia stopped short when she realized that she was speaking into a dead phone.

* * *

The president set the phone down and looked over at the initial casualty report from the artillery exchange in Korea. Then he removed the top page and looked at the estimates of the damage suffered by the two carrier groups in the Sea of Japan because of the earthquake.

The squadrons onboard both Nimitz-class carriers were down to 53 percent on the *George Washington* and 68 percent on the *John F. Kennedy*. There had been a loss of life of more than two hundred when the last vestiges of the tsunamis struck the two groups' smaller escort vessels.

The secretary of defense opened the door and stepped in. He looked subdued as he handed the president a note.

"The North Koreans informed us through the Chinese government that any attempt to reenforce ground or air forces by NATO or any of her factions will be construed as an imminent attack on North Korean forces and they will be forced to defend themselves."

"Jesus. What are the Russians and Chinese saying?"

"Nothing other than they support the North Koreans in the defense of the border and have asked us to show good faith and recall the task force heading for the Sea of Japan."

"Dammit, that's not exactly saying nothing." The president turned away, examined the note again, then tossed it onto his desk. "We have freedom of the sea here and I am not going to allow a buildup on the border to go unchecked. I can't," he said as he turned and faced his adviser. "The task forces continue. I'm not leaving those boys without naval support. Send a message to the Koreans that it is in their hands. Get away from the border. Allow relief efforts in and then we can talk."

He watched the secretary leave and then looked out at the clouded sky through the window. He shook his head as he was beginning to wonder if there was a serious attempt by an outside or otherworldly influence out to thwart his every move toward peace. He knew that he needed help from someone he trusted beyond any other in assessing all that was happening. He hoped he had it coming from Nevada.

EVENT GROUP CENTER
NELLIS AIR FORCE BASE, NEVADA

Niles attempted to smile but failed. He removed his thick glasses and rubbed the bridge of his nose.

"What are your immediate orders to the Group, Virginia?" he asked, finally looking up at the two women. "It's all over the news about that listening post in the Sea of Japan picking up those strange signals just before the quake hit. So that crazy bastard may have reason to believe the stuff he's spouting."

A knock sounded at the door and one of the secretaries stepped in and offered Niles a note.

"The president just sent this over, sir."

Niles took the offered note and excused the assistant.

Virginia calmly took a seat and then looked Niles straight in the eye.

"Thirty-two people, Niles—that's what we lost this morning in New York. Compared with the nation's losses in Korea and those two carrier battle groups, and all those poor souls in Korea, a very small number. I will follow orders of course and do what I'm ordered to do. But I refuse to just forget about our own people in New York."

Niles waved his hand for her to continue. He was still looking at the president's note.

"The science departments will be put to work finding out if this ridiculous claim by the Koreans could be true in the fact that the earthquake that struck there was manmade and intentional. But computer sciences will be allowed to have fifty percent of the computing power of Europa to help find the killers of our people, and to find out how they could have known about us, and why those artifacts recovered from Westchester were so important."

"Thank you, Virginia," Niles said as he replaced his glasses.

"It's not for you, or me, or even the Group. I just don't want to be the one to explain to Jack why we're not looking for these murdering bastards."

"My thoughts exactly," he said. Then he looked at Virginia closely and slid the note over to her. "But the priority here is no longer finding the murderers of our people. Keep that segment of research small."

"Why?" Virginia asked as she picked up the note and started to read.

"Because now we don't just have North Korea claiming this stuff; it seems the Russians also picked up a strange signal seconds before another quake. This one happened just an hour ago and explains the president's mood.

"What is it?" Alice asked.

"The Russian port of Vladivostok has just been wiped off the map."

The shipment of artifacts and maps had finally arrived and been transferred down to the sciences level to be carefully cataloged and photographed.

Sarah McIntire had been there at the dock to greet Jack, Carl, and Mendenhall and to offer her condolences on the loss of Lance Corporal Sanchez and the other members of the Group at the New York warehouse. Being secret lovers with the colonel had not prevented Sarah from getting an icy and distant look at first from Jack as she looked into his eyes. After a moment, he had come around and nodded his head and then lightly touched her right shoulder before moving off to report to Niles. Sarah had started to tell Jack that Niles had been ordered to Washington, but then she'd thought it would be better if Virginia informed him. After speaking with Carl for only a moment her curiosity had gotten the better of her and she'd taken the elevator down to level thirty-two to see the wonders that had been recovered in Westchester for herself.

Ten minutes later, Sarah was watching the Cataloging Department as they lifted items out of their transport crates. Others had joined her and were oohing and ahing at some of the more brilliant pieces. Soon the overhead speakers called most away, as the individual departments were receiving their new assignments, per the president's orders.

As a geologist there was one artifact in particular that Sarah spied that made her pulse race. Two men had lifted a large, framed maplike parchment from an art sleeve. As she stepped closer to the thick glass, she saw that it was a rough rendering of the world, as an ancient society would have painted it. The colorful scope of Europe, the Mediterranean, Africa, and Asia was almost as she knew them today, except for the strange ring of islands in the center of the Med. Depictions of North and South America looked as if the mapmaker had drawn them after looking into a fun-house mirror. They were wobbly and misshapen, as if a child had drawn them.

What really caught her eye and gave her the feeling that she should recognize something on the strange, ancient atlas were the lines that coursed through it. They seemed familiar to her somehow.

Sarah tapped on the thick glass and got the technicians' attention. The white-gloved navy specialist waved when he looked up and saw that it was Sarah. He knew her from Saturday-night poker. Sarah pointed at the eight-foot-by-five-foot map and waved for the two technicians to bring it closer to the glass. The men exchanged looks, shrugged their shoulders, then hefted the heavy frame closer so that Sarah could view it better. Then the man Sarah knew hit the intercom.

"I know what you're looking at. It's that strange island in the middle of the Med, isn't it?"

Sarah did not respond. She took in the strange lines, wondering where she had seen them before. Then she smiled thinly and looked at the man through the glass.

"What's that, Smitty?"

"That's what I'm saying, the island with the rings around it."

"No. I mean, yeah, that's a little strange, but I'm interested in the lines going through this weird world more than the ringed islands."

"Maybe some sort of latitude and longitude markings. They're a little screwed up, but that may be what they are." The tech looked from Sarah to the map he was helping to balance in front of the glass.

"Yes, they are latitude and longitude markings, but the thicker lines running beneath them—they zigzag crazily throughout all the continents and all the oceans. What in the hell are they supposed to be?"

The techs shrugged, and then as they saw their supervisor coming and they shooed Sarah away and lifted the large map over to a table where the photographer was at work.

As McIntire walked away, she could not help but feel that she knew exactly what those strange lines were. She tried to concentrate but the wisp of memory flickered just at the edges of her mind.

Jack sat at the conference table with the other department heads of the Event Group. Most were still curious as to why Niles Compton had been relieved and flown to Washington. Virginia had stunned them even further when she told the gathered doctors, physicists, engineers, and computer and historical staffs that they would not be devoting their full resources to looking for the people who had murdered their colleagues in New York. Instead, most departments were now under the direct, personal control of the president. When the protests started, Virginia rapped her knuckles on the polished table. As she did so, she took in Jack at the far end, who had not uttered a word.

"Everyone, listen. We are close to a full-scale escalation in Korea. Many soldiers, just kids for the most part, have lost their lives already. Soldiers like the ones we lost this morning. We will do as the president has ordered. The department heads excluded, they will report to Pete Golding in the computer center and he will coordinate the effort to find out who killed our people. The rest of your teams will put their effort on the problem of this wild claim of the Russians and Koreans. After the quake in the waters just east of the Russian coast, you can see why this is a priority."

"And *that* claim is outrageous, Virginia," Clark Ortiz of the Earth Sciences Department said. "A science-induced earthquake? Hell, even if someone could target something like a country, how in the world could we even begin to initiate a seismic event?"

"Lieutenant McIntire, any ideas on the geology side of things?" Virginia asked.

"We can model recent seismic activity on the computer, but to actually start an earthquake? No. It would take thousands upon thousands of pounds of explosive material to initiate something like that. Even that scenario would be no guarantee you would get as much as a vibration out of the known surface faults. The tectonic forces start well below most fault lines and can't be reached by anything outside of a massive drilling operation."

"So, you believe it not feasible?"

"Not to my understanding. But I would like to hear this mysterious monitoring tape the Russians and Koreans claim they have."

"I understand that the Korean government is making it available through the United Nations as proof that seems to indicate a rather firm belief in their claims," Alice stated from her seat next to Virginia.

"Then we start from scratch. Sarah, you will head up the effort here and be the team leader of the geology and engineering departments. In addition, I am throwing the entire weight of the Earth Sciences Department in with you. Your job is to find a way to manipulate the earth to move. If we can construct a working model, then maybe we can prove or disprove this claim. Prove it or lay it to rest quickly. Luckily, you will be coordinating with Director Compton; he will be your sounding board."

When the meeting broke up, with department heads moving off to give orders to their people, Virginia saw that Jack and Carl had not moved. Alice Hamilton stayed also, and was sitting calmly in her seat at the table with her pad and pencil in her lap.

"Corporal Sanchez was a great kid, Jack. I'm sorry," Virginia said as she held Jack's blue eyes.

"They all were."

"I know that. But I also know that Sanchez was close to you two; therefore, I am truly sorry."

Jack did not respond. He was freshly shaven and cleaned

and in his normal blue jumpsuit. He opened a red-bordered file folder in front of him, then picked out one and slid it across the table to Virginia. She looked from Jack to the picture and then closed her eyes.

"Not so secret anymore," Virginia read aloud and then slid the picture to Alice Hamilton.

"Someone knows about us and at least the warehouse in New York, and also the part of our national charter that states we are to be kept covert," Jack said, looking directly at Virginia, unblinking.

Carl cleared his throat. "This is unlike anyone we've come up against, Virginia. They hit us with complete surprise and they didn't seem to care that it was right in the heart of the busiest city in the world. Massive firepower and complete surprise— this was a pure military strike against the Event Group for recovering what we thought were just some stolen artifacts." Carl looked from one woman to the other. "This is more than just what we lost, but what we *could* lose."

Collins sat motionlessly, his face calm.

"What do you want?" Alice asked, cutting off Virginia before she could tell Jack what she had planned

"Simple: carte blanche. I want my entire Security Department pulled off every dig, university campus, and research site around the world. I want them here. We're going to need everyone. The country is almost at war and we have very few options as far as protecting this complex. If they have knowledge of one of our satellite facilities such as New York, it could be they know about the main complex. That strike this morning was not just to recover pretty paintings and suits of armor. What they were looking for is right here and they know it. Whatever they want, they want it badly enough to send a small army out to get it."

"But, Jack, this is the Group. We're situated underneath one of the most guarded air-force bases in the entire world. They couldn't possibly get through that security and get in here."

Again, Carl spoke up. "Forty thousand."

"Excuse me?" Virginia said.

"There are forty thousand policemen in New York City.

That small fact didn't seem to deter this force from attacking a building in the heart of downtown Manhattan. They assassinated a prisoner at a federal courthouse, and walked into the home of a senior FBI agent and murdered and tortured him and his wife."

"Do what you have to do to secure Group and its personnel."

THE LAW FIRM OF EVANS, LAWSON AND KEELER BOSTON, MASSACHUSETTS

The three white Chevrolet vans pulled into the adjacent parking garage and waited. This particular law firm was large enough that it had a private lot with an express elevator that led down to the large four-story brownstone that served the firm. The vans were nondescript and windowless. They were parked, their motors shut off. Now, they waited.

It was only a minute later when a black Mercedes SL pulled up and over the steep incline that served the lower level of the garage, which sat a full story above the firm. It backed quickly into a space that faced the three vans. The lights flashed once, then one more time. At that signal, the sliding side doors of the vans opened and ten men from each quickly stepped out. They were wearing black overalls and black nylon ski masks and each was heavily armed.

Lorraine Matheson, better known as Dahlia, watched the northeastern strike team of the Coalition expertly check their weapons on the way to the elevator. This would be a ruthless theft, acted out quickly and murderously. The men doing the job had become millionaires while in the Coalition's service. They paid for the best soldiers from around the world. These men were not timid in the taking of life, nor were they afraid to die. Danger was more of a drug to them and money was only a means to that drug.

One man exited the first van and approached her. He was dressed not in the BDU gear of her strike element but in a button-down shirt and sport jacket. He was carrying a manila envelope. She lowered her window and accepted the package. She opened it and looked through the abundance of photos. She quickly dismissed all the uniformed police. Then she saw three men who caught her attention. She went through the stack and found more eight-by-tens of the same three. She studied their faces and decided that she had what she wanted.

"These three men are not part of the NYPD. This one in particular." She tapped the man in the center of the first photo. "He is definitely no cop. Fax this to Tomlinson over a secure line and tell him I suspect these men were conspirators in the raid in Westchester and that they may be a part of this mysterious Group in the desert that the recently departed technicians told us about." Dahlia thought for a moment as she replaced the photos in the envelope. "Tell him they seem to be very resourceful and may be a problem. This one man in particular, I don't care for him at all."

The man saw her tap her finger upon a man in the picture.

"That's the one who scared me when he faced the camera. There is something about him. The only word that comes to mind is *menace*."

Dahlia studied the face closer before sliding it in with the others. She kept quiet as she passed the envelope back through the window. She did not want to say that she had been thinking of another word as she looked upon that man's countenance: *nemesis*.

The man took the envelope and disappeared back into the first van to carry out his orders.

The blond woman forced herself to relax, the image of the man and his two companions quickly fading.

Three minutes after entering the law offices of Evans, Lawson and Keeler, thirty-six employees, attorneys, and visitors were lined up and on their knees in the main meeting room. Their hands were on their heads, and most were in shock at the sudden death of their elderly security man. The former Boston police officer, who'd had the nerve to confront the leader of the assault, had been shot at point-blank range. He now supplied the example of what would happen to any others who didn't follow instructions. His body was still slumped on the floor just outside the meeting room, where many could still see the body.

"We carry no money here, and if it's revenge for something our firm has done in the past, I assure you that—"

"Your name?" the smallest man of the assault element asked. His 9-millimeter silenced handgun moved toward the well-dressed man who had spoken.

"Anderson. I'm a junior partner and—"

The women screamed and the men were stunned when the bullet hit the young man in the forehead, blowing his brains all over the white-painted wall behind him and knocking his body into the screaming woman behind him.

"You savage, why would you do that?" an elderly man demanded defiantly from his kneeling position.

"Your name?" the assailant asked in accented English.

Expecting a bullet also, the man faced the masked assailant. "Harold Lawson, senior partner of this firm."

"Good. Could you point out the other two senior partners, please? Most notably," the man pulled a scrap of paper from the inside of his black glove, "a Mr. Jackson Keeler."

Another man in his seventies cleared his throat. "I am he," he said shakily.

"You are the youngest son of Jackson Keeler the third, born in 1930?"

"Yes."

The smallish man nodded at two of his men and they moved forward to lift Keeler to his feet.

The man then looked at three of the female paralegals who were cowering together by the far wall.

"Mr. Jackson Keeler, you will be asked a series of questions about your father, your older brother, and also about your affiliations, most notably your private affiliations. You will answer these questions in the most direct and honest way possible. If you do that, this will not happen to any more of your people." The man quickly fired three shots at the cowering women he had picked out and lined up against the wall. The bullets struck

cleanly and the women were dead before they hit the expensively carpeted floor.

"You murdering bastard!" Keeler shouted.

The gathered employees and visitors prayed that Mr. Keeler,
whose father was the founding partner of the firm, was indeed
forthright in his answers.

"I believe we should retire to your office for our conversation."

As the two men with Keeler between them left the meeting
room, the smaller man hesitated and leaned closer to a large
man standing near the door and whispered instructions.

"Separate them into other rooms and dispatch them all."

The large man nodded and then looked at the hopeful men
and women around the meeting room. As the people watched
him, he gave them a reassuring smile.

Jackson Keeler was taken into his spacious office and was made
to sit down in his chair. The small man nodded to the two men
who had escorted Keeler in, and they left the office to join the
rest of their team.

Keeler closed his eyes when the killer removed the black
mask he was wearing, as if not seeing him would somehow
save his life.

"Relax, Mr. Keeler. Do you mind if I pour myself a drink?"

The older man opened his eyes in time to see the man with
the mustache pour a drink from the expensive decanters at the
small bar.

"The plate map, Mr. Keeler, where is it?" he asked as he
walked to the desk and set an identical glass of bourbon on the
maroon blotter.

Jackson Keeler picked up the glass and drained the bourbon
in one large gulp. He set the glass down with a shaky hand and
then wiped his mouth.

"Distasteful business, I know. But we do need to get this behind us and all you have to do is tell me where the plate map is."

Keeler knew that there was no use in denying the map existed or that his family indeed did at one time have it.

"I only know what my father told me when I was a young man. Anything other than that, I can't say."

The man took a small sip from his glass and then smiled. "That is good. You see, there is willingness on your part to get this bad business finished. Tell me, what was said to you by your father?"

"The item you are looking for, it's not here. It was sent to my older brother many years ago, before the war."

"Indeed? Please continue."

Keeler looked around, the hope of rescue now completely gone.

"The plate map was sent to Hawaii just before the start of the war and my brother was directed to give it to someone else. That's all I know."

The man finished his drink and then placed the glass back on the bar. He turned and looked at the old man but did not utter a sound.

"I know nothing else. Please allow those not involved with this to leave the building."

The man still said nothing.

The door to Keeler's office opened and Dahlia walked in. She nodded at the small man and then removed her coat, with his assistance. She smiled and turned to Keeler.

"Now, this is an honor. I never thought I would get to meet one of your kind face-to-face. I mean, my employer is a brother of yours, but to actually meet one of the last of the Ancients, well, I just can't tell you what an honor it is."

Dahlia turned and looked at the small man, who was watching her work with a smile etched on his harsh features. He shook his head negatively and then whispered something into her ear. The blond-haired woman turned back to face Keeler once again.

Dahlia looked around the richly appointed office, her eyes passing over the paintings and settling back again on Keeler. She removed her gloves and then sat in one of the chairs facing the old man.

"Your older brother, at least from what my employer's records show, was a nonconformist who didn't like the dirty little secret about the Ancients and wanted nothing to do with your family. Maybe the old boys and girls were a little too cowardly for his taste. Therefore, he went his own way. That makes me curious as to why your father would have sent him the plate map. You tell my man here your brother passed it on to another. However, your father would never have entrusted an item so valuable to an unworthy person. So I must conclude that it was passed to an Ancient, and I believe you know who that is."

"Like I told your assassin here, I don't know."

"Will you open your safe, please?"

"I don't have an office safe."

"Mr. Keeler, I have had a very long and tiring day. Must I order the deaths of more of your friends in the outer office?"

The old man lowered his head and knew he would have to give this woman the name she sought. The betrayal that he felt was choking him, just as it had his brother that night long ago in Hawaii.

"The map was ordered turned over to an Ancient."

"Ah, I knew your father was an astute man," Dahlia said as she smiled brightly. She then placed a black glove back on her right hand and held it out. Her man placed a glass of whiskey in her hand and then just stood there as she sipped. "I thought a drink would be in order. You don't know it, Mr. Keeler, but this is a very historic day." She smiled again and held the drink with only the one gloved hand. "The name?"

The old man lowered his head and then gestured to the far wall.

"Behind that picture is my safe. May I?"

"By all means, please."

Keeler walked slowly past the woman to a large portrait of his father. He pulled on the right side and the painting swung outward, revealing a small wall safe.

"Now, I wouldn't want you to open that and try and surprise us with a weapon. That would not be at all like your bloodline, would it? It would go against your nature to get directly involved."

"No weapons," he said as he reached out and started dialing his combination.

Dahlia nodded for the small man to step closer to observe Keeler.

The old man pulled the handle on the safe door as he felt the presence of the assassin as he stepped up behind him. He knew that he had to proceed delicately. He reached into the opened safe and started to remove a large book as he blocked the view with his thin frame. As he did so, he slipped his right hand under the thick pages.

The small man started to step forward to snatch the journal from him. Keeler had to think quickly before his deceit could be discovered. He allowed his knees to buckle; he moaned and collapsed, dragging the journal out of the safe as he did so. He fell to the carpet and rolled as if in the throes of a heart attack. Praying, he slowly and quietly ripped out the bottom of the last page and quickly slipped the folded paper into his mouth, between his cheek and dentures. He closed his eyes and waited.

The man rolled him over and pulled the journal from his hands. Keeler was breathing deeply, acting his part to perfection.

Dahlia held her hand out for the journal, looking at Keeler with the mild curiosity one would give an annoying child.

"Please assist Mr. Keeler to his feet and give him some water."

The small man heaved the thinner Keeler to his feet with not much grace. He placed him in a chair beside the desk and then poured him some water. Keeler in the meantime allowed his breathing to slow as his one-act play came to its end.

Dahlia was not watching him; she was already examining the thick journal with the name Jackson Keeler embossed in gold on the front.

"The location of the plate map is in here?"

Keeler nodded as he watched the woman, relieved that he had not been observed when removing the bottom portion of the last page. He accepted the water and drank.

"The names of your remaining brothers and sisters are listed?" she asked as she started thumbing through the pages.

The old man saw what she was doing and stood, allowing the glass of water to fall from his grasp. He stumbled forward angrily, still feigning weakness, until the smaller man stepped between him and the blond woman. He knew he had to stop her from getting to the last, incomplete and torn page.

"I am finished answering your questions. You have what you want, so please leave here."

His face showed no relief as Dahlia looked up in surprise and closed the book.

"Indeed, you have been most helpful, and I am so sorry for causing you distress."

Jackson Keeler, as afraid and ashamed as he felt, could not help but show a thin smile. He knew that he couldn't just let her walk out of there without letting her know that the book would now do her no good as far as the location of the plate map went.

"Van Valkenburg is the name you need to look up in my journal in order to find the location of the plate map."

"Very helpful once more. Thank you. Now, wasn't that easy?"

"Surprisingly easier than I thought it would be, miss," he said, the smirk growing on his age-lined face as he stood shakily before her.

For the first time, Dahlia felt uncomfortable as she watched the confidence return to the old man, who should now have been begging for his life.

"In all of your research of my brothers and sisters and the Ancient line we belong to, miss, did you not ever learn what ship my brother was assigned to? You now have the name of the man he passed the plate map to for security. Van Valkenburg was his commanding officer. The ship he captained was the USS *Arizona*." Keeler finally had to chuckle because, as sure as he was that he was a dead man, he knew that he had stunned the woman staring at him.

Dahlia clenched her teeth as she tried not to show the old

man any emotion, but, by the arrogant look on his face, she knew that she had failed. She leaned over, placed her unfinished drink on the desk, and, with the journal clutched in her other hand, stood. She pulled her glove back on and looked around at her man. The unvoiced order was clear.

Jackson Keeler, while still smiling, nodded at her.

"It has been a pleasure, miss. I assume you have resources to go digging around a national monument that has the potential to fall down around your ears at any time? A monument that is guarded twenty-four hours a day? Also one that is revered and is set in the middle of one of the most guarded harbors in the world?"

Dahlia turned and her smile had again spread brilliantly.

"The few brothers and sisters of the original bloodline that are left in the Juliai Coalition are far more resourceful than your cowardly faction ever has been. I will recover the plate map for them and your line will slip quietly into extinction. Even without the plate map, that fact alone may have been worth it to my employers."

"Someone will stop them; they always do."

"I'm afraid some stories just don't have the cavalry saving the day in the end. Mr. Keeler, you have been most helpful and informative. Now I would like to do something I so rarely do." She held out her gloved hand once more and her man placed his silenced weapon into it. "The arrogance on your face as you told me about the location of the plate map, well, it irritated me."

She raised the automatic and fired ten bullets into the thin body of the old man. He fell to the floor, where his blood spread into the thick carpet.

The look on Dahlia's face was blank. She lowered the weapon and held it out to her man, who took it from her grasp. He had never seen Dahlia do as much as speak in anger, so the display of violence she had shown was a side she had always hidden well.

"No, no heroic cavalry, Mr. Keeler." She started to turn but stopped short. "Our photographer is waiting outside. I would like him to stay here and check to see who shows up here. Tell him to stay at least twenty-four hours. He has the same orders as before."

With those orders, she turned and left the office. With her she carried the journal that would lead her not only to the location of the plate map and in turn the Atlantean Key, but the names of the last remaining Ancients.

CHAPTER

FIVE

RICHMOND, VIRGINIA

The sixty-six-year-old man sat and watched CNN without really seeing the images of North Korean troops on the move. The man knew that it was file footage, so he had no need to see the small disclaimer at the bottom of the screen. If there was one thing the man knew, it was the troop strength of the North Korean army; and he could clearly see that the uniforms worn by the PRK troops were old in style by at least fifteen years, thus he knew it had to have been file footage.

The glass of milk before him on the coffee table remained untouched since the housekeeper had brought it into him. The pills that kept his pain at a minimum sat unnoticed on a small silver serving tray next to the glass. Finally, the man blinked and brought his attention back to the screen when the announcer out of Atlanta switched from the deteriorating situation in Korea to happenings a little closer to home.

As for local law enforcement authorities in the Boston area, there was no clue left as to why thirty-one employees and clients of the prestigious law firm were found murdered execution-style in the most horrendous crime in Boston history. Authorities are baffled as to who and why—

Carmichael Rothman sat bolt upright, causing the pain in his upper back to flair excruciatingly when the camera panned to the front of an old brownstone office building. The gold script on the front of the building was there for the world to read. Ignoring the reporter currently framed in the camera's lens, he just stared at the names behind her. EVANS, LAWSON AND KEELER was only partially hidden behind the female newsperson, but Rothman saw the gold-plated letters clearly.

Still not hearing the words of the reporter, he absently reached out, took the three small morphine tablets from the silver tray, and shakily placed them in his mouth. He reached for the glass of warm milk, but instead of grasping it his fingers refused to open, and he succeeded only in knocking it over.

"Sir, are you all right?" The housekeeper had entered his study unnoticed and was at his side instantly. "Let me get a rag and I'll clean this up for you."

With the bitter-tasting pills dissolving in his mouth, Rothman violently shook his head. He slapped at the air as the elderly woman started to pick up the fallen glass. Finally, he managed to slap the housekeeper's hands away. She looked up at him, but his eyes were still staring at the television screen.

"Martha, get—Martha on the phone, immediately."

The housekeeper remained kneeling next to the coffee table. "Ms. Laughlin is on the telephone right this moment—that is why I came in: I didn't know if you wanted to be disturbed."

Rothman did not say anything. He just leaned back in the red leather easy chair and closed his eyes. The pills were slowly taking their desired effect and the cancer that was killing him momentarily eased his pain and released its hold.

"The phone, please," he murmured.

The woman stood, removed the wireless phone from its cradle, and placed it in his hand. With eyes closed, he started to gather his thoughts.

"Carr, are you there?"

At first, he didn't answer as he waited for his strength to return.

"Carr, this is—"

"I'm here, my dear. What are we to do?"

"Listen, you relax. I have our contacts in Boston sending me a few things from the crime scene. One of our informants absconded with evidence before his superiors found it. I do not need you collapsing on me because we have a lot to talk about in a very short time frame."

"I knew it wasn't a coincidence—the Wave is activated—I should have known right away—you should have also—what were we thinking?"

"Whoever the Coalition used was very good. Who would have believed they could track the Keeler line after all these years. Listen, Carr, we don't know for sure that whoever did this has gained any knowledge as to where the map is hidden. We just can't be sure."

Carmichael Rothman sat up and waved his housekeeper out of the room. Alert, he watched her leave and then watched as the two cherry-paneled doors closed behind her.

"We overlooked three coincidences when Korea, Iran, and now the Russian naval base were struck with no apparent aftershocks. Now this gruesome act in Boston that wiped out the last fertile line is just too much! They have the location of the map and probably our locations as well!"

There was silence on the other end of the phone as his point became clear.

"Martha, this is no time for secrets to be kept. We need help!"

"Yes, but whom—the new American administration? They will think we are insane when we tell them. Our assets in Washington cannot even begin to approach them. From my understanding, the new president has his hands overly full and he's not listening to a lot of reason right now."

The old man grew silent.

"We both have enough security around us to fend off an army. The Juliai would be foolish to come after us. We must assume they have the information they sought."

"So we do nothing as usual? We wait for our darker brothers and sisters to take control?"

"Our influence has waned, Carr. Our time has passed."

"That has always been our failing, Martha. Let others do the dying. We were always content to allow governments to stop the Juliai. Never once did our ancestors or we place ourselves in danger, or take even a stand. The Coalition has always been ruthless far beyond our understanding, yet we spring from the same fathers and mothers. I find this hard. I am old as you are. We are the last. Can we not just this one time assist with no thought to our own safety?"

The other end of the line fell silent. Carmichael Rothman sat and listened, but even as he did so, he felt his brave words starting to crumble in his memory. He and the Ancients had always been afraid of their far more aggressive brothers and sisters who had followed Julius Caesar down a path of separation and ruthless domination. Now, he sat there in his magnificent house and felt his desire for action failing.

"Carr, in the beginning, our side was no better than theirs. We were mirror images of one another. We were just as hateful as our ancestors were and that is *our* crime. Just because we are the last, does not mean anything. We will be hated for our pacifist leanings of the past by the entire world. I am just not brave enough for that. I'm sorry."

Rothman heard the phone line go dead. He felt the shame of their nonaction throughout history flood into his memory. He slowly placed the phone down and lowered his head.

So, the last two free-thinking Ancients would stand by and let the world come apart, only to have the Coalition pick up the pieces and put it back together again in their image.

Carmichael Rothman placed his head in his hands and sobbed, more ashamed than he had ever been. For the grandson of the man who had risked his life to thwart the Coalition over a hundred years before, this was too much to bear.

TASK FORCE 7789.9
USS *THEODORE ROOSEVELT*

Steaming at twenty-six knots, the *Roosevelt* was making good headway against the high seas, which were still a reminder of the massive underground quake of the day before. The Nimitz-class carrier and her escorts had been dispatched two days prior for deployment as a rear guard for the *George Washington* and *John F. Kennedy* groups, now in the Sea of Japan. Her latest flash message had ordered her directly into the hot waterway directly between Korea and China at flank speed. She was now cruising five hundred miles off the coast of Sakhalin Island.

Her captain was a man known for thinking outside the box. He was going to take a large risk, and a lot depended on the actions of the U.S. State Department. They were seeking permission from the Russian government to enter the Strait of La Perouse, a slim breadth of water between the Russian-controlled Sakhalin and the Japanese island of Hokkaido, and thus far the State Department had been thwarted at the United Nations Security Council by both the Russians and the Chinese—the two nations struck the hardest by the recent earthquakes. If the captain of the *Roosevelt* did not receive confirmation soon, he would have to alter course and head for the Sea of Japan through route farther south.

The skies were dark as the great ship plowed through the rough seas. Her smaller escorts were having a far harder time with the swells than the giant carrier was, but they were still keeping pace with the rapid pace of the *Teddy*.

As the captain sat in the large chair inside the command bridge, a signalman approached and gave him a contact report. He glanced at it and then looked at the sailor.

"Intermittent?"

"Yes, sir. The contact is low, possibly hidden by the rough seas."

The captain thought about bringing the ship to General Quarters but instead picked up the phone and contacted the ship's CIC.

"Yes, Captain, this is Commander Houghington. Our contact could be just a glitch because I don't suspect anyone would brave the seas at that low altitude."

"Conclusions?" he asked.

"Any action at this time is not supported by what we have,

Captain. The *Champlain* is monitoring the contact and will advise on any aspect changes."

"Very well. Inform everyone this could turn serious real quick."

"Aye, Captain."

The captain hung up the phone and bit his lower lip in thought. It was a bad habit and that knowledge had spread to his crew rather quickly. When he was like that, he was deep in thought.

"To hell with it. Officer of the Deck, bring the task force to General Quarters."

In the rough seas, the twelve ships of the large force came to life and men started running about, getting to their action stations. Word quickly spread that the group might be under surveillance at the least, or tracked by someone meaning them harm; at sea, both scenarios got the men's attention.

USS *LAKE CHAMPLAIN* (CG-57)
TICONDEROGA-CLASS AEGIS
MISSILE CRUISER

The heavy cruiser had joined the task force as a last-minute substitution and had arrived from her home port of San Diego just in time to meet up with the *Roosevelt* before they came in striking distance of Sakhalin.

In the combat direction center of the Aegis missile cruiser, the ratings were quietly watching their monitors. The deck officer was watching closely both the BQQ sonar and air-search radars. His eyes went from the subsurface search to the air search but were drawn more frequently to the air aspect.

"There it is again, sir," the air-search tech called out.

As the lieutenant commander leaned closer to the screen, the large blip disappeared.

"Dammit! If that's an aircraft, he's braver than me. Those seas are at sixteen feet."

"Last contact showed two hundred and thirty klicks and closing. Sir, this could be just ground swell and clutter."

"Well, the *Teddy* isn't taking any chances. They just launched her Alert One fighters to join the CAP."

As the officer moved to the subsurface-search screen, the green blip appeared and vanished once more.

GREAT DEFENDER FLIGHT, ECHO-TANGO-BRAVO, ONE HUNDRED KILOMETERS NORTHEAST OF THE USS *THEODORE ROOSEVELT*

The flight of six S-37 fighters of the North Korean air force skimmed the sea at wave-top level. If it had not been for the large amount of sea spray streaming from their fuselages, the newest line of stealth-technology fighters would have struck undetected. Still, that intermittent signal was enough to confuse the Americans.

Each of the six new fighters was armed with a single weapon: the SS-N-22 cruise missile. Western intelligence had recently dubbed the new Russian-designed weapon "the deadliest missile in the world." Code-named the Sunburn, it was capable of supersonic speeds and packed a punch that could singlehandedly sink an American Nimitz-class carrier. At this moment there were six Sunburns targeting the *Roosevelt*.

USS *LAKE CHAMPLAIN* (CG-57) TICONDEROGA-CLASS AEGIS MISSILE CRUISER

"We have multiple incoming targets, one hundred and eighty klicks and closing. Speed is estimated at Mach 1.2!"

The *Roosevelt* and *Lake Champlain* radars were picking up only four of the inbound targets because, after launch, one of the costly cruise missiles simply fell off its launch rail and hung from one of its explosive bolts. As it caught the air, it dragged the plane down and it splashed into the sea, cartwheeling the expensive fighter into the angry ocean.

Another of the Sunburns ignited, but then the warhead inexplicably detonated. Unknown to the manufacturer, a watertight seal that had been improperly installed at the Russian factory had corrupted the arming timer with seawater on the flight in. The resulting explosion took out not only the launching S-37 but its wingman. Both fighters disintegrated in an expanding wave of destruction that lit up the darkened sky.

USS *THEODORE ROOSEVELT*

The giant ship maneuvered to starboard at flank speed as the approaching missiles gained on it. Three of the Sunburns targeted the great carrier and one, the *Lake Champlain*.

As RAM (rolling action) missiles filled the gray sky around the task force from every warship in the group, the *Lake Champlain's* old Phalanx system started to track the incoming threat. The R2-D2 platform, named after the *Star Wars* character, rotated with the high whine of its turbine, and the six-barreled Gatling gun started turning in anticipation of placing its lethal rounds into the air.

The *Roosevelt's* captain saw what was going to happen.

"Helm, hard to port!" he ordered loudly.

The carrier started to turn, but it was too late. The first 770-pound warhead slammed into the vessel below the high-water mark amidships, killing four hundred sailors in the initial detonation. Fire quickly spread throughout the cavernous hangar deck. The giant warship shuddered and was actually lifted free of the sea as her keel bent and then straightened in a springlike action that came very near to breaking her back. As she settled back into the water, her crew waited for the second strike, which would surely finish her.

The *Lake Champlain* saved her. By splitting the two old Phalanx turrets between the second and third missiles, the *Champlain's* captain was hoping beyond hope to save the *Roosevelt* from the deathblow headed her way.

Another missile, aimed directly at the *Champlain,* was being tracked by their old but reliable Raytheon RIM-161 standard missiles. She started pumping the SAMs into the air as fast as her automatic loader could deploy them. Simultaneously, chaff and flares launched from their tubes and started to explode in an attempt to confuse the incoming Sunburn.

The first missile was just crossing the point of no return for the forward Phalanx. The depleted uranium rounds played out like water from a garden hose as it tracked. The cruise missile popped up in the last seconds of flight due to its programmed orders to target the *Teddy's* flight deck. At the last possible moment, five of the more than eight thousand uranium rounds in the air struck the large missile dead center and exploded it seventy feet from the carrier's large island structure. Fire and shrapnel from the momentum of the Sunburn spread destruction to the bridge area of the carrier just as she righted herself from the first strike.

The second missile was close behind, and just as the *Roosevelt* settled and her bronze propellers bit the sea, fighting for speed, the missile struck her at the stern. There was no detonation. The *Roosevelt* was hit with a dud missile. Thanks to the *Champlain,* thousands of men were saved.

The *Lake Champlain* wasn't so lucky. She attempted to turn to port just as the fourth Korean missile struck. The resulting explosion ripped through her midsection and blew out the other side. The worst effect was the downward trajectory of the expanding wave of destruction as it found a hole in the ship's design, the tunnel that fed missiles to the automated loader. The American missiles exploded in the main loading area of the cruiser and the rest of the energy traveled down into the bowels of the proud warship. The kinetic energy slammed into her lowest deck, disintegrating reinforced steel plates until it finally found the keel. The thick spine of steel simply snapped in half like a frail twig. The onrush of water weighted the forward half of the *Lake Champlain* and pulled it under, leaving the stern to catch up.

Two miles away, the USS *Theodore Roosevelt* was dead in the water with her fires belowdecks out of control. Other ships started making their way in to help as the shock of the Korean attack was quickly replaced by anger at what amounted to a sneak attack on the force.

The world situation was slowly worsening, per the plan. Meanwhile, across the ocean and half a world away, the Coalition was preparing to assault another, but very much older, ship still on the U.S. Navy active rolls: the USS *Arizona*.

CHAPTER SIX

The first female elected chancellor of the German state stood and walked to the podium. The dinner was a benefit for the German Red Cross and was a timely affair since the agency's resources had been stretched thin by the recent natural disasters in Asia and the Middle East. The chancellor was radiant in her black gown and she smiled brightly for the five hundred paying guests of the Red Cross. Her security detail scanned the forty round tables in the ballroom located in the newest of Berlin's luxury hotels.

The audience stood to applaud the woman who had so recently taken the country by storm, by word and vote. She had been elected on the peace vote just as her American counterpart had been, thus allying herself with American foreign policy.

She waved at the gathered guests and raised her arms in a triumphant gesture, which pleased the very rich in the ballroom to no end. Her black-gloved hand was richly appointed with a bracelet of diamonds, a gift from her husband on election day.

One man in the rear of the room just stood watching. The new chief of security for the hotel, a well-regarded man in his midfifties, watched as the left-wing bitch, as he thought of her, took in her glory. He sneered as he raised a cell phone to his ear and made a call. He nodded at one of the chancellor's security men who was covering the door; the man smiled and nodded back, never suspecting a thing.

"Yes," the voice answered.

"The chancellor is being well received," the security man said in perfect English.

"Very nice. Would you please send her our regards."

"I most certainly will—and my family, they will be honored by this?"

"They will want for nothing for generations."

The security officer closed the cell phone and placed it back in his suit jacket. He again smiled at the agent next to him and then moved off toward the stage, easily bypassing the standing guests and zigzagging around the tables. The mission he had volunteered for had been in the planning stages for ten years and he was well prepared. As a former German soldier and then later an intelligence officer, he was beyond reproach as far as his security clearance was concerned; thus, his advantageous position had been attained with no problem at all.

As he moved through the throng of people, he unbuttoned his coat, and that motion drew the attention of the chancellor's security detail on the stage. One officer saw the well-dressed man and knew him by name, and he knew that his hotel position required him not to be where he was.

The chancellor had finally persuaded the guests to settle in for one of her fiery speeches on the economy, the European Union, and the war on terror, when she saw the man approaching the stage. She watched as he stopped, and then a shot rang out from the left wing of the stage. The bullet caught the security man in the shoulder, but it wasn't enough to stop him from carrying out his mission for the honor of his Coalition-sponsored family.

The explosion from the eight pounds of C-4 plastic explosive disintegrated the first seven feet of stage, along with the new German chancellor. The security man along with ten tables in the front of the room vanished. The ceiling came crashing down into the guest tables in the center, killing a 110 more people.

The bomb squad would sift through the debris of the ballroom for the next week, and the only thing they would recover of the new chancellor was one gloved hand with a diamond bracelet still clinging to the silk.

With the major chess pieces in conflict across the board, and the occupied just surviving, the assassination had taken out the white queen, without any of the players really being aware of how their side of the board had been compromised. The chessboard was now in check because a large part of the western defense apparatus had now been removed from the board, and all it had cost the Coalition was one little black pawn.

LOS ANGELES INTERNATIONAL AIRPORT

The Boeing 777 was starting its takeoff roll. The livery colors were white on red and on the tail boom was the national flag of Japan. Prime Minister Minoro Osagawa was rushing home just after hearing the news from the Pacific. It had been a hectic day since the earthquake had taken a devastating toll on the northern tip of his nation. The prime minister had been trying to take off for four hours, but the Los Angeles area had been blanketed in fog for the better part of the day. Finally, his pilot had received clearance and was heading down the runway at 140 miles per hour.

The white, blue, and red Federal Express van had been parked in the long-term parking area of British Airways for the past five hours. The men inside had been patient and even joked about the L.A. weather, but they became serious as they received word that the prime minister's plane had been cleared for takeoff. Three men stepped from the large van, each carrying a large case. They heard the loud whine of a large aircraft as her engines spooled up. They were exactly 1.8 miles from runway five. A Coalition source had informed the fire team of the prime minister's imminent takeoff.

As the three men placed the cases on the ground and opened them, they could almost feel the power of the items inside. Each of the three cases held a weapon that once upon a time had terrified the bravest of Russian combat pilots. Because the Stinger missile employs a passive homing seeker, it is a "fire and forget" weapon, which needs no guidance from the operator after firing. Other missiles—ones that track the reflection of a designator beam—require the operator to maintain a lock on the target. This allows a Stinger operator to take cover, relocate, or engage other targets immediately after firing the missile. This is just what the men trained for in the months and years leading up to this day.

A fourth man had placed himself strategically in front of the van and was watching the sky through a pair of binoculars. He turned and looked at his three companions.

"Get a move on; here she comes."

The men had already placed the Stingers on their shoulders and were just waiting. An old woman walked by, pulling a suitcase on rollers. One of the men looked at her and winked. The woman didn't even know what the men held; she just hurried along a little faster than before, and she didn't look back.

Soon they saw the large Boeing plane take to the sky, and soon after that, the seeker tone sounded in their ears, meaning that the seeker head had locked on to engine one of the 777. First one, then the second, and then finally the third missile streaked out of the launch tubes.

The men lowered the empty tubes and watched in amazement as the small missiles climbed into the now-blue sky of Los Angeles. The white contrails were as clear as a stroke of paint as the missiles gained on their target. The scene was surreal and the men stood in awe.

Whoever the pilot of the prime minister's aircraft was, he was very, very good. The sensitive radar and threat detectors on the Boeing plane had to have alerted the pilot, and he swung the big plane over hard left and dived. In the tail boom, flares started to pop free of their launcher and chaff started bursting behind it. Tin foil would not fool the seeker heads of the Stingers, but the flares just might.

The leader of the fire team bit his lower lip as he kept the binoculars trained on the weaving and diving aircraft. The first

Stinger went for the flares and went off harmlessly a hundred feet from the tail. The second Stinger flew true to the target and struck the large General Electric engine. The third hit the left wing and ripped off a thirty-five-foot section at the end. The 777 dipped hard left and that was when the aircraft disappeared from view.

"Goddammit!" the leader said as he scanned the sky with his glasses.

Then they heard the whine of the aircraft as it fought its way back into the sky. The whole left wing was on fire and the aircraft was without a large portion of that wing. The large turbojet engine was still there but was a ball of fire as the aircraft tried to turn back into LAX.

The men watched in rapt silence as the plane, as if in slow motion, started to tilt over to the right, as the left wing could not hold up its end of the battle. The leader smiled as the 777 finally lost its battle with gravity and slid into a small strip mall and exploded. The leader closed his eyes as the ground trembled slightly from the distant impact.

The men hastily left the area as sirens finally started sounding. They did not bother to pick up the cases that had contained the Stingers because the equipment was untraceable, having been bought as surplus from several sources inside Afghanistan, where the Coalition had unlimited contacts.

With the deaths of two of the West's most influential leaders, the Juliai was now only four moves away from checkmate.

SITUATION ROOM
THE WHITE HOUSE
WASHINGTON, D.C.

The lighting was dim and the room deathly quiet as the president sat with his security council. Somewhere in the silent room, a pencil snapped in two. On the large high-definition monitor, a scene unlike anything seen since World War II was being played out in real time in the northern Pacific. The images were delivered from an overhead satellite and from a live feed from one of the ships of the task force. The directors of the CIA, FBI, and NSA, General Kenneth Caulfield of the U.S. Army, and the chairman of the Joint Chiefs were silent. The suddenness of the attack by the Korean air force had taken the gamers at the Pentagon by complete surprise and left everyone with a deep sense of failure.

As all eyes in the conference room focused on the scenes of destruction, the door opened and allowed in a flood of light from the offices outside. A small man dressed simply in a black suit and tie and white shirt quickly found a seat against the wall. Only the president looked his way, then quickly back at the horrendous scene.

"Casualties?" he asked.

"Preliminary reports from the *Roosevelt* are better than you would have thought. Thus far, four hundred and fifty-seven seamen are dead with a like number injured. At this time, we are not sure of the ship's survival. All assistance is being rendered by Japan, Australia, and England, whose small task force could be in the area in four hours," Admiral John C. Fuqua said from his spot at the table. "The Russians have offered moral support only at this stage due to the damage sustained at Vladivostok."

"Okay. What are we looking at for the *Lake Champlain*?" he asked.

"Thirty-three officers, twenty-seven chief petty officers, and three hundred and twenty-four enlisted men. She went down with all hands."

Niles Compton placed his arms on his knees and lowered his head. He had just arrived by helicopter on the White House lawn from Andrews Air Force Base, and walking in and seeing this brought what was happening into very real and deadly prospective.

The president gestured for the lights as the large screen dimmed and the horrific scenes vanished.

"Recommendations?"

"We have to defend our people, Mr. President, that much is evident," the admiral stated flatly as he looked the president in the eyes.

"Agreed. The rules of engagement have already been sent

to all American forces the world over," the president said, looking at the admiral and guessing at his next words.

"A change in our ROE will not be an adequate response, sir. We have to—"

"Start a world war, because that is precisely what we would be doing. The Korean consul and Chinese ambassador have notified us that the strike on our task force was defensive only and dictated by an overt act of war against *their* countries. No matter what we believe, and no matter how much we cry out our innocence, they believe they were hit intentionally by us, and if not us, someone in our sphere of influence. Who else would have the technology to do what they're claiming to have evidence of, if not the West?"

"Their claims are absolutely without scientific foundation. Our own people say that what happened could only be a natural occurrence," answered the director of the CIA, Charles Melbourne.

"Nonetheless, we have earthquakes without aftershocks and the evidence these people claim to have is just—" The president tossed his pen on the yellow pad before him and it landed on the casualty numbers he had circled several times. He closed his eyes in thought and left the question hanging.

"Gentlemen, this has to be thought out clearly. I have my doubts that the Koreans would have done this for any other reason than because they were pushed into it. It just does not make military sense. The move to hit that task force was an act of desperation on their part. I feel it. If it's a direct attack launched with some unknown science or not, it doesn't matter, gentlemen; they *believe* it is."

"We have to respond, we owe it to those boys." The admiral's voice was easy and steady but every man in the room could see that it was forced.

"First, I want a five-hundred-mile exclusion zone placed around our task force. I am ordering the air force to start low-level recon overflights of the North Korean rally points. I want preparations made and target packages on my desk in three hours in case Kim moves across the border. We *will* let him know clearly that this threatening gesture toward the South shall be met with unyielding force."

The president met every set of eyes in the room.

"The Koreans have said they are finished talking, but I will not allow them to once again start a bloody war without more facts to back me. I will make them see reason, but I need proof that these were natural disasters, or I need evidence of a crime, is this understood?" He was looking directly at the directors of the CIA and the FBI. "We are lucky the Russians have remained quiet on this tape of theirs. We can be thankful they are not adding fuel to Kim's fire, at least for the time being."

There were nods all around the table.

"We'll meet back here in three hours. Get me answers. Dismissed."

Niles received several curious looks from the security council as they broke up. He did not exactly avoid eye contact but did not outwardly look directly at them, either. He watched as the last member closed the door, then he looked at the president.

"It took you long enough to get here, goddammit."

Niles nodded. "My people needed their instructions. If we had not been so secretive about our friendship, I could have left much sooner. Especially now that I see we've got some real problems here."

The president smiled and then quickly stood and walked over to the director of Department 5656 and held out his hand.

"Don't want people knowing about how close we are. It could be bad for you on your end and me on mine. Secrets, the world runs on them."

Niles stood and took his hand. Alice had been right in her assessment about the president and Niles Compton. They were not only childhood friends but had attended Harvard together. The ROTC student and the computer-sciences nerd had been friends since they were eight and had been roommates together at the first of several colleges.

"I trust my people. You're lucky I caught on when you first arrived at Group," Niles said as he watched his friend wearily sit down.

"When I visited at the complex I thought it wise to play our friendship low-key. I didn't know if you had told anyone about us being friends. And then," he poured himself a glass of water from the decanter, "when this earthquake stuff started, I was bombarded from everyone from MIT to my own science advisers saying that the events were natural in nature and there could be no way they could have been manmade."

"And?"

"Niles, something's wrong here. I have a gut feeling—not really much to go on, I'm afraid—that something's happening here we don't understand." He took a drink of water and set down the glass. "I've been a soldier all of my adult life and this is just not right. The Koreans would never chance their annihilation on this. Regardless of what most people think of them, they do not act without cause, even if it is a ridiculous one."

"The Russians and Chinese—how are they reacting?"

"The Russians are just waiting to see what we do before committing one way or the other. China, well, the chairman condemned the Koreans for attacking our ships, but fell far short of telling their ally to back down. In other words, they're not sure either."

"What can I do to help you out?"

"Niles, you're the smartest man I've ever known. The people you've collected in that desert hamlet of yours are truly amazing. I need your brains. I need you here to help me get us out of this growing nightmare." The president slid a folder across the table to Niles and then looked away.

Niles read the report and then looked at the president.

"Both were assassinated today, only minutes apart."

"God, this can't be just a coincidence."

"The goddamn world's falling apart just like it's being orchestrated. It makes you think the North Koreans may be onto something."

Niles closed the folder that held the CIA report. "Pinpricks against the body," he said quietly.

"What was that?"

"Enough pinpricks will bleed a body, no matter how strong and powerful, until it's too weak to function."

The president did not have to ask any more. He knew that Niles was the man to turn to.

"Who do you have working on the murder of your people?"

"Colonel Jack Collins, the Group's security director."

The president looked at his longtime friend. "Collins is with you? I know Jack; I thought Congress and the Joint Chiefs crucified him a few years back for talking to Congress about the screw-up in Afghanistan?"

"They did. I got what was left. And he's still a better soldier than you ever were."

"What in the hell do you know about soldiering, you bookworm?" he shot back. "You're right about Collins, though." The president thought for a moment. "Dammit, Niles, I need you and your best people on this thing."

Niles stood and patted his old friend on the shoulder.

"I want my budget request fulfilled, Mr. President."

"You're a blackmailing little bastard!"

Niles patted his shoulder even harder.

"I ordered my people on it before I left Nevada. Still one step behind me on the uptake, aren't you, Jim?"

Both men grew silent as the vision of the burning *Theodore Roosevelt* entered their minds at the same time. Niles knew that the president was angry and wanted to hit back at someone. He just wanted to make sure that the anger was directed at the *right* someone.

CHAPTER
SEVEN

GOSSMANN METAL WERK BUILDING
OSLO, NORWAY

Coalitionist Zoenfeller, representing Austria, and the members from India, Canada, and Poland, along with main council, sat in the main conference room of the factory. Caretaker was on the main monitor from a location other than Oslo.

The richly appointed area was semidark, which was close in color to the mood of the four men and one woman gathered there. In front of each of them sat open file folders that had been forward to them from the Coalition's new headquarters in Chicago. The information contained in the folders was an insult. It bordered on treason and had been done so brazenly that the gathered members actually feared for their lives for the first time since the thinly veiled coup had started.

William Tomlinson was declaring war on the world almost three full years ahead of the schedule set by the whole of the Coalition members five years earlier.

"Caretaker, we have the grounds to remove Mr. Tomlinson from the council and expunge him from the Coalition, do we not?"

The elderly man cleared his throat and looked uncomfortable on the monitor.

"You have the right of law on your side as set down by Juliai writ. However, you gentlemen and lady," Caretaker nodded in deference to the Indian representative, "I'm afraid you will not have the votes. Many of your colleagues have joined the young American in his actions. I have learned they are very close to finding one or even all of the Atlantean Keys."

Zoenfeller could not help but notice that Caretaker kept saying *you* and not *us* or *we*.

The old man picked an eight-by-ten photo from the file in front of him showing the aftermath of the Korean air attack on the American task force and slapped it with his fingers. "This is madness! The loss of life on those two American warships was horrendous! He is weakening someone the Coalition needs to maintain continuity in the world until we consolidate."

Knuckles rapped on the table in agreement.

"It's not I you have to convince. I would recommend, secretly of course, that you contact the members of the Coalition who are teetering on the fence. Get them to commit to a more subtle approach. For now I must take my leave." Caretaker reached to turn off his laptop camera.

"Where are you going? We have other matters to discuss," Zoenfeller said angrily.

"Until you do receive the needed support of the rest of the Coalition, I am obligated to advise only the ruling body of the council. Thus far, with all due respect of course, you are not it. I am sorry."

With that quick apology, the image of the Caretaker of Coalition law vanished. The four members looked at the table in stunned silence.

Without preamble, a six-sided monitor slid up in the middle of the conference table. The test signal was a sharp and clear picture of a golden eagle on a red background. It soon vanished and the concerned face of Tomlinson appeared on the screen.

"Good morning." He looked at his watch. "Awful late to have a meeting the rest of us weren't informed of, isn't it?"

"You have done a grievous injustice to our plans. You have moved on the leadership of Germany and Japan, who are now stunned and running scared," Zoenfeller said as he stood and leaned over the table, making sure that his face was framed in the camera lens on top of the monitor.

"They are not running anywhere. Germany's replacement, a Coalition designee, is already in place. He has already issued a statement saying all is well, assuring the German people that the terrorist element he is holding responsible for the assassination will face swift German justice. Japan in the meanwhile has but one choice in this matter and can only turn to *our* candidate in the next few days. By Japanese law, they can do nothing else."

"You're going to bring the entire free world down around our heads!"

"You're worried about the attack on the American task force? Well, even that has its benefits. While it weakened the NATO response in Korea, it has also guaranteed Kim Jong Il's destruction sooner, rather than later."

"And how is that—by giving them the military courage to cross the border?"

"Exactly. The American theater commander, once the Second Infantry Division and its South Korean allies are overrun, will have no choice but to deploy battlefield nuclear weapons to stop them. As for Russia and China, they will soon cease to be of concern, as their countries lie in ruins, smashed beyond all ability to govern their own populations. There will be no assistance rendered to North Korea by her allies."

Zoenfeller sat back heavily in his chair, amazed at the calm demeanor Tomlinson was showing.

"After that, the assassinations will continue in later weeks until we have all of our people in place in the capitals of the West, and then our two-thousand-year-old charter will be fulfilled. We will have done what every Coalition Council has failed to do since the time of Julius Caesar. It gives me chills to think it was *our* Council that did this great feat."

The elder members looked horrified but remained silent.

"When the great Julius Caesar threw off the shackles imposed on him by the weaker members of our Ancient family, he couldn't have the foresight to believe the power his children would someday wield. His murderers, in their vain attempt to stop his desire for one rule for all the people, have finally led us to this momentous occasion."

Zoenfeller tried one final effort to bring the lion of the Coalition to the table of reason.

"Surely we can wait until the Atlantean Key is recovered. If we continue to accelerate beyond planning, things could spiral out of control and these great dreams of finally gaining all that was lost by our ancestors fifteen thousand years ago will be lost, possibly forever."

Tomlinson smiled and then looked into the camera. He now had Zoenfeller and the others right where he wanted them, and he would use the old man's fears and words to silence his voice in the Coalition forever.

"The recovery of the plate map is happening as we speak. The Atlantean Key will be found in no more than a week, and then our greatest enemies will be bashed to pieces by the very earth they walk upon."

"You have already been found out!" the old man said incredulously as he lost all control.

"You are referring to the supposed audiotape of the wave?" He laughed, and then he seemed to look into the monitor hard enough that the members thought he was staring directly into their souls. "The aerial platform will no longer be used. We will not need it. With the tone receptors already in place, we will strike at the world from a lair they would never, could never find—the very birthplace of the Wave itself."

Tomlinson saw the look of utter surprise on their faces. Even a few of his junior members were stunned.

"That's right. We have not only succeeded in finding part of the Ancients' city intact, we have already started naval operations to use the sunken city to conduct operations against Russia and China, even the United States, from one and a half miles below the floor of the Mediterranean."

Zoenfeller slammed his aged hand against the polished tabletop. "No! We won't allow it. If you destroy Russia and China, they will react. There are always survivors to a massacre and believe me they will want retribution. You have taken a carefully orchestrated plan and accelerated it until no one in the world will believe the Wave was a natural occurrence. We will stop you."

William Tomlinson smiled and leaned back in his overly large chair.

"I understand your timidity. All four of you have the Coalition's respect and gratitude for assisting us in planning the new order. I have tried to keep you informed out of respect, but we will not allow you to betray the new Reich. From the time of Caesar, through the Crusades, Napoleon, and even Hitler, we have strived to bring a sense of justice and continuity to all people and eliminate those that curse the name of order, that Gaius Julius Caesar saw in the barbarians of the world. Now, at the very moment of triumph, you have failed our cause. Old friends, you are hereby expunged from the Juliai Coalition. Your services to the Ancients will be remembered with honor and respect. Good-bye."

The monitor went dead. There was not even the image of a blank signal on in Tomlinson's place. Every member present on both sides of the Atlantic knew what was about to happen. It did not take long.

There came a light knock on the door. Without waiting for permission to enter, a thin man dressed in an Armani suit stepped in. He looked around the meeting room and then half bowed and then closed the door.

"I am here to accept your last requests, which will be written out on the notepads in front of you," he said with a thick Spanish accent.

Zoenfeller closed his eyes, and the others, including the woman from India, just stared at the man sent to kill them.

"I ask that you believe me when I say it is an honor to be chosen for this duty. You in this room are much respected, and Mr. Tomlinson offers his sincere gratitude for all that you have done for the cause."

They all saw that the man actually managed to look magnanimous and sorrowful as he pulled a large handgun from his suit jacket.

HEMPSTEAD BUILDING
CHICAGO, ILLINOIS

Tomlinson leaned back in his chair, knowing that he would never have to deal with the older faction of the Coalition again. Since the formation of the Coalition, after the split of the Ancients, never had they been so close to finalizing the plans for the formation of one order to rule all.

Tomlinson knew that some thought him mad or at the very least unbalanced. They also knew that he was the only man capable of carrying out the dreams of Julius Caesar and his original ancestors. Caesar had been a man of vision who wanted nothing more than justice for the children of the Ancients, to once again live in a world ruled by men of vision and race responsibility.

The thought that maybe theirs was a warped and intolerant view never entered their thinking. Tomlinson always tempered the argument with his own: absolutely nothing in this world had worked as men thought it would. Pure races and economic power equaled stability the likes of which the world had not known since the time of the Atlanteans. He was not a hater of lesser people. On the contrary, Tomlinson knew that every race had its place in the order of things, just as his ancestors and Julius Caesar had envisioned. They just could not be expected to reach beyond their grasp. The Coalition would be there to make sure they were fed, clothed, entertained, and taken care of. Their positions would be those of servants of the order and they would be happier for it.

His assistant who entered the office and made his way to the large desk interrupted his thoughts. That was when he noticed that Caretaker had not left after the meeting. He just sat quietly in the corner, watching him. Tomlinson looked at him and Caretaker just nodded his head.

"Sir, these were faxed to you earlier during your meetings. I thought you might be interested."

Tomlinson accepted the clear folder and then excused his

assistant. As he opened it, he momentarily turned his attention back to Caretaker.

"I'm sorry, I thought you had left. Can I help you with something?"

"As you must be aware, sir, as Caretaker of the law of the Juliai, I am obligated to remain at the chairman's side until dismissed for personal downtime. That is the way of things."

"I see. I didn't realize I'd been elected to such an exalted office."

"You haven't been. But I, like yourself, am a realist, and I feel it is only a matter of time before such distinctions are finalized."

As Tomlinson pulled the pages from the envelope, he had to stop and look closer at the older man before him. The surprise on his face was hard to hide.

"I would have thought you would be leaning more toward the letter of Juliai law. So you think we are taking the right path by moving forward with the attacks?"

"No, sir, it is not that at all. My job is to make sure you follow the path of the Coalition and its aims. You have not deviated from that as of this moment."

"Good, I am—"

"However, that does not presuppose that your plan will succeed. If there is a setback in finding the plate map, or the Atlantean Key, the plan must be terminated immediately. Then, after time has passed, a new council will start afresh. I believe that is a fair interpretation of Coalition mandate. The whole must be protected at all costs."

"You have made your point. Now, if you will excuse me, I have business to attend to that does not concern Coalition mandates."

Caretaker stood, buttoned his jacket, and left the office.

Tomlinson stared at the closed door for a brief moment and then looked at the faxed pages.

The photos were the first to catch his eye. The three men captured in them were formidable in stature. The notes tagged to each of the five photos said that they had possibly been involved with the raid in Westchester; thus, these men might have been connected with the botched attempts to collect the Key in Ethiopia. Dahlia claimed, in her attached note, that it was a logical step in the chain of actions to this point. She also wrote that she was hoping to run into these three again.

Another note was attached, reiterating what she had told him earlier about tracing the plate map to Hawaii. She foresaw no problems in attaining the artifact soon.

The second note had been timed thirty minutes after the first. This one made Tomlinson clench his teeth. He was not used to Dahlia making errors in judgment, but this time she had. Instead of making sure that Keeler's journal contained the complete list of the remaining Ancients, she had killed the man. She informed him that Keeler had ripped out the last page with the names of the surviving members of the children of Atlantis.

"Damn," he said as he laid down the note. The fact that they had missed a chance to rid the world of the remaining few old ones made his skin crawl.

As he shook his head, the picture of one man in particular caught his attention and he picked up the close-up taken from the second floor. The man looking out the landing window was a serious-looking man who was different from his companions: he was more focused as he looked around. This intrigued Tomlinson and he felt a chill pass through him as he memorized the face.

"If Dahlia is right, you have cost me valuable time, my friend," he said as his index finger popped against the fax paper right over the face of Jack Collins.

EVENT GROUP CENTER
NELLIS AIR FORCE BASE, NEVADA

Jack Collins and Carl Everett were waiting for the Europa technician to arrive from the computer center. Pete Golding was angry that he had to release one of his people from duties involving the investigation of the seismic occurrences, but he calmed significantly when he was told that it was Jack requesting the Cray-computer time to assist in the New York incident.

Everett looked at his watch, furious that it was taking so

long. Jack, meanwhile, was calm, his face showing none of the angst that Everett was dealing with.

"Damn techs, they think they run this place."

Collins finally looked at him without much emotion. "They do run this place."

"Yeah, I guess so."

Finally, the elevator that led down to the clean room opened and a familiar face stepped out.

"Ah, shit," Everett mumbled under his breath as he rubbed his forehead.

Dr. Gene Robbins was the assistant director of the computer center under Pete Golding. His performance in the use of the supercomputer Europa in the Event with the UFO a couple of years back had endeared him to Niles and the rest of the sciences departments. But he was a royal pain in the rear as far as Europa protocols were concerned, as Jack and Carl had found out personally.

The bespectacled Robbins looked up and grunted. "I should have known."

"Look, Doc, we don't have time for all of this clean-room stuff. We shaved this morning and are ready to go," Carl said as Robbins slid his ID card into the electronic lock beside the door.

"Gentlemen, today you don't have to put so much as a lab coat on." He opened the door and then stepped aside to allow the two very shocked men into the sanctuary that housed the Cray supercomputer Europa.

"What happened, Doc, you get electrocuted or something? I mean, you're almost like the rest of us humans."

Robbins pulled out one of the eight chairs that sat in front of the thick glass that housed Europa and her automatic program-loading system. He hesitated for a moment and then removed his glasses to look at the two men.

"Colonel Collins, Captain Everett, I requested this detail from Pete Golding. Sergeant Sanchez was always kind to us when he was on duty in the comp center. You see, while you only suspect we are human, he actually treated us as such." He placed his glasses back on and almost choked on the rest of his words. "He was my friend."

Jack stood silent and Carl felt like an ass. He just nodded and sat next to Robbins.

"He was a better and kinder soul than most of us jerks, Doc."

Jack nodded at Everett and took his seat.

"Think we start by digging into the New York Police Department files on the attack at the warehouse? Then maybe their crime-scene computer reports, blood type, ballistics, things like that?" Jack asked Robbins, who was already logging in to Europa.

Before Robbins answered, the large steel partition behind the wall of glass slid up, and Europa was there in all her glory. The automated loading system was idle, but her brain used her enhanced optics to view the three men.

"Good morning Dr. Robbins. I see we have company from the Security Department today. Colonel Collins, Captain Everett, how may I help you?"

Carl rolled his eyes at the female auditory system. He still wanted to get to know the person whose voice had been synthesized, because she sounded just like Marilyn Monroe.

Jack leaned forward in his chair and spoke into the microphone.

"Europa, we have lost many people to an act of murder and have many things to investigate and we will need you to break the security guarding police systems. We must find the people responsible for the deaths of Event Group staff. Is this understood?"

Robbins was curious as to why she didn't respond directly. The automated loader sprang into action as the robotic arms manufactured by the Honda Corporation started sliding programs into the bank of hard drives.

"Europa is ready to seek out your requested inquiries, Colonel. Shall we begin?"

Robbins smiled and looked at Everett.

"Europa was well aware of the murders because she references every daily newspaper in the world. She obviously knew the names listed in the reporter's story as killed and crossed them with her data files. She knows Event personnel have been lost."

Jack gripped the small microphone in front of him tightly at its base. His knuckles turned white as the pressure increased, but his calm features never changed.

"Yes, let's begin."

Sarah McIntire was getting frustrated with the twenty-five people in her group. Theories, no matter how far out, were discussed, and one by one they all lost credence.

Most present were of the opinion that earthquakes could not be manipulated short of placing a nuclear weapon beneath a fault line. Sarah thus far had to agree. Every computer model that Europa had built for them had failed. It was beginning to look as if they'd hit a dead end.

Virginia came into the room and kneeled next to Sarah's chair, and listened to the current argument of hydrodynamics and its effect on fault lines.

"Most fault lines are stable to the point where we would almost have to call them extinct, just a gouge in the earth's surface. While others, like the San Andreas, for instance, are active as hell. But we still couldn't get it to move unless the forces beneath it forced her to, by pushing water through the strata, weakening it, or an outright eruption of magma."

Sarah listened to the young professor from Virginia Tech whom the Group had recruited to earth sciences over a year ago. Then she smiled when Virginia mouthed the words *keep at it* and then moved to the door.

Sarah saw the young, long-haired scientist stand and go to the wall and pull down a large chart. It was a color picture of the earth laid out flat. Several hundred red lines were depicted as they coursed through the continents and oceans. They swirled and eddied, going in no particular direction.

"As you see, it's not just the fault lines around the world. It is my opinion that you have to attack not the faults, but the very plates beneath them that make the faults on the surface unstable."

Sarah closed her eyes. Something about the professor's explanation danced in her memory. She opened her eyes and looked at the chart that showed the world's known fault lines, but couldn't for the life of her remember what it was she had seen that connected the dots for her. She let the thought slip her mind as disagreement exploded in the room.

Jack watched as Europa entered three programs. Robbins did not understand what it was Collins was digging for. Even Carl was growing concerned.

"Europa, query: the two weapons recovered from the crime scene. They are definitely not in the inventory of Department 5656?"

"According to armory records, one Beretta 9-millimeter, serial number 587690, one Ingram automatic pistol, serial number 153694073-2, were not listed as issued to Department 5656."

Jack had one answer after hours of dead ends.

"Query: are you still into the ATF mainframe, Europa?"

"Yes, Colonel Collins."

"Can you check serial numbers against the two weapons you just gave us for stolen data?"

"Items were listed by ATF as destroyed by reclamation, batch number 45786-B90, on December 3, 1999."

"Both weapons were listed together in the same destruct batch?"

"Now that's weird. What would you say the odds were on that?" Carl commented.

"I wouldn't care to bet," answered Robbins.

"Europa, query: how many weapons in the ATF destruction batch dated 12-03-99?"

"Two thousand five-hundred, maximum weight allowance for melting furnace."

"Someone crooked at ATF, Jack?"

"Okay, we know where two of the weapons used against our people came from, but what in the hell does that get us?" Jack asked, instead of answering Carl's question.

"Europa, query: have you yet acquired access to the NYPD mainframe?" Collins asked.

"Yes, access was gained through unsecured backdoor in Albany, New York, used for the NYPD Widows Welfare Fund."

"Pretty good," Everett said, looking at Robbins.

"She has her ways," he said proudly.

"Has a ballistics report been issued on bullets removed from Event personnel?" Jack continued.

"A report has been generated by the team of officers assigned to case number 4564893-23 for Boston Police Department Robbery–Homicide Special Investigations Division."

"Why Boston?" Robbins asked, and then caught himself. "Europa, query: is there a case in Boston that warranted such a request for ballistics information?"

"Boston Police Department requested any ballistics match through the National Crime Database and received the NYPD report. Expended 5.56, 7.56 and 9 millimeter ammunition used in NYPD report matched exact specifications of ballistics report generated by Boston Police, Robbery–Homicide, dated this day."

"The bastards hit someone else up in Boston, Jack," Everett said as he leaned closer to the glass.

"Europa, query: is there a report of the crime filed by BPD?" Collins asked hurriedly.

"Formulating."

As the three men watched, crime-scene photos started to pop up at an incredible rate on the large monitor screen. Scenes of murder filled the frames. The corpses lay on bloodstained carpets in grotesque stillness.

"My God," Dr. Robbins said aloud.

"Looks familiar," Jack said beneath his breath.

"Europa, query: what is the location of the Boston crime scene?"

"Crime committed at the law offices of Evans, Lawson and Keeler, Attorneys at Law, located at 4967 Wayland Avenue, Boston. Thirty-seven known deaths occurred at approximately one forty-five Boston time."

"Europa, query: any motive stated for the murders at this time?" Everett asked, heading Jack off.

"Robbery has been listed as motivation for the deaths."

"Round up Mendenhall and Ryan, tell them we're taking a quick trip out to Boston. I want to see could have been so important that these bastards committed another slaughter of innocent people. Tell them to draw side arms and ammo from the armory. Inform Alice we need ATF identification. That should get us through the front door of wherever we need to go."

"You got it," Everett said.

"Is there anything I can do, Colonel?" Robbins asked hopefully.

"You've done enough, Doc. Just get back to Pete and help him. He seems lost without you in the comp center."

"Colonel, you watch your ass. From the looks of things, whoever these people are, they don't let anyone get in their way."

"Hmm, I know some people just like that, Doc."

Robbins watched the colonel leave and knew exactly whom Jack had meant. Everett joined Collins at the door and the two men left together to meet up with Ryan and Mendenhall.

"Yeah, I guess we do have people that are just as serious as those murdering pukes," Robbins said to himself and then closed the terminal with Europa.

CHAPTER
EIGHT

BOSTON, MASSACHUSETTS

Collins, Everett, Mendenhall, and Ryan stood outside the offices of the law firm Evans, Lawson and Keeler, easily identifiable to the public by the lines of bright yellow police tape surrounding the old brownstone. The Boston Police Department had several bright-light stands placed in front of the building and several uniformed patrolmen were watching the bystanders closely.

The black windbreakers the four men wore had ATF on the back and on the left breast. Jack walked to the front of the building and presented his identification.

"ATF out of New York," Jack began. He found that he didn't need even that small opening for the policeman standing on the large stoop leading into the offices. The man just pointed to the double front doors.

"Robbery–Homicide is set up right inside the lobby, mac. Coffee's there too."

"Thanks," Collins said and gestured for his three men to follow him.

The smell of death hit Jack as soon as he stepped inside. The fluorescent lighting illuminated the reception area of the prestigious firm and belied the fact that so much violence had taken place there less than twenty-four hours before.

"Coming onto scenes like this is getting to be a habit I can really learn to live without, Jack," Everett said, pulling his ID as a detective walked in from the long corridor behind the reception and eyed them.

"Still a hard world," was all Collins said in return.

"Can I help you?"

Jack looked at the man in civilian clothes with his shirtsleeves rolled up and saw that he was wearing a shoulder holster.

"ATF. Our people called today and spoke with a Captain Harnessy. We had a match hit on the ballistics report filed by your department."

"The warehouse thing, right?" the detective said.

"Can we have a look around?" Everett asked as he started to skirt the detective.

"We haven't finished the CSI yet, so—"

"Look," Jack leaned over and looked closer at the man's badge, "Lieutenant, we're willing to share our information and we do have a lot of it. Willing as long as we don't have to play any of these jurisdiction games. Believe it or not, we're on the same side here."

The lieutenant looked around and then nodded. "All right, but I go with you, and don't touch anything. My captain is a real stickler for this clean crime-scene stuff."

Jack smiled and started through the reception door. "I know what you mean; our director can also be a stickler for rules."

As they passed through the door, Carl stepped up and whispered, before the Boston cop caught up to them, "Especially if he knew we were here."

"Oh, man," Ryan hissed, as he saw the first bloodstain on the carpet, where the first victim had been killed.

"They capped the security guard here. The rest of the victims were split into six different offices and shot executionstyle."

Jack walked through the first door he came to, which was the main conference room. It looked to Collins that four or five people had been killed in the large room. There were stains on the carpeted floor and on the wall.

"The second batch of people died here, we think. One man, three women, all popped once in the head. The ladies were shot execution-style against the wall."

"Jesus, who in the hell are we dealing with here?" Ryan asked as he stepped from the room.

Mendenhall didn't say anything as he joined Ryan. The exact same thoughts had crossed his mind when he saw the death at the warehouse, and after two days he still could not fathom the type of man who would kill so callously.

"You claim the motive was robbery?" Jack asked as he followed the detective out of the room.

As they entered the hallway, several crime-scene people walked past with large cases. At the end of this line was a man in a white coat who snapped several pictures of a large bloodstain on the wall. As the five men walked off, the police photographer took several more shots and then left. He did not hurry or otherwise attract attention to himself as he made his way to the front after picking up a black case. He nodded at the uniformed officers outside and then moved past the onlookers, walked easily across the street, and disappeared.

Collins and the others were led into a very well-appointed office. A large bloodstain had soaked into the beige carpet in front of the oak desk. The detective pointed to a large portrait that stood out from the far wall. Jack saw the open safe built into a cavity behind it.

"The safe was found like that with only the fingerprints of the senior partner. . . ." He looked into a small notebook. "Mr. Jackson Keeler. Twenty thousand dollars in cash was found, along with several keepsakes and legal papers."

"What was missing?"

"We don't know at this point. Mr. Keeler has no living relatives, and his partners were among the dead."

"It had to be something pretty good to have murdered this many people," Ryan said as he looked into the safe.

"At this point it could have been anything, or nothing. Whoever killed Mr. Keeler took a lot of pleasure in doing it. He was shot ten times."

"So maybe they didn't get what they wanted. Maybe that's why he angered his killers," Everett commented as he looked at the large bloodstain.

"Did the bullets from Keeler match those of the others?"

"We don't know yet; he hasn't been autopsied yet. The coroner seems to be a little bit behind schedule. Guess he wasn't ready for the rush."

"Anything caught on security cameras?" Jack asked.

"No, the cables were—"

"What in the hell are you doing, conducting tours?"

Jack and the others turned at the sound of a booming voice with an Irish lilt. A large man stood in the office doorway with his hands on his hips, glaring at the detective.

"Captain, these men are from ATF and wanted—"

'I don't give a damn what they want. Get them the hell out of here! Did you know you have more people in here than Fenway! One of our CSI photographers was mugged outside just twenty minutes ago. We found him beat to hell. Now, all deals are off. You ATF guys go through channels."

Three minutes later, Jack and the others were standing on the other side of the police cordon.

"What now, Colonel?" Mendenhall asked.

"The coroner's office—maybe he has something we can use."

Their false ATF IDs worked again with no difficulty. The office of the coroner was packed with next of kin and extra medical examiners brought in from other towns to assist the Boston office with the massacre victims. Jack grabbed the first harried-looking white coat he could stop.

"Jackson Keeler—has he been autopsied yet?" Collins shouted above the din of crying family members and tired medical examiners.

The young woman wanted to pull away from Jack's grip, but when she found it locked around her wrist, she quickly looked at her clipboard.

"Number three. They're just starting."

Collins let the woman go and she dashed into a mob of

people and started explaining the hold-up on the identification process. The four men watched for a moment and felt for the families suffering from this cold-blooded tragedy.

They turned away and went to two side-by-side doors. One said EXAMINING ROOM 3 and the one next to it was marked VIEWING.

Jack chose the latter. As the four men entered, they saw two medical students standing at the glass. They looked at the four men in black windbreakers with the curiosity one would show a bug that had just crawled onto one's sandwich. Everett held up his ID and the two students swallowed and stepped to the far side of the glass.

Inside, the autopsy had already started. On a chalkboard in front of the stainless steel table was a hastily written identification: JACKSON KEELER, 78 YEARS, 4 MONTHS.

The speaker inside the viewing room was connected to the microphone used by the ME as he started to work on the elderly attorney.

Twenty minutes later, Everett leaned toward Jack.

"Well, I guess all we're going to get is the cause of death."

"Dammit. I was hoping something would come out of this," Collins said as he turned and sat in a chair next to Will and Jason.

None of the four men paid any attention to one of the medical students when she stood up and walked to the intercom.

"Dr. Freely, when your assistant removed the subject's dentures, something fell out of his mouth."

Everett watched as the assistant in the autopsy room bent over, retrieved something from the floor, and held it up to the light.

"Jack, you may want to see this," Carl said as he watched closely.

"It's a torn piece of paper. Looks like four names here; it's hard to make out," the assistant said, holding it in front of the ME.

Jack looked at Everett and they both made for the door.

"Ryan, you and Will go get the car started and meet us out front."

The ME was just reaching for the torn piece of paper when the door opened and two men in black windbreakers stepped in.

"Don't touch that, Doctor, please," Jack said.

"Hey, you can't be in here, there's an autopsy going on!" the assistant said as he tried to step in front of Everett, who just picked the smaller man up and set him aside.

Jack snatched a pair of rubber gloves from the counter and pulled the right one on and easily removed the paper from the shocked ME's hand.

"Call security and get these men out of here!" he said as he watched Collins hold the paper up to the light.

The assistant looked as if he wanted to follow the orders of his boss, but Everett was still standing in front of him with his brows raised.

"ATF, Doctor. We'll need this," Jack said as he lowered the paper and made for the door, followed quickly by Everett.

"What is it, Jack?" Carl asked as he caught up with Collins.

"Names; I can't make them out, but they are names. Keeler obviously didn't want his killers to have them, so he stuck them in his mouth before he died."

They were ten feet from the door when the large Boston police captain entered with the detective that who had given them the tour of the law office; they stood toe-to-toe with Jack and Everett.

"Hey, stop those men! They just took evidence from the autopsy room!" the whiny little assistant cried from the open door of the examining room.

"Okay, give it—"

That was as far as the police captain got, because right at that moment Jason Ryan pushed the double doors open as hard as he could, sending the two policemen sprawling onto the green tiled floor. Everett and Collins did not wait to offer apologies and followed the smaller Ryan out of the door and into the car, and Mendenhall sped away as if they had just robbed a bank.

As their car took off, another vehicle, this one a white van, pulled out and sped along in pursuit.

EVENT GROUP CENTER
NELLIS AIR FORCE BASE, NEVADA

Sarah had called a two-hour break for the science teams so that they could recharge their batteries. Thus far, the group had come up with no theory that would pass muster as to the validity of the manmade-earthquake theory. Virginia was very close to calling Niles at the White House and informing him that in the opinion of the Group, while not impossible to do, the expense and labor-intensive problems would be too much to overcome with today's technology. Which in and of itself was not gospel, but close to it, with the minds they had working the problem.

Virginia and Alice sat next to Sarah in the large cafeteria. They both had tea and they looked at Sarah's unfinished sandwich.

"Are we interrupting something?" Alice asked with her pleasant smile.

Sarah snapped to as if she had been in deep thought.

"Oh, hello, ladies. No, you're not interrupting anything more than the contemplation of failure."

"Failure? I wouldn't say that, Sarah. You weren't ordered by the president to start a manmade earthquake, only to prove if it could possibly be done by others. You failed at nothing."

Sarah looked from Virginia to the face of Alice and she smiled sadly.

"You know, this may sound strange, but I think it could be done. Oh, I know the North Korean claims are probably just a smokescreen, but I think the answers are out there and we just failed to find them."

Alice patted her small hand. "Well, don't take it so hard. You should spend the rest of your break down in the artifact-cataloging room—that's where the excitement is happening."

"Yeah, I was down there earlier and saw that large map and the other one with the strange lines running through it," she said, taking her spoon and playing with her cold soup.

"Not only that, but they came across scrolls from Rome. Julius Caesar, of all people," Alice said as she lifted her cup of tea and sipped.

"Caesar? Why would his scrolls be mixed in with the ancient texts? Don't tell me Jack and Carl screwed up when they crated them and just threw everything together?"

"No, no. That collector had them cataloged like that. Everything placed together by date. They're working on them now. There is really a lot of excitement, especially about those scientific scrolls and other things that are definitely strange," Virginia said. "So even if your team fails to come up with a way to start earthquakes, we still have plenty for everyone to do."

Alice and Sarah noticed that Virginia had lowered her tea and looked distant.

"What is it?" Sarah asked.

"Oh, I just realized how ridiculous all this is when you think about what's happening in the world around us. I mean we have kids, American boys, dying, and here I sit acting like a schoolgirl about a bunch of stuff that really means nothing when compared to the lives of people."

"Now who's being hard on herself?" Sarah said as she patted Virginia's hand.

"No, sometimes the foolishness of people makes me want to scream so loud I could shatter that glass."

Sarah smiled, but then a strange look crossed her face.

"What did you just say?"

"Oh, please, I could go on forever about the foolishness of—"

"Shatter glass," Sarah said instead of waiting for Virginia to finish.

"Excuse me?" Virginia asked.

Sarah picked up her water glass and looked at it. She then set it down and looked at Virginia and Alice in turn.

"What happens to a glass when an opera singer hits a certain decibel level?"

"Well, I've heard that they can . . ." Virginia trailed off as she thought about what Sarah had asked. "You mean sound?"

"Sound and earthquakes, Sarah?" Alice asked, lowering her teacup.

Sarah stood up and smiled.

"Excuse me, ladies, I have some calls to make."

BOSTON, MASSACHUSETTS

"Dammit!" Jack exclaimed from the front seat.

"What?" Will asked as he took a corner as fast as he could without losing traction.

"We should have brought a laptop so we could tie in to Europa!"

"Wait a minute, Will; pull over here by those kids," Ryan said from the back.

Mendenhall pulled into the curb and Ryan jumped out. Everett, Collins, and Will watched as Ryan spoke animatedly to them about something.

For the past fifteen minutes they had been trying to read the names on the wet paper, and now they thought they finally had all four: Henry Fellows Carlisle, Davis Cunningham Ingram, Martha Lynn Laughlin, and Carmichael Aaron Rothman. None of them recognized these names, but they meant something to someone, that much was clear. Jackson Keeler had wanted them protected enough to die for, and the people who had killed him had ruthlessly sought them.

"What in the hell is that flyboy doing?" Everett asked as Ryan finished with the young teenagers and then trotted back to the car and jumped in.

"Third and Argyle," he said, settling into his seat.

Everett looked at Ryan with a blank stare.

"You need a patch-in to Europa—well, there's a cyber café on the corner of Third Street and Argyle."

"You navy types never cease to amaze me," Jack said as the car sped away into traffic.

The man who had taken the photographs of Jack and his team at the law firm sat in the back of the white van and directed the driver to follow them into the heart of downtown Boston. The white lab coat he had used and the ID he had taken from the police forensics technician lay crumpled on the seat beside him. He was using a portable film developer on the pull-down table in front of him. The first photo of the man came out crystal clear as he pulled the still-wet eight-by-ten from the mouth of the machine. He snapped on an interior light and examined the face. He now knew for sure that it was the same man he'd seen in the warehouse.

He bypassed the five other shots on the reel, setting them aside as he placed the photo of Collins inside a scanner and closed the top. Then he opened his laptop and examined the black-and-white photo more closely. He centered the cursor on the identification badge and zoomed in a hundredfold. The name came into focus.

"John Harriman, ATF," the long-haired technician mumbled under his breath. "Let's just see if you are who you say you are, John."

The man picked up a cell phone and made a call. He gave the name and the department of the subject and then waited.

"There is no John Harriman at Alcohol, Tobacco and Firearms, huh? I kind of suspected that; this guy is a little too efficient for government work." The man thought for a moment. "Look, can you get a trace-visual ID on this man and see if you can come up with any matches? I'll wait."

The person he was speaking with was a deep-cover operative run by Dahlia and used sparingly because of his position in the federal records division. You didn't burn someone who was in a position to give you that kind of information.

The cell phone rang.

"What have you got?" He listened as he wrote down the information. "That's all? Colonel Jack Collins, U.S. Army Special Forces on detached service, and then nothing? I'll pass it along to Dahlia you were a *great* help," he said angrily.

"They're pulling over in front of that cyber café," the driver said.

"Park somewhere nearby and for God's sake don't be seen. These guys are starting to make me a little nervous."

The man opened the cell phone and hit a single number.

"Keyhole here. I'm faxing you some photos. Our friends from the warehouse are back. They went to the law offices and then to the morgue and they left there in one hell of a hurry. Listen, Dahlia, I used our source in federal records and we're dealing with an unknown here—a Colonel Jack Collins was ID'd. U.S. Army and a former Special Operations guy who is on detached service to an unknown entity, and I believe he and his men may have uncovered something from the coroner's office because they left there in one hell of a hurry. I'm going to keep a tail on these guys but I need some major backup. Is the Boston strike team still in town? Thank you. Now I'm going to see if I can eavesdrop on what they're doing. I'll call back."

The man shook his head, knowing that Dahlia failed to realize that somehow she had allowed a possible federal agency of unknown prowess to tag her movements. Oh, she acted calm enough, but then again she was safe in New York, while he had his ass hanging in the wind, tagging a damn Green Beret and his people who scared you just by looking at you.

"Damn, this is just too much," he mumbled as he brought his telephoto lens up to his eye and started perusing the café, looking for Jack Collins.

Jack felt exposed as he and Carl made the link with Europa. Everett kept an eye on the café's patrons to make sure no one moseyed by for a look-see. Luckily, most of the cyber kids were their doing homework or chatting up on MySpace and none of them seemed interested in the two adults. They were stuck in at a table that faced the rear of the café, so Everett kept most of his attention focused on the people nearest the plate glass window as Jack started his conversation with the Cray computer in Nevada.

Jack typed the names they had read on the piece of paper and asked Europa for any sort of record on them. It did not take her long on the first two.

HENRY FELLOWS CARLISLE, DECEASED, 81 YEARS OF AGE, DIED 1999. FORMER CHAIRMAN OF THE FELLOWS GROUP OF COMPANIES.

"Damn! Strike one," Jack said.

DAVIS CUNNINGHAM INGRAM, DECEASED, 90 YEARS OF AGE, DIED 2004. FORMER CEO OF INGRAM FIREARMS COMPANY, CEO INGRAM METAL FABRICATION, FORMER CHAIRMAN OF THE ADALAY SHIPYARDS IN MARYLAND.

"Strike two."

MARTHA LYNN LAUGHLIN, 1932–? CHAIRPERSON OF LAUGHLIN LABORATORIES, FOUNDER OF DEELEY PHARMACEUTICALS.

"Okay, that's better," Jack said, as he copied down the information.

CARMICHAEL AARON ROTHMAN, 1921–? FORMER CEO OF ROTHMAN INDUSTRIES, FORMER BOARD MEMBER GENERAL DYNAMICS CORPORATION, FORMER BOARD CHAIRPERSON LOCKHEED MARTIN AERONAUTICS.

"Whoa, that's a couple of heavy hitters," Everett said as he looked over Jack's shoulder.

"They sure are. They were the last two names on the piece of paper that Keeler hid in his mouth and also the only two that are alive."

"You think our attorney friend kept a list of his friends?"

"Or enemies. These two may be responsible for his death, and he wanted the authorities to get their names."

"Well, we're not in authority, but finder's keepers, Jack," Everett said.

Collins typed in the two bottom names and asked Europa for their current addresses.

"Virginia. So I guess we're headed south, huh?"

"Why not? Let's just go and ask them who in the hell they are and why their names are connected with over sixty-five deaths in the last twenty-four hours," Jack said as he terminated the secure connection with Nevada.

"Now, this should be interesting," Everett said as he led the way out of the café.

The man in the van had barely caught the last two names on the list and their addresses in his telephoto lens. He wrote them down and then picked up his cell phone and punched the one number as before.

"Martha Laughlin and Carmichael Rothman—mean anything to you?"

"I will pass this on to my employer."

"I suspect they're heading to the airport," he said to the driver. "Follow and confirm and then we're done here; Dahlia can have them."

HEMPSTEAD BUILDING
CHICAGO, ILLINOIS

William Tomlinson had decided to stay at the office and work on the final plans for staging the Wave operations from the sunken city where the Coalition would be protected by two miles of water and another half mile in seafloor. Ever since Caretaker had left for the night, he'd felt more at ease. He supposed that he would have to get used to the old man looking over his shoulder, but when you were used to privacy it was hard to take. As much as he needed some new rules and changes for the Coalition, he knew the value of tradition, and Caretaker was at least that.

His private phone line buzzed. He took a deep breath, tossed his pen onto the seagoing-operations plans for the Mediterranean, and picked up the phone.

"Yes."

"I'm afraid we have a problem that was not foreseen in your plans."

"I thought we had eliminated most of the obstructions, Dahlia."

"I have, but the items that were missing from Keeler's journal have turned up."

"Okay, Dahlia, bury them. And good work, by the way. How did you uncover their whereabouts?"

"They were hiding in plain sight in Virginia. We gave them too much credit for subterfuge."

"Live and learn. Get to them before they acquire the needed courage to do some name-dropping. Keeler's death may have made them nervous."

"William, we did not uncover the names."

Tomlinson sat forward in his chair. "What?"

"The people that showed up at the warehouse in New York—it was confirmed by my source that it was they who recovered the two names and addresses. They are on their way to Virginia as we speak."

The new chairman of the Coalition eased back in his chair.

"Salvageable. Hit these men in Virginia when they show up there. I want these pests out of the way. No, wait . . . I want to know when they arrive and enter one of the houses. I want to say good-bye to the two Ancients and to this . . . what is the man's name?"

"Collins; Colonel Jack Collins."

"I think it appropriate that I terminate this last threat. Very good, and I can finally say, very thorough work, Dahlia."

Dahlia ignored Tomlinson's snide comment.

"Now, I suppose you are off to Hawaii?"

"Yes, I leave within the hour. I will have my strike team in Virginia inform you on when to make your call. Good night, William."

RICHMOND, VIRGINIA

It had taken just two hours to fly south to Richmond. Jack had decided to go to Carmichael Rothman's house first, for no other reason than that Rothman was the last listed.

The countryside was beautiful as Mendenhall drove them through rural areas of large and very expensive houses. It was a full thirty minutes until they found the right address. The house was set deep in the woods and had a long concrete drive leading to it. The large iron fence coursed around the manicured lawns. There was a small building next to the thirty-foot-high gate and they could see two guards sitting inside.

"Tell me what-all you see, Lieutenants," Jack asked Ryan and Mendenhall.

"Ah, the test continues," Ryan said. "Well, besides the two guards, the gate is crash-proof. There are two-foot-thick steel posts descending from the gate to the cement, anchoring it firmly."

"There is a laser-security perimeter around the entire

property. They didn't hide the power source well enough, as it can be seen coming directly out of the gatehouse to the first laser reflector. Knock out the gatehouse, take the property," Mendenhall said as he pulled into the drive and stopped.

"Very good. But you failed to notice the small building across the street. It has no business being there. No house, no drive," Collins said as he watched the first guard come out to greet them.

"But plenty of extra guards ready to take back the gatehouse you guys just took," Everett finished for Jack.

"Oh," Ryan said. "How—"

"Separate power source. See the generator at the side of the building? No reason for that in a neighborhood like this. In addition, can you see the landline leading from the gatehouse to the structure across the street? This Rothman character takes his security seriously. But hey, you guys are learning the craft . . . almost," Everett said, looking at Ryan.

Mendenhall rolled down his window as the well-uniformed guard approached. Jack saw that the second guard had disappeared from the window.

"Can I help you?"

"We're here to see Carmichael Rothman," Jack said from the backseat.

The guard shook his head. "Mr. Rothman does not accept visitors. No exceptions."

Jack thought for a moment. "Inform Mr. Rothman we're here to see him about the death of Jackson Keeler."

The guard looked into the car. "I will inform the housekeeper. Please remain in the vehicle."

The four watched the guard turn and head back into the gatehouse and saw him pick up the phone. The other guard was still nowhere to be seen.

"We have company behind us and to the right. The large bush next to the gatehouse—the second guard, I suspect—and he has a rather large weapon trained . . . well, trained on the back of my head."

"It's that take-charge personality you have, Jack," Everett said as he slid farther toward his door.

"Funny."

Suddenly the large twin gates started to part. The guard reappeared and stepped to the car's front window.

"Please keep to the paved drive until you arrive at the front porch, where you will be met by Mrs. Laughlin, a very close friend of Mr. Rothman. I have been instructed to tell you that you have only one minute to convince Mrs. Laughlin of your sincerity. If you fail, we will remove you from the property."

The guard abruptly turned and walked back into the gatehouse. Mendenhall drove slowly through the gate.

"Lucky we have both of the people that interest us the most," Jack said under his breath.

When they arrived at the front porch, they saw an elderly woman standing in front of the ornate and gilded front doors. She slowly made her way down to the car as it stopped. Collins stepped out of the backseat and looked at the casually dressed woman, who was short in stature. She crossed her arms over her chest and waited for Collins to speak.

"Ms. Laughlin? Martha Laughlin?"

If the woman was taken back because Jack knew her first name, she didn't show it.

"Yes."

"My name is Colonel Jack Collins, of the United States Army. You were informed that we're here to see you and Mr. Rothman about the death of Jackson Keeler. I assume you have heard of this man?"

This time Jack saw the woman blink. That was all she did, but in that brief moment he saw sadness there, but not shock at the news of Keeler's death.

"Why is the army interested in the death of an attorney, Colonel?"

"You and Mr. Rothman's names were on a slip of paper Mr. Keeler hid in his person before he died. Do you know why he would do that?"

"Colonel, this line of questioning has no interest for me or Mr. Rothman. I do not see any reason to share information of a private nature with U.S. Army, which, as I understand it, is not tasked to do the work assigned to agencies far better equipped to deal with the matter of Mr. Keeler's death."

"Well, I can start with the death of thirty-six of my colleagues for doing nothing more than examining artifacts from antiquity."

Jack once more saw the woman blink, and now she switched the weight of her body from foot to foot.

"Artifacts. The army is dealing in artifacts now? Can you explain this sudden change of direction for a branch of the armed services, Colonel? I mean, with all that's happening in the world, I would think you would have your hands full instead of antiquing."

Jack smiled but said nothing.

"Very well, Colonel, you have piqued my interest. You and your men can come this way."

Jack watched the woman walk up the four steps leading to the door. He knew that she smelled something that didn't sit right with her. That and the fact that the woman was fully clothed at four o'clock in the morning told him that there was little relaxation occurring behind these closed doors. He waved the others out of the car and followed the woman into the house.

Two white vans pulled into the drive and waited for the guard to exit the gatehouse, while another van pulled in across the street. Four men exited that van and knocked on the door. As soon as it was opened they pushed the man who had answered backward and then tossed something inside and close the door again. They heard a muffled *whump* and then they pulled on black hoods and entered the building. Inside there were five men in total, the one who had answered the door and four other guards who had been sleeping in bunks that lined the wall. All were gasping for air. Very carefully and silently, the guards were dispatched with one round to the head in very short order.

Across the way, the first guard out to meet the white van met a similar fate. Shot once in the forehead, he fell backward and hit the concrete. The rear doors opened and two men exited and ran into the gatehouse. One soon reappeared and held up a hand and then closed it. The second man saw the signal and started firing with his silenced MP-5 into the bush where they had observed the guard previously when the car arrived. The man was satisfied when he heard a loud grunt, and then he made sure by going to the back of the bush and firing three more rounds into the guard who had thought himself well hidden.

The elimination of Rothman's security element was accomplished in thirty-two seconds. Then both vans, filled with fifteen heavily armed men, started making their way up the drive.

Jack, Carl, Ryan, and Mendenhall were led to a large den, where Martha Laughlin told them to take a seat at the large table in the center of the room. Then she turned and left.

Collins looked at Everett as he sat and nodded. Carl, with a blur of movement, removed his Beretta 9-millimeter and pulled the slide backward, chambering a round, and then allowed his hand to vanish beneath the table. Mendenhall did the same thing.

Soon Martha returned. She was helping a man who was fully clothed in slacks and a white shirt. He wore a dressing gown over his clothes and looked as weak as a newborn. The man, obviously Carmichael Rothman, was small in stature at only five-foot-five and he held the arm of Martha Laughlin as if he could fall at any moment. Collins looked at Everett, and Carl in turn felt silly for having his weapon out.

Jack stood and watched as Rothman was led slowly to the table. The old man did not meet any of his visitors' eyes as he slowly sat down. Jack sat too.

Martha stood by his side for a brief moment and then sat next to him. The man finally looked up and found the man who he assumed to be in charge. It just happened to be Collins.

"Jackson Keeler was . . . was our friend."

The old man said the words slowly, his eyes never leaving Jack's face.

"Why would he and other innocent people be slaughtered like that? What was being sought that all that blood would be spilled?"

Rothman looked from Jack to Martha, who squeezed his arm in support.

"If I ask you who you work for, Colonel, would I receive truth in your answer?"

"I work for people who lost thirty-six men and women to the same murdering bunch that killed your friend, Mr. Rothman."

"I see. That explains your interest in that regard." He turned and accepted two pills from Ms. Laughlin and swallowed them without water. "Martha here has informed me that you said your people were examining artifacts, I believe?"

Jack did not respond. He was not in Virginia to be questioned; he was there to get his questions answered.

"Could this be the artifacts recovered from New York, an account of which I have read in the newspapers?"

The four men before them sat motionlessly.

"I'm afraid the men who are responsible for the death of so many were not just after the names of Martha and myself. They were chasing something much more valuable to them. We were just a bonus. We knew our old friend kept a journal, and we couldn't convince him that it was dangerous, not only to himself but to others."

"Like you two?" Jack asked.

Martha smiled and her look never wavered away from Collins.

"Yes, like us, Colonel."

"There are people in the world, Colonel, who don't wear their intentions on their sleeve. Very powerful men and women who . . ." Rothman looked at Martha for support.

"They seek power and continuity. They want the world as a whole, a nice dream of one central government, but separate races. Their willingness to attain such a utopian society has been a rather ruthless one throughout the years. These are the people responsible for the death of your men and women and our friend. As I said, they have sought to bring about their way of life for many years. They actually have an ancient precedent of that utopian society, Colonel."

"Do you mean Atlantis?"

Martha went silent. Rothman only smiled.

"Colonel, you have said nothing, but told us everything," Rothman said, patting Martha's hand.

Collins and the three other men saw strength returning to Rothman. The pills he had taken must have been taking effect.

"I really didn't believe you and your people existed any longer. My father told me about a wonderful organization that was in existence many, many years ago. However, he lost track of your organization just before World War Two. Do not look so shocked, Colonel. It was the mention of artifacts that gave it away. For the life of me, I can't remember the name of your Group, though."

Jack remained silent but he see that Everett, Mendenhall, and Ryan were having a harder time of it.

"Yes, I can now see why you angered certain people. It was your organization that conducted the raid on their storage facility, was it not? No need to answer; your statement about Atlantis is circumstantial, but makes sense."

"You seem to be a very informed man, Mr. Rothman," Jack said, unsmiling.

"Yes." Again he patted Martha's hand. "We used to be. We are old now and just want the world to go on. Colonel, we are informed because at one time, very many years ago, my father assisted President Wilson in the writing of your organization's charter."

"Department 5656. The funny little moniker attached to that agency slips my mind, though," Martha said, looking at Rothman.

"What a wonderful concept, I have always thought, learning all there is to know about history and studying ways to prevent the horrid parts from happening again. Throughout our long lives and vast knowledge, your Group remained deeply hidden to the point that I did not believe it existed, even though my father said it did." He fell silent for a moment as he went into deep thought. "Group . . . Group." He smiled and slowly looked from face to face. "The Event Group!"

Jack exchanged looks with the others. They had come to get answers, but these two very strange people had turned the tables on them somehow and now they had guessed at one of the world's foremost secrets.

Rothman looked at Martha and seemed happy. They stared

at each other for the longest time and then Rothman turned and looked the men over.

"Do not worry, Colonel. Martha and I can keep a secret as well as anyone in the world."

Jack watched as Martha covered her mouth and he would have sworn that she chuckled at Rothman's small joke.

"Our time is short and Martha and I have wasted a lot of it because we do not normally interfere with the affairs of your . . . well, the affairs of the world. I think, though, and I'm sure Martha would agree, that you may just be the people who could assist us."

"Colonel, it's not just a coincidence that you and we have been thrown together. The situation in the world is dire and we believe we know who is behind it. I speak of the actions in Korea and the murders here; they are tied together," Martha said.

Jack was beginning to feel as though he had stepped down the rabbit hole. He looked at Carl, who was looking at Martha as if she were an alien.

Collins was about to ask just what in the world these two were talking about when a servant stepped into the den through the sliding doors and approached Martha. He watched as a concerned look crossed her face. She thanked the man and then excused him. She looked closely at Jack, then she stood and made her way to the small desk and removed the phone there and placed it on the center of the tabletop. Jack saw a flashing light, which meant that someone was on hold. Martha sat back and looked at their guests.

"It seems we have a call, Colonel. A gentleman has asked to speak to you, Carmichael, and me."

"Don't tell me the director has learned we took the plane already," Everett said, half joking, as he stood and went to the large window that looked out on the pool in the back. He gestured for Mendenhall and Ryan to cover the other windows.

"I assure you men that this property is well guarded," Rothman said as he watched the three men at the windows.

"Nothing personal, sir, but we have already discussed the

shortfalls of your security arrangements, and I'm sorry to inform you they are sorely lacking."

Rothman looked from Everett to Jack and nodded.

Martha reached out and placed the call into conference mode by pushing the flashing button.

"Hello," she said as if the call were anything but unusual.

"I assume I am speaking with Martha Laughlin?"

"I don't believe I recognize your voice."

"That is not a concern at the moment, Miss Laughlin. I take it I am being listened to by Carmichael Rothman and a Colonel Jack Collins?"

The three remained silent as Jack quickly glanced at Everett, who stood to the side of the window frame. He shook his head to indicate that the yard was clear. Jack did the same with Mendenhall and Ryan, who had a view of the front. They had the same answer.

"Your silence is answer enough. There is no need to tell you who I am. That does not matter. What does matter is that individually you three are bothersome, but together you are a threat. Colonel Collins, I do not know whom it is you work for, but as of this moment you will not interfere with me again. I suspect it was you and the three men you have with you that played the role of hero in Ethiopia. Well, I am here to tell you that such actions have an equal and far harsher reaction. This is a lesson I'm sure you have learned in the past few days."

"Something tells me you're not the type to carry threats out yourself. By the sound of your voice, I assume you order others to do the dangerous stuff while you manicure your nails and watch."

Martha and Carmichael watched Collins silently.

"Very good, Colonel. Your wit in times of stress tells me you are a man used to danger. The real point here is that I have the power to do it, as the body count of your people has clearly shown. Now, Carmichael and Martha, I believe you to be the last of our brothers and sisters. Mr. Keeler failed as his father and brother before him to protect that which was not his, nor yours. You may eventually guess at my identity and that is fine.

I do, however, know yours. You and your kind have always been sorely lacking in strength and you are no exception. Your forefathers should have remained with us, because as a split entity, you have no spine."

"We are aware of what you are doing and now have the *spine* to tell the world about you. We may have been weak in the past and allowed you certain liberties in regard to world affairs. Now that it only Martha and myself left, what the hell, we are letting the world finally know about you and your people and all the misery you have caused throughout history."

"Your story should make very interesting fodder, Mr. Rothman. Far more interesting is the fact that I would have looked forward to your explanation as to why you and your kind allowed it to happen without helping those poor, poor people throughout history. You and that bitch beside you deserve to die with the colonel and his backward monkey-people."

"Hey!" Ryan said from his place at the front window. "Monkey-people?"

"Good-bye . . . Oh, one last item, Colonel. Tell your men at the windows to duck."

The line went dead just as the windows on every wall in the den exploded inward in a hail of bullets. Jack threw himself to the floor, crawled quickly to Martha, and pulled her roughly out of her chair. Mendenhall duckwalked from his spot at the now-nonexistent front window, pulled Carmichael from his chair, and then covered him with his body.

"I think you pissed him off, Jack," Everett said as he fired three quick rounds out the window frame and then pulled back.

"That's what monkeys do," Collins said as he looked at Martha. More bullets flew through the windows and slammed into the expensive paneling. "We need a not-too-obvious way out of here."

"There is a passage that Carmichael uses to reach his helicopter at the back of the property. It's through the basement, but the electric car is on tracks and only carries two people at a time," she said, as something hit the table and thumped to the floor.

Jack looked until he found the object and then decided very

quickly that he had no time to dispose of it. Suddenly Ryan was there; he picked up the grenade and threw it out the window, barely missing Everett's head. They heard the *crump* of the grenade as it went off in the pool.

"Colonel, this place has too many holes in it; maybe we should move someplace else," Ryan said as he hit the floor next to Jack.

"As I said, you're learning, Ryan. Come on, we're heading for the basement. Help Mendenhall with Rothman. Swabby, we need cover fire now!"

Everett fired six quick shots out the window and then turned and fired five more out the window that Ryan had been covering. He heard someone outside cry out in pain and then was quickly rewarded with a hundred return rounds slamming into the walls and artwork around them.

"Go, Jack!" Carl shouted as he quickly placed another clip into his Beretta and repeated the same sequence of cover fire.

Collins pulled Martha to her feet and ran to the double doors of the den. He opened the doors and went into the long hallway. He slammed Martha against the wall and waited for Ryan and Mendenhall to get Rothman out of the den.

"Get the hell out of there, Carl!" Collins ordered. "Lead the way, Ms. Laughlin."

Jack fell in right behind the older but agile woman as she went from the hallway into a large kitchen. Ryan, Will, and Rothman caught up through the swinging doors and then Ryan turned and held the door for Everett, who fired three times at an unseen entity behind him.

"At least ten, maybe more, Jack, and they're hot on our ass," Everett shouted and then quickly fired five times through the swinging doors. Another yelp of pain and then blood ran underneath the door. "Not bad for monkeys, huh?"

"This way," Martha said as she pulled open the door leading to the basement.

Jack pushed Will and Rothman ahead, and then Ryan quickly went by and down the stairs just as Everett ducked and the swinging door above him jerked as ten bullets punched through the wood.

"These guys are getting serious, Jack."

Collins fired his entire clip through the splintered doorway and then pulled Everett after him.

Once in the spacious basement, they heard the attacking force above them as they moved about. It was only a second later when they heard several objects bouncing down the stairs. Collins and the others ducked quickly behind one of the reinforced concrete walls as the three grenades detonated. Shrapnel spread out in a deadly arc and punctured everything exposed in the basement.

"It's right there. There's a small landing; the tracks and car are there behind that steel door," Martha said as she pointed.

"Carl, move in and check it out and make sure these guys didn't come across that little bit of information, too."

"Right," Everett said as he moved to the door and quickly opened it. He jumped out and made ready his response, but there was no fire. "It's just stairs, Jack."

"Get going, all of you. Mr. Ryan, assist the lady."

The others quickly made for the door and the stairs beyond. Jack waited one minute and then turned and followed.

A moment later, they found themselves a hundred feet down in the earth, staring at a small electric car that sat on tracks. The small tracks led upward and they saw light illuminating the tracks.

"Okay, Ms. Laughlin, you and Mr. Rothman get moving. We will cover you for as long as we can. But pretty soon these guys are going to smarten up and cut the power, so send that thing right back here." Jack looked at the locked door, just waiting for a satchel charge to blow it inward. "If for any reason we get separated, you have got to tell your story, either at the White House, where my director is—his name is Compton—or out at Nellis Air Force Base. If that's the case—"

"If that's the case, I know the base commander there. I got him appointed to the Academy," Rothman said.

"That's nice," Everett said as he pulled Rothman to the small cart.

The four men watched as the two old people moved off in the electric cart. Martha turned and Jack would have sworn she mouthed the words, *I'm sorry.*

Several explosions sounded through the steel door as the assault on the basement began in earnest. Dirt settled onto them from the tunnel above and around them.

Jack looked closely at the incline of the small tracks as they disappeared into the distance. Then he made a decision.

"Look, I don't feel like waiting here for our company to just drop in. Let's make this more expensive for them and head up toward the surface. Maybe we can pick a few off."

"I'm for that," Everett said as he caught a clip of ammunition from Mendenhall.

"Then let's catch the number nine, boys. Will, lead the way."

As they started out, they heard the first real explosion against the steel door. Jack motioned to Everett to catch up with Mendenhall and Ryan.

"Dammit, that's enough! Let me take the risks once in a while."

"That's an order, swabby. Now move it."

As Everett obeyed, Jack hunkered low and waited. He did not have to do so for long. He heard whispered orders as the attackers made it through the steel door. He cocked his head to listen. Jack knew that he was high enough on the incline of tracks that he was not seen. He would have to make that advantage count. The first four men came into view. They wore black Nomex and covered like professionals—two men forward, two squatting and covering. He waited for the optimal shot.

As the first two went low to cover the second, Collins aimed and fired at the two, who had just stood to run. He fired four times. Both men crumpled and fell onto the tracks. Then he adjusted and fired at the kneeling men before they knew what was coming. Two shots apiece. But this time only one man fell. The other, on the right, was only wounded and he nearly made Jack pay for missing. On full automatic, the man fired as he fell backward. The bullets hit the metal track to Jack's front and then stitched their way up into the concrete wall of the tunnel.

"Dammit!" Jack said as he quickly recovered and took hurried aim and fired. His rounds caught the man in the thigh and then the stomach. He was rewarded by the view of the man dropping his weapon and letting out a sigh.

Suddenly more men appeared and this time they let their automatic rifles do the covering. Bullets started hitting everywhere and Jack knew that he did have a chance to get off any return fire.

Everett had caught up with Mendenhall and Ryan just as the firing below began.

"Dammit. You two get to the top and find the damn light switch. These guys are well-equipped enough that they probably have night-vision gear." He looked at his watch. "Give me exactly three minutes and then hit the lights. Thirty seconds later, turn them on again. Got that?"

"What if there's no switch at this end?" Ryan asked.

"Then you may be moving up in rank real quick."

"Really!" Ryan said with all the false levity he could muster.

Jack knew that he was in trouble. He would stop for a split second and then fire blindly, hoping to hit one of the assailants with a ricochet. Then he would run, stop, and do the same again.

As he turned a third time, the lights went out.

"Oh, oh," he said to himself.

As he strained to listen, he remained perfectly still. He could hear quiet orders being voiced by whoever was in charge; he also heard the noise of men as they shuffled around in the darkness. He aimed toward some of that noise but held his fire, hoping that his eyes would adjust to the sudden darkness.

The withering fire opened up right at Jack's position. Chunks of concrete flew and struck him as he tried to back off on his stomach. The assault was too accurate for men blinded by darkness; they had to have night-vision goggles. Which he knew spelled disaster for him.

Above the din of exploding rounds, Jack heard a familiar voice.

"Stay down, Jack, and be ready!"

Suddenly, the lighting in the tunnel came to glaring life. The men in black Nomex screamed out as the brightness struck their eyes after being enhanced a thousandfold by the ambient light devices. Men fought as they tried to raise the single-lens goggles.

Everett, who was only ten feet from Jack, opened fire with deadly accuracy. Jack didn't hesitate as he sighted and added his 9-millimeter to the fray, hitting screaming men in their chests, faces, and arms. The two military men had caught each of their supposed killers in the open.

Three men turned and ran back the way they had come, but the rest would never return to the man who had ordered them to Rothman's house.

When it was over, Jack stood and hurriedly replaced his spent clip. He scanned the area around him and then looked at Everett.

"When in the hell are you going to follow orders, Captain?"

"Maybe when you start giving me orders that make sense by allowing me to assume some of the risk, Jack."

"Okay, Captain," he said, letting a smile finally crease his tanned face. "That wasn't a bad makeshift plan, by the way. Especially since we didn't know if they had night-vision gear. Also the part of the plan where you assumed Ryan would find the right switch for the lights."

"Nah, I knew he would just hit them all; the odds were with us."

Collins stared at the empty cart and the open door. Mendenhall and Ryan stood next to it and they did not look happy.

"The helicopter?" Jack asked.

"Gone," answered Ryan.

"Maybe that bad guy on the phone had a point about those two, Jack," Everett said. "I mean, leaving us to fend off the wolves while they run is not the makings of people with a whole lot of character."

Jack grimaced and then looked at the others.

"Well, we learned a few things. Let's go home and see what comes of it. We'll call the locals and use Europa to see if we can pin some names to the Virginia hospitality down in the tunnel."

"Yeah, we learned a few things all right, like not to trust anyone over fifty," Ryan mumbled as he turned and left.

CHAPTER
NINE

Sarah had been on a conference call with Bell Labs for four hours and had even awakened the chief design engineer for Bose. She had to run some questions by the chief engineers of both facilities after Niles Compton, in Washington, had pulled some powerful strings and cleared the way for her to speak directly to the labs. When she was done with her questions, the Group's Engineering Department ran her theory in model form on Europa.

With some success in the theory end of things, they needed an actual working model to prove it sound. They set up a mechanical model inside one of the many workshops of the complex. They had engineered two sandstone slabs, each eight inches thick, and it was these strange items that the Earth-Sciences team was currently examining as the communications division hurriedly set up their equipment to be used in the experiment.

"I don't get what you're suggesting, Sarah," said the young doctor from Virginia Tech. He looked over at a room monitor and into the face of Niles Compton, who was on the line from the White House subbasement, where he had set up shop with the new science adviser to the president.

"I think I do, and if she can pull this off, we have at least a theory to advance to the Russians and Chinese, and maybe, just maybe, they can convince the Koreans," Niles said from Washington.

"The key here is our naval-communications gear." Sarah nodded at the com techs and they gave her a thumbs-up.

The summoned scientists and engineering personnel assigned to the earthquake investigation stood around the lab, and all were wearing goggles. Most shook their heads in doubt at what Sarah was trying to do. Most of them had heard of sound as an impact carrier, but few believed that it could actually be used in real-world situations. As they watched the final connections being made, each was handed a pair of earphones and earplugs. They were instructed by the communications men—an army sergeant and a navy signals man—to insert the ear-canal plugs first and then place the headphones over them.

Sarah was nervous but she knew that this experiment should work. She was standing next to Jerry Gallup, who held a PhD from Harvard in telecommunications. He had informed her, after seeing Europa's results, that she had a very viable theory.

Sarah thought briefly of Lisa Willing, her roommate who had been killed in a field operation close to three years before. She was in communications and had once that sound decibels could penetrate aggregate formations in just the same manner as an opera singer could break glass when a certain pitch was reached. It was very rare in that scenario, but she and Gallup had received startling information from Bell Labs and the corporations of Audiovox and Bose that such theory was in practical use inside their own labs.

Sarah watched on closed-circuit television as Professor Harlan Walters of the University of Hawaii and director of the Trans-Pacifica Institute of Seismic Studies on Oahu started the experiment.

"Okay, I think we're set to begin," he said from Hawaii. "The hydraulic rams you see on the bench are set at scale level to two hundred billion metric tons, an estimate to be sure, of the pressures some of our continental plates induce on their leading ledges. The two sandstone slabs that you see represent the plates. The hydraulic rams are exerting this pressure on them at this moment, just as our real plates are doing below our feet. Now on top of these sandstone slabs we are placing a piece of granite with a hairline surface fracture that will act as our fault line."

Sarah looked at the sound technicians and nodded on her cue from Hawaii.

As the gathered witnesses watched, the communications men placed small domes in a long line two feet from the surface crack of the granite and then attached electrical leads to them.

"Now, what you see being done is the small domes placed on the granite have what the audio scientists call 'sound-inducing tone forks.' A small electrical current is sent through to the forks, which will act just as a real tuning fork will when struck; only we will control the amount of vibration by electrical current, thus controlling the power of the decibel output. While no sound-wave energy will be strong enough to damage strata that are as hard as granite, our intention is not to attempt that. Instead, we will strike at what supports the granite, or the upper crust of the earth, the actual tectonic plates that support the upper crust and are responsible for continental movements throughout earth's history. Since these plates all have leading edges that are uneven and the thickness varies to some degree, we presuppose that they can be attacked, for use of a better word, by audio waves."

There was loud mumbling as people in the engineering lab disagreed with one point or another about the theory.

"Lieutenant McIntire, you may begin," the professor said from Hawaii.

"Sergeant, if you will start the decibel assault on the plates, please."

A large console hurriedly pieced together by the Communications Department came to life. The sergeant and naval signals man started manipulating the knobs and switches that would activate the current, which would in turn start the minute motion of the forks inside the small domes.

One woman—a young first-year PhD from Stanford—shook her head and became unsteady on her feet. When she became nauseated, she was assisted out of the lab by another lab technician who was not feeling well.

"Some of the wave will escape. It will affect people differently, as our inner ears are not identical. Some will feel queasy and light-headed, while others may feel nothing at all. Once we interview survivors of the quakes and determine if any of them felt these same symptoms just before the earthquakes hit, that will add punch to the theory," Walters explained over the closed-circuit television link.

Sarah winced, as she too had felt uncomfortable as the wave started its assault. Then she felt better after a moment.

"They will start adjusting the pitch of the wave at this time," she said. "The pitch refers to whether the sound is a high or low note. High frequencies create high pitches and low frequencies produce low pitches. The human ear can process frequencies between twenty Hz and twenty thousand Hz. These are audible sounds. Sound waves with frequencies above twenty thousand Hz are called ultrasonic. Dogs can hear sounds up to about fifty thousand Hz. So a whistle that only dogs can hear has a frequency higher than twenty thousand but lower than fifty thousand Hz. Sound waves with frequencies below twenty Hz are called infrasonic. We will begin at the lower end of the ultrasonic scale and work our way up."

At first, they watched the sandstone a foot beneath the slab of granite and connected by several steel rods holding them together. Nothing was happening. A white cloth was placed under the stand-in for the tectonic plate to catch debris, so that they could see clearly any small granules of sand that fell.

"Take the wave to five hundred thousand Hz, please," Sarah ordered.

As the two technicians adjusted the frequencies on their makeshift board, a few more people in the room started to feel the effects. It was nothing that they could really describe as they placed their hands on their heads and temples. Another tech was feeling it in his stomach and his dental fillings, and all symptoms ended in a nauseating cramping.

As Sarah and Virginia watched, they saw the first grains of sand start to hit the white cloth. Then more and more granules started to fall. Then a small piece about one inch thick fell off the bottom of one of the sandstone slabs. Then another, even larger section fell free at the opposite edge.

The hydraulics kept up a steady pressure, pushing the two sandstone slabs together with great force.

Sarah nodded and the power was increased. More large pieces from both ends started to fall. The leading edges started to crack as the sound bells penetrated the granite and passed through it to strike the sandstone below. Suddenly, the leading edges went with a loud snapping sound as they mimicked the movement of the continental tectonic plates during an actual seismic event. As they broke apart, the hydraulics continued their pressure, thus moving the connection rods attached to both sets of stone.

"My God," Virginia said to no one but herself.

The connection rods pulled inward as the sandstone beneath came apart and suddenly the granite with the weakened fault on its surface cracked with a loud pop, as the fault line in the granite completely separated and then broke into two pieces, one half sliding completely over the other. As the pressure continued from the sandstone beneath, the entire structure of granite caved in.

The room was silent as the hydraulics shut down. The experiment had worked. As some of the professors and techs smiled and patted Sarah and Professor Gallup on the back, they saw that Sarah in her triumph was not smiling at all. She slowly removed her headphones and looked at the engineering model. She turned to Virginia.

"We may be in serious trouble," she said as she turned from Virginia to the monitor that would pass her image on to Niles in Washington and Harlan Walters in Hawaii.

"But, Sarah, it worked. That proves that—"

"Dr. Compton, please listen closely to what Sarah has to say. I just thought the same thing myself," Walters cut in.

"Director, the experiment was a success, yes, but it proves one thing: if these incidents were created by human manipulation, we are sitting on a time bomb."

"How do you mean?" Compton asked.

"When the plates move, even if it's only measured in mere feet, it would be enough to cause a fault line to fracture, creating an earthquake. If the wave is increased and the plate crumbles, by, say, a mile or maybe two, the main reaction of any fault that the assault is directed at may not just take out the desired targeted area, but continue on down the line. Another, even worse reaction could be thousands of miles away on the other side of the plate. Do you see what I mean? Because the actual tectonic plates aren't elastic in the least, they will pull at another point, affecting every fault line along the way."

"God," Niles said. "Virginia, get a copy of the experiment over to me double quick."

"Yes, sir."

"Dr. Compton, someone out there may be playing with a doomsday weapon that could crush an entire continent.

"Or open up a hole in the earth's crust large enough to swallow an ocean or a continent that may not have been an intended target," Walters added bleakly.

Second Lieutenant Will Mendenhall yawned as sat at his desk inside the security center on level three. He'd been virtually sleepless since the return flight from Virginia.

He yawned again as he was filling out the new duty rosters for the expanded staff brought in from field operations. The colonel was uptight about their little secret in the desert, now known to the man on the phone the night before.

The door opened and Lance Corporal Donny Sikes stuck his head in.

"Sir, field-unit three is reporting a helicopter flying over the north range."

Mendenhall looked up and wondered how an unauthorized aircraft had entered the restricted area without the Nellis air police being all over it.

"Have you monitored anything on the radio from base security?"

"There was nothing on the airwaves, sir. No authorization and no order to vacate the airspace."

"Is the air force asleep up there?" Will asked as he stood and made his way into the command center.

The lance corporal went to the large bank of monitors and gestured at the correct screen. Mendenhall watched as a large helicopter circled the old World War II hangar that the Event Group used for clandestine entry of large loads into the secret main facility.

"Europa has identified the craft as an executive-style Sikorsky S-76. The number on the tail boom is 4907653, listed as corporate 310 out of Virginia. Privately owned, and the listed owner of title is Carmichael Rothman of Rothman Industries."

"I'll be damned; the chickens have come home to roost."

"Sir?" the lance corporal asked, confused.

"What ground-security team is the closest?"

"Three, sir; they have the craft covered, three Stingers are currently tracking the inbound. With the mood the colonel's in, I thought it better to err on the side of covering our asses."

"Good. Now get onto to Nellis base security and ask why they allowed a civilian aircraft onto the northern firing range, and find out why that same craft is in a no-fly zone."

Yes, sir."

Mendenhall watched as the helicopter started to settle onto the scrub of desert three hundred feet from the hangar. Gate one was a kill zone for Event security, but Mendenhall was not one to order the death of people just for being stupid, or cowardly. Instead, he watched as the large helicopter landed. As the rotors slowed to an acceptable speed, a door opened and a set of steps automatically lowered. Then a woman appeared and she was holding the arm of a man who looked unsteady on his feet. Mendenhall visually confirmed the identities of the two people and then quickly took the field radio from the desk at his side.

"Team three, observation only, safe your weapons. I repeat, safe your weapons."

"Roger, weapons safe, observation only at this time."

Will relaxed when team three confirmed that they were nowhere in sight because they were invisible against the terrain of the high desert. Dug in and deadly, as their training dictated.

As the elderly couple walked away from their transport, the large Sikorsky started spooling up, kicking up sand and scrub as it went. Carmichael Rothman held on to his hat and Martha Laughlin bowed her head as the helicopter lifted off and peeled away to the north.

Mendenhall was amazed as he saw that the man and woman were just standing there looking at the hangar and not moving. They seemed to be looking at the hidden camera just inside the old structure. Just standing and waiting.

He reached out, picked up the phone, and punched in the clean-room section, where he knew his superiors were.

"Collins."

"Colonel, you'll never guess who appeared out of nowhere at gate one. You have to see this."

"Pipe it down, Will."

Mendenhall tapped a few commands into the duty sergeant's keyboard and the live video feed wound its way to Jack in the Europa clean room.

"Got it. Fill me in, Lieutenant."

Mendenhall described everything they had on the helicopter and security situation, and as he did so, he watched the old couple on the screen. They still had not moved and they did not speak to each other. They were just waiting, just as if they knew that the Group was watching them.

"Bring them in with all due courtesy and take them to the holding room," Jack said. "I'll be right up. Inform Captain Everett to meet me there. And, Lieutenant, no one talks to them, and they talk to no one, clear?"

"Yes, sir, we'll put them on ice," Mendenhall answered, and then he said to himself, "Before they decide to split again."

Martha Laughlin and Carmichael Rothman sat in a small white room. The hoods that had been placed on their heads upon entering gate one had been an inconvenience, but they had endured it without complaint. Two large marines in blue jumpsuits removed their coats after they had walked through a body scan hidden in the seemingly simple doorway. The weapons search was conducted without the usual full-strip search.

The special room they were taken to was stun equipped, meaning that they would be gassed at a moment's notice if they were deemed hostile during their interview. As they sat and waited, another man dressed in blue overalls, this one with a U.S. Army insignia, brought in two glasses of water for the two visitors. Rothman used his water to wash down two morphine tablets that security had allowed him to keep.

The door opened after ten minutes and Everett followed by Collins stepped in. They both wore the same blue jumpsuits as the other military men and women, with their officer's rank being the only difference.

Jack looked into their eyes, one face at a time, and then he punched a button on the tabletop.

"For the record, your names are Carmichael Rothman and Martha Laughlin, correct?"

"Correct," Rothman and Martha said simultaneously.

"And I assume you know you have entered a restricted area of a United States government reservation—am I correct on that point also?"

"You are."

"Can you tell us how you received permission to enter restricted airspace?"

"Not officially, no, I cannot."

"You are protecting a United States Air Force officer, I assume, namely the commanding officer of the Nellis base, but we'll take that little crime up later."

"Yes, Colonel Collins, we may, but you'll get no admission from me as to who my friends are. He happens to be a very nice young man and all I had to do was explain why we needed to be here. After all, you told us to come," the old man said and winced as he did so.

"You're in pain; may we get you a doctor?" Carl asked.

"I have seen many doctors, Mr. Everett, and they also know I'm in pain, will be for the next eight to nine months. They guarantee the pain will stop at that time."

The two officers said nothing. They understood that this man sitting before them had a death sentence over his head.

"As I said, we will talk about the base commander's impropriety at another interview. Right now, I would like to understand what kind of people would leave the men defending their lives behind when all they had to do was wait," Jack said, looking from Martha to Carmichael.

"To put it frankly, Colonel, we did not know your capabilities at that time. You were in a rather bleak situation and the knowledge we carry needed to be saved, thus it looked as if we left you in a rather bad situation. Now we understand that your abilities far exceed first impressions. Now we must get on with the business we have come to discuss. Things that could have been said last night before the Coalition tried to murder us," he said as he reached over and took Martha's hand.

"The Coalition?" Everett asked.

"The phone call last night was from a member of the Coalition," Martha answered. "I do not know exactly which member, but he was definitely Coalition."

"Again, what is the Coalition?" Collins asked.

"The Coalition is a new incarnation of an older group called the Juliai. You see, Colonel, when you look deeply into money, corporations, conglomerates, and the like, you may find that the wealthiest of these individuals are Juliai, or Coalition. They are secret and have been since the time of ancient Rome." Martha looked at Rothman for the briefest of moments. "Their aim, at least at first, was the control of wealth. With that, the control of people first, and then governments would naturally follow."

Jack had seen Martha's brief look at Rothman during her explanation at that very moment and knew she had left something out. For now, he kept his silence.

"The original Juliai started at the time of Julius Caesar. It was his brainchild, Colonel. He was born unto a great family of an ancient and lost civilization. When Caesar became power-hungry, this family split into two separate entities. The Juliai, named after his own family, became lustful for true power over the world. The other faction, led by his co-counsul of Rome,

Pompey Magnus, tried to stop Caesar, but the newly pro-
claimed emperor went to war and killed Pompey and most of
his followers."

"The Roman civil war was about power between the two
men," Everett said.

"History has always been shaded by those who are the vic-
tors. Surely you have learned this in this magnificent facility,"
Martha said as she smiled. She nodded to Rothman to continue.

"The few remaining followers of Pompey banded together.
Hiding from Caesar and the Juliai Coalition was not easy.
Some had to become a part of that power-mad society. Until
finally they saw the Coalition's power under Caesar was rising
beyond all effort to stop it. Therefore, they acted. The followers of Pompey struck Caesar down just as the history books
will tell you. The history passed down to us didn't outright lie
in telling it this way, they just omitted some of the facts as to
the why of it."

"How do you know all of this?" Jack asked.

"It was our group that broke away from Caesar. Jackson
Keeler, his father, his brother, they were our people."

"What separates you from the rest of the world?" Everett
asked.

"Let's just say for the moment that we are different from
you and the Colonel here." A light seemed to come to Martha's
eyes, as if she'd hit on a thought. "For instance, the artifacts
your men confiscated in New York? Well, in a way they belong
to us, Carmichael and myself, that is."

"You're the real owners of the stolen artifacts?" Jack
asked.

"Yes . . . well—"

"For the sake of argument, yes, we own them," Rothman
answered for her. "Now, the newspaper accounts of the attack
on your facility in New York stated that only hard artifacts
were stolen—armor, swords, pottery, things of that nature. The
news reports never mentioned anything about histories, scrolls,
maps, or diagrams. Please tell me that they were not present in
New York."

Jack did not answer their question. He was far from satisfied that these two people were being straight with him. He
just watched the pair.

"Colonel, this is most important. Last night you proved to
us that you are indeed capable men; let us prove to you that we
are also of some value. Do you have the scrolls?"

"Yes."

Everett and Collins saw the relief on their faces when Jack
answered.

"In that case, we can prove to you the fantastic story we
have to tell," Martha said, squeezing Rothman's arm.

"Who in the hell are you people?" Jack asked calmly but
firmly.

"Last night Carmichael and I reached a rather bleak cross-
roads. Our kind has always been content to allow your people
to deal with the Coalition in their own ways, using your own
devices. We were never brave, not like you and the captain
here. We just wanted to live and blend in. Carmichael made me
see last night after we left you and your men behind that this
cowardice could not continue. We have had renegades in our
family before who tried to help the world in small ways fight
against people such as the Coalition, but they were few. But
Carr convinced me your Group could be trusted with the truth
of things."

Jack and Carl exchanged a look that begged the question,
What in the hell is going on?

"Carr is dying; I imagine you have guessed that. I am
doomed also. We are the last of our kind. The Keelers were the
last family that was capable of having children, Jackson being
the last. Our line may have continued a bit further, but Jackson
Keeler lost his brother in 1941 at Pearl Harbor. He may have
been capable of having children like his grandfather, but we'll
never know."

"This is making no sense at all," Everett said, frustrated.

"We are the last people of Pompey, the group that split off
from the Juliai over two thousand years ago. Now, we have in-
bred with other Pompey families until the practice weakened
our bodies' ability to reproduce."

"I find your story hard to believe," Collins said, wanting to stand up and leave these two nuts alone with their fantasies.

"We knew you would. Nevertheless, you will believe, Colonel. We will make you." Martha looked at Carmichael and gathered strength. "The Coalition is entering its final days also. They may have one or maybe two generations left to them, but they are finished, just as we are."

Jack finally made at least the edges of the puzzle fit together.

"You are one and the same, the Coalition and you, the same bloodline."

"That is correct. However, it is not the whole tale. As I said before, the scrolls in a roundabout way belong to Carr and me. The Coalition can claim them as theirs also. It was our ancestors who made the scrolls you have in your possession. They made them as far back as fifteen thousand years ago."

"You're not saying—"

"I'm saying exactly that, Colonel. You saw the large relief map in New York, I presume." She stopped and looked at Rothman, hesitating before saying it, hoping the old man would relieve her of that burden.

"What Martha wants to say, Colonel Collins and Captain Everett, is that we and a few members of the Juliai Coalition are the last descendants of a civilization that dreamers and fanciers of fiction call Atlantis."

Jack and Carl were patient as they listened to the strangest story they had ever heard. They were stunned at the history Martha and Carmichael recounted as to how two thousand of their ancestors had been hidden away as small children, saved from the destruction of Atlantis. Their small society had learned to blend in with humankind as a whole, but kept themselves separate and pure through inbreeding. With the initial intent not ever again to allow such arrogance to enslave the lesser people of the world, the Atlanteans became observers of the destructive societies around them. Until, that is, the start of the Juliai, who remembered the power of rule.

They had made minor attempts to sway power to their side

of the game board many times, but had never chosen a proxy wise enough to handle the money and power they offered. From the Holy Roman Church, to Spain, England, Napoleon and Hitler, they had failed at every attempt. While race purification is a goal of the Coalition in all its forms, it never was the intention of the ruling body to eliminate races as a whole. In their eyes, that would have been foolish. Why eliminate those who can best serve the ruling class? Keep them fed and allow them their liberties and they will fall in line. Theirs was a class system of master and serf. If you know you are the master race, does it take a brilliant mind not to say it to those who are not? Alternatively, is it not far wiser to allow the illusion that all people are of equal value?

Jack and Carl exchanged looks of incredulity when Martha stopped her version of a world-history lesson.

"We need to bring the people that murdered your friend, his employees, and our people to justice. Not the ravings of a subsociety that could never pull off what you are suggesting. The murder of innocents is what concerns me," Jack said.

"No, Colonel, there is quite a bit more that should concern you," Martha said as she offered Carmichael another morphine tablet. "We suspect the Coalition is bypassing a proxy nation this time around and making a play for their form of domination directly. One that makes mankind rely on *them* instead of governments."

"Time is now growing short, young man. They are already replacing world leaders with their own people, two already and more to come. It is right there in the newspapers."

"What are you talking about?" Collins asked.

"The assassinations in Germany and Japan—link those with the earthquakes and then the murder of Jackson Keeler. The pieces fit."

"In your warped Picasso-painted puzzle, maybe," Everett said.

"The explanation is not a simple one, Captain. All of our lives, from childhood to adult, stories have been passed to us. Tales from our ancestors handed down word of mouth, generation by generation, that told how our ancient civilization was lost beneath the sea. One was the tale of a great weapon that used the very power of the earth to destroy its enemies. A machine that was capable of making the earth tremble and move under the feet of whole armies and destroy them."

"We're getting a little off the beaten path here. I mean, fairy tales? Now, come on," Everett said, but Jack placed his hand on Carl's arm as he started to rise and leave.

"Continue, Martha."

"The scrolls were originally found by a man, an archaeologist who was part of our society. He sought out the financing of the Coalition in a vain attempt to bring the two sides together in a mutually beneficial endeavor—his archaeological dig to find the hidden scrolls. Well, he did exactly that: he found them. They were unearthed in Spain, right where the old tales said they would be. Only in the scrolls, the Coalition discovered the design for the Wave of the Ancients, the very same device of legend and the very weapon that destroyed Atlantis thousands of years before."

"Are you buying this, Jack?" Carl asked, but he saw that Collins was listening intently.

"The device was going to be built and tested. At least that was what this simple man of science suspected from his financial backers, the Coalition. The design was incomplete because of three lost items that control the device used in creating earthquakes. They were known as the Atlantean Keys. Industrial blue diamonds that were so large that none has ever been unearthed to match them. Two of these diamonds were lost with our civilization, while one other was buried in secret . . ." Martha looked at the two men closely in hopes of a reaction, "in Ethiopia."

Everett suddenly became still in his chair. The story had just taken a more realistic turn toward the area of believability.

"The discoverer of the scrolls knew that he could not allow this device to be constructed. Therefore, he absconded with the map found with the scrolls. A bronze plate imbued with strange properties that held the exact coordinates of where to find the buried Atlantean Key. The plate map was sent to America."

"The family Keeler," Jack said.

"Correct, Colonel; the father of Jackson Keeler, to be more precise. Well, after the disappearance of the only means to discover the hiding place of the last Key, the poor professor was murdered and the scrolls disappeared until you uncovered them in your daring raid. However, that did not stop the unscrupulous men of the Coalition. It is told that a German industrialist built the audio-wave weapon anyway. Only instead of using the giant blue diamond, he used a crystal and based the Atlantis design in that. Without looking at the scrolls. We know nothing of the details of the engineering. His experiment occurred on a small island in the Java Sea. A place called Krakatoa."

Jack glanced at Carl and allowed him to state the obvious.

"I take it you really need that blue diamond in order for it to work?"

"Yes. However, Carmichael and I believe they are not waiting for the Key to be unearthed. We were told that the weapon would work on a small scale and still be able to target areas indirectly. We have learned this from Coalition members that have left their society from time to time. The earthquakes in the Middle East, the strikes in North Korea and Russia—coupled with the murder of Jackson, it adds up to Coalition involvement."

"Wait. You're basing all of this speculation from a story handed down to you? You're just guessing at this weapon's strength and the entire story on just hearsay. That's a stretch," Everett said.

"Normally I wouldn't expect you to believe it, Captain Everett, but in this case it's just a bit more than mere hearsay. The professor that discovered the maps and the scrolls and studied the designs in detail was named Peter Rothman—Carr's grandfather. The man the Coalition murdered in their pursuit of the weapon."

Everett remained stock-still and Jack nodded in understanding.

"Okay, so it's a little more than hearsay. Sorry to hear about your grandfather," Everett said, feeling like an ass.

"What would be the gain if North and South Korea went to war?" Jack asked, to get the conversation moving again.

"The gain is a weaker United States, Colonel, one that would no longer have the moral high ground on any world matter. With the harvest failures in Russia and China and their capitals and major cities leveled by earthquakes by the Atlantean Wave, the governments would not survive unless they were propped up by someone, or some entity."

"The Coalition," Jack said.

"Correct."

"Why the murder raid on Mr. Keeler's office?"

"That is the point we need to get to," Martha said. "As you know, the plate map was sent to Jackson Keeler's father. Just before the Coalition traced it to him with the help of the Nazis, he sent it away to a secure location. His son was the first recipient and then it was given to another Ancient for safekeeping."

"Who was it given to and where is it?" Carl asked.

"Where it's been for the past seventy years, young man: in a safe."

"Where's the safe?" Jack asked.

"Aboard a warship of the U.S. Navy—the very ship Jackson Keeler's brother was assigned to. Lieutenant Keeler did as instructed by his father and passed it to a secret member of the last family of Atlantis—the captain of his ship. The plate map remains onboard to this day."

"What warship is still active where the plate could be after all of these years?" Jack asked, perplexed.

"The USS *Arizona*," Martha answered.

Jack and Carl looked away from the two old people and stared at each other for a moment. Collins wanted to say something but was speechless. Everett, on the other hand, was not.

"Jesus, Jack."

Collins and Everett were almost running down the hallway to get the information to Niles in Washington, when they heard a female voice call out from behind them. Jack saw Sarah

McIntire running toward them, but the two military men did not slow down. Collins just waved her forward.

"Don't have time, McIntire," was all he said when she breathlessly caught up to them. "You'll be given a new assignment as soon as we clear it with Virginia and Niles. You're going to start reading some ancient scrolls."

"But, Jack, we have a sound theory about the earthquakes. We now know that they were possibly manmade and they may be caused and activated by—"

"Sound?" Jack said, cutting off her dramatic news.

Sarah skidded to a halt. "How in the hell did you know that?"

"Two Ancient Atlanteans told us," Everett said as he continued walking.

Sarah watched the two men hit the elevator button and she ran to catch up.

"I think you have to explain that 'Ancient Atlantean' crack to me, boys."

Virginia felt out of place as she sat at Nile's Compton's desk. She was looking at a monitor that showed the faces of Martha and Carmichael and shook her head as Jack explained.

"And you're convinced they're speaking the truth?" Virginia said, not taking her eyes off the old couple.

Jack tossed a rubber-band-restrained scroll of paper onto her desk. "According to voice-stress polygraph, yes."

"We have to get this off to Niles and hope he can convince the president of its validity."

Virginia finally turned away from Martha and Carmichael on the wall-mounted monitor and tapped in her commands on the computer. After a moment, another monitor came to life and Niles was there, looking haggard and worn.

"What have you got?"

"Niles, as you know, Sarah here has come up with the way the earthquakes could have been initiated. But Jack here has just confirmed the theory *and* the people responsible for it."

"What?"

Collins stepped to Virginia's side to see Niles. Sarah was

biting her lower lip as she looked at Carl, who stood grim faced.

"Niles, get to the president and make him understand that we now know something of the people who are responsible for all the unnatural phenomena happening around the globe. They are also the ones that hit our team in New York and also murdered Agent Monroe and his wife."

"I'll do my best, but Jesus, this is like something out of a bad spy movie."

"Maybe, but I believe them, Niles."

Niles just nodded and then the picture went blank.

An hour later, Alice brought in coffee for the four people in the conference room. She stood next to her seat and looked from Sarah to Jack to Carl.

"You three did a good job. If you don't need this old woman, I think I'll stroll down to security and take our guests Martha and Carmichael to the cafeteria. I'm sure they think our hospitality is left wanting to some degree."

"Just call and ask them to meet you there; they just may already have the keys to all the doors anyway," Carl quipped.

"What do we do now?" Virginia asked, as she sipped her coffee and grimaced, finding out that she didn't want it at all.

"We have alerted the National Parks Service in Honolulu and they will add on extra security until a detachment of marines arrives on station. The navy will provide around-the-clock surveillance and backup, and Carl and I are going there in about thirty minutes. Carl has asked for SEAL Team Six to standby also. These people do not mess around when it comes to getting what they want. Ask Niles to get his old friend the president to get clearance to dive on the old girl. The Parks Service is cooperating fully but is still very picky when it comes to the *Arizona*."

"Well, it is a naval gravesite," Sarah said.

"Nonetheless, we have to dive on her. We must secure that plate map for two reasons. One—it proves that the Coalition is behind this mess, and two—we can't let these power-mad people get their hands on it."

"Good luck. In the meantime, I'm sure the FBI and the rest of law enforcement are going to be quite anxious to get the names of the men and women of this so-called Juliai Coalition," Virginia said as she finally slid her coffee cup away.

"Carmichael and Martha only have the name of one American Coalitionist that they know of through rumor only, a William Tomlinson. They think he's a pretty high up in their ranks, but are not sure. That's it."

"Lieutenant Mendenhall is about to throw the hatches of this place down tight, no one in or out. We just don't know how much knowledge these people have and what information they gained by torturing our people in New York. We have to base our reactions on the message left to us at the warehouse," Everett said, as he and Jack stood to go.

"We have redistributed the brain power around here now that we're relieved of the earthquake question. Sarah and the rest will be put to use with historical forensics, engineering, and reading ancient languages and deciphering the scrolls and maps. We need to know exactly what kind of science we are dealing with here."

"Well, if anyone can get a jump on fifteen thousand years of history, it's this Group," Jack said, standing up to leave.

"You two be careful, I know how much bullets are attracted to you. One of these days one may get up close and personal," Sarah said as she locked eyes with Jack.

"Are you kidding? We're faster than a speeding bullet, more powerful than a loco—"

"Go catch your plane," Sarah said, cutting off Everett's teasing.

PART III
Ancients
Rising

CHAPTER
TEN

William Tomlinson sat in his ornate study with several of the key Coalition members. One fellow was an American named August Nelson, a former World Bank president who had been on the Coalition's payroll since 1969. He had funneled billions of American dollars and euros through the world's checks and balances in order to finance the immense payroll outlays for a private military the size of the Japanese defense force.

There were others of the Coalition inner workings who were key to the final plans being made, but it was the Englishwoman, Lilith Anderson, better known in the inner circle as Dame Lilith—which was a title actually bestowed by the queen herself—who brought the concluding stages of the Mediterranean operation to a resoundingly satisfactory finale.

"Dame Lilith." Tomlinson raised his glass of hundred-year-old whiskey. "Your Crete operation has gone off without a hitch. The way you have hidden our real intent on the island is astounding. I toast you, my dear, dear lady."

The magnificently dressed woman of fifty nodded her head and returned the gesture, smiling.

Tomlinson lowered his glass and looked at the eight-by-ten

photos once again. "Unbelievably, there are entire sections of the dome still intact. I can even see columns inside it."

"As you can imagine, a great percentage of the dome didn't hold up to the tremendous forces that destroyed the island, but there are clear areas that were protected by the magma flows at the time of the island's demise. The old maps transcribed have shown us invaluable spaces that may hold some fascinating variables as far as possibly discovering the third Key—a nice backup just in case your operative, Dahlia, has any—misfortune in Hawaii. For instance, we believe the ruins of the large building, very hard to see in the initial photographs, may be what was described as the Empirium Chamber, the very seat of their government."

"Magnificent! And when do you think we'll get more than just a probe inside the dome?" Tomlinson asked, ignoring the slight about Dahlia's and her chances.

"We estimate sixteen hours, and we'll have people inside," answered Dame Lilith as she placed her drink on the table to her right. "But I must caution you that the initial testing of the air quality is disappointing. The environment is toxic to the extreme, but thanks to the tunnel opening we are starting to pump fresh air into the city."

"We expected as much. We could not very well expect part of an ancient city covered by magma and a trillion tons of rock and debris to be a Garden of Eden. How soon can we expect our equipment to be placed inside the magma chamber and city dome?"

"Our submersibles are inspecting the exposed section of the Crystal Dome as early as tomorrow. If they believe that exposed area will continue to withstand the pressure of the Mediterranean, we can start transporting the Wave equipment down the largest shaft on Crete in less than thirty hours."

"August, will we have added security in place by that time?" Tomlinson asked, sipping his drink.

"Yes, I believe so. Five hundred defensive troops on Crete itself, with another one hundred in the chambers below when the time comes; these of course will be our finest soldiers, the elite."

"Antinaval assets?"

"Already in place. If any navy or air force in the world starts poking around the area, they will have the surprise of their lives. They would be foolish, with our batteries of hidden SAM sites. I believe we are adequately covered until such time when we need not hide any longer."

"How exciting! Great moments started by great people, eh?" He raised his glass again.

After the toast was finished, Dame Lilith leaned forward in her chair. "William, I apologize for making light of Dahlia's abilities in the matter of recovering the map plate. I know it upset you. Its procurement is so very vital to our plans. Tell us, can she recover it?"

"Dahlia at this very moment is scouting the situation and should have a report forthwith."

"You have been right about everything thus far. We will never doubt your leadership. You have thought this out thoroughly and have earned the respect of all of us now inside the inner circle. Ours is the just way, the only way. The world needs us," Lilith said, and this time she raised her glass in tribute to Tomlinson.

They drank and relaxed, and Tomlinson held his audience captive with words.

"When the outside world learns of our plans, anyone outside of future history will think us some sort of James Bond bad guy, a mere cliché of evil. Little do they know this early on that we mean only good for our world. The changes in the way people live have been needed for more time than we will ever truly know. They are subservient to men and women who will drain them of even the minimal standards of a good life. While we will see to their every need, and give them the one thing governments cannot guarantee, a future. They just need to be led. They *want* to be led."

"Hear, hear!" they all said loudly as Tomlinson stood proudly.

"Here's to the man who will lead us all into our future, our destiny, William Tomlinson, to a brave new world!" Dame Lilith toasted.

"A brave new world!" They drank.

* * *

Later that evening, only four people sat in William Tomlinson's den. They were the true leaders.

"William, you have something to tell us?" Dame Lilith asked.

"We noticed you waited until the others left to pass on whatever it is on your mind," said August Nelson.

"We are moving operations to Crete much sooner than I said to the others. Once the Black Sea sound domes are in place, it will be the safest place to be when we strike at the heart of Russia. I have made a decision and I want your comments. I have planned a false strike at Russia. We will use Russia's paranoia against her. I am downing the Wave aircraft with all the equipment onboard."

"What would be the use of that?" Nelson asked.

"The livery colors of the aircraft will be changed to those of the U.S. Air Force. The blame will fall directly into the lap of the United States, and that will give us extra time to find the Ethiopian Key. I see no disadvantage in this action; it may even force the Russians' hand and make them move militarily in some other region, thinning America's military even further. Assets, I remind you, would be used against us. I must admit to you that I expected a harsher reaction from the new administration after the *Roosevelt* incident and the downing of those American and Japanese aircraft. Thus far, the president has been very restrained."

"Your changes have been timely thus far. Of course, whatever you think is necessary. We are still very much headed in the right direction and it will not take much more to make this new president take firmer action against those he sees as aggressors. This may be the straw, if we can get the Russians believing and retaliating."

Tomlinson nodded in thanks to Dame Lilith and August Nelson for seeing his plans clearly. He was about to stand and get a refill of whiskey when a light knock sounded on the door. Caretaker, just in from Europe, stepped in and closed the double doors lightly.

"Mr. Tomlinson, you have an important call from your asset in Hawaii, sir."

Tomlinson watched as Caretaker brought him the phone, then he nodded for the man to leave. He watched the older man slide his study doors open and then exit, ever careful not to divulge too much information to the man who could tip the balance of power in the Coalition with just a few words against him.

"Yes, Dahlia, we were just speaking of you. How is the operation proceeding?"

"We move in twelve hours, but that's not why I called you. I wanted to tell you personally that our attempt to kill the men responsible for Ethiopia and the raid in Westchester has failed."

"I see," Tomlinson said as he poured his drink.

"That is not all. We managed to follow the helicopter used in their escape and now they are under the protection by the same group of men at a secure location at Nellis Air Force Base in Nevada. William, it would be most difficult to get to the Ancients or Colonel Collins there."

Tomlinson looked around at the two people who were watching him closely. He smiled at them as if he were receiving good news. "Is that right?"

"You seem to be taking this matter extremely well, since these two Ancients are undoubtedly spilling a lot of information to that colonel and whoever it is he works for. Information, I may add, that could be very detrimental to your health. You must assume you have been compromised and leave your home immediately."

"You are sure of this?" he asked, losing his smile at the others.

"I won't sit here and debate the validity of my surveillance techniques with you. If you had paid me fully in advance, this conversation would have ended two minutes ago. As it is, you still owe me a considerable sum. In addition, I was not told about these mysterious men that seem to show up at the oddest times and are very, very good at what they do. Your intelligence in this matter was sorely lacking. Therefore, William, I suggest you leave before several nasty men from the FBI and some Virginia farmers show up at your door. I'll report when I have the plate."

Tomlinson blinked as the connection terminated. He hung up the phone and half smiled as he looked at his two Coalition colleagues and then around him at the ostentatious study. He knew he was going to leave everything behind that his family had worked for, for centuries, and he was angry.

"I'm afraid Dahlia has informed me that our old family members Carmichael and Martha have taken a trip to Nevada and are more than likely breaking their tradition of silence about their heritage. I must assume we are, or soon will be, compromised. We must leave immediately for Crete, as it has now become a sanctuary earlier than we thought it would have to be."

"We knew this day would come," Lilith said as she set down her drink and slowly stood. "I will miss the lifestyle and titles, I must admit."

"We can commiserate on the plane later. For now, we must evacuate." Tomlinson made for the study doors, then stopped as he placed his hands on the doorknobs. "August, leave a defensive team here and tell them nothing. I also want a large surprise waiting that will show the authorities they have a fight on their hands. I want the destruction of my own home and everything I possess to show my dedication and firm belief to our cause. Also, get Operation Boomerang launched immediately and order Professor Engvall to prepare for his move to Crete."

"I will order it," August Nelson answered, as he placed a reassuring hand on Tomlinson's shoulder. "And Professor Engvall is already safely in Crete, supervising the unloading of the Wave equipment."

With one last look at his American home, William Tomlinson left, knowing that he would not return until the Coalition was in control not only of the United States but the entire world.

UNITED STATES AIR FORCE FLIGHT 2897 HEAVY, TWO HUNDRED NAUTICAL MILES FROM SAKHALIN ISLAND (OPERATION BOOMERANG)

The Boeing 777 weapons platform that had initiated the attacks in Iran/Iraq, Russia, Korea, and China had undergone a radical change during its layover in Jakarta. The Wave equipment remained inside and intact, and the outside of the aircraft had been repainted, from the livery colors of a commercial carrier to those of the United States Air Force. Every Russian fighter pilot in the world would recognize the blue-and-white paint scheme, and that was just what William Tomlinson and the Coalition wanted.

The pilot and copilot onboard had explicit instructions to turn on the Wave Decibel Transmitter remotely just as they crossed over Russian airspace. The system could do no harm because the frequencies had been changed in Jakarta to new, benign settings, and now all that would happen was that the Wave signal would be broadcast in the open—directly into the ears of Russian listening posts.

The airliner was equipped with military-style ejection seats in the cockpit; the pilots would eject when they made first contact with Russian air-superiority fighters. Within thirty minutes of ejection, a Coalition trawler would pull them from the rough sea. Dangerous, to be sure, but they each would receive a two-million-dollar bonus.

"We have company and are being painted," the copilot said in heavily accented Bulgarian from his position in the right seat.

AIR DEFENSE FLIGHT TANGO-ABEL SIX, TRAILING U.S. AIR FORCE FLIGHT 2897 HEAVY

"Roger, we have attempted contact and have had no reply to our instructions," said the leader of the flight of four MIG 31s.

"Can you identify the aircraft? According to commercial routes it should be an American Airlines flight out of Fairbanks, Alaska, over."

"Negative. We have visually identified aircraft as that of a U.S. Air Force 777 transport conversion, tail number 6759875. We will attempt—"

The Russian colonel yelped as the penetrating Wave signal burst through his headphones.

"This is Tango-Abel lead; we have picked up a strange audio tone emanating from the American aircraft, over!"

"Tango-Abel, lead, lock on to, and destroy target, immediately!"

"What? They may just be off course—"

"Flight leader, destroy the target. This command is from the highest authority!"

The MIG 31 slowed and took up station half a mile from the American 777. He ordered his wingman to lock on and fire. The Russian colonel heard a clear and long signal from his missiles' seeker heads as they both locked on to the large GE engines.

As soon as the Coalition pilot saw the incoming MIGs on his radar, he set the controls to automatic pilot and made ready for his ejection. He and the copilot wore cold-water survival gear and were equipped with a life raft.

"We are ready. Stand by to eject. Eject, eject, eject!" he shouted out as he pulled the ejection seat's yellow-and-black-striped release bar.

Nothing happened. He pulled again and still nothing. The copilot pulled the dual handle on his and had the same result. Both men started to panic, as they knew they were only seconds away from a fiery death. In their terror, neither knew the men who had paid them so handsomely had betrayed them. The Coalition needed American-uniformed pilots to be discovered if any wreckage was ever found, but the men had never questioned the need for such an elaborate ruse as the uniforms.

The missiles flew off the rails. The first heat seeker struck the port engine mount just below the long, wide wing of the Boeing plane, while the other hit the engine itself. The next two, fired by the copilot, struck the remains of the already damaged wing and the giant plane rolled over in the sky and nose-dived two miles down into the sea.

The Russian pilot angrily pulled his face mask away. He was confused as to why the American pilot had not attempted to break away and try to avoid the missile attack.

It was as if he had wanted to die.

THE WHITE HOUSE
WASHINGTON, D.C.

Niles sat on one of the ornate couches in the Oval Office and watched the president listen to his opposite number in China through an interpreter. His old friend was about to put the medicine into the mouth of the president of the People's Republic of China first, before feeding him the sugar. The Chinese ambassador to the UN Security Council, with Russian backing, had been claiming a horrible accident since early morning concerning the air-to-surface encounter with North Korea.

"The Korean assault on our task force was an overt act of war and the American people insist I respond in kind. Now, for me trying to keep the peace, the world press is crucifying me! Your ally's actions were wrong in the least and criminal at the most. Either you will get Kim to listen to reason or we can carry this madness to its obvious conclusion."

Niles watched as his oldest friend's knuckles grew white on the handset and he saw the jaw muscles working at a furious clip.

Now the sugar, Jim, offer the sugar, Niles thought.

"We have evidence of an outside entity being responsible for these quakes and it is being forwarded through official channels now. Official and not private, for the reason that I want it to leak out, because the world must know that we were not responsible for these quakes that your ally North Korea is blaming us for. If you do not heed the evidence we send to you, Mr. President, circumstances will force me to defend this nation's soldiers, seamen, and airmen as well as those of our allies, and I will do so with vigor. Do we understand each other clearly?"

The American president listened to the return tirade and then closed his eyes and visibly relaxed.

"Have your people study the names and evidence we have sent and then I will await your call. Until then I have ordered our military to set DEFCON Two for defensive reasons. No more American lives will be lost without us shooting back." Again he listened to the other end of the line. "Very well. I will await your decision."

The president slowly placed the phone into its cradle on the coffee table in front of him. The secretary of state, newly arrived from his address to the United Nations, where he had condemned the actions by Korea and the unhelpful silence of both the Russians and Chinese, awaited his new orders.

The president looked at his watch and then glanced at the director of the FBI, who sat off by himself in a small chair to the sofa's left.

"When will you round up this man in Chicago?"

"The HRT unit is in place as we speak. They should have break-in in exactly ten minutes," he answered as he looked at his wristwatch.

"Good. Mr. Secretary, you may proceed back to the UN and address the Security Council and lay out all the evidence that Dr. Compton has provided you. I understand his people are working on learning more background on the technology used and the people using it. I believe it's time to share what little we do have on this Coalition faction. Mr. Director, take that son of a bitch in Chicago alive if you can."

"Yes, sir, that is the plan."

The president felt in control for the first time in days. He nodded his thanks to all in the room.

"Gentlemen, with the exception of Dr. Compton, you are excused."

The secretary of state along with the directors of the FBI and the CIA stood and left the room, excited to be moving against the man who might have been responsible for the American lives that had been lost.

When the door closed, the president half slid down into the sofa. He rubbed his hands over his face and then looked at Niles. "This job really sucks, bookworm."

"You're the one who wanted it. By the way, thanks for giving Colonel Collins a blank check as far as Hawaii goes."

The president raised his chin once and then let it fall again to his chest. Then he half smiled.

"You may have saved our bacon, Niles. Tell your people . . . tell them—"

"You can tell them when this thing is over, Mr. President. All they have done is what they've been doing for a hundred years."

"I just hope I can face them and others when this is over. As of right now, I'm responsible for getting a lot of American boys getting killed."

Niles leaned forward and looked at his friend. "That's not true." He looked at his watch. "The man responsible is just about to realize that it's he who's not the secret any longer."

5708 LAKESHORE DRIVE
CHICAGO, ILLINOIS

The Hostage Rescue Team (HRT) of the FBI was in position. As Agent in Charge George Weston watched the thermal monitor from the large house across the street, he was confused as to what he was looking at.

"Walk-in freezer?" he asked the technician sitting at the bank of monitors.

"Probably; by far the largest one I've ever seen. Then again, look at the house—who has that much money?"

"Evidently this Bozo does. Anything changed in the last two minutes?"

"No. We still have three hot bodies in the room the house specs say is the den, and three in the kitchen."

The AIC was worried about the room that the thermal scan was picking up, shading it a solid blue on the monitor. The warm bodies were easy to discern, but if someone was in that cold room, his team would not know it until they broke in.

"Is there any movement at all from the warm bodies in the den and kitchen?"

"None."

The AIC raised his walkie-talkie. "Red One, are the sniffers picking up anything?" he asked. He watched the monitor that showed the green night-vision image of the HRT Red One unit, whose job it was to check for minute traces of explosive materials by using the "sniffer," a small portable computer that smelled the interior air that escapes around windowsills and doorways. They were able to get so close because, surprisingly, the arrogant Mr. Tomlinson had no security grid around the house.

"Negative. Clean, cool air only; no nitrates are indicated and no chemical trace other than household deodorant and disinfectant are evident," the field tech answered.

He made his decision even as his eyes moved to the cold spot in the house.

"Okay, advance technical units move away. Strike team, we're a go in two minutes, on my order and by the book."

He did not need a response from the HRT as he saw that they were moving into position. His eyes moved to the cold spot and he frowned. He then forced his eyes away and saw the window, door, and upstairs teams reach their IPs.

"Stand by . . . Move, move, move!" he said into his radio.

As the command team watched from across the street, the first team used a ram to break through the thick double doors and then a flash-bang grenade flew inside, and then smoke canisters quickly followed. The flash and boom echoed loudly even from across the way as agents dressed in black charged through the door just as more smashed through the front and back windows. Up on the roof of the three-story house, a rappeling unit jumped from the expensively shingled roof and smashed through the upstairs windows.

Two full detachments of HRTs, one from Chicago and the other from Kansas City—a full twenty heavily armored and armed men—were inside the large residence in less than thirty seconds.

As he watched through the window, forsaking the monitors, Weston saw more flash-bang grenades go off. He was relieved when there was no initial gunfire coming from the large mansion. *Maybe this traitorous bastard Tomlinson will go down without a fight,* Weston thought.

"Down, down, down on the fucking floor," came the shouts over the open microphones of the assault element. "One, study is secure. Kitchen is secure; five men and one woman in custody."

"Is Tomlinson one of them?" he asked, looking at the monitor that showed the cold room on the thermal camera.

"One, Tomlinson is—"

Suddenly and without warning, the Tudor mansion disintegrated. The explosion was so powerful that the entire HRT assault element vanished in a microsecond. The explosion ripped through the mansion and blew outward toward the surrounding homes.

Weston was killed a split second after he saw the thermals on the cold room suddenly go red. The house they had borrowed for a command post blew apart and collapsed. The two houses in the back and two on the sides of the Tomlinson residence blew inward and started burning. All told, with the sacrificial lambs the Coalition had left inside the house along with the twenty assault members of two HRT units and fifteen other FBI agents and Chicago police officers, forty-one died in the explosion.

After Tomlinson and the other Coalition members had left the house on Lakeshore Drive, a Coalition courier had delivered a special package to the huge walk-in freezer in the kitchen. This package was protected behind freezing temperatures and a tight seal, so that nothing the FBI had in their bag of tricks could detect it. One hundred seventy-five-pound boxes of C-4 exploded with the flick of a switch twenty miles away at O'Hare International.

Tomlinson tossed the long-range remote to the steward and looked away. He reached for his drink as the Boeing 777 started its takeoff roll. As the large plane lifted off and started its turn north over the lake, everyone onboard was looking out the right-side windows of the aircraft. In the distance, they saw the small, brightly colored cloud rising above the rooftops of the very rich neighborhood they had recently left.

Dame Lilith was the first to turn away from the scene, and she looked at Tomlinson. He calmly took a sip of his drink, stretched out on the long leather couch of the richly appointed aircraft, and then looked over at her.

"How long until our teams can be in action in Ethiopia after we receive the plate map from Dahlia?" he asked as he placed his drink on the long table in front of the couch.

"Six hours," she answered.

"Good," he said as he smiled at Dame Lilith. "All in all, even with the loss of my home, it has not been an entirely unsatisfactory day."

CHAPTER

ELEVEN

PEARL HARBOR
HAWAII

Inside the solemn enclosure of the USS *Arizona* memorial, Jack was listening closely, but that didn't stop his inner furnace from burning hotly as he stood beside the eighteen U.S. Navy divers. The meeting of the National Parks Service, the Mobile Diving and Salvage Unit—or, as Carl Everett had introduced them, the "Mudzoos"—and the eight-man U.S. Navy SEAL Team Four, which had flown out with Collins and Everett from Coronado, California, had been in progress since the sun set low in the Pacific.

They were listening to the special assistant to the secretary of the interior talk about the remains of the crew onboard the USS *Arizona*. The secretary finished and then a park ranger took over the briefing. So far, everyone in the group was going, with the exception of Jack, the assistant secretary, and two other park rangers. This exclusion was not sitting too well with the colonel.

"By the time you enter the water, it'll be full dark. Keep in mind, we have mapped where we believe most of the old ordnance is, but there are always surprises inside the old girl. It's as if she still thinks she's fighting the war," the park ranger giving the briefing looked at the faces around him, "and she has every right to think that way. She's earned it."

The divers and SEALs nodded in understanding. Jack could see the respect that everyone in the room had for the *Arizona*. It was as if she were a sick woman and everyone was there to take care of her. They also knew what was at stake, and the respect they had shown thus far belied the fact that they knew, no matter what, that plate had to come to the surface. When the president orders something done, you do it.

"Why was the captain's safe never opened before? It's my understanding that the National Parks Service has made several forays into the cabin," Everett asked as he zipped up his wet suit.

"Because of respect and privacy, it's that plain and simple. The captain was the only one with his personal safe's combination, thus the items inside are his own. We had no right to enter it. Captain Everett, you and these men have to get a clear understanding of what we have here. This warship is still on the rolls of the United States Navy, she is alive and you will respect her as a fighting combatant," ordered Richard Chavez, head ranger of the memorial. "Believe me, if it's in our country's best interest, the old girl will give up her secrets willingly. Ghastly, but that's the way it is."

Again the men nodded in understanding. They all knew that military battle sites had a way of causing deep, soul-searching experiences, and none of them came close to scoffing at the idea of the *Arizona* being haunted.

"Okay," one of the salvage divers said. "SEALs are outside, conducting security sweeps. When we dive, they will relieve the UDT already providing security. The eight-man Underwater Demolition Team will then board the memorial platform and await demolition orders *if* needed. Let us hope that is not where we're headed."

"The Mudzoos will then try to cut the safe open and remove the item in question," Everett said, taking over the secure portion of the briefing. He looked at the schematic of the *Arizona* laid out before them. "Now, we will execute the dive through this gangway here," he said, pointing to a starboard stairwell.

"That will lead us down to the second deck closest to the bridge. I'll carry the DET cord and two quarter-pound charges of C-4; if it's not enough we can always send up for more—let's just hope we don't have to use it down there. Now, Ranger Chavez, the length of the companionway isn't that far?"

"Right," answered Chavez. "Thirty-five feet to the captain's stateroom."

Everett was satisfied and he looked at his dive team. "Ready?" he asked, looking at his watch.

Heads nodded around the large table. Everett then turned to Jack. "Hopefully, we'll be right back, boss."

Collins nodded, accepting Carl's decision that, with his limited dive experience, he could cause more harm than good. Jack knew that he was right.

Everett turned to Ranger Chavez. "Permission to board the *Arizona*?" he asked officially.

"Permission granted, Captain."

The SEALs and Mudzoos came to attention and then moved to the memorial's railing. For the first time in more than sixty years, American sailors would board the *Arizona*.

Dahlia watched from across the harbor. The powerful night-vision binoculars she used allowed her to see clearly the eight navy SEALs, two National Park rangers, and eleven navy salvage divers slide over the side of the memorial. The SEALs were clearly identifiable by their plain black wet suits and the arms they carried. She adjusted her view and saw four men watching the divers from above, on the observation deck of the memorial.

She lowered her binoculars and brought up a small electronic-file device. She hit Saved and several pictures started flicking across the small screen. She finally came to the image she wanted and looked closely at it, then looked at the lone figure standing in the open on the memorial.

"Damn," she said, recognizing Colonel Jack Collins immediately.

It was now obvious to her that he was responsible for the navy having beaten her team here. He must be in custody of the two Ancients, she thought. Regardless, she decided that the strike element she had assembled should be sufficient and was satisfied that they could retrieve the plate map, so she raised her radio.

"Recovery One, you are go for incursion."

She lowered the radio, raised her binoculars, and watched a fifty-man team slide away from the much smaller memorial for the USS *Utah,* a former battleship turned target ship used in the training of the newer, faster, Pennsylvania Class Battlewagons of the 1930s. The *Utah,* also sunk on December 7, 1941, was lying on her side on the bottom of Pearl not far from the *Arizona.* She provided the perfect location for the attacking force to enter the murky waters unseen.

The fifty-man assault-and-recovery element were excellent divers. All were former naval men from various countries. Their pay for this mission would be quite enough to retire and live a life of luxury. They would earn it.

As she trailed her team, she was happy to see no trace of them as they swam south from the *Utah.* They were using special rebreather units that allowed no telltale air bubbles to escape the completely closed-loop systems. Dahlia then moved her glasses to watch a special three-man team on Ford Island, not far from the *Arizona.* The image was in a sickly green ambient light, but she was clearly able to see one man as he reached for his radio. She smiled as she heard three distinct clicks transmitted. The three men had successfully severed the electrical cable that supplied power to the underwater sound and laser-fence security system guarding the *Arizona* from treasure hunters and souvenir seekers.

"Now, bring me my retirement," she said as she adjusted her view to the memorial; she was satisfied as she watched the four men remaining on the observation deck.

Except for the pain-in-the-ass Colonel Collins, whom she knew to be one of the most formidable men she had ever seen, the men did not look like much of a threat. She and her small five-man team should have no trouble removing them from the surface equation.

* * *

Jack Collins looked at the names of the dead on the memorial
and thought about how they had died. A surprise it had been,
sudden and unexpected. Jack had always hoped never to lose
anything as valuable as his men's lives in battle, but he was
also wise enough to know that was one wish never granted to a
leader. All one could do was be vigilant and try never to be surprised as the brave men on the *Arizona* had been. He turned
away from the names and looked out on the harbor lights and
Honolulu glimmering in the distance.

He raised his radio and depressed the Send button three
times. Then he heard a return three clicks and was satisfied
that his own surprise was ready.

Everett was the fifth in line as they passed over the *Arizona*'s
forward number-one turret. Although he had expected to see
it, the scene was still something out of a ghostly dream as the
handheld lights they used played over the rifled barrels. Marine growth had done nothing to diminish the menacing opening where at one time, long ago, one-and-a-half-ton shells had
exploded out of the massive guns.

As they approached the starboard gangway next to the old
bridge tower that navy salvagers had cut away almost sixty-
five years before, the water seemed to become even blacker,
giving every man on the excursion the chills.

The eight SEALs relieved the UDT element and Everett
watched as they slowly made their way to the surface. The
SEALs, armed with UPPs (underwater-pressurized projectiles) took up station patrolling the waters outside the great
warship. The weapons they carried were multibarreled spear
guns that could rapid-fire fifteen ten-inch-long darts at anything threatening the team.

Even in her deteriorating condition, the *Arizona* was still
something to behold. Her dark skin was alive with marine life,
and as he slid a hand along her starboard railing, Carl knew
that she was truly still alive in more ways than one. With well
over three-quarters of her crew still inside, how could she be
anything else.

In the blackness of the harbor waters, a gaping maw slowly

came into view in the dim lights ahead, and the gangway quickly followed that. The steel steps that led belowdecks were still intact and, if it had not been for the rust, looked as if men had used them just that morning.

The lead ranger went in first after attaching a nylon cord to the railing. The others followed slowly at five-foot intervals. Everett felt the minute pressure build as they descended into the darkness that led to the second deck of one of the most famous ships in history.

As they traveled down the passage, Ranger Chavez dropped a small dive marker about fifteen feet in and then turned to face the men following him. The Mudzoos knew what was happening, but Carl was curious as the yellow-green dye marker rose into the water of the passageway as if it were a ghost. Someone tapped Everett from behind. A navy salvage man had seen the questioning look on his face, so he had written something on his plastic board with grease pencil.

"*Arizona* crewman in the silt," it said.

Everett personally could have gone all night without knowing that, but he knew that they had to be warned, so as not to disturb the area. He knew why diving on the *Arizona* was limited to personnel of the U.S. Navy and the National Parks Service only.

As he passed over the yellow-green marker, out of respect, he looked straight ahead and not down at the thick bed of silt where one of the *Arizona's* boys lay. Carl was then startled when he looked ahead of him and saw at least twenty more of the markers rising like small ghostly signals. He realized then that they were inside a most hallowed place.

Ahead, Everett knew, the rest of the *Arizona* crew lay where they had fallen at battle stations and awaited the arrival of their brothers of the modern U.S. Navy.

A thousand yards from the stern of the *Arizona,* the Coalition assault team split into two groups. They would strike the old ship from two sides. One team of twenty-five would follow the Americans inside and strike there, and the other element would hit the SEAL security team in the waters surrounding the dead battleship. Then they would wait and take anyone who might escape the bowels of the vessel. The few men left on the memorial were not their concern. They would hit and hit hard and be away before the Pearl Harbor U.S. Marine contingent could react.

Everett watched as the captain's cabin finally came into view. It had seemed like a mile when it had been only thirty-five feet of dark passageway. The door to the cabin was wide open, and as they watched, a small blue-finned fish swam out as if curious at his nighttime company.

As the only diver who knew approximately what it was they were searching for, Carl would be one of only six allowed into the cabin of Franklin Van Valkenburg, who had been the commander of the USS *Arizona*.

As the initial team entered the cabin, Everett was shocked to see that the closet with the remains of uniforms still hanging. The sea had not eaten them as it had so many of the other things onboard. Carl hoped that the sea life had left them in respect to the ship's captain.

Everett continued looking around as the others went to the main bulkhead that separated the cabin from the next space. As he looked over the stateroom, he saw the phone off its hook, and then before he knew it two more yellow dye markers rose from the deck; two more bodies here. Who were they? It was a known fact that the captain had made it to his command bridge, had been seen there moments before the destruction of his ship. Therefore, who these men could have been was a mystery.

The rest of the captain's cabin was losing its fight with the waters of the harbor. The rich paneling that had covered the steel-encased room was all but gone.

Everett recalled that Martha and Carmichael had said that Van Valkenburg had been one of *them*. However, unlike Martha and Carmichael, he had done his duty to the human race, as well as to Keeler's brother.

A bright light suddenly filled the dark cabin. Carl had to turn away as the cutting torch flared brightly as the Mudzoos went to work on the small safe.

As he looked away, he saw the round porthole, one of the only ones he had observed not covered by a protective steel hatching. A form suddenly crossed the murky glass. It was only momentary, but he was sure that it was someone in the water outside the hull. He turned back to the cutting, unnerved by the dark figure he had seen outside the porthole. Then he reassured himself that it must have been one of the SEALs in the water. However, he could not help but have a momentary SEAL-trained reaction that something was not right about the blurry figure he had seen, and that something kept playing on the fringes of his mind.

The battle outside the *Arizona* started before SEAL Team Four knew it was upon them. The black-suited and -helmeted assault element of the Coalition fired their first volley from thirty yards away through the darkness of the harbor. Before the SEALs could respond, three of their team were down. There had been no warning from above by the rangers monitoring the laser fence that guarded the site.

The team leader, a chief petty officer named "Breeches" Jones, was a wily veteran of many Persian Gulf excursions. The one thing that no SEAL team had ever done in their storied history was fight an actual undersea battle. He quickly saw the dark figures ahead of him branch out as his remaining four men returned fire at the advancing group. He raised his M1A1-56 dart rifle and rapidly fired six of the tungsten steel projectiles at the closest of the attackers. Two of the darts struck home and the dark-suited figures became still and started to sink.

The chief then saw at least twenty more bad guys swim out of the murk toward the outnumbered SEALs. The attackers were armed with the same weapons the SEALs had, and Jones saw that his only choice was to make for the superstructure of the *Arizona* and swim over to the protection of the far side. He saw two of his men break over the top. Then they quickly returned and were waving him back. The route was cut off by more attackers.

Suddenly, the routine security operation had turned into a life-or-death struggle and Jones's team was losing.

* * *

Inside the captain's cabin, Everett was still thinking about the figure he had seen through the porthole. Then what he had seen finally dawned on him. No, not what he had seen, but what he had failed to see. He would regret not acting fast enough for years afterward. There had not been any air bubbles trailing behind the blurred figure he had briefly viewed. Everyone on the dive was using standard diving equipment because when you were diving on a dangerous wreck, air bubbles could be used to let a team member know that you were in trouble. Just as he started to move and warn his companions, the safe door popped free of its hinges.

As Everett moved forward quickly to let the salvage divers know they were not alone, two of the deadly darts struck one of the navy divers from the companionway. Carl made it to the four other men and started pushing them in the opposite direction; he was gesturing and waving them away when three more darts sliced their way through the water and struck three of the salvage divers.

The remaining team members needed no more coaxing to turn and swim to the passage opposite the main companionway. Everett, thinking about what he was there for, quickly reached into the open safe and felt around until he pulled out an old plastic-covered map and chart case. He hurriedly dropped them into the silt and then felt around the safe again. He felt something spongy at first and then underneath it was hard and rectangular. He pulled it free just as a steel dart pinged off the door frame of the safe. He did not stop to see who had almost killed him; instead, he kicked out with his fins and made to follow the rest.

The attackers charged the captain's cabin in pursuit. One diver saw the map case lying half buried in the silt. He reached down, claimed the case, and then kicked his fins to follow his team.

Jack had seen the UDT team away for a well-deserved rest and was walking along the memorial deck when he suddenly saw emergency flares start to glow below the waterline. Bright yellow dye markers then started reaching the surface. He did not hesitate as he reached for his radio and depressed the Talk key; this time the signal was two short and one long. At that moment, he heard sharp cracks start peppering the concrete memorial. Small-caliber silenced rounds started chewing up the radio, map table, and other equipment. Two bullets struck the assistant interior secretary and he fell dead three feet from Jack as he hit the wooden deck.

"Are you armed?" he called out to two prone park rangers.

"No!" one said as he covered his head.

"Great!" Collins said under his breath as he pulled a 9-millimeter automatic from his coat. Only five minutes before, the UDT had left the memorial to take a break.

Before they knew what was happening, a rubber Zodiac assault boat with its loud outboard motor bumped the memorial and three men poked their heads through the slats, giving them a good view of the interior. One of these smashed the tinted glass and started to climb in. Collins took quick aim and fired one round. His aim was true and the attacker's head jerked back, then the man fell backward through the slatted opening.

"You two, get to the far end and into the water and get the hell out!"

The two park rangers rose. One fell immediately as five bullets stitched his backside. He fell into the other man and they both went down. Jack started to crawl in the prone position toward the fallen men as twenty more rounds plunked into the wooden flooring beside his head. He rolled quickly and on instinct let loose three rounds in the direction of the gunfire, and an attacker in black Nomex clothing fell from the side of the memorial.

Just as Collins turned back to the rangers, he saw three of the attackers rise from the opposite side and step onto the platform. He aimed and fired, striking the first man in the groin, doubling him over. Then one of the other two emptied a magazine of bullets into the ranger who was lying helpless at their feet.

"Damn," Jack said as he started to roll on the hard deck, turning over and over, giving very little for anyone to aim at until his body slammed against the harbor-side wall of the white-painted memorial. He turned and fired five times into the thirty-foot-high window and watched as the tinted glass exploded inward. Then, with three shots over his shoulder, Jack rolled into the oil-laced water of the harbor.

The memorial had been lost to the enemy just as the upper deck of the *Arizona* had been quickly overwhelmed.

The five remaining SEALs dived into the first opening they could, the empty barbette of number-three gun mount. The gaping hole was where one of the fourteen-inch mounts had been located. It had been removed shortly after the attack on December 7, then relocated to the coastal defense battery on Oahu. As the five SEALs dived quickly into the interior, twenty of the deadly darts pierced the dark waters behind them, striking the rusting steel of the number-three barbette.

Everett and the navy salvage team swam quickly down the emergency passageway of number-two deck. At every opening they passed there had been at least a two-man team waiting for them with deadly and accurate fire from the outside. It was clear to the trailing Everett that there were far more bad guys than good. They had lost three of the navy salvage men and Ranger Chavez in the first of these unexpected assaults without any return fire. Everett concluded that the SEALs outside were either dead or fighting for their lives just as he and his men were.

Carl used his dive knife to bang on the steel bulkhead until the men ahead of him stopped and turned. They had been heading for the stern companionway that led to the open water of the harbor, where he knew that attackers were waiting to ambush them. To punctuate this thought, four men in the same-style wet suits as Everett's team were wearing came bursting into the hatchway from above. The men started to scatter until they realized that this was what was left of the SEALs' security element.

Everett waved everyone over to the open hatch, which had been frozen in that position since 1941. The chief and the remaining SEALs turned and started pumping darts into the massive barbette opening of number-three gun mount to cover the salvage team as they entered the hatch.

Carl was the last to enter the hatch following the SEALs. He stuffed the plate map into the back of his weight belt so that he could pull himself into the hatch. Just as his fins disappeared through the opening, ten darts ricocheted off the steel around the hatchway. One of the deadly projectiles hit his right fin and pierced it, knocking him sideways. Everett's luck was holding as he went deeper into the darkness of the *Arizona*.

As the survivors dived into the real heart of the ship, the attacking Coalition force hesitated only moments before following. Soon the entire force of forty-two men entered the bowels of the ship in pursuit.

The great gray lady was crewing live Americans once again, but she was old and tired and very near collapse as the remaining men swam for their lives into her darkened belly.

Jack dived under the concrete memorial and came up under her frame to catch a breath. He held his Beretta up out of the water, ejected the nearly spent clip, and silently slipped in one of his spares. He shook his head in anger after losing another three people to the Coalition.

He heard loud talking as more men entered the memorial from the harbor side. Where in the hell had they come from? The afternoon search of the harbor had been thorough; they had made sure that all the tourists had exited the area and there were no surprises awaiting the dive team.

As Jack moved from frame strut to frame strut, he heard equipment smashing and men walking overhead. He spit out some of the foul-tasting water, then froze when he heard a woman's voice.

"I am speaking to Colonel Collins. I know you are the military officer that was at the warehouse in New York and Mr. Keeler's offices in Boston."

Jack did not move. The gentle lapping of the water underneath the memorial masked his breathing, but he was still prepared to dive deep if bullets started punching their way through from the deck above.

"I know that your facility at Nellis has Ms. Laughlin and Mr. Rothman under quarantine. They tell the wildest and most fanciful stories, don't they? They really are quite insane, you know. It must be the inbreeding."

Jack's eyes followed the voice through the decking above his head. The woman was moving left to right and coming very close to the spot where he had rolled into the water.

"I must tell you, and whatever entity you work for, that you have caused me concern here. This was supposed to be a no-violence endeavor. Your interference will just be the cause of more deaths."

Jack thought he had a good spot where he could shoot through the deck and hit the woman, but then he decided to hold his fire. He wanted her alive because now he knew that she was at least culpable in the murders of his people.

"We will get to the two Ancients eventually, Colonel. It's just as the message I instructed be left for you in New York stated: *You're not that secret anymore.*"

Jack closed his eyes in anger as he heard her arrogant chuckle.

The dive team, or what was left of them, was holed up in the ship's number-three galley. They had lost one more SEAL and another three salvage divers on their way in. Everett and the rest of the team were fast running out of darts, just as the enemy seemed to have an endless supply.

Carl took a quick head count and saw that they were down to two SEALs and five unarmed navy divers, plus himself and one park ranger. They had their backs up against a solid steel bulkhead behind good protection; a large cast-iron stove was stopping most of the tungsten darts. Now they would be picked off one at a time or they would run out of oxygen. Neither fate suited him all that much.

Growing angry at the no-win scenario, Carl reached for his plastic writing board and quickly wrote, "What is above the galley?" He quickly showed the board to the others.

The park ranger quickly wrote, "Number eight antiaircraft mount."

Carl pointed to a large hole in the steel ceiling of the galley. What he was indicating was the hole that the 776-pound aerial bomb dropped by a Japanese pilot over sixty years before had made in its plunge into the forward magazine for number-two gun mount. As they looked upward, they could see the open water through two decks.

Carl used his thumb and index finger to mimic a gun, asking for the two remaining SEALs to cover him.

The chief held his board up and quickly wrote, "No way, there are at least thirty to forty attackers in the galley and companionway!"

Everett looked at the jagged hole again. He thought he could squeeze through. He handed the bronze plate he had removed from the safe to the park ranger and then quickly started to remove his tanks. The others looked at him as if he were nuts. The SEALs turned and fired off a few darts and then reloaded their last tube of ammo. Before Everett removed his mouthpiece for the last time, he wrote on his board, "If I'm lucky, you'll hear three taps when I get there—get everyone inside the big ovens and cover up!"

With one last look at the incredulous faces of the salvage team, Everett started taking deep breaths. Then he removed his mouthpiece and tapped the chief on the shoulder. The two SEALs popped up and started pumping darts into the darkness of the mess area, not really knowing if they would hit anything. The idea was to keep their enemies' heads down until the former SEAL followed through with his crazy plan.

Everett held on to a flashlight as he pushed up hard with his legs. His body left the deck and he almost made it into the large hole in one fell swoop, but his shoulder hit one of the jagged edges and his momentum stopped cold. He felt a dart plunge into his neoprene wet suit and lodge in the soft folds of his side; luckily, it was only skin it caught. He adjusted his angle and kicked with his fins, and the dart in his left side hit the opening on the way through. The sudden flare of pain almost caused him to expel the precious air he had stored up in his lungs. Nevertheless, he kicked once more and he was through.

Carl shone his light around. He was in a small crawl space between decks and he hurriedly looked around for the ladder he hoped led out to the antiaircraft mount. He suddenly saw it about six feet away. It went upward and in the opposite direction; and went down toward what he was hoping to find. He just hoped he remembered the schematic correctly.

As he descended into the hold, his captured breath was expanding in his chest. Carl eased up and forced himself to slow, lowering his blood pressure intentionally and allowing small amounts of air to escape his lungs. As he used a handrail to guide him, he saw ahead through the light a small hatchway that was bent almost double, but still open. That had to be the small locker that served the number-eight gun mount. He just hoped that salvagers had left what was stored there intact as too dangerous to be moved. As he held the sides of the hatchway, he pulled himself into the armored locker.

The eeriness he felt inside was palpable. He shone the light on the deck and saw the bubblelike rise of steel where the explosion below had buckled the deck above. The forces involved had been so tremendous that the armor decking had separated into layers.

Carl looked around. Time was running out as his lungs were starting to ache as he continued to expel air a small amount at a time. Still he did not see anything that he needed. The armory looked to be empty. Then he saw them. They were in the silt of sixty-five years' accumulation, buried like the men around them, and were like skeletal fingers poking from a grave.

Before he could reach even for one, he started to grow dizzy. He shook his head and looked around him. Calmly and orderly he checked every upper corner of the locker. Finally, he saw something that could help him. There, hanging from the ceiling, was a vent cover. It was off and it angled downward. He just prayed his luck held. He kicked to the vent and tore the remaining small rivets free, then stuck his mask up and inside. He worked his way up and then the large ventilation shaft angled back and out of the locker. Where it angled, he found what he desperately needed: air. Air that had been trapped long ago and could not escape due to the particular curvature of the vent.

He took a deep breath, expecting a horrible stench, but instead it was as if he had opened a door to a springtime day. The smell was a pleasant one, like that of a bakery not far from the house where he'd grown up. The air that filled the vent had come from the ship's bakery. On the morning the *Arizona* died, the cooks and bakers just at that moment had been serving breakfast. He was grateful as he filled his lungs with the aroma of long-dead biscuits and cinnamon rolls.

When he had his fill, he replaced his mask and backed out of the shaft. He then aimed for the deck and retrieved five of the items he had come for.

The SEALs were out of darts. They turned back to face the others and could see their faces through the glass of their masks. It was over. The park ranger, knowing that the map could not be allowed to fall into an aggressor's hands, raised the bronze plate and started to bring it down onto the corner of a steel table, hoping to damage it enough to be useless.

As he was starting to bring down the plate map, three loud taps sounded in the overhead. The ranger remembered what Everett had written and went straight back to the large ovens. He opened the first wide door and squeezed inside; the others soon followed. Several darts bounced harmlessly off the cast iron as the second of the large oven doors closed.

The attackers soon felt comfortable enough to show themselves as dive lights came on, and several even smiled behind their rebreather masks at the inane attempt of the navy men to hide at the last possible moment.

Above them, in the hole made by that fateful Japanese bomb, Carl Everett was about to deliver another kind of projectile. He had found three five-inch antiaircraft rounds in the silt. He had taken these and tied them off with the det cord that he was assigned to bring along with the quarter-pound charge of C-4 to open the safe if need be. Then he attached the small charge to the large rounds and made fast the blasting cap. He hoped he wouldn't kill everyone along with his targets. Everett started to run out of air just as he started his makeshift plan.

The Coalition assault team were starting to swim forward with the arrogance of the victor when they saw something slide down from the steel overhead. The thirty men of the inside team stopped and looked on and then finally one of them turned his light onto the strange object. Eyes widened in horror as they realized what they were looking at: three large bullet-like rounds tied together by yellow detonation cord attached to an explosive charge. Their eyes followed the cord up into the gaping hole, and then they froze as they saw Everett in the void beyond.

Everett saw the attackers look up and knew that they had seen him. He quickly waved his hand in a good-bye gesture, then turned his hand over and flipped the stunned attackers the bird. Then he twisted the small electrical switch for the detonator. He pulled away from the hole as the charge raced through the det cord to ignite the blasting cap stuck into the small charge.

The C-4 went off, striking the cordite inside the shell casings, and that set off the warhead of the five-inch antiaircraft shells. They exploded downward into the stunned Coalition divers and struck the deck below them, creating a manmade fusillade of shrapnel that struck everyone in the attacking team. Half of them were killed immediately, while others were just maimed, while still others only had their eardrums punctured. The force of the underwater blast was so great that glass face masks imploded into their flesh of their wearers. Silt was cascading around the mess area and galley, looking as if a deep London fog had rolled in.

Above, the detonation lifted Everett from the crawl space and smashed him into the deck above. The last of his air was forced out of his lungs. He gathered what senses he had left and shot through the hole and into the clouded mess area. He did not clear enough vision to see around him, but he knew that there were dead men floating all around him as he made for the galley. Once there, he found his discarded tanks and placed the mouthpiece into his mouth and inhaled deeply.

When that immediate need was satisfied, he went to the large ovens and gave a silent prayer as he opened the first door. A finned foot immediately smashed his face mask. He yelled, spitting out his mouthpiece, just as the chief saw who it was. Everett was waving desperately for them to get out before more company could show up.

Below the monument, Jack was still holding one of the support struts when his body lifted in the water. Large bubbles started to rise around him as air and cordite escaped through the open and empty bridge area of the *Arizona*. He heard running feet and shouts above as men looked into the water.

It seemed like ten minutes later when Jack heard men shouting out to people unseen to raise their hands. Then he heard curses, and he knew that the dive team had surfaced right into the waiting hands of their attackers. He closed his eyes and cursed, knowing that he had no choice now. He could not wait on the failsafe he had set up earlier. He slowly made for the outer wall of the memorial and brought himself out into the open night.

Once out in the clear, he held on to the memorial with one hand and pulled himself around to the window he had broken earlier. He raised his head and looked over the edge into the interior. It was indeed worst-case. He saw Carl, his hands on his head, with the rest of what was left of the dive team. Bloodied and weary, they were being pushed and beaten with assault rifles.

Jack shook his head. He was tired of hiding. He brought the pistol up, but then hesitated as he saw the woman. Dressed in black pants and a black leather jacket, she stood in front of one of the rangers, removing something from him. She held it up to the light and then brought it down reverently.

"Thank you for recovering our lost artifact. You have been most helpful."

That was enough. As far as he could tell, the woman was without a weapon, so he aimed at the two men on her left, who were busy looking after the devastated dive team. He started to squeeze the trigger. That was when all hell broke loose around the *Arizona* Memorial. Unseen and at Jack's orders, a platoon of U.S. Marines had been dispatched from Pearl and left to stand guard just to the dock side of the USS *Missouri.* The great battleship had shielded the strike force as they approached after Jack had used his radio to alert them when the attack had begun. It had seemed like they took their own sweet time, but Collins knew that they could not have just come barging in like the cavalry of old.

Several Zodiac attack craft circled the memorial as Everett ordered the remains of the dive team down. Automatic fire was striking the white memorial from marines firing from their own moving platforms. Collins used this diversion to open up from close range from his position behind the enemy. He dropped six before they knew that they had an antagonist in the rear.

Soon the Zodiacs started screaming for the gangway that led to the memorial. They exited the boats and started forward, firing as they came on. Seeing that her situation was hopeless, the woman started to turn and run. Jack fired his 9-mm and the round struck just where he had aimed it, in the woman's calf. She fell and the plate map went sliding away as it struck the deck. She immediately got up and limped until she found an open slat. She dived in toward the land side of Ford Island.

Jack gained the platform and ran for the plate. He took it and then looked for Carl. He was relieved when he saw his friend standing. They locked eyes. Jack threw Everett the plate Frisbee-style, then Jack dived through the opening after the woman

Everett ran to the window, holding the plate and his injured side, and saw Jack's form as he swam after the woman who had just gained the swampy shore area of Ford Island.

Collins easily followed the woman through the darkness.

She was leaving an easy trail to follow in her panic to escape. He heard her clearly through the bushes and cattails ahead. Then he heard a splash as she fell into the wet weeds.

Dahlia was looking around in panic when she saw the figure standing in the moonlight.

"Don't just stand there, you—" she started, and then she saw that the figure was wearing civilian clothes, and then she knew. "I have very valuable information to trade for my life, Colonel."

The dark shape did not move. He just raised his weapon and ejected the spent clip. Then, with deliberate slowness, he inserted his last one. He charged the slide forward and chambered a round.

"You need to know that Tomlinson didn't die in Chicago. It was his plan all along to leave the States; he has no need to be here any longer," she said as she was suddenly praying that someone, anyone, would show up and stop what she knew was about to happen.

"You're not so secret anymore."

"What . . . I . . . please, you need me." The pleading in her voice was clear.

The last of the marines' gunfire ceased and several loud whistles and sirens from the harbor patrol blared as Pearl woke up to the assault on their revered *Arizona*.

"I need my people back. Can you give them to me?"

Dahlia saw the raised gun and finally knew what it was like to face imminent death. This man was going to murder her.

Jack raised his weapon and fired.

The three Coalition divers had come close to catching Jack unaware. At the last second, the light from the rising moon caught the glass in one of the face masks of the divers. Jack had just enough time to fire directly over the head of the woman, who had thought for sure the American colonel was going to murder her.

The first of the Coalition divers went down with a hole placed cleanly into his forehead, but the other two ducked into the

murk of Ford Island. Jack dived for cover just as twenty silenced rounds whacked the damp soil around him. As he looked
up, he saw the woman disappear into the cattails and reeds. He
took quick aim and fired five times at the spot where she had
vanished, but the area had suddenly become motionless.

As Collins stood, helicopters started shining large search-
lights around the area of the memorial. He reached for his radio to inform them to search Ford Island for the woman and at
least two Coalition men. As he raised the small radio to his
mouth, he realized that it was not going to work. He had been
in the water so long that seawater had shorted out its workings. Collins reared back and threw it into the reeds.

At that moment, Everett broke through the reeds and saw
Jack.

"Jesus, Jack, I thought you bought it. The woman?" he asked
as he walked forward.

"Order a sweep of the area. Maybe they can find her, but I
suspect she has nine lives."

"Yeah, maybe, but with you taking shots at her, I bet she's
only got one or two left."

Dahlia was getting her leg tended to by one of the few survivors of another botched raid. Because of this colonel, she
was on a losing streak. She winced as the diver placed pressure on her wound as he wrapped it.

Three of them had managed to evade the massive search
for the attackers by marines and shore patrol. They had
crawled through mud and mosquitoes to a waiting boat and
slowly made their way to the dry-dock facility across the
harbor. From there it had been a terrifying game of cat and
mouse as they barely managed to hide from patrols looking
for survivors. Dahlia knew that she was now one of the most
wanted women in the world, and she owed it all to Jack
Collins.

Once in the city, the men who had saved her took her to a
safe house that she had prepared just in case something like
this happened. She stretched out on the couch with her injured

leg up on the arm, in the dingy room with a small automatic in her lap. Having a weapon was distasteful, but if Collins came through that door, she promised herself, she would put a bullet into his brainpan.

When a knock sounded at the door, Dahlia took the gun and aimed. Using the barrel of the weapon, she gestured for one of the men to answer. She doubted very much that Collins or the U.S. Navy would be so polite as to knock. One of the divers opened the door, and she relaxed as three men came through. They all were worn and tired. However, one man was smiling.

"And what is it that makes you stand there grinning like a fool?" she asked.

"You may find this of value. A nice second prize," the man said as he tossed the map case to her. Then he accepted a glass of water from one of his companions. "We almost didn't make it. The Honolulu policeman who stopped us won't be hula dancing anymore."

Dahlia opened the aged plastic case. The smell was atrocious as she looked from the Coalition diver back to the items inside. She slowly pulled out several charts and maps. There were also handwritten notes. She looked at the map and her eyes widened.

"It looks like you just may have tripled the bonuses of every man in this room." She smiled at the words written on the map of Africa.

"Then it is important?" the man asked, lowering his glass of water.

The men looked at the colored relief and saw the written coordinates placed there by the hand of Franklin Van Valkenberg, captain of the USS *Arizona*. In the weeks that he had possession of the plate map, he had figured out its secret and soon had calculated the resting place of the Key, exactly where Dahlia knew she and her men would be in the coming days.

She picked up the cell phone and pushed a single, special number. The man answered on the first ring.

"William, we have the location of the Atlantean Key."

Dahlia hung up, then picked up the gun and smiled as she

thought about Colonel Jack Collins. She knew that with the plate map he would come looking for the Atlantean Key. As she tapped the barrel against her muddy cheek, she thought about that bullet she would place into the colonel's head.

"This is one killing I do myself, free of charge."

CHAPTER

TWELVE

THE WHITE HOUSE
WASHINGTON, D.C.

The president sat silently watching the live C-SPAN feed from the United Nations in New York. The ambassador from North Korea was berating the Americans from the podium.

"They just threw out the evidence we sent them," the president said to no one in particular. "The Chinese were not able to convince them of the truth, or they're just not hearing it."

Niles watched the angry animation of the Korean ambassador, but what was more important to Niles was the way the Chinese delegation sat stoically, not moving an inch as their ally decried what they perceived as a South Korean and American conspiracy to weaken the People's Army to the point of total collapse. The ambassador even threw in the disaster at the Russian port of Vladivostok for good measure. Damn! The president needed the Russians' support, but Niles as well as the president knew that this was a backlash action over the harvest and grain shortages.

Previously, the American secretary of state had told the world about the true nature of the Coalition that was truly responsible for the seismic attacks. Armed with only circumstantial evidence, and with the ambush in Chicago on record, even allies of the United States had looked on with skepticism.

The president could endure it no longer and snapped off the television.

"We can't stop them if they come across the border, can we, Ken?"

"The delay in moving in our sea power has seriously damaged our reaction time. Our pilots and the Japanese are running nonstop from Kempo, they're beat, and it's even harder on the aircraft."

"So there's not a whole hell of a lot we can do about it," the president finished for him.

"We have options, Mr. President.

"Ken, you know me—until they threaten to push the Second Infantry Division into the sea, *that* option will not be discussed, not with the world thinking we're behind these disasters."

Admiral Fuqua stood and paced to the far wall and looked at a portrait of General George Washington. Compton had briefed the admiral on his SEAL- and salvage-team losses at Pearl and knew his anger.

"Admiral, do you have something on your mind?" the president asked.

"I see no way out of this outside of nuclear weapons' use."

The room erupted as most thought that the admiral might be intentionally goading the president.

"Gentlemen, let the admiral voice his opinion," the president said.

"We can't take more carrier groups from their current deployments," he said, turning to face the room. "Hell, it would be over by the time we got them in theater anyway. But we can"—the admiral turned again and faced the president directly—"pull everyone out."

The gathered military men just stared at the admiral as if he had lost his mind. However, Niles could see the brilliance of the statement as soon as the admiral had said the words. He nodded as he listened.

"As a navy man, I know what we face in Korea is a funnel which will slide thousands upon thousands of young men into uncertain hostilities, and in the end someone, maybe even us, will push that button we've feared since we were crawling under school desks as children during air-raid drills."

The president watched the admiral walk back to his chair and sit. He swallowed and looked from face to face.

"In the end, we would prevail—I truly believe that—but at what cost? I say we place the emphasis on the North Koreans by pulling back the Second ID and the South Korean army. Pull them all the way back south of Seoul and let them set up defensive positions there, and let the world see us do it."

"Brilliant!" Niles said, to let the admiral know that he, for one, did not think he was nuts *or* defeatist.

"That just may read like an invitation to Kim Jong Il to come through the door quicker than he otherwise would," General Caulfield said.

"Maybe," said the president. "But it would go a long way to demonstrate to the Chinese and Russians that we have no designs on Korea, or themselves." He looked at Niles, knowing that the emphasis for getting them out of this mess might have just landed in the Group's lap. "How soon can we get the orders out to the Second ID to pull back from the DMZ?"

"They can be on the move in six hours. I'll order the overflights stopped, border patrols only. Admiral, you can order the two carrier task forces to hold station at their current location."

"And I'll announce to the world that we're pulling back. Let's just hope we can take the sword out of the Korean hand without getting ourselves cut to pieces," the president, said looking from the general to Niles.

The door opened and the president's secretary entered and handed him a communiqué.

As the men in the room watched, he crumbled the paper and tossed it onto the coffee table, almost smiling at the way things were developing.

"The Russians are claiming they have downed a U.S. Air Force 777 cargo-conversion aircraft in their airspace." He looked up with red eyes. "They claim they have some of the wreckage in their possession and proof that the aircraft was attempting to use the Audio Wave against their nation."

"Impossible! The air force didn't—"

The president glared at the air-force chief of staff. "It doesn't matter, General. Whoever this Coalition is, they just outplayed our move."

Niles looked down, knowing that the Coalition might finally have severed any chance they had at ending this thing peacefully.

THE DMZ (THE BORDER BETWEEN NORTH AND SOUTH KOREA)

Major General Ton Shi Quang had relieved the previous commander after the artillery exchange between the Americans and the forward shock troops. As he sat in his command bunker, he saw that his troop and tank buildup was nearly complete. He saw that overwhelmingly he outnumbered the two armies gathering to the south and knew he could crush them within two days without help from the American naval and air forces. He outgunned the Americans five to one in tanks. The deciding factor would be as it always was—the ground soldier. In that arena, he had a fifteen-to-one superiority, and unless the United States and their southern lackeys did the unthinkable, he would be in Seoul having lunch on the second day of battle.

"Intelligence report from Pyongyang," his orderly said stiffly.

The general did not like to have his thoughts disturbed and gave the colonel a stern look as he reached for the flimsy paper.

American defensive troops of the Second U.S. Infantry Division appear to be falling back from frontal positions. The South Korean army, after initial hesitation, has also begun what seems a possible withdrawal. Stand down from all offensive operations until tactic can be analyzed.

The lead military-council member of the Great Leader's inner circle had signed the message.

"Analyzed? This is obviously a trick by the imperialists!

What are they thinking in Pyongyang? Are those old fools falling for this? They only wish us to believe they are falling back. This is obviously a ruse to create more time to bring up what I suspect will be a preemptive strike on our People's Army by nuclear forces!"

The colonel shot a worried look at his commanding general; the horror of what he was saying was clearly etched on the man's sharp features.

"I'm sure the council has taken that into consider—"

"I will not allow the Americans a first-strike opportunity here." The general looked at his watch. "Inform command that we are in receipt of the message."

The colonel hesitated before departing with his orders.

"Go!"

"That is all, General? Pyongyang will want to know how you plan to deploy for defensive purposes."

The general slapped the large map table in front of him, knocking several of the small models from their positions.

"Defensive positions?" the general said loudly. "That particular word has no meaning for me. Now send off the message that we are in receipt of the new orders, and that is all!"

The general watched him go. If the American forces were actually moving back from the lines, it would give his armor a running start and thus be unstoppable. He placed the disturbed models back onto the table and they formed a three-tank regiment spearheaded right at the American and South Korean lines. If the Americans did not start this, he would.

HOTEL DE PALAZZO
ROME, ITALY

One of the oldest and finest hotels in Italy was emptied of guests upon the Coalition's arrival; in the small print of several international contracts, they owned it outright. They also owned most of the local police, and that, coupled with the ties they had with certain people in the Vatican hierarchy and the Italian government, allowed them a free hand in running their illicit operations.

William Tomlinson stared out the window at the Coliseum only six blocks away. Their Group had its roots not far from that ancient and revered place. The Juliai had learned early on in that wealth was power, the only true power on earth.

"How excited you must be, William—finally, the Atlantean Key within reach," Dame Lilith said from her chair in the main parlor of the suite.

Tomlinson turned from the window and his view of the Coliseum. He smiled politely and took in the woman's lovely features.

"Yes, of course. I was just lost in thought. The thing that is most exciting to me is the knowledge that we will soon be stepping fifteen thousand years into the past, our past and no one else's. To the place our ancestors once dwelled and where our blood was born."

"It's so sad that there are not many pure-bloods left in the Coalition. We have been watered down so. At least those that remain will have this opportunity, all because of your foresight, William."

"Too kind, Lilith," he said as he turned and walked to the bar.

"Something far more pressing is troubling you. Tell me?"

"It's Dahlia's report. I received the full text this morning just as we landed. The plate map was not recovered," he said, turning to Dame Lilith. He held up a hand when she suddenly sat up in her chair. "Calm, calm . . . Dahlia recovered something far better and less time-consuming than the plate map. We have a true map. A map made by the very man the plate was sent to. However, you are right—I am troubled. The American government recovered the plate. It is now in the possession of the same group of people that have sheltered Laughlin and Rothman."

"William, this is indeed serious. They will come after the Key. How soon is Dahlia arriving in Africa?"

"Soon, very soon," he said as he poured Lilith and himself a drink. "We may have an opportunity here. The people of this secret group that have become such a troublesome lot will undoubtedly lead the charge to Africa for the diamond. As a matter of fact, Dahlia has virtually guaranteed it," he said as he turned and offered Lilith her drink.

"What are you suggesting?"

"Without the risk of losing the Key, I want these men eliminated. Dahlia is of the same opinion." Tomlinson sipped his drink and then smiled, embarrassed for what he was about to say. "You've known me since I was a child, Lilith. I have never shown fear in any arena. However, these men that have been in the way since Ethiopia . . . well, I fear them. It's like they have been placed here just to stop me."

"I've never thought you a mystical person, William. These men just happened to be in the wrong place at the wrong time. A chain of events allowed them to become very lucky people. That is all."

"Thank you for easing my mind, but I would still feel better having them out of the way. Dahlia believes an ambush could be set up without endangering the diamond. As you know, I am an opportunist. This is one of those—"

A knock sounded at the door, interrupting Tomlinson. He placed his drink on the sideboard and straightened his suit jacket. He composed himself and answered the door.

Caretaker half bowed in greeting. August Nelson was behind him and looked very much agitated over something.

"Gentlemen, we were just discussing the plans for the recovery of the Key. Come in, please."

Caretaker entered, followed by Nelson. He bowed and smiled at Lilith and then turned to Tomlinson. Before he could say anything, August Nelson blurted out a stream of words.

"The American president has done the unexpected, William. He is—"

"Please, Mr. Nelson, calm yourself. I will inform Mr. Tomlinson of the facts. There is no need to be so emotional."

Tomlinson looked from the red-faced Nelson to the calm demeanor of Caretaker, a man he had never once seen flustered.

"It seems the American president has withdrawn his forces from the disputed line in Korea, sir."

"Impossible! He would never allow the North Koreans into the South; the United Nations and South Korea would crucify him."

"It seems to be gaining a widening support base in the

United Nations. It is seen as a sign of nonaggression by the Americans."

"The plan banks on a conflict, William. This is serious, very serious."

Tomlinson looked almost sadly at Nelson. The man was not as strong as he had hoped. He would have to deal with that issue another time.

"Gentlemen, please sit down and have a drink." He gestured to the bar, and Nelson made a beeline to it. Caretaker sat in a chair.

"There is some rather good news: it seems the Russians have bought into the ruse you created with the Wave aircraft. They were nowhere near the UN council chambers today."

"You see, Nelson, you have gains and then losses, but the market always settles." Tomlinson retrieved his drink from the sidebar and then glanced at August Nelson. The man would have to be replaced with another true-blood, one who had a little more intestinal fortitude. Reactions like his worked like a plague around other members of the Coalition.

"William, this is not the stock market. We are dealing with dangerous nations here who have armies under their command. I wish now that—"

"I think it's the right time to allow you into the world of intelligence. Both you and Caretaker have been most patient."

Caretaker sensed a shade of patronization in Tomlinson's tone but decided not to comment.

"The war in Korea will start very, very soon, gentlemen. It will happen regardless of what the American administration does or does not do. They are helpless in the matter. North Korea will attack."

"You have an assurance of this?" Caretaker asked.

"I have more than that, my dear Caretaker. I have the general in command of all North Korean forces, Major General Ton Shi Quang."

Caretaker leaned forward in his chair, a surprised look on his face.

"I am rarely, if ever, surprised in this position, Mr. Tomlinson. However, in this case I am happy to say I did not see that statement coming. Someday I would like to learn how you gained access to a closed society and purchased the services of this man. Please, is there is anything else?"

Tomlinson looked at Dame Lilith and wondered if he should impart the knowledge he had confessed to her about Dahlia's ambush plans. Lilith saw his look and shook her head almost imperceptibly.

"No, Caretaker, I believe you are now up to date on everything in my bag of tricks." Tomlinson smiled and once again walked to the bar. "Now please, Caretaker, toast the recovery of what we have sought for thousands of years, the Atlantean Key."

"For that item alone, Mr. Tomlinson, I will indeed have a drink."

"Imagine no more country-versus-country nonsense. Only one system to govern, a new Reich that the people can call whatever they choose, and everyone working together to fulfill a destiny that was cut short fifteen thousand years ago." He handed Caretaker his drink.

"To Atlantis," they toasted.

CHAPTER THIRTEEN

EVENT GROUP CENTER
NELLIS AIR FORCE BASE, NEVADA

Ryan had pulled the shift security from the complex and ordered a full detail to meet Jack and Carl at the airfield. Twenty heavily armed men accompanied the two men and their very valuable cargo. The large group took no chances as they entered the massive, dilapidated hangar of the main gate for the complex.

Ryan and Mendenhall met the colonel and captain at the elevator. The two men and their security looked small in the cavernous lift used for the transport of large artifacts into the underground facility.

"Lieutenant," Jack said as he stepped from the lift.

"Colonel, Captain, exciting trip, I understand?"

"It seems it was mission standard for us anymore," Everett said as he spied Virginia Pollock exiting the elevator from the complex below.

"Glad to have you two back in one piece. You had us worried, as usual," she said, approaching the men.

"Well, here's what the hubbub was about." Carl handed her a large case.

She accepted the case and then looked at the two officers. "All those deaths for this . . ." She handed the case to

Mendenhall. "Will, make sure Pete Golding gets this right away down on level eighteen, lab six; he's waiting on it."

Mendenhall took the case and Ryan made his exit with him.

"The president has placed a lot of emphasis on making sure the Coalition doesn't get their hands on the diamond. Niles wants us to get it and has promised you all the support you need."

Jack nodded and started for the elevator. "So the president has bought in fully to the theory of the quakes?"

Virginia pushed the Down button on the pneumatic elevator for level seven. She then related the horrid facts of the Tomlinson raid.

Jack and Carl were silent as they stepped into the elevator. Virginia followed and the doors closed.

"The Russians downed what they believe is a U.S. Air Force aircraft carrying strange equipment. They say it was transmitting the same type of audio signal as the tape in the Sea of Japan."

"These people are still a step ahead of us, maybe even two or three," Everett said as the elevator arrived at level seven.

"Mr. Everett, get with Ryan and give me a duty roster and pick a strike team ready to leave as soon as the science teams get this plate thing figured out. Virginia, what archaeologist and experienced dig people can you afford to part with?"

"Well, I think we'll send the same people that were just there, Sandra Leekie and her team."

"That's fine, but cut it to bare bones, Doctor. I don't want any kids on this trip."

"Do you expect the Coalition to find you, Jack?"

Collins had started to turn and leave for the security offices but stopped short.

"Ask the FBI if these unconscionable bastards do the unexpected. Yes, Virginia, they will be there waiting for us. They failed once getting access to that diamond; I don't think they will stop now."

The fifteen-thousand-year-old bronze plate, centered on the lab table in the middle of the room, was a mystery to the brilliant minds studying it. Several technicians from the Archaeological Studies, Forensics, and Mathematical Engineering departments surrounded the amazing find, mystified by its workings.

The plate itself was unremarkable in its design. It was comprised of two sheets of thinly plated bronze sandwiching a thinly shaved quartz crystal. A 3-D image supplied by Europa was projected onto a wall screen, and all the other departments, including Mechanical Engineering and Nuclear Sciences, were studying the strange plate from their own labs.

Linguistics experts were poring over the symbols etched into the bronze facing of the plate, while engineers examined a small clamshell-like protuberance in the exact center of the object. The clamshell bulge was on both sides of the plate and was three inches in diameter.

Pete Golding and Sarah McIntire had stopped by the lab to see the amazing find brought back by Jack and Carl. They were taking a break from leading the scroll search with one hundred others. They stayed back and out of the way as the other qualified scientists assigned to the plate map studied it and spoke quietly among themselves.

Pete stepped back farther to get a look at the strange design. What little hair he had was askew and he was chewing on a pencil. He was just getting ready to turn away and retrieve Sarah when a thought struck him out of nowhere. He turned slowly and looked closer at the clamshell centerpiece. He cleared his throat.

Martha and Carmichael were there, too. They were studying a linguistics report of the strange symbols when they heard Pete trying to get everyone's attention.

"The centerpiece of the object—have you, ladies and gentlemen, formed an opinion on this?"

Virginia Pollock, who was sitting next to the two Ancients, turned toward the director of the computer center.

"As with the other symbols on the facing of the object, the conclusion is it's a three-D symbol for the sun. If you look closely at the etched portions of the plate, the exact match is the sun, which is clearly next to that of the quarter moon. The lines at the center of the sun may just be artwork placed there by the whoever etched the symbols."

"Clamshell," Pete mumbled, still chewing on his pencil.

"Excuse me?" one of the design engineers asked from his spot next to the map.

Not all those in attendance inside the lab understood what Pete had said.

Sarah tapped Pete on the shoulder and pointed to the pencil in his mouth.

Pete slowly understood and removed the pencil. "The sun, as you've deemed it, in the center of the plate—it resembles a clamshell aperture."

Martha glanced at the strange-looking director of the computer center and then tapped Carmichael on the arm to get his attention.

"Professor Golding, your science is an exact one, but sometimes ancient technologies are not. If you would step closer to the plate, you will see that the etched lines on the depiction of the sun are perfectly matched. No one in antiquity could get separate sections of metal to match so perfectly that there is no discernible separation between the two. Believe me, Professor: the lines are etched into the bronze."

Pete looked at the scientist from the Mechanical Engineering Department and then stepped closer to the plate. Sarah bit her lip, knowing that the Golding was overstepping his territory. She looked at Virginia and gave her an uneasy smile.

Pete looked very closely at the bulge and then at the symbol for the sun at the bottom of the large plate. He stepped to the opposite side of the lab table and looked at the bulge from that side and then at the bottom of the plate. There were no symbols there. There were, however, two small points of bronze protruding from each of the plate's lower corners.

"Lens cap," he mumbled.

"Pete, don't you and Sarah have a team on level fifteen you are supervising?" Virginia asked.

"Wait, please." Carmichael Rothman was looking at Pete intently. "Young man, did you say 'lens cap'?"

Pete looked up from the plate and pushed his glasses back up his nose. "Yes," he said, trying to focus on the older man.

"Pete, I appreciate you help here, but this is not a clamshell aperture," said an exasperated engineer. "The edges fit too perfectly. Look." He produced a small jeweler's screwdriver, placed the tip on one of the eight line etchings, and probed around it. He tried to push in and lift, but the small screwdriver could find no place to wedge against for advantage in prying the section apart. "You see, it would have to have been engineered on a modern CNC machinist tool."

Pete looked from the engineer to Sarah, who was just getting ready to pull the tired computer man from the lab. She did not try, though, as Pete shook his head.

"The symbols on the front are not duplicated on the back. The only things on the reverse side are the clamshell—or sun, if you prefer—and the two small points sticking out of the lower corners of the plate."

"We noticed the points of bronze. They are possibly casting marks from when the plate was forged," the same engineer said as he looked at the others for support. He received nods of agreement from everyone.

"I'm sorry, I don't believe those two points are casting marks from a mold. They do resemble something I work with quite often, though."

"What is that, young man?" Martha asked.

Pete looked around the lab until he found what he was looking for. He smiled uneasily as he unplugged a handheld buffer and then looked at the electrical cord. Then he cut the three-pronged plug off with an exacto knife. Then he split the black cord in two, one positive and one negative. Then he attached one end to the lower-left piece of bronze and then repeated the process on the right. He wrapped the wire around them several times.

"I cut the plug off because I don't want to fry what's inside . . . if anything. So . . ." Pete looked around and saw what he wanted. "Young lady, can you pass me the battery from that digital recorder, please?"

The technician removed the back of the recorder and handed Pete a double-A battery.

"Most kind, thank you. This may be enough, but I'm not sure." Pete placed one end of the wire on the positive side of the battery. Then he looked up at the men and women around him. "Okay, here we go," he said, as he placed the other end of the split wire onto the negative post.

As all eyes focused on the plate, nothing happened. Pete adjusted the wires on the battery for a better connection and . . . still nothing.

The man from mechanical engineering who was closest to the plate smiled. "It's all right, Pete; at least you eliminated the idea from future consideration. The lines are just lines and not separate sections." He tapped the bulge in the plate. "They are too precise to—"

A small *swish* came from the plate and several people actually gasped in surprise. The small clamshell spun in a circle from right to left and opened, revealing a crystal protuberance front and back.

"Well, in a way you were right—the engineering did not allow for the sections to separate, but it did allow for them to expand and open. Huh!" Pete said as he stepped closer to the plate and looked.

"I'll be damned," the engineer said.

"Don't feel bad—your tapping the aperture may have freed it. After all, it has probably been fifteen thousand years since it was last opened."

Sarah looked from Pete to Virginia. They both smiled as they realized that sometimes experts could be too close to the objects they studied, while an outsider could come in and see something they could not. Pete Golding, though, was not an outsider; he was a man who had a brain that could think far faster than most. He was almost on a level with Niles Compton.

Pete released the electrical cord and the clamshell remained open. Then he stepped to the front of the plate and examined it again.

"These symbols don't match any other in the history archives and not even those hieroglyphs we studied direct from the scrolls we uncovered?" He turned to face the two Atlanteans. "And these symbols mean nothing to either of you?"

"We are not familiar with them, no."

The professor of ancient languages, who had spent several hours with Carmichael and Martha learning the basics of the dead tongue of Atlantis and who had used a combination of written words and hieroglyphs to make it easier to study the written language of the scrolls, turned back to the plate and pushed his hand through his hair.

"We're stumped, Pete."

Pete walked up to the plate and ran his fingers first over the symbols and then slowly over the center hole, where the sandwiched crystal protruded. The other technicians looked at him and shook their heads, thinking that the computer wiz was only in the way. His fingers slowly felt the deep lines of the symbols and then he stepped back and looked at them.

"Okay, Virginia has explained we're extremely short on time. Therefore, we must find the closest examples of what they are through other means. First, let us concentrate our . . . excuse me . . . you must concentrate your efforts on the crystal inside. The bulge at the center, front and back, is key. We now know that, since the clamshell aperture was there for protecting. My guess is that it is a lens of some sort." He looked around, hoping that the other scientists were not taking offense.

"Keep going, Pete, you seem to be on a roll," Virginia said from her seat.

"Europa, query," he said as he straightened up and examined the 3-D virtual reality projected on the screen. "Analysis of x-ray of crystal between the two bronze halves, please."

"Exact number of crystal flaws found in five separate depths of crystal is seven billion fifty-two thousand."

"Explain depths analysis, please."

"Flaws found at 1.7, 1.8, 2.7, 2.9, and 3.1 centimeters of plate crystal depth and 1.9, 2.1, 2.5, 2.8, and 3.2 centimeters in width."

"This can't be," Sarah said from her position in front of the projection. "If the crystal is flawed with natural fractures or formation abnormalities, they wouldn't be located at exact depths and would be far more random in the width; they would be throughout the crystal and certainly not at certain depths only."

Pete Golding listened to Sarah's expert geological explanation but did not comment. Instead, he examined the flaws as seen from the front and the side projections as sent through Europa from an electron microscope and x-ray imager.

"Gentlemen and ladies, let's return our efforts now to the symbols one last time. As I said before, we will find their closest relations in the linguistics family from other languages and symbols from the ancient world."

Several members of Ancient Languages Department looked from one to another, but they stepped aside in deference to Pete's genius for thinking beyond the norm.

"Europa, query: the three symbols arrayed at the bottom of the plate below the exposed crystal at the center." Pete removed a small penlight from his many pens and pencils in their plastic holder in his shirt and clicked it on and shone the bright beam through the center hole, producing nothing but regular light on the other side. "You stated in your report earlier that there is no reference in the linguistics historical record for any word, symbol, or hieroglyphs known, is that correct?"

"Correct, Dr. Golding."

"Query: what are the closest hieroglyph or symbol matches to the three symbols as taken from all known civilizations throughout history, preferably the earliest examples?"

"Formulating," answered the womanly voice of Europa.

Sarah walked over to stand next to Martha and Carmichael and looked at them with a questioning glance. They both shrugged, but were also curious as to where Pete was going with this.

"There is only one familiar symbol recognizable in the historical-linguistic record. The centerline symbol designated number two bears resemblance to ancient Sumerian symbol for 'storm,' as taken from hieroglyph discovered outside present-day Iraq in 1971."

Pete ran the word repeatedly in his mind as he paced in front of the image on the screen. Then he walked over and shone his penlight through the hole once more. Then he smiled and stood straight and looked at Sarah.

"There's no way those flaws could have been a fluke of nature and just happened to be formed naturally?"

"Impossible. I couldn't even begin to calculate the odds of their being at five exact depths."

"This is impossible," Pete said, smiling. "Europa, query: at current magnification level of electron microscope, is there any indication of any other flaws in the sandwiched crystal?"

"None, Dr. Golding."

"Please order the electron microscope to repeat the side scan of the interior crystal and raise the magnification power on each pass and continue side scan until a flaw in its thickness is detected. Continue until magnification power hits its limit."

"Pete, you're losing me and everyone else here," Sarah said, but as she looked from Pete to the smiling couple next to her, she became aware that all three were thinking the same thing.

"Microscopic scan complete. Five distinct engineered sections found at setting one million times power."

"What?" one of the engineers exclaimed. "That's impossible. We're not even capable of this today!"

Sarah and most of the others were confused by all this.

"Europa, enlighten our audience as to the sections mentioned."

"Five sections, engineered as separate crystal shavings, placed together as one flat surface, indicating that earlier flaws are not flaws as previously reported, but surface symbols etched onto the five separate crystal plates."

The projection changed and Europa produced an animated image showing the sides of five separate crystal surfaces being placed together to form one flat, almost-solid crystal plate. The image rotated and they saw what they had once thought were flaws inside the sandwiched crystal plates at the depths had Europa reported.

"That is impossible. Even today, we cannot get two surfaces that flush without major separation throughout each of the joining surfaces. The engineering is impossible!"

Pete was looking at the rotating image and smiling.

"Nonetheless, there it is." He turned and looked at Martha and Carmichael. "An amazing race of people, to be sure."

"But why do this? What in the hell is this thing?" the head of Linguistics asked.

"I believe what we're looking at is an ancient visual disk. Just like what we use today in the computer center," Pete said. "Can we get some electrical leads and attach them to the bronze connection at the back of the plate, please."

As the engineers rolled over a large box that supplied twenty-five thousand volts of mobile electricity, Pete tried his best to explain his theory.

"The middle symbol that Europa said has a resemblance to an ancient Sumerian hieroglyph for 'storm' . . . Well, if you see what I see, it becomes apparent. The rounded objects that look like hills or mountains are actually clouds; thus, Europa saw the "storm' of Sumerian origin. However, the zigzagging line beneath is a stumper. I believe that it's not just any storm, but an electrical storm. Lightning, if you will. And this line here," he pointed to the thin line with two dots on the front and the back, "we didn't recognize it because it's a view from the side of this very bronze plate before us. See here, in the center of the plate are the two crystal protuberances. Ladies and gentlemen, what those are is a lens, pure and simple."

"A projector?" Sara asked.

"Not only have we a projector but also video disk inside the projector, dear Sarah. And not only that—I believe, rudimentarily speaking, of course people who invented this were using a rough form of electrical power."

Several people started saying things like *impossible* and *no way,* but Pete only smiled while looking around the room.

"Can we also bring the portable laser over, please," he asked the mechanical engineers, who did as he asked. "Europa, remove the current images from the screen, please." The images of the plate vanished. "Could we dim the lights? I really don't know how efficient this will be."

The lights lowered and Pete attached the two electrical leads to the sides of the large plate. "What we are doing is supplying electricity to the conduit of the device—in this case, bronze, highly conductive and efficient, more so than our small battery. By doing this, I believe, we are exciting something that was placed on what we thought were small scratches or flaws on each of the crystal plates that are meshed together. Now we will place the laser and shine it through the aperture of the centerline crystal, or what the Ancients used as a lens."

Pete turned on the electrical power and then maneuvered the laser head close to the plate and centered it on the lens. On the other side, a very blurry light appeared on the screen. Pete first pulled the laser back from the hole and the projection worsened. Then he adjusted again, this time bringing the laser head up until it almost touched the crystal protrusion. Suddenly the image cleared and about twenty schematic drawings appeared. Map locations and what looked like numbers and more symbols. However, as the images solidified, they could clearly see that the center of the picture was an exact duplicate of the ancient map recovered from Westchester, New York. The Mediterranean was there, and located in its exact center were the ringed islands of Atlantis.

"Can we bring up the electrical power, please, by say, oh, five thousand volts?"

Suddenly they heard a low swishing sound and the lens turned in its plate, swirling outward and simultaneously becoming more concave. Then the green and blue images rounded and the pictures seemed to leave the projector screen altogether and form a three-dimensional hologram. The gathered scientists were stunned as locations in Africa, Spain, and then Atlantis itself floated in front of their eyes. They could even make out a huge aqueduct that rose a thousand feet above the sands of the Nile Delta and stretched across the Mediterranean to the island.

"The billions of microscopic scratches inside the sandwiched crystals—when put together, they form these holographic images. When separate, they are flat and meaningless. The lens must be layered in differing thicknesses to create the hologram. The mathematics involved in that alone are purely in the realm of Einstein. Their crafting of crystals is one of the keys to their civilization."

One of the four mathematicians clapped once and actually stepped inside the huge hologram.

"What do you see, Professor Stein?" Virginia asked.

"When Pete mentioned Einstein, it struck me. These symbols at the bottom of the hologram—I believe it is a key to their mathematics system. It's very close to the system we have today. You won't believe this, but I think these here . . ." He pointed to the symbols in the center of the floating hologram and then suddenly pulled back as he felt foolish thinking that he could touch the image. "Anyway, I will swear on my PhD that these symbols are their prime numbers. The same as ours as demonstrated by Euclid in 300 BCE—two, three, five, seven, eleven, thirteen, seventeen, nineteen, twenty-three, twenty-nine, and so on."

"And these numbers dead center of the map in the Med, and these two sets, one in Egypt, one in Ethiopia, and one other on the outermost eastern ring of Atlantis . . . this is where Crete would be today?" Pete asked.

"I don't know yet, but I think we can figure this out rather quickly. These were brilliant and advanced people, but now that we know they used the same prime numbers as us, we can crack this thing rather quickly."

Virginia walked up to the hologram and ran her hand through the green and blue images. Then she focused on two areas of the Atlantis map.

"This area looks like it could be the only remaining part of Atlantis above water; you're right, it could only be Crete." Then she moved her hand and indicated the area that Stein had indicated in Egypt. "I'm sure—no, positive that these are coordinates. Moreover, Professor, you are right, they do use the same prime-numbers system as our own. These are longitude and latitude."

"You're right, young Virginia. If I read this right, it's 25.44 north and 32.40 south. Europa, can you verify location of coordinates, please."

"The indicated coordinates 25.44 N, 32.40 S, is location in southern valley in the nation of Egypt, valley is named on local and world maps as Valley of the Kings, named so for the—"

"The Valley of the Kings," Martha said from her chair, cutting short Europa's lengthy answer.

With so many images emanating from the ancient disk, the one that took up the largest space was the giant depiction of the ringed continent. The great center of it was the capital, and far below it—miles down, it looked to be—were great caverns with a multitude of tunnels and passages.

Sarah saw something that caught her attention.

She put her hand through the projected image of Egypt, then stepped to her left and looked at the symbols surrounding modern-day Crete and the Valley of the Kings. Another image showed what looked like giant stairways spiraling down into the earth, and at the bottom of these, one in Crete, one in Egypt, were great tunnels running to the centermost island of Atlantis. *No,* she corrected herself, *running* under *Atlantis.*

"What in the hell are we looking at here, Sarah?" Pete asked.

"From the scrolls that we've deciphered thus far, we have learned that slaves were abducted in many countries, mysteriously disappearing from time to time. Now look at this, the Valley of the Kings, where the pharaohs were laid to rest before their trip to the underworld. Now, I think we may have found the front and back door to that underworld—doors to a city and civilization that sank almost fifteen thousand years ago."

Virginia was not listening. She once more ran her hand through the floating hologram, this time through the terrain of Africa.

"For the moment, everything outside of the scrolls must be placed on hold. I need the exact coordinates for this location here. My guess is it's Ethiopia," Virginia said as she turned to face the others. "Pete, thank you for leading us through this. You can poke your nose in anywhere you want from now on."

Pete reddened as he nodded his thanks.

"I will now alert the president and Director Compton in Washington that I am officially calling an Event alert." She turned to Pete once again. "You will have to do without Sarah for the time being. Get with the Cartography Department and Europa and get me those exact coordinates in Ethiopia ASAP, I mean right now!"

Men and women started to move and Pete shot through the door as Virginia picked up the phone and pushed the Intercom button.

"Attention to all departments: an Event alert has just been called. I need Colonel Collins and his discovery team to report for briefing in ten minutes. This is no drill."

The Event Group went into action on all levels of the complex. Alice would get the official guidelines for the discovery team to Europa, and then orders would be sent out to be displayed on departmental computers for whatever actions their divisions had to take.

Most of the people left the room, but Sarah stayed where she was, looking at a strange pattern of lines that were grouped into fours. One of them was shaped roughly like the North American continent, while the other groupings were unfamiliar. For some reason, that same flickering thought entered and then left her memory just as fast. She decided that it was nothing of value at the moment and moved off.

Down in security, Jack heard the announcement of the alert and looked at Carl from over his desk.

"Only sixteen hours; not bad," Jack said.

"So, you expect to meet our blond-haired friend in Ethiopia, huh?"

Jack had stood and started for the door, but he stopped at Carl's words and turned, and his look was intense.

"I'm banking on it, swabby."

Five minutes later, Collins and his discovery team were in logistics, drawing supplies for the dig in Ethiopia, when the next announcement went out.

"Attention, Event Order has been canceled; Discovery Team Phoenix security element is to stand down. Dig team will continue to prep. Colonel Collins and Captain Everett, report to the main conference room."

Everett looked at Jack. "What kind of happy horseshit is this?"

Virginia was pacing in front of the large monitor on the far left side of the conference table as Jack and Carl entered the room. Alice was jotting down notes and looked small as the only one sitting at the large table.

"Niles, Jack and Carl are here. You explain this to them."

Collins looked at Virginia as he took up position in front of the high-definition screen.

"Niles, what's going on? We have to be on a plane in about twenty minutes," Jack said, looking at Niles's tired face.

"Jack, you and your team have been ordered to stand down by the president. He feels that the importance of getting to that device dictates that this be a military recovery operation."

"What in the hell are we, rent-a-cops?" Everett asked angrily.

"Captain, you are not aware of the pressures we have building here. I was not about to add to the president's burden by arguing the point any more than I have." They saw Niles force himself to calm down. "Look, he knows what kind of a job you two did at Pearl; if it wasn't for that, he would never have fully realized the importance of this device the Coalition seeks. The Security Council would feel better having a Special Operations team sent in with Professor Leekie."

Jack knew there was no use in trying to argue the point. He took a deep breath to calm himself because he thought that Niles had more than likely fought hard and lost the argument with the president.

"Jack, have you heard of a Major Marshall Dutton?"

"Jesus," was all Jack said as he lowered his head.

"Who is he, Jack?" Carl asked.

"A career officer who's by the book and very, very, predictable. Niles, didn't they learn anything by having the FBI blown to hell and watching a SEAL team get decimated by these people? We're dealing with an element that knows how to do one thing particularly well, and that's killing."

"I know, but I can't sit here and argue with the Security Council about the classified details of our Group's security element and their prowess."

"The woman in Hawaii—she's not going to let us just waltz into Ethiopia and take the item they desperately need," Jack said as he looked around him and then back at Niles, on the monitor. "She's going to be there, Niles. Ethiopia isn't large enough to hide a bunch of Americans out digging in the sand."

"Colonel, this Major Dutton is being briefed on enemy capabilities. The situation outside of the actual dig is out of our hands." Niles looked around him as if he were a conspirator in a grand scheme. Then he faced the camera and raised his left eyebrow.

Alice smiled from her place at the table. "Pay attention here. I know that look," she whispered.

"Colonel Collins, during the formal request for the dig, the president spoke to Vice President Salinka of Ethiopia, who granted our request on the spot. He cited the deed you and your vacationing revelers pulled off by saving those students on the Blue Nile. He requested during the meeting that you come back to Ethiopia and receive his personal thanks for saving the life of his only daughter, Hallie. So, I am ordering a forty-eight-hour stand-down period for rest and recuperation for Captain Everett, Mr. Ryan, Mendenhall, and you. I figure you could go fishing again. Perhaps the same spot where you caught your last big one."

Collins and Everett turned away from the monitor and left the conference room without another word.

Virginia crossed her arms and looked at the screen. "I'm beginning to think you're picking up bad habits from those two."

"I haven't a clue as to what you're referring to. Now, I have to go, the North Koreans have just sent five more divisions south from Pyongyang."

With those words the monitor went dark, and with it the good feeling Virginia had about Niles and his subterfuge. Time was in short supply, and the Coalition and North Koreans controlled the clock.

AMERICAN EXPEDITIONARY FORCE
BAKER-ABLE, FOUR MILES EAST
OF ADDIS ABBA, ETHIOPIA,
FIFTEEN HOURS LATER

Dr. Leekie and her team of four Event Group specialists guessed the age of the ruined mosque at close to twenty-three hundred years. The once-great minaret and tower were but a ghost of the former structure, having fallen into the sands many hundreds of years before the founding of America. The foundations and walls that remained upright allowed the wind to howl through them with soft moaning sounds.

There were aspects of the mosque that confused the professor. The surviving walls had been constructed around the time of Christ, plus or minus a few hundred years, she estimated. However, the foundations were much older. Leekie could not say how old they were because they were built in a style she had never seen before. They were not Roman or Greek and certainly not Egyptian.

"Not much to look at, is it?" Ryan asked, lying prone between Jack and Carl as they watched through binoculars from a rise of sand.

"Not much," Everett mumbled in answer, gazing at the professor down below, about a quarter of a mile away.

Professor Leekie was taking measurements inside the ancient mosque with the help of two of her archaeology team and Will Mendenhall, whom Jack had snuck onto the team as an archaeological assistant. The Ethiopian laborers hired by the professor for the dig stood watching from under a date tree

"I have to tell you, Jack, I sure hope you're wrong on this one. The way that Major Dutton has his men deployed, they're very exposed. Mendenhall keeps looking around and he doesn't look too happy."

Collins lowered his binoculars and glanced at Everett, but hesitated as he noticed Ryan in his new desert wear, complete

with zinc oxide on his nose and a blue baseball cap with a
white kerchief attached to the back to protect his neck from
the sun. Jack shook his head and then raised the binoculars
again.

"Mr. Ryan, since you're dressed for it, go a thousand yards
to our rear and watch the desert to our back. If Dutton won't
deploy his men properly, we will."

Ryan turned and looked at the vastness of the wasteland
behind him with a frown. "What desert?" he joked.

Leekie was just rolling up a tape measure when Major Dutton
and his platoon leader approached.

"The laborers are going to have one hell of a time digging
through this sand. I would have expected better soil for a burial spot," Leekie said as she shaded her eyes and looked at the
stern countenance of Major Dutton. "Are you sure you have
the coordinates my people gave you correct?"

"In my line of work, miss, reading a map is fundamental,"
answered Dutton as he looked away.

"It's Professor, or, if you prefer, just Leekie."

"Ma'am, I would appreciate it if you would get on with
your survey. This was not supposed to take as long as it has."

"I won't go into a long and boring speech about the dan-
gers of ancient burial sites, Major. One wrong move and we
could have the entire area collapse under our feet."

"Well, have you *anything* to report?"

"Not yet," she answered, and then she waved the diggers
over and used the interpreter to order several pilot holes dug
in the sand for her equipment to take readings.

"Major, we will be placing portable ultrasound units at the
base of what's left of the foundations and inside the remains
of the prayer tower. If there's something buried here, that
should tell us."

Jack had moved away from Everett and stood watching the
eastern part of the desert. The midday sun was a killer as he
stood still and listened. He had that old prickly feeling in his
stomach that told him they were not alone in the desert. For

the life of him, he could not tell where a potential enemy could hide. There was very little cover, just scrub and sand. The Blue Nile was more than a kilometer away, and any force coming from there would have given ample warning to the op team at the mosque site.

He shook his head as he started to turn, and as he did so he saw a mark in the sand. It was only a track, but it was one with which he was familiar. He did not want to lean down and examine it in case eyes were on him, so he removed his sunglasses and stretched, and as he did so he eyed the track more closely. It was a track in the literal sense: padded and linked; the sort of track used on a bulldozer or a backhoe. It had been brushed over but not completely wiped from the desert floor.

He replaced his glasses and turned back to the mosque. He had just confirmed that the dig team was not alone in the desert. Jack also knew that they had arrived too late.

As he casually walked back to where Everett was watching the camp and mosque, he reached into his pocket and felt the reassuring touch of his panic button.

Professor Leekie was getting frustrated with her equipment. She slapped at the laptop computer she had perched on the broken wall and cursed.

"This damn sand is so thick, it's almost impenetrable."

Dutton was just returning from the perimeter of the encampment, where he had checked on the positions of his twenty-five-man team. He shook his head after hearing Leekie curse her equipment. He saw her assistants return from laying their last remote ultrasound probe in the ruined tower of the mosque.

"Fifteen thousand years ago this area was forest land with compacted soil good for trees and plants. This equipment should have no trouble penetrating a few lousy feet of sand to reach the old earth beneath."

"What's the matter, Professor Leekie, modern science failing you?" Dutton asked with a smile, masking his ire.

"If we have to use the laborers to remove six or seven feet of sand before we can search, we'll be here forever. Let me try the probes attached to the walls; their base should be closer to that ancient topsoil—at least two thousand years closer."

Dutton heard Professor Leekie curse again:

"Damn, I'm getting a better reading, but there's still nothing there. No metal and no empty space that would indicate a shaft or cave. . . . Damn, I thought . . . Oh . . . Just damn!"

One of the Event Group assistants slapped his head with his palm. "Just a sec, Doc. I didn't switch on that last sonic probe."

Leekie shook her head and watched as the young man trotted back to the base of the prayer tower and vanished through the arched doorway. She wanted to shout out that it wasn't necessary but then decided that they had to be thorough, at least.

"All right, Doc, it's on," her assistant called out from the tower's opening.

Leekie switched the mode over to the frequency of the last probe. When the picture came onto the screen, she saw only a rounded blackness, as if she were looking into an old well. She tapped the laptop once again in anger.

"This thing, I swear—" She looked over at the base of the prayer tower. It was *round*. Then she looked at the screen again. The darkness there was round, too. She looked up suddenly. "There's nothing!"

"Well, maybe your people were wrong and this is just a wild goose—"

"No, I mean there's nothing there! The ultrasound probe isn't picking up anything under the sand inside the prayer tower but empty space!"

"What are you saying, Professor?" Dutton asked.

"I'm saying that the empty space I'm looking at is a covered shaft of some kind and it's deep. Damn, this may be the place. The mosque is here to cover the opening!"

"I was informed that no one knew about this spot until recently," Dutton stated. "You said earlier this burial site predates all religions. So why is there a mosque here?"

"Who knows? Maybe it wasn't a mosque to begin with. Maybe it was something else long ago and future generations just added to the foundations." Leekie's pretty face lit up with the answer to her earlier question concerning the age of the mosque and its foundations. "My God, that's why the foundation and wall ages don't match. Don't you see, it all fits! The people of this area, never knowing an original structure covered the ancient burial site, have used this place repeatedly. They never knew that a structure was here literally thousands of years before their civilization was even born."

"Okay, you sold me, Professor. What are you waiting for—let's recover this device," Dutton said, impatient to be out of there.

"I can't believe it," Leekie said, slamming her laptop closed. She smiled and jumped up and slapped the reserved Dutton on the shoulder. Then she ran to get the diggers to unearth the shaft inside the smashed prayer tower.

"She's excited about something," Jack said, adjusting his field glasses. "She must have discovered the burial site."

Carl watched Leekie as she hastily gave out orders; the reserved professor was more excited than any of her colleagues at Group had ever seen her before.

"Damn, Jack, you didn't say she gets to keep the diamond, did you?" Everett asked.

The Ethiopian diggers worked within the confined space of the ancient and collapsed prayer-tower base. The sun was now beyond its zenith, which cut the heat significantly. The sand was loose and hard to keep out of the hole they were digging. Finally, a shovel struck something hard with a loud ping—a sound that Leekie had always equated with finding buried treasure.

Three workers went to their knees and started shoveling the remaining sand out with their hands, until they hit a smooth surface. Leekie squeezed her way through the workers and knelt, brushing away the last of the sand.

"A cover stone," she said barely above a whisper.

"What's a cover stone, Doc," Mendenhall whispered beside her.

"In ancient times, civilizations such as the Egyptians and Greeks used cover stones to . . . well . . . cover anything buried. They were a deterrent to grave robbers and usually had curses written in their language warning an intruder that foul things and horrible deaths would befall them if they removed the cover stone."

"I guess that's you, huh, Doc?" Mendenhall asked, becoming nervous when she mentioned the word *curses*.

"Yes, that's me, Lieutenant."

Leekie instructed her team to remove the large, flat stone from the hole. Three Americans plus Will started pulling and prying with long-handled steel bars. The stone moved easily, and Leekie was surprised at the ease of removal after thousands of years.

"Can we get some lights over here?" she called out.

In minutes, several high-powered lights were shining down into the deep shaft. Leekie pulled a long tube filled with green liquid out of her pack. She snapped the inner casing inside the tube, then shook the liquid inside to life. When it began to glow bright green, she tossed it into the hole, where it soon struck bottom.

"There's flat flooring beneath. This is definitely a man-made excavation."

Mendenhall watched as Leekie removed a small device that resembled a flashlight from a case, turned it on, and pointed it down into the shaft. A thin red laser caught some of the swirling dust, making the beam visible. She turned it off after only a second and looked at the readout on the handle.

"It's only seventy-five feet deep. We can rappel down."

Mendenhall wished the colonel were there to lead this side of things, but he couldn't dwell on that now as he reached into his rucksack and brought out his gear used for a short rappel.

"That cover stone *was* blank, right, Doc?"

Ten minutes later, Mendenhall and two of the Green Berets had hammered their rope stakes deep into the soil closest to the tower's foundation. Then they tossed their ropes into the shaft. Will pushed off first from the edge, quickly followed by the two Special Ops soldiers.

Will let the rope play through his belly ring smoothly, hitting the sidewall only twice to cover the seventy-five feet to the bottom. He held his position two feet above and examined the packed earth in the green glow of the nightstick. He saw solid footing below and then allowed the final feet of rope to slide through his gloves. He hit bottom and immediately shone his flashlight around the large chamber. A moment later, the two soldiers hit bottom and joined him.

"Holy shit," Mendenhall said as his light caught the large and intimidating features of two statues along the far wall. "I think we hit the right spot."

"Now, that's impressive," one of the soldiers said as he looked at the closest twelve-foot statue. "Who is it?"

"Zeus," Mendenhall answered. "Listen," he said.

The two Special Forces men quieted as they shone their lights around the earthen room. The twin statues of Zeus, on either side of a long and dark corridor, watched them as they looked around. Will shone his flashlight down the eight-foot-high corridor and caught sight of a sloping ledge in the distance.

"When these guys dug a hole, they really dug one," Will said as he glanced down and noticed something in the outer limits of his light's range.

"What in the hell—" He leaned down and felt the dark earth. It was wet, and as he held his fingers to the light, he saw that they were red with blood. It had been there for a while but, without the sun to dry it out, remained moist. As he aimed his light around the ground, he saw that he was standing in a large stain that had yet to soak entirely into the soil.

One of the soldiers stepped past Will and started forward.

"Major Dutton wants this recon done ASAP," he said as Mendenhall reached out and tried to stop him.

Leekie had briefed every team member who was to enter the dig about the intelligence of ancient people when it came to protecting their property.

The staff sergeant had taken only four steps, and then his fifth footstep depressed a patch of soil covering a pressure plate with a connection to a sealed ceramic jar. The jar broke and released salt acid that had become stronger over the centuries. It burned through an ancient spun cable of copper, which snapped with a loud *ping* and sent a solid wall of razor-sharpened bronze down on top of the soldier.

Mendenhall watched in horror as the fifteen-foot-wide wall came down, slicing cleanly through the soldier's body, the backside of which stayed upright. The wall stayed in place as the horror of half a man peeled away from the wall. Will ran forward and started to bend down, but then he felt it was a waste of time. Instead, he placed his hands against the razor-edged wall and pushed up. The wall slid into the cave's ceiling as easily as a window blind. Once Mendenhall saw the other half of the soldier, he turned away, but not before he thought about the bloodstain that he'd seen moments before the sergeant tripped the booby trap.

Mendenhall slowly pulled the 9-millimeter from the back of his pants and looked around with renewed interest, knowing that they had not been the first to enter the cave.

Leekie was staring down into the hole and was becoming anxious when there was no immediate word from Mendenhall. She stood and brushed sand from her pants and then left to find her rapelling equipment. When she returned, she climbed to the edge of the tunnel after tying her rope off to the spikes.

She smiled at her American team members and was about to push off from the edge when the world exploded around her. She was thrown over the lip of the shaft by a blast she never saw coming. Her belly ring caught the rope but her momentum, plus her weight, was too much for the twist of rope to catch and she fell down the shaft.

She felt the rush of cooler air and came awake enough to reach for the rope. Her grasp slowed her momentum, cutting her speed in half, and then by a quarter, until her back struck the cool earth below.

* * *

The Special Ops team returned fire at the low-flying helicopters after the first volley of Hellfire missiles struck the low foundations of the mosque. The old AH-1 Cobra attack helicopters were legend in aviation and had earned the respect of ground soldiers the world over.

The Coalition pilots chosen for this ambush were very good. One was Israeli trained and the other British. They attacked Major Dutton's ground element with devastating effect. Twenty-millimeter explosive rounds struck positions and tore into flesh and sinew with ease. Dutton was lucky thus far, as only three of his men lay dead after the first pass of the two Cobras. The major saw that they could not stay out in the open and ordered the platoon to the protection of the crumbling mosque.

Once the major had dived behind one of the low foundations, he pulled out a small transmitter similar to the one Collins was carrying. He pushed the Transmit button and said two words: "Feather River!"

The first of the two Cobra gunships came low over a scrub dune and loosed a barrage of rockets that struck the crumbling walls of the mosque. Several soldiers and diggers were buried alive as the explosions tore through the ancient stone.

"Are you ready for the surprise of your life, assholes?" Dutton screamed at the second Cobra as it made a low pass and started strafing positions where his men had dug in.

There was a low rumble coming from the south and Dutton smiled in anticipation. *These jerks don't know who they're messin' with,* he thought.

Mendenhall and the remaining sergeant ran back the way they had come, jumping over the line of pressure devices that activated the deadly trap and separated the cave from the manmade excavation at the rear. The slope was all but forgotten when the attack started above them. Heavy thumping and explosions sounded as they came closer to the shaft. Mendenhall reached Leekie first and knelt beside her. The Special Forces sergeant looked up the shaft and saw a body fall against the opening and drape over the edge for a moment, then fall toward them.

"Look out!" he called.

The sergeant pulled Will and the unconscious Leekie clear of the hole just as one of the Ethiopian laborers hit the ground with a large hole in his chest. The young sergeant quickly ran forward and checked the man.

"He's dead," he said and then ran for one of the dangling ropes.

"Well, the doc's alive, just had the wind knocked out of her," Will said as he looked up. "Hey, don't do that!"

The sergeant had reached one of the ropes and had started to pull himself up, ignoring Mendenhall's order.

"Sergeant, I order you to—"

The sergeant suddenly fell back down. He hit with a thud and Mendenhall saw the perfectly round hole in his forehead.

"Dammit," he cursed. He then quickly gathered Leekie up and made for the darkness of the cave.

Collins was just getting ready to move down to assist the defense of the mosque but Everett forcibly stayed him with a hand.

"Jesus, Jack, we have company!" he said, looking through his binoculars.

Collins focused his field glasses to the left and saw several vehicles approaching the area between the low dunes. Then he looked skyward as the roar of jet engines screamed above them. Two F-15 Eagles were making a run on the attacking Cobras. This was Dutton's sure-fire backup plan. Jack again lowered the view of his glasses and saw that the vehicles had stopped and men were removing tarps from the backs of trucks.

"Damn! It's an ambush!" Jack said as he clenched his teeth. "They were expecting Dutton to have air cover!"

Everett followed Jack's lead and focused on the vehicles.

"SAMs!"

"Those Eagle pilots are sitting ducks," Collins said as he dropped his glasses and reached for the radio on his belt. He turned to the frequency that the expedition used and hit the Transmit button.

"American aircraft, this is friendly asset on the ground to

the south. Abort your attack run, I repeat, abort your run, we have mobile SAMs tracking you from—"

Collins stopped talking because he knew he was too late to save the Americans as four brown-painted missiles left their launch platforms.

The two F-15s screeched in low and the lead pilot targeted the first Cobra in line. He was about to fire his 20-millimeter cannon into the thin armor of the attack chopper when his threat receiver started going crazy. The American pilot was too late. As he started to abort his attack, two SAMs apiece tore into the planes' airframes.

Major Dutton, in his anger, actually forgot where he was for the briefest of moments and stood as the American aircraft disintegrated right before his eyes. As he cursed the trap that had been set, his body jerked as ten 20-millimeter rounds tore through his body. The stream of death reached out toward the mosque and the remnants of the Special Forces team.

"Ryan!" Jack called as he stripped his pack away, opened it, and pulled out several extra clips of ammunition for his Beretta. "Get over here."

Everett anticipated Collins's order and started stripping away all his unnecessary gear. He reached into his pack and pulled out an MP-5 with a folding stock. He took out a bandolier of ammunition and slung it around his neck. Then, as Ryan approached, he tossed him his pack.

"Weapon and ammo only," Everett said as he placed a magazine into the MP-5 and charged the handle, chambering a round.

"Damn, what in the hell did I miss?"

Jack reached into his pocket, pulled out his small transmitter, and hastily broke off the plastic cover that protected the red button inside. He pushed the button until it clicked and then tossed it away. He chambered a round into his Beretta and then looked at Ryan and Everett.

"We have a quarter mile to cover. I don't know if the doc is still alive, but I know Will must already be inside of whatever

Leekie found in the tower's base. We have one goal: make sure these bastards do not get the diamond. Ready . . . Go!"

The three men broke and ran toward the mosque.

Four additional mobile SAM vehicles arrived and took up station behind the same dune that had hidden the first four. A Land Rover broke free from the group of trucks. The small vehicle headed for the mosque and the attackers did not see the three Americans break and run for the site below. They kept to the backside of the dunes as they ran.

The Land Rover was equipped with a .50-caliber machine gun that was perched on the top, and a gunner started firing at the few men left inside the mosque's walls. The two Cobras kept swooping in and firing streams of 20-millimeter rounds into the piles of rubble.

The four-wheel-drive SUV stopped only fifty feet outside the walls and the gunner continued to fire into the ruins. One Special Forces sergeant stood and loosed a full magazine at the Coalition vehicle and managed to drop the gunner, while the rest of his bullets ricocheted off the Rover's armored skin and glass. A circling Cobra fired its remaining rockets and killed the sergeant before he could take cover again.

The vehicle slowly started to advance when the return fire from the mosque fell off to nothing. Three men jumped out and ran for cover. One of the Cobras took up a hovering position a hundred feet over the mosque and covered the ground team as they cautiously approached.

Suddenly, the last remaining Green Beret stood and arrogantly aimed a small tube at the hovering Cobra. The Stinger let loose with a screech as it left the launcher. The three men fired at the man who stood bravely watching the missile's exhaust trail as it tracked the Coalition's Cobra.

The Cobra pilot turned as soon as his missile-warning system lit up. He popped chaff and flares in an attempt to escape. However, the distance was far too short and the Stinger was fast. The small but powerful missile made impact on the engine housing on the starboard side and tore through into the engine itself. The warhead detonated and blew the engine and rotors entirely free of the airframe. The attack chopper simply fell one hundred feet into the largest section of the mosque and exploded.

The three Coalition men ducked the flying debris and then quickly recovered. The first man to fire took a quick and terrible vengeance for their downed pilot. He fired and struck the last of Major Dutton's ground team. The man fell through the tower doorway and lay dead in the sand. The three men stood and waved the second Cobra in to safeguard them as they checked the ruins for survivors.

Collins, Everett, and Ryan saw the Green Beret attack on the Cobra as they neared the last dune before they had to break cover.

"Good for him," Everett said as he saw the chopper explode.

The three men slowed and then slid into the sand as they came to the edge of last dune. Jack looked around and saw the last of the three attackers enter the tower base. He grimaced as he heard shots fired and screams of men as they were shot down in cold blood.

"Goddammit!" Jack said as he ducked back. "Dutton should have known better. With the mosque around them, they could have held off a brigade for half a damn day. We've got to take out that last Cobra."

"The only way we can do that is have a bunch of bullets shot at us."

"I've got to take the Land Rover; we need that fifty-cal."

"If we had just one damn grenade," Everett said.

"Mr. Ryan, you're the fastest. If I take out the fifty-gunner from here, can you sprint the distance before another takes his place?"

Ryan was breathing heavily and it wasn't just because they had run a quarter of a mile. He was frightened.

"No; I would have to start before you take a shot. It won't take long for someone to pop up and start shooting at us again. I'll run, and when he turns to fire I'll take him out. That will give me about twenty yards to cover and the time I need."

Collins looked at the small navy pilot and nodded.

Everett shook his head and tossed Jack the MP-5. He knew that Ryan had never lacked for balls, but what made him so convincing was that he was always scared to death. Scared men got the job done.

"Don't be shy about wasting ammo, flyboy—empty a full magazine of nine-mil through that sunroof of theirs," Everett said, and then he pulled out his own Beretta.

"Right," Ryan said as he looked at the colonel. "Don't miss, or my boat-surfing days are over."

Collins was silent as he extended the retractable stock and then wrapped the MP-5's shoulder strap around his forearm. He raised the rear site and adjusted for distance. Then he placed the stock into his shoulder.

"Okay, Colonel," Ryan said, taking three deep breaths. "Do some of that black-operations stuff you're famous for," he said as he suddenly burst free of the dune and ran as if the devil himself were chasing him.

As luck would have it, Ryan broke cover just as the remaining Cobra turned and gained a better vantage point. That was where his luck ended. The gunner on the top of the Land Rover must have had excellent instincts for danger, because before Ryan had taken five steps the gunner started turning the heavy weapon his way. To Ryan it was as if everything went into surreal slowness as he awaited the large-caliber rounds to hit his small body and tear it apart.

Jack kept both eyes open as he aimed. In his peripheral vision he saw the long barrel of the .50-caliber turn in Ryan's direction. Collins took a breath and then allowed half of the air out. Then he sighted again, taking his time. The sight was center-lined on the man's throat. Jack figured that the MP-5 would bolt up at the split-second discharge of the bullet, so he accounted for recoil and pulled the trigger.

Ryan saw the gunner smile as he continued to run. He knew the man had two fingers on the triggers of the machine gun, so he concentrated on running even faster. When he was sure he was done for, Ryan felt something buzz past his left ear. Just when he wondered if the colonel had forgotten about him, he saw the gunner's head snap back, and then the barrel of the

.50-caliber slowly rose into the air as the man fell back into the sunroof.

Ryan covered the remaining distance without a rational thought in his head. Just before he reached the Land Rover, he knocked his sunglasses off and then hit the bumper perfectly and bounded up and onto the roof. He actually started shooting before he had aimed into the cab, and several bullets hit the roof with a loud thud. Then he adjusted and fired directly into a man who was rising to take the gunner's place, and then he shot the driver, who was quite shocked at his own death.

Jack stood and along with Everett made a dash for the mosque. At the same moment, the last Cobra completed its turn and saw the two men break from the sand dune. It banked hard and made a run for the sprinting men.

Ryan saw the Cobra, but it had not seen him. He jumped through the sunroof and landed on something soft and wet. He took the handles of the large weapon and hoped he remembered how to fire the thing. He was short enough that he didn't need to lean down to bring the barrel into the air. He aimed at the attacking Cobra and fired. The first five rounds flew out of the barrel and then the weapon jerked out of Ryan's hands, almost breaking his fingers. He cursed and took the .50-caliber again and aimed. He braced himself this time and cut loose a long stream of bullets. He saw the tracers and adjusted his fire until it crossed paths with the slow-moving Cobra just as it started firing its 20-millimeter cannon at Collins and Everett. Ryan's fire hit the cockpit and smashed through the canopy glass and into the pilot and the weapons man.

Ryan's jaw fell as he watched the Cobra turn over and fall away. The rotors smashed into the scrub and the small helicopter erupted in a fireball.

Fifty yards away, Jack and Carl had stopped and were looking at the downed Cobra and then back at Ryan. The small navy man waved quickly and then ducked as small-caliber rounds struck the Range Rover from the rear. When Ryan turned, he saw ten men running in his direction. It crossed his mind for a split second to turn the machine gun on the charging

Coalition men, but he decided that he had pressed his luck just as far as he could for the day. He hopped out and ran to the mosque.

Collins and Everett ran through the opening of the tower base and slammed right into two Coalition men who had entered unseen. Everett slammed the man so hard that he hit the rounded wall, and when he rebounded toward Carl, he shot him three times. The other didn't live quite as long, as Collins in a last-second move raised his 9-millimeter and shot the man twice in the head. Everett almost shot Ryan as he entered the tower base.

Jack didn't wait for the others as he wrapped one of the three ropes around his right boot once and then took up a large loop in his right hand. Then, without hesitation, he pushed off into the shaft. Ryan and Everett followed. Ryan didn't know how to rappel without the proper equipment, so he just grabbed the rope and went hand over hand until it started cutting and burning. As he slid down the rope, he passed Everett and Collins and hit the bottom with a thud.

"Dammit," he cried out as he rolled onto his stomach. Everett and Collins landed softly next to him and removed the ropes from their feet. "I think you forgot to train me on that little trick with the rope," he said as he started to rise, wiping blood from his hands.

"Sorry about that. I Didn't think we had the time to show you," Jack said as he took the 9-millimeter from his belt.

"Damn, it's dark," said Everett as he tried to penetrate the darkness around them beyond the light shining down the shaft.

Above, they heard the sounds of many vehicles approaching the mosque.

Jack's foot struck something and he reached down and saw that it was a field pack. He held it toward the sunlight and saw that it was marked with Leekie's name. He opened it and fished inside until he found what he was looking for. He brought out a phosphorescent flare and struck it. He held it up and the darkness gave way to bright light.

"Whoa, I think this may be the place," Everett said as he took in the statues.

Jack looked down and saw one set of tracks leading away from the antechamber of the cave.

"Looks like another opening there, Jack," Everett said as he pointed his weapon at the large opening.

The three men started forward slowly. They walked along the stone-and-earthen walls carved to resemble pillars. There were strange designs etched into them that depicted bulls, disks of a blazing sun, and women and fighting soldiers in armor. Hieroglyphs identical to those they had seen on the scrolls they had recovered lined the walls.

"Ah, Jesus," Ryan said, disgust edging his voice.

Jack held the flare closer and saw the horrible death that had befallen one of Dutton's men. The two halves of his body lay crumpled side by side as if they were just laundry waiting to be picked up.

"Watch where you step," Jack said as he threw the flare down and struck another. He held it close to the dirt floor and saw the sun designs on the packed earth. "Look," he said as he pointed the flare at the ground. Then he looked up and saw a large slit in the natural rock formation where something was hidden, just waiting for someone to step on the sun designs on the ground.

"I wish Sarah was here, she knows these traps far better than us," Ryan said as he slowly backed away from the dead man.

Collins hopped over the line of pressure plates after making sure that one trap didn't lead directly to another. They slowly and cautiously entered what they had thought was another cave, but as the light struck and dispelled the blackness, they saw that it was a manmade extension of the natural cave. Jack could see where the ledge sloped steeply down in front of them.

"Listen," he said.

"Running water," Carl ventured. "A lot of it."

As they entered the larger excavation, Jack felt the same feeling he'd had earlier in the desert above. Eyes were on them. He tried to see beyond the steep slope, but there was nothing.

"Lieutenant?" he shouted.

"Colonel?"

It was Will Mendenhall, his voice echoing off the walls just below the slope's edge. He stood, lowered his 9-millimeter, and took a deep breath.

"I'm sure glad to see you guys."

"Is Leekie with you?" asked Jack.

"She's right here. I thought we were going to make a last stand. I was going to take as many of those bastards with me as I could."

The professor limped up the slope and joined Will.

"Glad to see you made it, Doc," Collins said as he stepped forward.

"Major Dutton, his team?" Mendenhall asked.

Everett just shook his head.

"Damn."

"What have we got down there?"

"You're not going to believe this," Mendenhall said. "Show 'em, Doc."

Leekie gestured for the men to follow. She veered to the right side of the slope and then asked Jack for the flare. She touched it to a small ledge and the entire slope lit up with a ring of fire. The ledge, as it turned out, was a trough filled with something ancient, the smell of which was horrible. Everett, Ryan, and Collins watched as the ring of fire illuminated a series of ornamental pillars that lined each side of the slope, which led to an underground river that raged in front of them. The cool waters fell from a great waterfall that exited an opening sixty feet above. As the water from above struck below, it misted and then disappeared as it entered a natural cave that had stalactites and stalagmites lining the upper and lower edges, making the cave seem as if it were an open mouth full of very sharp teeth.

The vision on the other side of the river was what caught their attention. Placed at the very water's edge on the far shore was a small temple of marble and sandstone that gleamed in the flare's false light. Inside, they could see a giant bronze bull, head and right leg bent as it pawed the ground, just as if it were frozen in time while in the act of attacking.

"Now that is something," Everett said, gazing at the incredible sight.

Mendenhall took Collins by the arm and leaned close.

"I didn't want to tell the doc this earlier, Colonel, but we weren't the first ones here."

"I figured as much. I saw some heavy-equipment tracks in the desert. That, coupled with the fact that the Coalition hit so fast and hard, tells me they were nearby, just waiting to spring their ambush."

Everett heard the last of the conversation as he stepped up.

"If we recovered the plate map, how in the hell did they get here first?" Will asked, looking from Jack to Carl.

"I don't know. After searching for it for thousands of years, they suddenly pop up out of nowhere. Did we miss something in Hawaii?"

"No one from Leekie's group entered before you, Lieutenant?"

"No, sir; I and two Special Ops men were the first."

Leekie and Ryan joined the group.

"What are we waiting for? Let's get what we came to get," she said as she looked at the serious faces of the three.

"I'm the strongest swimmer, Jack; I'll get a rope across and tie it off," Everett said.

"Yeah, just don't end up in Cairo in that current."

Ten minutes later, after Everett had given them all a scare by not coming up for six minutes, they saw him break the surface of the river a hundred yards downstream of the temple. He rested for only a moment before he worked his way back along the slim shore. He tied the rope off to the first pillar in line and made it fast. He then waved the others into the water.

Everett looked around the base of the temple for anything that resembled the trough that Leekie had ignited, but found none. He did, however, find torches, last lit when the foul place had its secret first placed there. Carl pulled his Zippo lighter out of his pocket and reached for the first of the ancient torches. He placed the flame next to it, then hesitated as he saw that it was made from a human arm. The skeletal hand of it held a small bowl. Carl hit it with the flame and it sprang to life with the same awful smell as the trough across the way. He lit all the torches that lined the walls of the temple.

Leekie and Ryan, tied together, were the first to traverse the rope hand over hand. Mendenhall and Collins followed. Everett was at the shore's edge to assist each out of the water.

They rested for only a moment and then made their way to the temple steps. The men allowed Leekie to examine the marble steps first so that they wouldn't make the same mistake as the sergeant had made back in the first cave. Then, she waved them forward. It was Jack who noticed that, for having been buried for close to fifteen thousand years, the temple was in remarkable shape.

Leekie was the first to enter the temple. Everett had retrieved a torch and Jack lit off one of their last flares as they looked on with amazement at the work that had gone into building such a thing beneath the earth. Spaced around and in front of each pillar, lifelike statues of men stared out at them with blank eyes. Some were dressed in ancient armor, others in the flowing robes of a politician. Most were impressive in looks but small in stature. The largest was of a bearded man, a soldier perhaps, with a battle helmet in the crook of his right arm and in his left a bronze spear, which stood out brightly against the white marble of his body. The statue was only five foot seven inches high, much taller than its adjoining companions.

"If these were men of Atlantis, they weren't all that impressive in size," Ryan said, feeling even taller as he stood next to the largest statue. He had no way of knowing that the statue was once of Talos, the last of the great Titans.

"Well, ancient man was a very small creature compared with humans today. Even in biblical times men rarely, if ever, topped a height over five-eight," Leekie said, looking at Ryan.

"Jack," Everett called as he and Mendenhall stood in front of the giant bronze bull.

Collins joined them as Everett shone the torch over the

lowered horns of the beast. Jack saw two notches about fifteen inches wide on each of the horns.

"Professor, could you look at this," he called. "Could these notches have held something?"

"Dammit!" Leekie said as she looked at the horns. "The blue diamond was more than likely cradled by the two horns."

"Maybe they were just—"

"It was very difficult removing the diamond from its locked base on those horns, I assure you." The female voice, raised over the sounds of the river, caught them off guard.

Collins, Everett, Ryan, Mendenhall, and Leekie took cover behind the pillars. Jack ventured a look across the river and saw fifty men slowly coming down the slope. The blond-haired woman was behind them, walking slowly with the use of a cane. The soldiers stood silhouetted in the light of the fire ring. She gestured right and then left as her men took up positions in various places on the slope.

Jack looked at his watch and saw that he desperately needed to stall the woman.

"I was hoping you drowned at Pearl Harbor," Jack called out.

"Almost, Colonel Collins, almost," Dahlia said as she paced to her left behind the wall of soldiers. "The Atlantean Key is safely where it should be. We recovered it only ten hours before your arrival here."

Collins did not respond as he reached into his pocket and pulled out a second transmitter, which he had hoped not to use. He looked at the excavated ceiling, hoping that it was mostly earth and not rock. He needed a ground-penetrating signal to pierce through to the surface. As he thought about how he was going to put the transmitter in the right spot, Everett joined him, after sneaking behind the temple.

"We're trapped like rats—there's no way out in the back—"

He went silent when he saw what Jack held in his hand.

"Oh, shit."

Everett recognized the small electronic marker that had a counterpart: one attached to a thousand-pound ground-penetration bomb called a bunker buster.

"I take it you alerted the air force already?"

"Just before we broke cover in the dunes. Niles insisted we have a failsafe."

"It would have been nice if the diamond was still here," Everett said, not taking his eyes off the remote signal.

"It would have been, swabby, but what the hell."

"Yeah, what the hell."

Collins walked to the front of the temple.

"Where did you take it, if you don't mind me asking?"

Dahlia smiled as Collins walked slowly down the steps of the temple. The man's arrogance was beyond anything she had ever seen. She came close to laughing at the bravado of this bastard.

"This isn't the movies, Colonel. I do not tell all even though I am sure you're living the last moments of your life. Just rest assured that because of your failure at the *Arizona,* the world will—"

Collins raised his weapon and fired as fast as anyone could have thought possible. The first bullet tore through one man's ear and struck Dahlia. It grazed her left shoulder just outside the protection of the vest she was wearing. The rest of the rounds struck men and dropped at least five of them. The commotion gave Jack the time he needed as he reared back and threw the designator across the river. The laser was broadcast on both sides, front and back, so he knew that it didn't need to land upright to work. The device landed about twenty feet up the slope.

"What are you waiting for?" Dahlia screamed, angered almost to the point of hysteria. "Kill that son of a bitch, kill them all!"

Jack hit the temple steps just as large chips of marble started flying. He rolled until he was safe behind one of the thick pillars.

Everett was stunned at what had just happened. Jack had caught even him off guard. He had thrown the transmitter as far as he was able to, giving them hope that they could survive what was coming. Carl fired five rounds into the swirling mist of the falls and hit three of the men.

Ryan and Mendenhall added their fire to Everett's and to-

gether they kept the Coalition mercenaries moving and duck-
ing. Jack looked for Dahlia and finally saw her crouching low
beside the fire trough. She was directing something behind
her. Jack looked up the slope and saw a man place a tube to his
upper shoulder.

"Get down!" he cried.

The LAWs rocket was old, but effective. It streaked out of
its launch tube and struck a pillar at the front of the temple,
smashing it, bringing some of the marble roof down with it.

Jack took careful aim and fired. The man holding the tube
in the shadows across the way crumpled as the bullet hit the
thickest part of his body; the stomach.

Dahlia saw the man lean forward and slide down the slope.
She shook her head in anger, then stood and fired her own pistol at the temple.

Collins saw his chance, lined her up, and pulled the trigger,
nothing. He cursed and ejected the spent clip and inserted another. He brought up the Beretta, but Dahlia had lowered her
frame once more.

AIR FORCE FLIGHT 2870 LIMA-ECHO
OPERATION HEAT LIGHTNING
THIRTY-FIVE THOUSAND FEET

The aircraft was a B-1B bomber. In its belly was just one large
egg it needed to drop—the bunker buster. It was there just as a
last ditch effort in stopping the Coalition from obtaining the
diamond just in case it had not been recovered by Major Dutton and Professor Leekie. Niles knew that it was a last-resort
type of mission and called for only if there was no other way.
So, naturally, when the air force informed him of the bomb
drop, he lowered his head, thinking the worse.

"We have a painted target," said the pilot as he pickled his
load off.

The bomb-bay doors opened automatically and the thousand-
pound weapon fell free.

"We have a clean drop and designator is receiving target
information."

"I hope someone down there knows how to duck," the copilot said as the B-1B bomber turned for home at Diego Garcia.

Dahlia waved forward more men with LAWs rockets. As the volume of Coalition fire increased, she knew she was close to ending the luck of this Colonel Collins. Her embarrassment would be erased and she would be able to look at herself once more without the shame of Collins around her neck.

She smiled, as the pitiful return fire was so ineffective that her men were starting to take chances by standing and taking better aim, pinning Collins and his few men down. It was now only a matter of time. Dahlia saw the men above her on the slope arming the rockets, and when she looked back down the incline she saw one of her men kick something along the ground. It was just dumb luck that she had seen it at all. The black case gleamed in the firelight flickering onto the slope as it skidded to a stop not five feet from her position.

Her eyes widened when she recognized the transmitter. Dahlia knew it was a geo-positioning transmitter, the sort used as a portable ground-penetrating lasing system.

"That crazy bastard is trying to kill us and himself!" she screamed indignantly as she broke free of her safe position and ran down the slope toward the return fire of Collins and his people.

The signal of the laser beacon was weakened by the topsoil and sand above it, but it was enough for the seeker head located in the nose of the bomb to lock on to. Small fins fore and aft maneuvered the fat weapon onto its glide path. This particular smart bomb was the largest in the U.S. inventory capable of guided flight. Falling from a height of thirty thousand feet, it had little trouble penetrating the thickness of the earth.

The world above and in front of them came crashing down. The bomb exploded off-target two hundred feet behind where the slope started in the natural portion of the cave. The fireball killed every man on his feet and buried the rest. The pillars of the temple cracked and started falling as Jack and the others broke for the water below them. They felt the heat burn their skin as they dived just as the earthen roof came cascading down.

Collins was the last to dive into the water and it was he who saw Dahlia as she was catapulted forward, cartwheeling through the air. She landed in the rushing torrent of water and immediately disappeared. Collins dived in and grabbed a handful of hair. He pulled her to the surface just as they shot into the mouthlike cave, and then the world around them went dark.

Jack held on to Dahlia as he tried to relax his body and allow the current to take them where it wanted. His only struggle was to keep the unconscious woman's head above water. At certain points, he found, the harsh current went far beneath the underground roof of the ancient river as it sped along. He saw momentary flashes of light ahead and heard the shouting of the others above the din of the rushing Blue Nile. Bright mineral deposits gleamed wetly as they screamed passed.

Jack's shoulder struck a stalactite and he careened into the smooth, age-worn wall, then a rip current pulled him and Dahlia under. Collins thought that this was where the river disappeared far below the desert and would not rise again until its waters mixed with those of the surface Nile far from where they were.

The roar of the river was growing even louder as Jack came close to passing out for lack of air. Suddenly the dark world filled with light and the waters warmed by twenty degrees as Jack kicked upward. The great current died out as he broke the surface into bright daylight. As he took in great gulps of air, he was never so glad to see the sun as it set low over the western horizon.

As he placed his arm around Dahlia's neck and started kicking, he felt hands and arms around him, pulling him through the water until his feet started dragging in the mud. He was pulled onto the hot sand lining the river. He heard Dahlia coughing and throwing up water next to him and he angrily shoved her body away from his own.

"Damn, Jack, you caught the biggest fish in this damn river," Everett said as he leaned down and made sure that the woman wasn't going to choke to death. "Freshwater piranha, I believe."

Collins coughed up water and rolled onto his stomach. Then he turned and looked at Everett.

"Next time we stay and shoot it out. That was not fun," he said as he looked beyond Carl. "We lose anyone?"

"All accounted for. Will broke his nose, Professor Leekie is crying about losing the temple, and Ryan is bitching that he lost his wallet, but it looks like we'll all live."

Jack pushed himself into a sitting position and looked from Carl to the blond woman lying on her stomach.

"We better find a phone and pass on the bad news."

"Think she'll talk?"

Collins stood on shaky feet, trying to clear his head. Then he looked down at the woman, who was just coming to.

"Yeah, she'll talk, or she may find herself being left in a country where people disappear all the time."

AMERICAN CONSULATE
ADDIS ABBA, ETHIOPIA

Jack, Carl, Mendenhall, and Ryan were standing behind the two-way glass looking into the interview room. Virginia, feeling sick after her supersonic flight from Nellis onboard an F-15 Eagle, was to handle the interview with Lorraine Matheson— Coalition code name Dahlia—who was presently sitting in a straight-back chair with her hands cuffed to its armrests.

In Nevada, Sarah and her geology team were watching the video feed in hopes of gaining an advantage in their scroll research.

"And they developed this Wave technology from copies of the same scrolls we have in our possession?" Virginia asked, with her arms placed firmly across her chest. Her demeanor was calm, but inside she was seething that this woman could order death and assassination as easily as ordering breakfast.

Dahlia was dressed in the same clothes she'd been wearing

when she was apprehended. Virginia understood, from a woman's point of view, that this was grating on her.

"Yes."

Jack had received Dahlia's background check from Europa, who had hacked the FBI mainframe and pulled out her rather mundane file from its stored archives. Lorraine Matheson was the daughter of a wealthy author and was a graduate of U.C., Berkeley. She had squandered some years at the CIA as a researcher before finding the job boring. All through her young life, she had tried to be the exact opposite of her left-wing father and friends. She had eventually quit the CIA and drifted into freelance work in 1978. That was where her file ended.

"We know that certain members of the Coalition are related by blood to other Ancients, so they have heard the same stories about the Atlantean Key and the Wave being the cause of the destruction of Atlantis. Why does this Tomlinson believe he can control it?"

"His science teams estimate that the Wave will be enhanced by twenty million decibels, and the tone grooves on the diamond are a pinpoint decibel control for specific faults and their geologic makeup. That's all I've learned from Tomlinson; he's rather tight-lipped about his plans."

In Nevada, at the mention of geologic makeup, Sarah started thinking. The familiar thought was again at the edge of her memory, then it was gone.

"What is the Coalition's ultimate goal in all of this madness—to take over the world?" Virginia asked.

"You really don't understand anything, do you? The Coalition is out to eliminate the leadership of nations that are a drain on the material wealth of others. They play games with the support offered by building up armed forces used for only one purpose: the subjugation of their own people. Tomlinson seeks to eliminate them from the world stage. Not their people, as in the past attempts, but their leadership."

"If this is so, why the assassinations of western leaders and why a war in Korea that could bring down or weaken the United States?"

"The United States has always favored the status quo of the world. A weakened America will be swayed to mind its own affairs. Leaders financed wholly by the Coalition will receive the wealth of the world—food, money, and comforts will be supplied to their people. You see, why conquer when you can purchase. The use of the Wave is for those countries that will not let go of the old ways. It's expeditious," Dahlia said with a smile.

Jack and Everett walked in and handed Virginia a file folder.

"Before we concern ourselves with the real questions you will be asking, have you delved into the more recent materials concerning your friends the Ancients?"

Collins just looked at the woman, not really concerned with what she had to say about Martha and Rothman.

"I think you may be somewhat shocked that they are not the innocents you may have been led to believe." Dahlia raised one eyebrow and smirked.

Virginia sat in front of Dahlia and looked at her without saying anything for a moment. Jack and Carl stood with their backs against the glass and waited.

"I believe at this point I should be asking for legal counsel," Dahlia said, looking from face to face.

"Nah, we don't use 'em," Everett said from his place next to Jack.

Virginia opened the folder and pulled out a sheet of paper, then turned it around and laid it so that Dahlia could read it clearly.

"Do you recognize the letterhead on this document?" she asked.

The seal of the president of the United States was embossed at the top.

Dahlia looked and then leaned back in her chair. "Yes."

"Do you see the signature?"

"I have."

"This document clears you of all crimes committed in the United States and her allied treaty nations. In essence, Ms.

Matheson, you are hereby pardoned before the facts are brought to public knowledge of the brutal crimes committed against the citizens of the United States. It is a document the new president did not want to sign. Am I clear on this point?"

Dahlia didn't blink an eye; she only waited.

Virginia frowned and placed the letter back into the file folder and started to stand. She was playing this out like an experienced trial lawyer.

"You are clear," Dahlia said before Virginia could stand.

"Good." She removed the letter once again and slid it over to the woman. "Now, the sooner you answer a few questions from my two colleagues here, the sooner you can sign this and then take that much-needed shower and change of clothes you're desperate for."

Collins walked over behind Dahlia and removed her right handcuff.

"Where is he?" he asked, still standing behind her.

Dahlia looked at the document in front of her and then up at Virginia, avoiding Jack as much as she could.

"Crete."

"Why Crete?"

"Because that's where the Coalition will make their final assault."

"How many?" Jack asked, finally turning around.

"Far more than you can handle. I believe your armed forces have far more pressing issues in Korea at the moment, as per Tomlinson's plan."

"How many?" Jack persisted.

"Two thousand defensive troops; I don't really know."

"Equipment?"

"I don't know."

"Again, why Crete?"

"You won't be able to get to them there. He's deep underground," she answered, finally looking Collins in the eyes, and then she smirked.

"Why?"

"To use the Wave, complete with Atlantean Key. He will

attack Russia and China. That is everything I know."

Virginia placed the pen on the presidential decree. "Sign it."

Dahlia scribbled her name, never looking away from Collins.

Carl walked over and took the pen, then undid the other cuff. He helped her to her feet and pulled her toward the door.

"Come on, petunia, let's get you to a bar of soap. You're a little ripe."

Before Everett could pull her through the door, Dahlia stopped and turned to Jack.

"I can't resist, Colonel. I do have one more piece of information. Why Crete, you asked," she said, starting to laugh. "Tomlinson is in a city that sank fifteen thousand years ago. Good luck assaulting *Atlantis,* Colonel."

Everett pulled Dahlia away, but her laughter lingered.

EVENT GROUP CENTER
NELLIS AIR FORCE BASE, NEVADA

Sarah was in the examination room, deep in thought as she perused one of the ancient scrolls as one of the professors from the Ancient Languages Department sat beside her, explaining a strange design pattern.

"How they even knew about the North and South American continents is anyone's guess. They must have had exploration vessels that at the very minimum rivaled the Vikings' ship design."

Sarah was only half listening as the small memory of the Wave pattern still flickered just beyond her grasp.

"Now, this particular pattern here, according to Europa, is a close match for the continental plate that North America sits on. I say 'resembles' because the fault lines listed by these swirls and valleys are not accurate, nor the ones here, closest to Russia. I really don't know what they are. Without some understanding of their science, we may never know."

Sarah turned to the professor. "Excuse me?"

"Without some understanding of—"

"No, not that. You say Europa didn't recognize the fault

lines on the scroll the Ancients created?"

"No, she didn't. The blue swirls listed are accurate faults, but the thicker red lines are a mystery. So either the Atlanteans knew something we didn't and placed faults and plates that we can't see today, or—"

Sarah jumped up and ran out of the clean room. She took the elevator down to the engineering lab, where Pete Golding was still studying the plate and its hologram. Sarah ran right into the middle of the floating map and started looking for a design she had seen earlier.

"Sarah, what's the matter?" Pete asked.

Sarah finally found the design she had seen during the demonstration. It was a Key they hadn't recognized earlier. As she examined it, Pete started looking over her shoulder.

"This fault pattern here, Europa has confirmed it is accurate. This line here beneath it is the continental plate, the same here in Europe and Asia. I didn't recognize patterns in the shape of the continents earlier—only the North and South American plates, because of their unique shape. What's confusing me is that this same pattern is on the map Jack recovered from Westchester. Now that I see it on the hologram, I can tell it runs *under* both the faults and the tectonic plates. Now look at this," she said to Pete as her fingers traced a series of lines that led from one plate to the next, to the next, and so on. Some of the lines branched out and dwindled to nothing, like the branches of a tree, while the thicker, stronger lines connected the tectonic plates of the world by underground magma veins.

"What are you saying?"

"Somehow, the Atlantean scientists found a way to map what we can't do today. They found out that all the continents and the plates they sit on are in actuality connected."

Pete looked closer at the design, then his eyes widened as he finally pieced together what Sarah was driving at.

"Any massive assault on one tectonic plate could trigger a chain reaction around the world."

"Wouldn't the Coalition . . . wouldn't they have seen this?" Pete asked.

"Not without this three-dimensional design they wouldn't. They didn't have the plate map, so they could never have known about it."

"Oh, Sarah, if they use this device on any of these major plates—"

"They could either shift entire continents . . . or blow the planet to hell."

THE WHITE HOUSE
WASHINGTON, D.C.

The most important meeting in the long and storied history of the Event Group was about to begin. The president's National Security Council was about to be formally introduced to several of the Event Group members. The Group's background would remain hidden from them, as the council thought they were to be briefed by Compton's secret think tank. Nevada and Ethiopia could see the council via video link.

"Ladies and gentlemen, we are very short of time here. The briefings will be short and to the point. Questions will be relayed to me and I will ask them," Niles said, sitting at the head of the table next to the president.

"Secretary of Defense Johnson, if you please."

"As of this moment, the situation in Korea, while not yet stable, has cooled somewhat. We have pulled back all defensive troops from the border and have entrenched around Seoul. The armored divisions of Kim Jong Il have not made any threatening gestures as of yet, but CIA reports there is tension between Kim and at least one of his generals in the field. We will get more on that in the next few hours. On reinforcing, we have deployed the Hundred and First and Eighty-second Airborne to act as rapid deployment out of Japan."

As everyone watched, pictures started flashing on monitors in Washington, Nevada, and Addis Abba.

"The Chinese and Russians are massing heavy bomber and fighter forces at their Pacific bases. They are not lowering their defense status even with the Coalition evidence we have provided them. We have the *Eisenhower* and *Nimitz* carrier groups steaming for the Sea of Japan, but it will take at least five more days to deploy them defensively." The secretary paused and removed his glasses. "We are spread thin. If anything outside of Korea erupts, we will be desperate to cover it."

Niles nodded in thanks. Then he turned to the head of the FBI. "Any word on the forensics end from Chicago?"

"We have concluded that none of the bodies found inside the house are that of William Tomlinson. We must surmise he escaped," he said angrily.

"Mr. President, my people have come up with several pieces of information that will be important to this meeting. I ask that close attention be paid to the military aspects of what is said because the shortages the secretary of defense spoke of are a very serious problem if what we think is happening is accurate."

The president nodded.

"Several of you know Colonel Jack Collins. Colonel, explain what you have uncovered on the Coalition and its whereabouts, please."

As briefly as possible, Jack explained what they had learned about the Coalition thus far. He explained the confrontation and failure at Pearl Harbor and the results of Dahlia's interrogation. Then came the shocker.

"In essence, the Coalition is going to strike at the Chinese and Russian nations within a short time frame. We have traced the Coalition hierarchy to a base on Crete, and this base is heavily defended."

"Ken, we need intelligence on this Crete operation as soon as possible," the president said.

The chairman of the Joint Chiefs nodded. "I will order photo recon overflights immediately."

"May I recommend satellite surveillance only, or we may tip our hand that we know where they are," Collins stated from the Ethiopian consulate.

"General, this will involve retasking a few satellites. You better get Space Command on it right away," the president ordered.

"Now, Jack, do we have any ideas on how we can assault the island with the few assets we have in the area?" Niles asked.

"A nuclear strike is out of the question because of the civilian population. Even if we could manage evacuating the populace, we believe the Coalition operation is under ground—very deep under ground, where air strikes are not possible. I'm afraid we have to do this the hard way."

"Colonel Collins, on Dr. Compton's recommendation, I am placing you in command of all operations *outside* of the actual assault. General Caulfield will coordinate with field command. Gentlemen, plan it well."

The president didn't say it outright, but he had just ordered the planning stage for the invasion of Atlantis.

PART IV
Atlantis

CHAPTER
FOURTEEN

THE DMZ (THE BORDER OF
NORTH AND SOUTH KOREA)

Major General Ton Shi Quang was looking at the opportunity
of a lifetime. The Americans had retreated without a shot fired,
leaving positions that had been prepared since the end of the
conflict in the 1950s.

Thus far, he had been on the phone no fewer than five times
to the Great Leader himself, telling him that he could make an
offensive run right around the Americans and destroy the South
Korean army, which was setting up defensive positions two
hundred miles farther south. The American Second Infantry
Division would be completely cut off, where they would die or
be forced to surrender.

Of course, Quang knew that he wouldn't be there for the
great victory or when the Americans started lobbing nuclear
weapons onto his troops. Instead, he would be far from the
battle zone, waiting for his Coalition partners to make him a
very, very rich man.

Still, the Great Leader was hesitant, as if the Americans
were starting to get the full truth through to his addled brain.
He could not allow Kim to fade in his desire to get retribution
for the earthquakes. The Chinese and the Russians had swayed
him in order to allow things to settle over the last two days.

General Quang now had to start the war in earnest, which was what he was being paid for.

He studied the intelligence reports and matched them with the large sand table. The Americans had left close to two thousand troops behind to guard combat engineers who were undoubtedly laying traps and tank obstacles to slow him down. As commander in the field, he had the option and the right to attack these troops if he thought them a danger for any future attack.

"Colonel," he said as he looked at the terrain just across the border.

"Sir," the thin officer said, standing at attention.

"I want a three-tank-brigade thrust in sectors three, eight, and thirteen. Catch the Americans unaware before they can finish with their traps. I want the men and equipment they leave behind destroyed. Then order the brigades to hold position south of the border."

The colonel could not hide the shock on his face. He stepped up to the sand table and looked at the positions the general had ordered taken.

"Are we acting on orders from Pyongyang?"

"My orders are defensive in nature, Colonel. I do not need Pyongyang's permission. From this moment on, we will observe radio blackout. We'll receive only."

"But, General—"

"Carry out your orders, Colonel, or I will find an officer who will!"

The colonel saluted and left the bunker. If he hadn't known better, he would have believed that the general was starting it, rather than trying to prevent it.

The war was now on, whether Kim Jong Il or China wanted it or not.

EVENT GROUP CENTER
NELLIS AIR FORCE BASE, NEVADA

The computer center was abuzz as the crystal-clear imagery of Crete started coming in from two KH-11 Blackbirds in

geosynchronous orbit over the Mediterranean. Europa was a
great help in her microsecond washing of the pictures, which
cleaned them up to maximum enhancement. The pictures
were being relayed to Jack, Carl, Ryan, and Mendenhall in
Ethiopia. The images of the bright blue waters looked inviting
until they saw the tracks in the sand and large tents and metal
buildings at the island's southern end. Camouflage netting hid
equipment that stretched for fifteen kilometers around the
centermost portion of Crete, but it was the tracks in the sand
that had Jack's attention.

"What do you think, Jack?" Everett asked.

"Not good, swabby, not good at all," he answered, and then
he hit the intercom for the direct link to the Pentagon. "General Caulfield, do you see the tracks leading to the camo netting, satellite designation one through sixteen?" Europa had
designated the sixteen centerline camouflage nets as 1 through
16 and the figures popped up on the monitors in red.

Collins and the general had seen enough of the tracks in
Saudi Arabia and Kuwait to recognize them immediately.

"I would say we have good old-fashion SAMs underneath
the netting."

"I agree," said Caulfield.

"General, the plan for taking the beach could become very
costly."

Caulfield had worked out his end of the plan with the navy
and marines and knew that it was hasty but as good as they
could get with the current Mediterranean assets.

Jack had informed Niles that he and his element would
concentrate on the Egyptian tunnel they had discovered on the
bronze-plate hologram; they were hoping that it led to the Coalition. The theory was that the tunnel had once been used for
secret travel and survival of their hierarchy. The linguists,
along with Carmichael and Martha, had been working nonstop to decipher the details of the map.

"It will be very costly, Colonel, but while we're keeping
their heads down at the front door, your team just may slip in
through the back door."

"Agent Dahlia has indicated that the Coalition has at least a brigade-size force for beach defense and a minimum of thirty advanced warplanes hidden somewhere in the region. Has the navy decided what other surface assets they can give us?"

"We have the Royal Navy, but not much else."

"Damn," Everett said as he looked at the waters surrounding Crete.

"All we have currently in the Med is the Tarawa-class Assault Ship *Nassau* and the Wasp-class USS *Iwo Jima*. The beach assault will comprise the *Iwo*'s eighteen hundred marines, supported by the *Nassau*'s eighteen hundred in a follow-up second wave. The two assault ships, plus whatever we can get through Italian airspace, from Aviano, will supply air support. We're just too damn low on assets in the area."

"My team is en route to Aviano as we speak. The navy has pulled SEAL Team Six out of Afghanistan and the survivors of SEAL Team Four from San Diego. The backdoor force will be supplemented with men from our Group and by a company of marines from the two attack carriers. We'll be going in light and fast."

"Right, get me your final plans as soon as you have studied the intel from Space Command more closely, and then I'll brief the president."

"Yes, sir."

Jack switched off the intercom and looked at his three men. "A lot of people aren't coming back from this one. I want you to know that you don't have to—"

"This speech really gets boring, Jack," Everett said; Mendenhall and Ryan looked at Collins as if he had insulted their mothers.

Collins just nodded.

As they looked at the map, Sarah McIntire walked into the room and saluted Jack.

"My team is ready, Colonel," she said.

Jack nodded. "Will, you and your protection team of ten men will accompany the lieutenant and her geology and pale- olithic team to the Valley of the Kings. The president has called in a favor from the Egyptian president to get the team into the valley to find that back door. You will have no other backup, and I expect you and her to get in and get out safely and report. After you've located the subterranean gateway, we move in."

"Yes, sir."

Collins looked back down at the map and avoided Sarah's eyes. She wanted him to look at her again with something more than a military bearing, but she could see that he was forcing himself not to.

"Good luck, Lieutenant. Your transport is waiting."

She saluted again, but when Collins did not look up, she turned and left. Everett, Ryan, and Mendenhall turned to face Jack.

"Little cold with her, weren't you, Jack?"

Collins just closed his eyes and said nothing. Then he straightened from the map and looked at Mendenhall with his piercing eyes. The look alone said it all. His orders were clear.

"I'll watch her, Colonel."

Jack just nodded, not trusting his voice because of the fear he felt.

CRETE
COALITION SITE 1

Tomlinson stared down the long shaft, the sides of which were shiny from the equipment used to widen it from its original series of stone arches. The rebar used to shore the downward-spiraling tunnel made it seem like a thirty-five-foot-diameter spiderweb. Tramcars sat at the entrance ready to transport the final troops and Wave equipment down into the city, of which 2.2 square miles was indeed dry, as they had hoped. All thought of the missing Dahlia was now far from his mind.

This was the pivotal moment in the history of the Juliai. Whole nations would be placed under the umbrella of the Coalition, which would dictate to the world the Ancients' laws of a demanding new society, a model of which had once been the city and civilization right beneath his feet.

Tomlinson shivered in the wind as he saw the shaft that would lead to his lost city. From there all things would be righted.

THE WHITE HOUSE
WASHINGTON, D.C.

"Your people really came through, Mr. Director, I want you to know that," the president said as he looked through the window at the protesters out on Pennsylvania Avenue.

"Don't get all mushy on me. I still want my budget."

The president shook his head, then turned and sat in his chair.

"So, even if Colonel Collins finds this back door, what if the tunnel has collapsed in the thousands of years since it's been used?"

"Good question. It's all just best-guess, Mr. President— that's all historical science ever is. But if there's a way in, Jack will find it."

Niles yawned and cleaned his glasses. "What bothers me is the fact that we had a group of citizens in this country and in other free nations who knew about this Juliai Coalition for almost two thousand years and didn't do anything to stop them. As much as they have helped, I can't excuse the arrogance of these . . . Ancients."

"What should we do with them?"

"Nothing. They're old and the last of their kind. They just need to go away."

"Niles, you know that if Colonel Collins can't find a way down, those marines are going to have a tough time of it on Crete."

"I know it," Niles answered. He knew that the president was fishing for reassurance that Collins was as good as advertised.

The intercom buzzed and the president quickly picked it up. "Yes, put him on."

Niles heard the change in the president's tone of voice and sat up.

"When and what is the force?"

Compton watched his friend place his free hand on his forehead and then hang up the phone. He looked at Niles and then stood and walked to the window once more.

"The North Koreans have come across the border with a small force. The details are sketchy and they don't know in what strength yet. The original assault is by a three-pronged group of armor we hope is just a probe, or something to elicit a response. Now there are indications that other units of the People's Fifteenth has started massing north of the DMZ."

Niles knew that the worst-case scenario was happening and there wasn't a damn thing the president could do but fight back.

"Come on, Jack," he whispered to himself.

THE VALLEY OF THE KINGS
LUXOR, EGYPT

The only difference in the ancient valley since the time of Howard Carter, who discovered of King Tutankhamen's tomb in 1922, was that there was a literal traffic jam of people with permits issued by the Egyptian government seeking the archaeological riches of the valley.

Sarah, Will Mendenhall, and twenty Event Group security men and women were being escorted through the valley by Professor Anis Arturi, the director of information for the city of Luxor. He was not a willing partner in their endeavor to find the gateway to Atlantis. He knew only that the president of Egypt himself had ordered him to watch the Americans and indulge them in their search for a tomb of some significance to the desert government.

They had been on station for four hours, but the coordinates of the Atlantis plate map did not match with what they had hoped to find. Instead of the longitude and latitude being in the valley where the tombs were located, they found themselves on a flat piece of sand-swept desert with not so much as a date tree for a hundred miles.

"Not exactly Times Square here, is it?" Will said as he checked his global positioning link on his laptop. The eight other Land Rovers were idling behind them as he and Sarah got their bearings.

"There isn't one landmark for miles around."

"I can now see why this doorway to the underworld has never been discovered."

The headlights started to pick up the sand as it blew across the desert. The wind was increasing in velocity and the guide and the Egyptian professor started squirming in the backseat.

"We should be heading back; these windstorms can be quite dangerous in the valley."

Sarah turned and looked the man in the eyes. "We haven't found what we came to find and we won't be leaving until that happens." Sarah had a momentary flash of Jack and the rest waiting on the USS *Iwo Jima* for their report. If they did not find the doorway, Jack would be going on the assault of Crete with the marines. There was no way she would stop looking.

"Will, drive south, very slowly."

"But, madam, there is no road, we are off the track. We cannot go further into the plain!" Professor Arturi said as he looked out into the darkness.

Mendenhall rolled his eyes and then put the large Land Rover into first gear and started forward. The wind picked up in violence as if in warning as the small line of vehicles moved onto the plain of Luxor.

Two hours later, Sarah was biting her lip. They had come across nothing even remotely manmade in this horrid area of Egypt. They had traveled in a zigzag pattern and had even spread the vehicles out in a straight line in case they had overlooked something.

"Stop and let me take another bearing," Sarah said as she placed the laptop on her knees.

The wind was howling at sixty miles per hour, rocking the Land Rover on its springs, and the windows were starting to pit from the abrasive sand. Will felt movement and thought at first it was just the wind. Then it happened again. He felt it in his stomach first, and as it increased he grabbed the steering wheel.

"Did you feel that?" he asked Sarah.

"What," she asked, her face aglow with the brightness of the screen. She did not turn away from the positioning report.

Mendenhall looked around and peered outside. He turned on the spotlight and shone it around, but he still could not see ten feet in front of the vehicle. Then he let go of the wheel and light handle when he felt the truck lurch again. He knew then that somehow it had slipped downward.

"Uh-oh," Will said when he felt it again.

"What in the hell was that?" Sarah said, looking up when the laptop jumped in her lap.

"We must leave this spot. There is quicksand all over this area; I told you it was dangerous to leave the road!" Arturi whined.

"Will, get us moving."

Mendenhall put the Land Rover in gear once more and it started to struggle forward. Suddenly the rear end went down into the sand and the two men in the back screamed. Then the vehicle rolled to the right, then to the left, and then the front went down into the sand. The laptop slid off Sarah's legs as she reached for the radio. Then the Land Rover rolled nearly upside down and then quickly straightened before vanishing into the sand.

The security personnel in the convoy could not believe their eyes as they left the safety of their own transports and ran for the spot where the lead vehicle had vanished.

Sarah and Will Mendenhall had disappeared into the soft sand and there was not so much as a tire track to say they had ever been there.

USS *IWO JIMA*, 100 KILOMETERS WEST OF CRETE

Jack listened to the final plan for the invasion of Crete. He was impressed with what commanding Marine Corps General Pete Hamilton had devised with the commander of the Joint Chiefs.

"It all boils down to the defenders taking the first piece of bait we throw into the water."

Collins nodded at the logic. "If they take your bait, that will expose all of their batteries before our people begin the assault."

"These are mercenaries—not unlike the terrorists we have tangled with—and I have learned that although it's hard to get inside of their heads, they can be expected to do one thing when the shooting starts, and that's to shoot back. Surprise is key; if we achieve it, we have a fighting chance."

Jack nodded and looked at his watch.

"Worried about your team in Egypt?" the general asked.

"If we have to depend on taking the front door and using that to gain access to their underground center instead of just holding it, we could be in for a long-running and very costly battle."

The marine general nodded in understanding.

Jack walked away from the planning table and cornered Everett.

"Nothing from Sarah and Will?"

"I've got Ryan babysitting communications, but there's one hell of a storm over the search area and they may not be able to get any signal out."

Jack looked at his watch for the hundredth time.

"Jack, Sarah knows what she's doing. Unless she's been swallowed up by the desert, there's no way she'll fail us."

FORTY-FIVE KILOMETERS SOUTH OF LUXOR, EGYPT

The eeriness of the sudden silence did not set well with the occupants of the Land Rover. Sand completely covered the vehicle and the air was growing foul.

"We are doomed because you refused to listen to the people who have lived here for thousands of years!" Arturi said, wiping sweat from his brow.

Sarah looked into the backseat and saw through the dome light that the guide was taking the situation far better than his boss was.

"We have twenty men up there that will get us out. What we don't need is for you to go and lose your cool," Will said, when he saw that Sarah had little patience with the Egyptian.

Suddenly they felt the Land Rover slide farther into the quicksand. Sarah saw long-buried, skeletal-looking bushes slide by the window in the wrong direction and she was worried that very soon they would be too deep to get out without the use of heavy equipment.

"The air's getting a little ripe in here, why don't you open a window," Mendenhall joked.

"Don't do that, you fool—do you wish to kill us all!"

Sarah looked back at Arturi, then back at Will. They both laughed at the same time.

"You are crazy, both of you, laughing at a time like this!" the professor said with as much indignity as he could muster.

"Mr. Arturi, the more you speak, the less air we will have to breathe. Take a hint from your man there: relax."

Sarah's words sounded good, but she knew that they were in a very serious situation. The vehicle was sliding deeper and deeper into the loose sand, one or two feet at a time. It as was if the very ground beneath them was spilling into some unknown abyss.

"Uh-oh," Mendenhall said again as the rate of their sinking increased.

Sarah closed her eyes and thought of Jack. The first thing to enter her mind was the base fact that he would be killed in the assault because they had failed him. The second thought was more personal in nature. The last time they had been together at dinner, she had chided him for being so straight and rigid all the time. She now regretted doing that.

Suddenly the descent stopped as the rear end of the Land Rover sank far lower than the front.

Will looked at Sarah with wide eyes. "I guess this is—"

He stopped speaking when he saw that Sarah's was looking beyond him through the driver's window. All she could do was point with her finger.

Will turned, not knowing what to expect, and his heart rate

increased tenfold when he saw the stern countenance of a white face and blank, hollow eyes staring at him at him through the window.

In the backseat, Arturi yelped in terror.

"What in the hell is that?" Mendenhall asked.

"Oh, my God," Sarah said as she leaned closer to Will and shone a flashlight on the face in the window. "It's Apollo!"

"What?" Will asked.

"This is important, Will. What in the hell is it doing here, at the very spot the coordinates said the front gate was supposed to be? Over the years the movement of the desert must have swallowed it up, along with everything the Ancients had marking the place!"

"This is Egypt, young lady, not Greece. Why would a statue of Apollo be here?" Arturi said, when his heart had resumed its normal function.

"Listen, jerk, I know Apollo when I see him. The winged helmet, the—"

Suddenly the guide screamed. Sarah turned and saw what he was frantically pointing to. The rear window of the Land Rover was no longer covered in sand. She could make out ancient-looking timbers. Sarah now understood the reason why the vehicle had sunk beneath the sand. The weight of the Land Rover on the ground had broken support timbers lining the top of a cave or excavation. The sand had started filtering through until enough had vanished beneath them to take the vehicle down. They were no longer sinking because they had been stopped by the remaining timbers that now crisscrossed the back window.

As she shone her light on the rocklike timbers, she saw the cracks not only in the window but in the ancient wood itself. The weight of the Land Rover was starting to crack the remaining petrified wood.

"If this is the spot, it must mean that that timber is—"

"Fifteen thousand years old," Sarah answered Will as the age-hardened wood snapped and the Land Rover, with the great statue of Apollo in escort, started a free fall into the blackened underworld of Egypt.

TWO AND A HALF MILES
UNDER THE ISLE OF CRETE

The large tram system built by Coalition engineers saved hours upon hours of travel time into the bowels of Crete, but it still took close to two hours to reach the bottom. Tomlinson and the other Coalition members were tired and their nerves were on edge as they had received word that a naval task force was headed their way.

Tomlinson seemed not to care about the developing situation as he stood at the door, looking out at the amazing sight before him. Large banks of floodlights illuminated the most amazing scene in human knowledge.

"Oh, my God," Dame Lilith said in wonder as she stood next to Tomlinson and saw what he was looking at.

The Coalition Council watched as workers labored to clear a passage through the crumbled world of Atlantis. Columns the size of which none of them had ever seen before were lying on their sides. Giant statuary of the ancient Greek gods, most without limbs, heads, and bases, were prevalent throughout the city. Buildings lay where they had crumbled and giant mold spores covered most of the marble ruins.

Three great pyramids dominated the distant skyline next to the far side of the great Crystal Dome. A once-great aqueduct system at least four hundred feet high ran through the dome and ended abruptly where it had crumbled not far from the middle and highest pyramid. The magma of the original eruption had sealed the hole that the waterway ran through.

Tomlinson took the first step onto the soil of the world's most ancient roadway. He felt the thick cobblestones beneath his feet and knew the power of the place. The floodlights could show only swatches of what must have been a grand view. Giant lakes of seawater had formed when the great city went under.

"Now, that makes me quite nervous," Dame Lilith said, looking up.

Tomlinson followed her gaze to the darkened sky of the great underground ruin. The lights from below barely illuminated the

Great Crystal Dome. Buried under two hundred feet of Mediterranean seabed, the water still cascaded through large cracks in the crystal and its protecting covering of rock and sand.

How many billions of tons of seabed must the architecture be supporting? he wondered.

"After close to fifteen thousand years, why hasn't the water completely flooded the domed area?" Caretaker asked as he studied the geodesic structure.

"Look," Tomlinson said as he pointed to steam rising from a thousand different areas. "The water is boiling off from the magma activity beneath the city. The pressure inside the dome must be considerable, and it assists the structure in supporting the tremendous forces arrayed against it."

"That would explain the horrible humidity and pressure my ears are feeling. But just how stable is the city?" Lilith asked.

"Strong enough to support the weight of the world. What amazing ancestors we had!" he said as he stepped farther into the great city.

A smaller dome, which had once been lined with the largest pillars of all, took up the furthermost portion of the city. The building beneath that dome had been crushed during the final cataclysm that had claimed Atlantis. Tomlinson smiled when he saw the structure through the lights.

"Have the excavation start there, but only after the Wave equipment has been installed completely. That is the priority."

One of the Tomlinson's engineers approached them after hearing his comments.

"Sir, we have started placing the Wave equipment in the remains of what must have been a huge lake near the center of the city. It seems to be the most stable area. Professor Engvall has started connecting the last of the Wave cables."

"Excellent. I want everything up and running within three hours."

"The cables?" Lilith asked.

"The Black Sea connection has been made." Tomlinson looked at her and then at the others. "Did you doubt that we would accomplish our goal?"

He turned and started walking to where a hundred workers

were gathering to break into what the ancient scrolls had described as the Empirium Chamber.

THE SOUTHERN GATE

Sarah felt herself being shaken by Mendenhall, who was calling her name. Their plunge through the darkness had ended with a sudden, bone-crunching impact into the pile of sand that had fallen beneath them from the desert floor. Then the Land Rover had rolled off the pile and hit a hard-packed surface, and that was when Sarah had hit her head.

Sarah rubbed her neck and opened her eyes. She thought she was blind for a moment until she heard Will speaking.

Mendenhall finally managed to find a flashlight and click it on. "The Rover's battery must have been torn loose from the fall." He shone the light first on Sarah and then on the two in the back. They were shaken but still alive. "At least we have air. Hot air, but breathable, I think."

Sarah tried to open her door. She pushed until it opened with a creak. She slowly climbed out and bent at the waist until she felt better. She rubbed her neck and then looked around in the darkness. She turned and felt around in the interior until she, too, found a flashlight. She turned it on and threw the beam around. Her mouth fell open in wonder.

"Jesus," was all she could say.

The light picked up a smooth surface beyond the massive pile of sand from above. The light bounced back from millions of tiles—small, colored ceramic pieces that described a life long dead, an ancient people seen at work and play. Scenes depicted the building of great monuments that, Sarah was sure, must now lie in ruins somewhere below. She looked around and saw a cobbled road that sloped downward. Then she knew that they had found the door that led under the sea and exited into the bowels of the city described by the plate map.

As the two Egyptians finally stumbled out of the backseat, a tremendous cracking sounded above them. Sarah and Will shone their lights up and saw to their horror that the giant statue of Apollo had lodged against one of the broken beams of petrified wood. Mendenhall ran and tackled the two shocked men as they were brushing themselves off, clearing them from the Land Rover just as ten tons of Apollo crushed the vehicle flat.

"Hey, is anyone alive down there?"

Sarah jumped at the sound of the bullhorn. She shone her light up at the spot that they had fallen through. The sand had drained away from the giant shaft, leaving a gaping hole in the ground above. What looked like a million tons of sand had fallen through with them when the unstable ground let loose. The effect was what Sarah imagined being caught in an hourglass would have been, with the beams stopping the sands from pouring in.

Above them, the Event Group security detail stood in the windstorm, shining their flashlights onto the very strange scene far below.

"Radio Colonel Collins, inform him in code we have found the road to Atlantis!"

"Yeah, and watch out where you step!" Mendenhall added.

Ten V-22 Ospreys, the tilt-rotor aircraft used by the U.S. Marine Corps, set down the last of the one hundred U.S. Marines and U.S. Navy SEALs who had been assigned to Jack. The president of Egypt, believing in the sincerity of the American president, had volunteered the forty vehicles that the Operation Backdoor assault element would use.

In the three hours since they had discovered the ancient gateway, Sarah and Will had been busy. With the help of her team and some very expensive equipment borrowed from the archaeological sites in and around the Valley of the Kings, they had widened the gate and actually improvised a ramp they could use to get into the wide avenue of the tunnel.

As the V-22s lifted off to return to the *Nassau* and the *Iwo Jima* for the main part of the operation, Sarah met Jack, Carl, and the major commanding the marines with a crisp but tired salute.

"Lieutenant McIntire, this is Major Gary Easterbrook; he's in command of the marine element."

Sarah saluted the major as he examined her work, then he returned her salute as he looked into the wide opening that led away into darkness.

"Any idea how far it goes?" the major asked.

"Well, according to the plate map, about two hundred miles," Sarah said, looking at Collins.

Carl looked at his watch and grimaced. "That's going to be cutting it close, Jack. We have only five and half hours until daybreak."

"Morning Thunder begins at exactly 0630 and we don't even know if this place leads anywhere any more important than a Starbucks," Jason Ryan said, adjusting his pack over his black Nomex BDU.

"We won't find out until we get our asses in the snake hole," Jack answered. "Major, your men will follow my team and we'll follow the captain here and his SEALs. They'll be traveling far faster in their jeeps than us in the two-ton trucks. Captain Everett and his team will be in advance and clear any obstacles they may come across. I need a clear roadway, Captain."

"Got it. We'll clear what we can and try not to cave the entire thing in on top of us," Carl answered as he raised his hand and signaled his team of forty SEALs and four specialists to come over.

"I can't help but think this is a wild goose chase, Colonel Collins. I mean, why not concentrate our efforts with the rest of the assault on Crete? We may end up missing the whole thing going through this way."

Jack looked at the young major and then removed his Mylar helmet. "Listen, our forces are getting ready to get their asses kicked all over the known world, and this operation could be the one wild card that the Coalition does not think we have. According to some very smart people, if they start the Wave again, it may not stop at just their target—it could continue until it starts the whole tectonic-plate system moving. So unless you want Gary, Indiana, to wind up where the Arctic is now, we'd best get through, no matter what lays in wait."

He turned to Carl and stuck out his hand. "Good luck, swabby."

Carl took the hand and then smiled. "This is probably no worse than some of the bars I'm known to frequent, Jack." He smiled at Sarah and then at Ryan. "Now don't you guys stop off at Denny's or anything, we may need you before too long."

They watched as Carl led his team over to the five jeeps.

The four officers saluted Collins and started for their vehicles as the first of the SEALs entered the darkened passageway to the oldest city in the planet's history. Whistles sounded in the dying wind as the main assault element climbed aboard their transports.

Like thousands of years before, western man was once again attacking the civilization of Atlantis. Sarah McIntire looked one last time at Jack and then prayed for a different outcome this time around.

CHAPTER
FIFTEEN

AVIANO AIR FORCE BASE
ITALY

After a personal phone call from the president of the United
States and an hour and a half of arguing, the Italian government finally granted permission for the most important aspect
of Operation Morning Thunder to overfly Italian airspace. The
president dropped certain names of people connected with the
Juliai Coalition who happened to be members of the Italian
parliament—names supplied by Martha and Carmichael. Fear-
ing a repeat of what had happened in Germany and Japan, Italy
became very cooperative.

The ten aircraft in question, hidden secretly at Aviano for a
full day after having been flown in during the hours of total
darkness, ten F-22A Raptors, America's fifth-generation fighters of the newly activated 525th Fighter Squadron, would play
a pivotal role in the opening minutes of the attack. Meanwhile,
the big surprise would come from the American air base at
Diego Garcia, where two B-2 Spirit stealth bombers would be
the first of America's warplanes to lift off.

As the fighters were made ready in Italy, the pair of B-2s
were already rolling down the darkened runway at Diego
Garcia.

USS *IWO JIMA*
ONE HUNDRED KILOMETERS
OFF THE WESTERN SHORE OF CRETE

Marine Corps General Pete Hamilton was on the flag bridge when the captain of the *Iwo* handed him a cup of coffee.

"We just received word that the first element of Morning Thunder cleared the runway at 0345 hours," the captain said.

General Hamilton sipped his coffee and looked out at the calm Mediterranean. He did not respond at first, only nodded. He knew that if their ploy didn't work, the landing force would not only have to deal with a stiff land defense, they would have to dodge an attack from the air.

"Thank you, Captain." He placed his coffee on the arm of the large chair. "Signal *Nassau*, Casper the Friendly Ghost has levitated."

"Aye, sir. Should we also signal Backdoor that Morning Thunder is off the ground?"

"If Colonel Collins started out on time and they're where they should be, he and my marines won't be able to receive you." He looked at the captain and shook his head. "Backdoor is on its own. No message."

The captain saw that the general was off in his own world, worrying over the time-worn problems of how to kill your fellow man without losing too many of your own, or of your enemy. The captain knew that very few men in the violent history of the world had ever found out how to do that.

USS *CHEYENNE* (SSN 773)
LOS ANGELES–CLASS
ATTACK SUBMARINE

The third piece of the surprise was the *Cheyenne*. The Los Angeles–class nuclear attack submarine had entered the Mediterranean through the Strait of Gibraltar three hours before and had run at flank speed until she reached her initial point. The captain of the *Cheyenne*, Peter Burgess, had received his orders the night before and was baffled as to why his boat was ordered to the relatively quiet Mediterranean when the world was getting ready to tear itself apart on the other side of the planet. Then he read the coded orders and his anger became an uneasy self-rebuke. The *Cheyenne* was ordered to launch all twelve of her Tomahawk cruise missiles at the island of Crete at exactly 0600. All twelve Tomahawks would be air-burst HE (high explosive) shots.

As he brought the *Cheyenne* up to periscope depth, he knew that whatever enemy was at those coordinates when the cruise missiles arrived was in for a major hurt.

"XO, open doors on vertical tubes one through twelve and spool up the birds."

125 MILES INSIDE THE ATLANTEAN ACCESS TUNNEL

The second element of Operation Backdoor was cooling its heels. For the past thirty minutes they had been at a standstill, since Everett had called Jack and told him that they had a major blockage of the passage and would have to blow an ancient magma flow from the tiled roadway.

While they waited, Sarah took pictures of the tunnel and its ornate wonders that depicted Atlantis in mosaic relief throughout the gateway. There were scenes of teachers instructing the young. Some depicted great battles fought with barbaric people; most brutal of all were the scenes showing the barbarity toward the lesser people of the world.

"Looks like these people were a little harsh on their neighbors," Mendenhall said as he saw the mosaic of slaves as they went about harsh work in the fields and buildings of Atlantis.

"It was a different world for those people. To be as advanced as they were, they had to have existed for at least ten or fifteen thousand years. As for their obvious brutality . . ." Sarah remembered that Mendenhall always looked at such things this from a base point of view. Either you were good or you were bad. There was never, ever anything in between.

"What do you suppose those are?" Collins asked, coming up from behind.

Sarah saw where he was pointing. She walked over to Collins, bent down, and placed her hand over one of many crystals about two feet in diameter placed into the tiled walls about five feet up from the cobbled floor.

"They look like lights," Collins ventured.

"Hey, the colonel is brighter than I thought," Sarah quipped.

Collins looked at her expressionlessly.

Sarah cleared her throat and then took out a small hammer and chipped away at the clay tile around the crystal. She finally managed to pop it free and held it in her hands.

"See, it's been beveled into this shape—very efficient for amplifying light. It would have taken very little electricity to ignite this filament here." She probed a small copper wire attached to a larger one running through the tiled wall.

"Electricity again?" Jack asked.

"Yes. These people were as active as ConEd."

"If they were so smart, how come they didn't have a train running down here?"

Sarah didn't answer Jack's question because she was thinking. Suddenly she pushed the light crystal into his hands and then ran to the back of one of the two-ton trucks and removed a spare battery from the back. She relieved Jack of the crystal and ripped free the thicker copper line, part of which was so old that it crumbled in her hand. She laid the crystal aside, opened up her battery-operated flashlight, and emptied the batteries out, then unscrewed the lens cap. She easily popped free the two small wires and then attached them to the copper line that ran chainlike to the other crystals embedded in the walls. Then she kneeled by the battery and hesitated. She split the flashlight wires farther apart until each end could reach a battery post and then she attached them.

Jack was amazed when the crystals in line lit up like a row of Christmas lights until they disappeared down the long tunnel.

"Uh, did someone trip the house alarm?" Everett asked over the radio.

Jack smiled and raised his radio. "Advance one, that's a negative. We had one of our electricians just throw a breaker switch," Collins answered, just as they heard and felt a rumble from below.

"Understood. Get your team moving. We just cleared the road down here, continuing on."

Jack clicked his radio twice and ordered everyone to the vehicles. Then he looked at Sarah with his left brow raised.

"Think you're pretty smart, don't you?"

She batted her eyelashes, smiled, and then moved off.

Jack shook his head and ran to his vehicle. He raised his radio. "Captain, we have to push it. Things are going to start going boom pretty soon."

ATLANTIS

"You think this is a waste of time?" Tomlinson asked Caretaker without turning around to face him.

They watched the engineers clearing the last of the debris from the entrance to the Empirium Chamber.

"I have no comment one way or the other, sir."

"Then why don't you go eat some cheese and drink a glass of wine with the others?"

"I have no taste for such things."

"Mr. Tomlinson, we are through the outer wall of the Empirium Chamber," the lead engineer said as he removed his hard hat and wiped sweat from his brow. "We have four men inside setting up some klieg lighting; we still may have a very unstable situation in there. In addition, we may have found another extensive cave system under the building. My echo-sound people tell me it goes down at least a mile and a quarter."

Tomlinson looked from the engineer to the set of twenty-foot-tall bronze doors that had bowed when the Empirium had collapsed. He could wait no longer. He ducked his head and entered the fifteen-thousand-year-old structure.

"Is he crazy? I told him it may be unstable," the engineer said to Caretaker as he approached the Empirium.

Caretaker's face was neutral as he looked into the blackness beyond the doorway. He had been watching Tomlinson closely ever since he had demolished his home in Chicago. The signs were small and had not been noticed by the others, but he had seen a change in the usually unflappable Tomlinson. When he spoke, his eyes moved too quickly from person to person, as if he was waiting for the first sign of disagreement from them. Caretaker believed that the pressure was mounting for the new Coalition leader. This seemingly obsessive desire to enter the old seat of the Atlantean government was just the latest. He smiled and looked at the engineer.

"*Unstable* may be the operative word," he said to himself as he followed Tomlinson inside.

The large lights cast eerie shadows on the broken columns and marble that lay crushed beneath most of the collapsed ceiling. A few of his archaeologists and paleontologists started filtering in to look at this marvel of history.

Tomlinson had to smirk when Caretaker ran one of his hands across an overturned marble table and grimaced at the millennia of dust.

"I always said you could never trust a man that didn't like getting dirty once in a while."

Caretaker did not bother to look at Tomlinson. "Is that what you say? Well, here is what I say: I believe you should be working on finalizing this last assault of yours and not out sightseeing."

"Can't you feel it? Where else but here could the power of this civilization be governed but the Great Empirium of Atlantis?"

"If we don't use the Wave soon, this just may be the only place you are allowed to govern."

Tomlinson knew that Caretaker was right. With his new feeling of rejuvenation, he looked around one last time at the Empirium Chamber, not noticing the skeletal form at his feet or the broken marble tile that hid the secret entrance to the underground world beneath.

THE ATLANTEAN ACCESS TUNNEL

Fifteen thousand years of leakage had formed long stalactites that hung from the high ceiling, each dripping with water that found a way in through course rock and magma from the Mediterranean, two miles above their heads.

Sarah and the other scientists back at Group had been right: in the three hours they had been in the great tunnel, Carl and his SEAL teams had come across numerous parts of the outer islands—the three great rings that had guarded the capital. There were large and small pieces of great columns, bath-houses, petrified trees, and roadways, all interspersed with giant deposits of ancient molten rock that made the landscape they had come across look like vast lakes of rippling water. The upheaval and death throes of this civilization had been of such violence that Everett could only imagine.

The inefficient lights provided them with horrific views of the cataclysm. Skeletal remains were everywhere, half buried or crushed by the very island they had lived on. It was as if the place had folded up and over the capital, and then the whole mass had sunk to the bottom of the Mediterranean.

"Captain, you have to see this," the SEAL lieutenant said as he approached. "This operation is done."

Carl quickly saw the reason for his dire comment. Standing in front of them, blocking their way, were the entire outer edges of the city of Atlantis rising four hundred feet into the air. Their way was blocked.

THE WHITE HOUSE
WASHINGTON, D.C.

The president was watching the C-SPAN coverage of the special UN meeting. He watched the Russian ambassador to the United Nations present their case.

As photos of the aircraft parts from the downed Boeing 777 were shown from an easel, he was reminded of the Cuban missile crisis, only this time it was the Russians who had the sympathy of the body politic. The president winced at the way his government had been set up.

"Our pull-back didn't convince anyone. All it did was corner our men into a tighter situation than before. Now we have a million refugees on the roads south from Seoul, clogging up reinforcements, and at the first sign of an offensive move, which I am compelled to order, the Chinese will rush across the border just like in 1947."

"We have to invite the Russians and Chinese in," Niles said, looking at the president.

"What?"

"Our KH-11 is over the Med; when we hit Crete, we have to get the Russians and Chinese to watch what's going on."

"What makes you think they don't have a spy bird over right now and just don't care what we're doing?"

"Because if they did, they would know our evidence is linked to what's going on. They're smart enough to see what is happening if it's right there before their eyes. Mr. President, if the Russians and Chinese really wanted to believe Kim or the evidence they have, they wouldn't wait, they would have hit us already. They *want* to believe us."

The president snapped off the television.

"You know what's happening better than anyone. If I can get you into a room with the Russian and Chinese delegations and get a live feed to you, can you convince them? I mean really convince them?"

Niles removed his glasses and shook his head. "I can sure as hell try."

205 MILES INSIDE THE ATLANTEAN ACCESS TUNNEL

Jack looked at the mountain of rubble before him strewn with giant boulders, parts of the island and most of a city or small village comprising its bulk. As he examined the wall before him, he even saw three of four ancient wooden ships.

"Before you ask, Jack, we don't have enough explosive for a quarter of that thickness," Everett said as he joined him at the blockage.

Collins looked at his watch. Forty-five minutes until the attack commenced. That meant that his element would not be able to relieve any of the pressure on the marines at the front door.

"I'm at a loss," Jack finally said.

Sarah was staring at the massive roadblock. She examined the rubble that lined the tunnel from top to bottom, where most of one section of the island had crashed through the crust and into the bedrock of the seafloor. She then noticed one of the giant stalactites that hung from a massive broken column. She tilted her head as she watched the runoff of seawater from above as it added to the mineral deposit.

"I know that look. It says either you have to go to the bathroom or you have a serious thought," Mendenhall said.

"Smart-ass," she answered as she continued to watch the runoff above her. Her eyes went to the roadway and then followed the water as it disappeared somewhere ahead. "Come on, funny man."

Mendenhall followed Sarah until they came to the inside wall of the tunnel. Sarah bent over, then went to her knees as she ran her hand over the broken cobblestone of the roadway thirty feet from the start of the blockage.

"These were a highly advanced people," she said.

"Yeah, advanced enough to blow their continent to hell."

"These tunnels were designed to run under the Med. What would they have to have installed to control the leaking? I mean, no matter what, if you tunnel under a body of water, you are going to have leaks. Just look at the Chunnel; the French and the British have major flood control built in."

"Yeah, but I don't get what you're driving at."

"Jack!" she stood and called out.

Collins saw Sarah thirty feet away and he and Everett trotted over.

"Make it quick, Lieutenant. In case you hadn't noticed, we have a major problem here."

"I think I'm aware of that. Carl, we have shape charges, correct?"

"No, but we have the training to create some conical charges, or directional explosions if that's what you need."

"Can we blow straight down?"

"Easy; but why would we want to?" he asked.

"I want to because I have faith in the engineering of the

Ancients," she answered, looking from face to face of the men standing around her. "What does every major city, every highway, have that controls water runoff?"

Jack smiled and Carl slapped his forehead.

"A sewer! These smart bastards had to control the leakage you have whenever you tunnel under a body of water. Jack, we go through the sewers! We don't go through but *under* the blockage!"

Everett slapped the SEAL lieutenant on the shoulder and got him moving to bring up the explosives they would need.

"I guess we'll have to thank the Atlantis Department of Water and Power," Mendenhall said.

"Not bad, shorty, not bad at all," Jack said to Sarah.

CASPER THE FRIENDLY GHOST
THIRTY THOUSAND FEET
OVER THE MEDITERRANEAN

The two B-2 stealth bombers made a wide turn to the south after their five-hour flight from Diego Garcia in the Indian Ocean. Their part of the mission would look as if the opening phases of the attack had originated in Aviano, Italy, a vital, imperative deceit.

"Casper One Actual to Casper Two, thirty seconds to launch point."

"Casper Two, copy, starting the music at five, four, three, two, one, bomb-bay doors opening on automatic."

The bomb-bay doors of the two giant aircraft, which resembled bats, opened to reveal a darkened interior. The automatic carriage that held each of the twelve Tomahawk cruise missiles started turning like a rolling lottery drum. At the bottom of each cycle, a BGM-109 Tomahawk Special radar-manipulation weapon fell free. As each engine ignited, the stubby wings and tailfin popped free of the outer body. A split second later, a strong signal started to pulse through the dark sky ahead of them. In all, twenty-four weapons shot through the thin air on a course for Crete.

"Casper One to Thunder One Actual, Heckle and Jeckle flight is now airborne. Casper One and Two, RTB at this time, good luck, Thunder One."

USS *IWO JIMA*

Marine General Pete Hamilton received the message from the lead B-2 and watched the night sky around the *Iwo*. The ship was coming to life in the early morning hours. Tilt-rotor craft abovedecks along with sixteen Seahawk helicopters were spooling up their engines and the marine assault force was in the process of loading.

Belowdecks, the sea-assault force was loading onto the Landing Craft Air Cushion (LCAC). This would be a lightning strike. The LCAC was loaded with four fully manned armored assault vehicles, while the four M1 Abrams tanks would be deployed from the USS *Nassau*.

The general looked from his wristwatch to the captain of the *Iwo*.

"Order *Cheyenne* to attack," he said far more calmly than he felt.

One hundred feet below the surface of the Mediterranean, Captain Burgess received the extremely low-frequency message (ELF) from the *Iwo*.

"Weapons officer, you have permission to launch vertical tubes one through twelve, empty 'em out. Diving officer, after launch, take us down to four hundred feet, heading two-three-zero at six knots."

CATAPULT FLIGHT

Flying at wave-top level, the flight of ten F-22A Raptors from Aviano, Italy, screamed over the Mediterranean at Mach 1.5. The internal weapons bay of each stealth fighter was full of air-to-ground munitions.

ATLANTIS

Tomlinson was personally overseeing the placement of the Atlantean Key. He was so excited that he could barely contain his feelings. He even looked kindly upon Caretaker and the other Coalition members as they watched the final parts being calibrated. His smile faded when he was handed a topside report.

"Twenty-four? I guess we don't rate any higher than that with all the trouble in the world. We were right: the Americans are spread too thin to adequately deal with us."

"What is it, Mr. Tomlinson?" Dame Lilith asked.

"It seems we have become a nuisance to our American president after all. Radar has picked up a force of twenty-four fighters inbound from Aviano. They're not even bothering to hide their presence."

"I see. And your plan for this is—"

Tomlinson looked at Caretaker and smiled. "To destroy them, what else." He turned away and raised his radio to his mouth, the whole time watching Professor Engvall install the Key. "Commander, defend the island; defend it vigorously, please."

Above, former Soviet Air Force General Igor Uvilinski lowered his radio and looked at the radarscope one more time.

"The SAMs will strike first and then our Migs will take care of any American that makes it out alive," he said, raising his field glasses to the camo netting three hundred yards away. "All air-defense units lock on to inbound targets and fire at will."

Around the center of the island, twenty-five SAM batteries fired, as each of their missiles locked on to an incoming warplane.

A hundred miles south, following the exhaust trails of the SAMs as they streaked through the sky to meet the foolish American pilots who so brazenly thought they could attack Crete without a fight, the lead flight of twenty Coalition MIG

31s based out of Libya saw the first of the antiaircraft missiles take out the first five targets. The lead pilot smiled under his mask. At this rate they would not have much to clean up.

As the flight leader watched the fighters break through the SAM screen, he became curious as to why they were not taking evasive maneuvers to avoid further contact—a decision that was very brave of them, but also very foolish.

"Lead, I have a visual on the targets. They are not American fighter aircraft—they are cruise missiles!"

The leader heard the call. He had been duped into believing that the cruise missiles were a fighter flight. As he thought this, he heard his missile-threat warning system go off with a piercing screech. He looked at his radar but it was clear. *Where is this threat coming from?* he asked himself.

At a hundred miles away from Crete, the flight of ten F-22A Raptors popped up from the ground clutter of the sea and fired off twenty AMRAMM missiles, then went low again and continued to streak toward Crete.

Before the lead pilot of the flight of MIGs knew exactly who and what was attacking them, AMRAMM missiles started to slam into the engines, wings, and fuselages of his squadron. The Americans had somehow enticed his men to attack what they thought was a poorly disguised flight of fighters, having their cruise missiles emit a high frequency "ghosting" as if they were manned aircraft, radar signature and all.

The pilot's next thought never made it to the formation of a question in his mind as the lock-on tone became even more insistent just as he finally saw the telltale radar-guided AMRAMM. The flight leader's MIG came apart exactly one minute after the attack had begun; after ten years of training and payment to an air force consisting of very well-paid mercenaries, the Coalition fighter squadron had ceased to exist.

As the MIG wreckage struck the sea below, a new and even more amazing sight graced the Mediterranean as twelve water slugs breached the surface one right after the other as the

Tomahawk cruise missiles of the USS *Cheyenne* flew to a hundred feet before leveling off. The stubby wings, air intake, and rear stabilizers popped free as the missiles started their runs for the SAM sites that had been tracked by the *Cheyenne* when they launched against the decoy cruise missiles, their target being the Coalition air defenses.

The defensive SAM sites started tracking new targets. These were not giving off false radar bounces and they were anything but incoming aircraft. The commander of the SAMs knew that they were under missile attack. However, before he could give the order to target the Tomahawks coming from the *Cheyenne,* his radar commander called in ten new targets to the east of Crete and coming on at Mach 1.9—more than twice the speed of sound. The Coalition general knew that the Americans had outsmarted him. To split his remaining SAMs among the two incoming sets of targets was to guarantee that half of the bogeys would get through.

"Sir, the incoming targets to the east are intermittent, not a strong bounce-back. I suspect another trick," his radar officer reported.

Yes, the Americans made the mistake of showing their hand earlier, he thought. Obviously, the targets that had swung around to the east for the attack were nothing more than the same type of missile that radiated like a fighter signature. They hoped to fool them into firing on them again.

"Once too many times to the well," the commander said. "Target only the western bogeys, ignore the eastern threat."

As he watched, SAM after SAM lifted off its launch rails and streaked into the sky headed west. Almost immediately, the general started receiving reports that the incoming targets were being struck without evasive maneuvering. The general raised his field glasses and looked to the lightening western sky. He saw a sky burst as something went down in flames.

"How many targets have been destroyed?"

"Six—there are six still incoming!"

The general closed his eyes and lowered his glasses for a moment. He then brought them back up and looked into the eastern sky and saw, in nightmarelike slowness, that the aircraft he thought had been decoy missiles were actually fighters. The first of the ten F-22A Raptors, acting as a Wild Weasel antiradar attack plane, launched its missiles. He lowered his glasses again before the nine others started launching their long-range ordnance. Right at that moment, the remaining six cruise missiles he had mistaken for manned aircraft screamed overhead and then air-burst over the SAM batteries. Then the first antiradiation Snake Eye struck the radar and command bunker.

The population of Crete, around 650,000 people, awoke to the tremendous explosions at the center of their island. The cruise-missile airbursts were an added bonus for the American commander. He actually did not think any of them would get through to their targets. The downward pressure of the warhead explosions drove the batteries into a crumpled heap along with the crews who operated them.

The ten F-22A Raptors tore over the island and fired on anything that moved. Either the Coalition troops were running around dazed or they made their way to the giant opening of the excavation.

The sound of helicopters came with the first rays of the sun. V-22 Ospreys and U.S. Marine hovercraft were making a run unopposed to the beaches of Crete.

The Second Battalion, First Marine Expeditionary Force (recon) was starting the land-assault portion of Operation Morning Thunder.

THE UNITED NATIONS
NEW YORK CITY

The special conference room had been set up at a moment's notice. The American ambassador had finally talked the delegations from Russia and China into attending, along with any military attachés they chose to bring.

As the live feed from one of the KH-11 satellites continued to show real-time visuals, the room remained silent as a tomb. The destruction in the opening moments of the attack stunned the gathered attachés and diplomats.

Five minutes later, Space Command reported that the Blackbird was drifting out of visual range of the battle and could not maintain the live feed.

"What you have just witnessed was an attack by Coalition forces on military units of the United States. A force you did not believe existed, a group that has made the United States look guilty at every turn in this very murderous game they are playing. Moreover, what is worse is the fact that we have intelligence that states they are going to strike your homelands within the hour. Earthquakes designed to destroy your way of life and take away any offensive military capabilities you have. They are going to make China and Russia so weak they will no longer be a threat to their long-range plans of dominating your societies."

The Russian ambassador silently stood and then looked back at the large screen on which he had just watched many people die. Then he nodded at Compton and left the room with his military attaché close behind.

The Chinese delegation sat for a moment. The ten men did not exchange words; they only looked at Niles, gauging his words and watching for the moment when a lie would be detected in the American's face. Slowly, the ambassador rose to his feet, followed by his entourage.

"If you will excuse us, we have much to absorb and much more to discuss with Beijing. Thank you for our inclusion in this briefing."

Compton watched them leave and then harshly pushed a chair out of his way as he grabbed his coat. Their honesty seemed that it would only delay the inevitable.

The president would have to defend those boys in Korea, and Niles knew that this would mean the world would then go to war.

An hour later, Compton was sitting with the president and the National Security Council in the subbasement of the White House.

Niles thought it ironic that the two parties most involved in the conflict were both buried below ground and waiting for things to play out above. He also knew that the Coalition would not be content to wait things out—they were going to strike; and it looked as if Jack and his team wouldn't get to them in time to stop the Wave from unleashing its devastating effects.

On the large monitors placed at the four corners of the room, Marine Corps General Pete Hamilton was seen on a live feed from the USS *Iwo Jima*.

"Yes, Mr. President, the second assault wave is ashore. We have curtailed the Sea Harrier and Raptor strikes on the island for lack of viable targets. The civilian population has cooperated thus far, and I am using two companies of marines to safeguard the indigenous personnel. That will make the tunnel-assault force light, but we'll have to do it with what we have on hand."

Every man in the room had been impressed with how the plan had unfolded thus far, but the real nut remained to be cracked.

"Any report from Operation Backdoor?" Niles asked from his seat away from the table.

"None. Since we have had no contact, as operational field commander, I must assume they have not reached their objective, dictating that we attack the front door with everything we have."

Niles lowered his head in thought. Only he knew that Collins had never failed at a mission he'd set out to complete.

"Thank you, General. We had one last go at the Russians and Chinese and it looks like they'll have none of what we're selling. So, good luck and Godspeed," the president said as he ordered the satellite feed terminated.

"What's the latest from Korea, General Caulfield?"

"Still just the one spearhead has crossed the border. We have learned that the commanding general has finally crossed with them and is leading the assault. We have a mixed bag of intelligence, some saying that this general," Caulfield looked down at his notes, "Ton Shi Quang, is acting alone and against orders from Pyongyang. Other intel says he is acting directly on Kim Jong Il's orders. In any case, his spearhead will meet up with the Second Infantry Division's armored forces ten miles north of Seoul. Satellite imagery has given us a grim picture of what's to come. The North could cross with thirty-five divisions at any time."

"We all know I cannot let the South Korean government fall. The painful truth of the matter is that we are a prisoner of our own past. We would betray those that have died there in hot war and cold. Either we stop them any way that we can, or half those boys will be overrun."

The faces around the room could not bring themselves to look at one another. Niles stood in frustration and paced.

"Admiral Fuqua, do we have a capable sub in the area?"

Fuqua stood up and looked from Caulfield to the president. "Yes, sir, USS *Pasadena*."

"She is carrying *special* ordnance onboard?"

"Yes, sir, she is."

"She is to stand by for orders." He looked at Niles and then back at his military advisers. "But first, I want every fighter from Japan, the carrier groups, and Korea in the air. Before I commit to a nuclear option, I want to hit them conventionally with everything we have. Simultaneous with the air strike, I want the Second ID to advance to meet the spearhead. Make up the orders. I want them on my desk confirming a nuclear-strike alert."

"Yes, Mr. President."

Niles closed his eyes. The words *nuclear strike* were out in the open.

Jack Collins was their last hope for peace.

THIRTY MILES SOUTH OF THE DMZ, SOUTH KOREA

Major General Ton Shi Quang had just received the orders he had forced his Great Leader into giving him: "Attack with all offensive forces under your command."

The Coalition's bold plan for North Korea was finally becoming a reality and was going to pay off far better than they had ever thought. Now he would order his army forward to crush Seoul and he would be far away by the time the Americans were forced to do what he knew they had to do. Long before the mushroom clouds started to spread along the border, he would be a thousand miles away.

"Order the armored spearheads to advance at all possible speed; they will now be supported by the whole of the People's Army and air forces. Also inform my helicopter pilot I will be touring the advance from the air."

After his aide left to give the order, the general looked around and was content. He nodded as he looked at the sand table once more as the small models of tank forces from both sides were very nearly converged.

"Too bad; I believe we would have had a fighting chance this time around," he said to himself as he pulled on his gloves and walked away from the People's Army forever.

CHAPTER

SIXTEEN

THE ATLANTEAN ACCESS TUNNEL

The last sandbag went on top of the eight-pound charge of C-4 explosive. The echo-sound machine that Sarah had insisted on bringing had shown a large cavity underneath the roadway, but it could not tell them anything other than that. The hollow spot could mean almost anything, and Jack knew it. Their entire participation in this attack depended on what was down there.

"Fire in the hole!" one of the SEAL team shouted.

Ryan and Mendenhall covered Sarah as the loud *crump* was somewhat muted by the pile of sandbags that directed the blast downward. The tunnel shook, and they feared collapse until it settled.

Collins shone a large light down inside the hole they had made and saw that there was indeed a bottom, and that was a start. He started peeling away equipment, but was stopped by Sarah, who had started handing off her own equipment to Mendenhall and Ryan.

"Excuse me, Colonel, but I think this is my area of expertise, remember?"

"Sorry, Lieutenant, I believe your job description is now that of an instructor in geology," he shot back, knowing that Sarah had originally been trained as a U.S. Army tunnel rat—

what the army euphemistically called a person dumb enough and small enough to wriggle into places where only bad things could be lurking.

"She's right, Colonel. And not only that, your going down first is a little off the beaten path for a command-type person such as yourself," Ryan said as he, too, handed off his equipment to Mendenhall. "And I believe this mission also calls for a gentleman of my . . . uh . . . limited stature."

Jack looked at his two officers and then over at Everett.

"I hate to say this, and I really do hate it, but Ryan's right, Colonel."

As Mendenhall accepted Ryan's field pack, a small CD player fell out along with several CDs.

"You didn't!" Will said, looking at Ryan.

"Yeah, the colonel's music; it brought me good luck back in Africa."

The marine major looked at the five people in front of him and then turned to the SEAL lieutenant.

"Just who in the hell are these people?" he whispered.

"I don't think we want to know," the SEAL answered.

Hands-free SEAL headphones and silenced MP-5 machine guns were issued to Sarah and Ryan along with four pounds of C-4 and several flares.

"Kind of reminds me a little of Arizona a couple of years back," Sarah joked, but then she looked around and saw the serious faces of the others. Mendenhall looked downright angry at the comparison because they had all lost friends there and he didn't want to lose these two here.

"Just watch your ass, Lieutenant," Jack ordered.

Sarah shone her light into the hole and started down the ladder into the darkness below. Will slapped Ryan on the back and then stepped back and allowed him to follow.

"Okay, Major, let's start getting our equipment off these trucks and get the men stripped down to something that'll allow them to fight in this heat. Upper-torso body armor only if they so choose," Everett ordered, as Collins watched the two lights disappear down below.

* * *

At several places in the first hundred feet, the sewer walls had given way to forced magma movement. Sarah thought it was lucky beyond measure that the entire system had not filled up with the flow of hot stuff. One of the first sights they saw were skeletal remains. It looked as if the bodies had been citizens and soldiers. Some had the barest of armor still attached, literally, to their bones. Others had the bronze chest plates and grieves melted onto them.

"Sarah, stop!" Ryan said.

Sarah stopped in her tracks. They were close to a turn in the ancient sewer system. She looked back at Ryan and saw that he had his gloved hand placed against the tiled wall.

"Feel it?" he asked.

Sarah placed her hand on the wall. She felt it immediately. It was the same sensation as one would have if she placed her hand against a subway tunnel wall.

"What do you think?"

"I can't place it. It's not moving, but it builds in intensity and then settles before starting up again."

"Construction?" Ryan asked.

"Maybe. Come on, let's get our asses down the tunnel and find out."

Sarah turned and started making her way along faster. Soon she noticed that with each step she took, her feet were sinking into ever-deeper water that had accumulated. This did not bode well, but she decided not to say anything to Ryan.

Five minutes later, Sarah's shoulders slumped as she saw the cave-in from the roadway above. More parts of the ancient city had spilled into the sewer system. Columns, pieces of roadway, marble, sandstone houses, and more skeletons littered the sewage passage ahead.

"Damn, we're not catching any breaks here," Ryan said as he stood next to Sarah. "I better let the colonel know the bad news."

Sarah just nodded as Ryan started making the dreaded call. While he did so, Sarah popped a white flair and tossed it onto the rubble pile just above the lapping water.

Sarah shook her head, and that was when she saw it. Smoke

from the flare was rising, and then about five feet up it was suddenly sucked into the debris. She tilted her head and watched just to make sure, then she reached out and grabbed Ryan's shoulder.

"Hold one, Colonel," he said as he looked at where Sarah was pointing. "Colonel, let me get back to you."

As they advanced, Ryan popped another flare and tossed it onto the slide. Sure enough, they both saw the large hole. It looked big enough for both of them to slip through side by side.

Sarah laid her MP-5 against the rubble and started climbing. Ryan watched for a moment and then followed. She shone her helmet light into the hole and then, unsatisfied, used her large flashlight.

"It looks likes it goes all the way through. This is too much to ask for. How in the hell was this thing formed?"

"Don't look a gift horse in the mouth—"

"You mean 'maw', don't you? Because that's what it looks like, a maw."

"You have such a way with description, Sarah old girl," Ryan said as he pressed his throat mike and held on to his MP-5 somewhat tighter than before Sarah's comment. "Colonel, we have a way through. Start sending the men down."

As Collins and the others hit the tunnel floor, Sarah started through the hole in the debris field. She had Ryan stay behind to assist with getting the troops ready for a tight squeeze and a long crawl out. She cursed herself for not having worn her knee pads, because every sharp rock and jagged piece of marble seemed to find a soft spot on her knees.

She was near the end when she noticed a large niche in the side of the tunnel. As her helmet light hit the spot, she saw bones of fish, humans, and material of some kind, and what looked like paper, or was it papyrus, she couldn't tell. She reached out and looked at the shredded paperlike material, then looked over the bones more closely. They were mostly ancient human remains. However, interspersed with these were fish bones and other animal skeletons. Then her eyes widened when she saw the gnaw marks on them, deep gouges that had to have been made by enormous teeth.

"Yuck," she said.

When she turned to make her way past the site, something hard and heavy fell on her from above. She screamed when she saw the incisors, teeth as long as two butcher knives, directly in front of her face. She crawled backward, and the skeletal remains of the giant rat rolled off and lay beside its ancient nest. The giant must have lived in the rubble for years after the destruction, feeding off the dead and then the fish that were trapped in the cave-in, and then it must eventually have starved to death.

She shone her light ahead and saw that the rat hole dug long ago might have saved their mission. The light picked out the tunnel's end. She keyed her throat mic.

"Okay, Jason, send the cavalry in."

OPERATION MORNING THUNDER
THE ISLE OF CRETE

The marines of the advanced recon unit started easing their way to the giant cave opening of the tunnel. Several small-arms shots rang out; they were quickly silenced by marine counterfire. Within ten minutes, the site was secured and word was sent to the *Iwo,* offshore, that Operation Morning Thunder was starting to make its way down the tunnel.

As the radio message went out, a marine squad passed a checkpoint that they didn't know was there, and with orders directly from Tomlinson, one of the survivors of the beach defenses pushed a button.

Standing on the flag bridge of the USS *Iwo Jima,* General Hamilton flinched at the explosion in the center of the island. As he watched, he slammed his fist into the steel railing, as a nonnuclear mushroom cloud rose from the excavation site. He closed his eyes and cursed. He turned to see the navy bridge staff staring at the scene in shock.

"Captain, get me the beach commander on the horn if he's

still alive and get our Seabees moving, I want that area secured and the excavation opened up. Also get me National Command Authority on the line, tell them that Operation Morning Thunder has not, repeat, ha*s not* secured the front door."

"I hope Colonel Collins is having a better go of it than we are. Operation Backdoor has now become our last chance."

ATLANTIS

Tomlinson listened to the survivors of the beach defense and was satisfied that the marines could not get to them before the Wave activated. He nodded and then turned to Professor Engvall.

"The blue diamond is in place?" he asked.

"Yes. We have been generating for the past hour on the smallest setting. I just need to know which connections to attach."

Tomlinson smiled and looked from Engvall to Dame Lilith and Caretaker.

"The orders remain the same—China and Russia . . . also the eastern United States."

"Strikes in the United States are not called for at this time. We have weakened the U.S. far too much as it is," Caretaker said, stepping forward.

"The transmission lines have been laid, the amplifiers are in place, and the Key can reach them with no problem."

"But—"

"Enough! Professor, begin your countdown in one hour."

Dame Lilith, Caretaker, and the others watched as Tomlinson disappeared back into the broken Empirium Chamber, where he had been holed up most of the morning.

"I'm worried. The plan does not call for American escalation at this time," Lilith said, looking at Caretaker.

Caretaker watched as Tomlinson retreated with his hands held behind his back, then he answered Lilith.

"He's under stress, but right now our lives and, I daresay, the very life of the Coalition rides on *his* shoulders. Hitting the States may not be a bad idea at this time. It may take their determined minds away from us."

Dame Lilith watched as Caretaker turned and walked slowly away, just looking at the ruins of the capital city of Atlantis as if he were on a stroll in Piccadilly Circus.

She looked around at the Crystal Dome rising far above her and the ruins that surrounded her.

"I was just concerned . . . you won't tell William I doubted him, will you?" she called after Caretaker.

Just as she said the words, she felt the hair on her arms stand straight up and suddenly felt slightly nauseated. She knew then that the large generators had started up and the Wave was building into Thor's Hammer like the anger of a caged tiger, and that tiger very much wanted to be let loose.

CHAPTER

SEVENTEEN

SOUTH OF THE DMZ
SOUTH KOREA

The general in charge of the three-pronged attack raised his radio.

"For the honor of the People, I give the long-awaited order: Commence the artillery barrage of Seoul!"

From behind the DMZ, five thousand artillery batteries opened fire, sending rounds into the American line of defense.

SITUATION ROOM
THE WHITE HOUSE
WASHINGTON, D.C.

As the president watched the large viewing screen, the numbers and field units of the North Koreans started changing rapidly. Icons symbolizing artillery were flashing red; the ones indicating the three-pronged spearhead started moving also, along with thirty-five divisions north of the border.

"They're on the move," said General Caulfield.

Niles Compton watched the president, who sat with his eyes closed.

"We have major air assets lifting off from all the eastern Chinese air bases. It looks like over five hundred aircraft of

every variety. Should I order our fighters in from Japan and
notify our carrier-based planes, Mr. President? They're loiter-
ing a hundred miles off, over the Sea of Japan,"

The president stood and put his large hands into his pockets. He glanced at Niles for a moment and then looked at the
monitor. The red icons of the North were moving very rapidly.

"Take note: the North Koreans have crossed the thirty-
eighth parallel in force and are now, and have been for hours,
in noncompliance of the treaty of July twenty-seventh, 1950.
The Second ID and the air forces of the United States are
hereby ordered to defend South Korea from the Democratic
People's Republic of North Korea. If the People's Republic of
China crosses into South Korea, American aircraft are to attack them."

CRUSADER FLIGHT, TWENTY-SEVENTH FIGHTER SQUADRON OUT OF KADENA AIR FORCE BASE, OKINAWA, JAPAN

The twelve F-22A Raptors had been based in Japan for the past
eleven months and were now grouped with thirty-five F-15
Strike Eagles, thirty-five Eagle air-superiority fighters, and
twenty-five F-16 Fighting Falcons of the Japanese defense
force. As the fighters cruised at twenty thousand feet just east
of Korean territorial waters, they received the order that shook
every man in the flight. The lieutenant colonel flying as the
lead asked for confirmation twice to make sure he had heard
right. "Attack all North Korean forces south of the thirty-eighth
parallel. Attack any air assault by any foreign government. Commence unrestricted warfare against all ground units south of the
border."

As the colonel looked at his scope, he counted fifty-plus
Chinese MIG 31s and an equal number of North Korean aircraft ready to cross into South Korea.

"This is going to be messy," he said to himself.

* * *

The spearhead and lead armored element of the People's Army opened fire from a ridge overlooking Qua Shan village. There were no reports of enemy emplacements, but the overzealous general left in charge was taking no chances. He thought that he might as well level the village while he had the chance, with their air power soon to arrive.

"We have incoming aircraft from the west, General; they are squawking People's Republic Air Force."

The general looked down from his armored personnel carrier and nodded at his courier.

"Good. Have ground control direct them to the first American defense line. Inform them I will lay green smoke."

"Yes, sir."

It happened so suddenly that the American colonel thought that his air-search radar was not operating properly. The entire Chinese force turned away and started flying northward, away from South Korea. He watched to make sure it was not a trick. When he saw the MIGs continue northward, he smiled.

He was further shocked when his radio came to life on the frequency that was supposed to be secure: "American flight commander to the south, the People's Republic of China apologizes for the closeness our training flight came to South Korean airspace. We are returning to base at this time."

"All elements of Crusader are to attack. I repeat, attack!"

The first thirty-five F-15 Strike Eagles banked hard and dived for the earth.

The North Korean general turned in his turret and smiled. Now the Americans would feel the full force of the Great Leader's might. He looked through his glasses and froze. American F-15s were screaming toward his positions unopposed.

"General, the Chinese have left the area and our own air support has been ordered to stand down. The Americans are attacking up and down the line. U.S. carrier aircraft are hitting our artillery positions on our side of the border. Pyongyang is ordering a general retreat!"

To augment the disastrous report, five T-80 tanks exploded

only a thousand yards in front of his command vehicle. As he ducked, he saw the American fighters pull up after their attack. There were more explosions as more tanks met the same fate. The Americans had acted swiftly and caught them off guard.

"This is madness," he screamed as he saw antipersonnel cluster munitions fly into the back of his lines where his infantry had been mobilizing for the assault.

As the general watched, the spearhead that had been rolling through unblemished just five minutes before lay in a smoking ruin all around him.

SITUATION ROOM
THE WHITE HOUSE
WASHINGTON, D.C.

Things were moving too fast for Niles to keep up. One by one, the icons marking the forward advance of the North Korean assault slowly started to disappear from the map.

"Mr. President, it's been confirmed: the Chinese have exited north of the thirty-eighth parallel. They are returning to Chinese airspace!"

"I guess they decided we weren't lying after all!"

Compton heard the relief in the president's voice, and he himself felt like jumping up and whooping, as many of the generals and admirals were doing.

"American and Japanese air strikes are heavily damaging all forward units in the south. The Second ID is moving unopposed into the DMZ. It has been confirmed that Kim Jong Il ordered his troops north of the thirty-eighth parallel."

"Sir, we have a message from the Russian president; he's asking if they could render assistance to our marine force on Crete," the national security Adviser read from a note. "Also, the Chinese ambassador just issued a statement saying that the People's Republic has no intention of aiding this lawless act of aggression by Kim Jong Il and the People's Army, and is insisting that his army stand down in this time of world crisis."

The president sat hard into his chair and looked at Niles. "It seems your words meant something to them, Niles."

"No, Mr. President, the images of kids dying on Crete did the convincing. The Russians and the Chinese do not like to see civilians dying."

"Still, old boy, you may have saved our collective asses."

Niles stood and walked over to the president's side of the conference table and knelt beside his chair.

"Mr. President, this is just a stay, not a pardon. If we don't stop the Coalition from using the Wave against these people, they're not going to give a damn who's guilty or innocent. They now know their main enemy is on Crete and they will destroy it with nuclear weapons if they have to. We would do the same if we were losing cities. Our people beneath Crete still have to stop the Coalition from attacking their countries."

"But now that the Coalition knows they are found out, why would they continue?"

"The Coalition has survived through worse many times. They will attack and then disappear, only to resurface with new identities and the same hidden wealth, and they will still win by offering financial assistance to the countries that are devastated. They have been planning this thing since the end of World War Two."

The president stood among the gathered men and women of the Security Council, who were still smiling from ear to ear. Then he looked at the threat board; down at the bottom sat the small island of Crete.

"Niles, I've heard about his prowess in the field, but tell me again how good your Colonel Collins really is."

CHAPTER EIGHTEEN

OPERATION BACKDOOR
CRETE

It had taken far longer to get men and equipment through the small access tunnel, or Ratzville, as the men were calling it, than they had originally thought. A full fifty minutes had been wasted as they struggled through the filthy tunnel. When they finally made it out, the lead SEAL unit reported that the sewer shaft was clear for at least two miles.

"Ryan!" Jack called over his shoulder.

"Yes, sir?"

"The marines having any luck with the radios yet?"

"Negative. We can't even get the local Atlantis AM station," he joked, but stopped smiling when the marines around him looked on with sour faces. "No, nothing, Colonel."

Jack looked at his watch. Almost a full hour and a half since Morning Thunder had kicked off.

"Jack, are you feeling that?" Sarah asked. "The Coalition has started the Wave."

Collins didn't say anything; he knew that she was right. He was feeling it in his inner ear, just as Sarah had said he would.

"Look, when this thing starts, you watch your ass. I don't want a dead girl—" Jack caught himself. "Just watch your butt, Lieutenant," he said quickly and then walked off.

"What does the colonel have to say?" Mendenhall asked, walking up to Sarah.

"Nothing important, I guess."

ATLANTIS

Tomlinson was sitting in the now well-lit Empirium Chamber. The engineers had shored up what they could and roped off the worst areas. He had watched the men working without comment until his eyes had settled on something jutting from a large slab of marble. He had been looking at it for well over thirty minutes, mesmerized by the sight of the skeletal arm and hand. There was a mold-covered bronze knife clutched in the blackened fingers, the bones still curled around the hilt. He was content just to look and wonder who the person had been.

"Sir, we are ready. Power is at one hundred percent and we have full continuity in the power lines to the Black Sea and Lake Shiolin."

Tomlinson, without looking up from the hand and knife, smiled. "You forgot the Long Island Sound, Professor; is that line also active?"

"Yes, sir. The amplification modules are placed one mile from the Davidson fault line and thirty-three miles from the continental plate."

"Very good. That should create quite a headache in the financial district, wouldn't you say?"

"It should, yes," Engvall answered as he turned and slowly walked away.

Tomlinson looked up, but all he saw was the professor's backside as he moved into the shadows of the Empirium Chamber. Then he lowered his head and stared at the arm and hand again. He tilted his head and seemed to be somewhere else.

The Atlantean Wave equipment with the five massive fifty-thousand-watt generators had been placed inside a natural bowl surrounded by solid rock. The hole, it was surmised, must have been a manmade lake fifteen thousand years before. A 180-foot statue of Poseidon had once sat in the middle of the lake, rising 100 feet into the air. Poseidon, the Greek god of the seas, now lay in a crumpled heap around the sides of the dry lake with only his island pedestal still in the center.

Technicians were working at a hundred monitoring stations inside the bowl and another twenty sat at stations on the hundred-foot tower. They all knew that the power they were about to unleash could not be calculated in normal terms because of the added power of the Key; with its intricate tone grooves and strange properties, such power usage was unknown.

After studying the Key's grooves, Engvall knew that the decibel level they had used before paled in comparison to what the Ancients had accomplished. They had duplicated only 3 percent of what the Atlantean Key had in its etched surface. The power of the diamond was awesome. They had placed the blue diamond in its cradle for only a moment in the initial test; when they had all felt the strength of the device as it started emitting a tone that they could not hear. So far, thirty men and women had reported to the makeshift field hospital where some of the troops from above were being treated, which upset Tomlinson no end, due to the fact he had wanted the cowards, as he called them, kept separate from the scientists, lest they cause doubts about their security.

The way in which the tones would be taken from the magical diamond was far different from the stylus method used in ancient times. Engvall had come up with an ingenious design that would flood the rotating diamond inside its chamber with plasma, which would ensure that there were no impurities on the surface of the grooves. Then the chamber would be flooded with ozone and electrified. The tones would then commence, carried electrically from the diamond chamber through the connecting lines and onto their long journeys to their target cities.

Each section of the diamond had been broken down into smaller sections by the Ancients. Each one was designed for a specific stratum of different tectonic plates; in other words, they had a section of tone grooves for the granite and sandstone base for Long Island Sound and the same for the paneurasian plate, comprised of compacted granite, slate, marble, and sandstone.

Depending on the density of these materials, the Ancients had calculated the specific tone-groove-decibel level for that attack area. An electronic cable, the type that was found on every PC in the world only larger by a 100 percent, was running from the diamond's cradle to their coordinated continental cable.

Engvall now knew that the blue diamond was the only substance on earth that would hold up to the tones themselves without cracking. *Amazing,* he thought as he watched the chamber from a distance. This was why the grand experiment at Krakatoa had failed so spectacularly, when a large crystal was used instead of the blue diamond.

As Engvall watched from his perch high above the emptied lake where he and his special assistants would monitor the Wave as it radiated outward, he felt just as Tomlinson had said he would feel—like one of the gods of old with the power of the earth at his fingertips.

However, as he looked out at his creation, the thought of the destruction of Atlantis, Krakatoa, and the innocent deaths in China, Russia, and Iraq registered in his mind that he wasn't a god at all, just a man following another man. As he watched Tomlinson slowly leave the Empirium Chamber far below, he could not help but think that the man he was following was slowly becoming unbalanced, as were the many men who had come before him who had dreams of subjugating the world.

THE WHITE HOUSE
WASHINGTON, D.C.

The president was taking many different routes in trying to explain to the Russians and Chinese what the plan was for rooting out the Coalition members who had burrowed deep into the ground. Because of a solid argument from Niles, the president had not included the information regarding the discovery of Atlantis. So far, what they had come to terms with was the fact that the 650,000 inhabitants of Crete would have to be evacuated immediately. NATO and Russian warships and every passenger liner and ferry in the Mediterranean were being utilized to this end.

The situation in Korea had stabilized to the point where the Second Infantry Division with reinforced armor of the Fourth ID had reoccupied the border, and the North Korean army had recalled the surviving elements of the three-pronged attack into the South, though most of them wouldn't be coming home.

American airpower, without the added element of China to cope with, had manhandled and mauled North Korean airpower and artillery units so badly that his generals had persuaded Kim that they had no friends left at this point, and the only thing to do was end this thing. The Chinese still had not sent official word through diplomatic channels that they fully bought the American explanation, but they would assist in stabilizing the region until things could be made clear.

A tone sounded and a small light went on in the corner of the laptop Niles had placed on the table before him. Virginia's image from Nellis flashed on the screen.

"Niles, Pete Golding is on the line. I'm going to conference his monitor in with yours."

The screen was split so that Niles could see both Virginia and Pete from the Event Group Center at Nellis Air Force Base.

"Niles, we have a very bad situation," Pete stated flatly with no emotion in his voice. He was crumpled-looking, with part of his white shirt collar pointing up.

Niles closed his eyes. "What have you got, Pete?"

"We have deciphered some of the scrolls that Jack recovered. Niles, it's not the power of the blue diamond that is flawed, it's the great chart—the map the Ancients created that depicts the fault lines and tectonic plates. We've advanced in most areas since the Atlanteans' time. They were amazing to be sure, but one area they failed at was that these plates are conjoined, they are connected, some just below the crust, some as deep as the mantle. It took us a while to figure this out because the Atlantis language is some parts hieroglyph and what we call Linear B and—"

"Pete, for God's sake, what in the hell are you saying here? Forget the damn linguistics lesson!" Niles said irritably.

"Niles, if they use the Wave with the added power of that

diamond and its tone design, it will set off a chain reaction that could bring this planet to its knees. We could lose entire continents, crack them wide open, flip whole continental shelves, crack the world down to its core. Whatever you consider hell to be, this damn device could make it happen!"

"Jesus," Niles said.

"We now know that the Atlanteans, for whatever reason, tried this once, fifteen thousand years ago, and look what happened: the entire world was changed."

"Get me Europa's model and your figures."

"What are you thinking, Niles?" Virginia asked.

"What am I thinking, Virginia? I'm thinking the president may have no other choice than to bow to world pressure and smash Crete and everything under it, including Jack, Carl, and those young marines."

THE ATLANTEAN TUNNEL

The heat inside the sewage system was getting unbearable, but Jack could not afford to call for a halt to the march. The hundred marines had managed to make the best time possible under the circumstances. Giant walls of ancient magma had cracked and poured through in a thousand different areas. In many areas it looked as if the tunnel itself had been lifted up and dropped, to become a twisted and jumbled mess. All the while, they could feel the Wave building somewhere through the dense rock strata of the underground maze.

Sarah caught up with Jack and took long strides to keep up with him.

"Jack, it seems we're too deep," she said breathlessly.

"What? What do you mean?"

"I've been keeping track of our progress. We may be as far as a mile too deep. Have you noticed that the symptoms of the audio tones have lessened? Look around; men are making better time because they aren't feeling the effects in their inner ear. No nausea."

Jack stopped and raised his radio.

"Backdoor One to Two Actual," he called on the radio.

"This is Two, go ahead," Everett answered from somewhere up ahead.

"Two, our lieutenant here says she believes we've gone too deep."

"She may be right. We're starting to get magma vents here and the heat's up by thirty-five degrees in the last quarter mile."

Collins lowered the radio and watched as several of the marines walked doggedly past him.

"Wait a second, One. The SEALs are saying we have a large cavern ahead. . . . Jesus, Jack, you have to see this!"

Collins clipped the radio to his belt and then trotted forward after ordering the marines to take five minutes' rest. Sarah, Ryan, and Mendenhall followed Jack.

They climbed over a sloping mound of solid lava and finally spied Everett, who was talking with the SEAL lieutenant. They were standing in a natural alcove overlooking their new discovery. Twenty phosphorus flares glowed brightly from below and afforded a shadowy view of hell, highlighted by terrible orange and yellows of Satan's waters.

"Oh, my God!" Sarah said as she leaned over, placed her hands on her knees, and looked out over the vast chamber below.

The flowing river of lava was just that—a large ribbon, twenty feet wide, that stretched the entire length of the ancient excavation. The manmade structures inside were torn and broken; pillars of immense size had tumbled to the stone flooring. Littered among these ruins were hundreds and hundreds of skeletal remains that had melted into the stone to become one with floor they lay upon.

Collins looked around the upper reaches of the chamber and saw giant beams of scaffolding. There was a rail system capable of holding thousands upon thousands of tons. In addition, lying on its side at the bottom was what that system had once held— a gigantic wheel. The spikes arrayed around this object were as big a mystery as the wheel itself. It lay half buried in the debris that had shaken loose from the cavern's ceiling.

"What in the hell went on here?" Everett asked as he spied

the arms and other skeletal parts protruding from the lava that had flowed over them.

Sarah was looking at the arrangement at the top of the giant cave. The ancient copper wires hung limp and grime-covered, and the copper plating attached to them was green with mold and corruption.

"This is the Wave chamber, a giant power-generating system. Jesus, Jack, this place was responsible for the death of Atlantis," she said as she straightened. "This diagram was in one of the engineering scrolls you recovered and the plate-map hologram, we just didn't know what it was. The whole of Atlantis must have come down on this place, and the weight of the island must have pushed this place miles under the sea."

Jack was watching the SEALs as they reached the bottom of the cavern, then he turned to Sarah. "Did the diagrams show any way out of here?"

"I don't know. We were in such a rush, Jack, I'm sorry. But listen, if this is truly the Wave chamber, Atlantis has to be on top. We have to find a way up; there has to be a connection."

"Well, we're not going to find it just standing here. Will, bring the troops in."

As Collins started down the sloping trail to the bottom, Sarah and the others became aware of the death that surrounded them in this ghastly place. Thousands of people had been killed in this tunnel while trying to escape the final decisions of their gods. The marines tried to step carefully, but many bones, petrified, snapped beneath their boots.

As Jack gained the floor of the chamber, he saw a particular set of bones that made him stop to examine them. The bronze armor was like others he had seen above, mostly melted into the stone. The skeleton was larger than most he had seen, and remnants of blue cloth could be seen cloaked around its shoulders. The helmeted head was still intact and lay staring up at him. The blue horsehair plume was as viable as it had been the day this man had fallen. It was covered in grime, but it was enough to tell Jack that this was a fellow soldier from a time ten thousand years before Moses.

As he gathered his thoughts and stepped over the remains,

his boot came down on a smaller skeleton. There was no way to
know that he had just given the final insult to the very necro-
mancer who had invented the Wave, the great Lord Pythos,
whose broken and twisted arm was still in the grasp of the last
of the Titans.

As they followed Collins in a straight line, Sarah doubled
over in pain at the same moment as half of the marine force
did the same, some vomiting, others dropping their gear and
grabbing for their temples in agony. Even Collins had to lean
against a stone wall hard enough to send his helmet rolling.

"Jack, the Wave is building fast! They're going to attack!"
Sarah yelled as she finally gave up and vomited.

Tomlinson watched the technicians as they monitored their
boards. High up in the control platform, he, Caretaker, and
several other Coalition members, including Dame Lilith, were
amazed at the power being created by the generators, which
seemed to have doubled in strength as soon as the blue diamond was connected. The time it had taken to recut the blank
ends of hardened diamond to fit the new cradle designed by
Professor Engvall had delayed the attack by more than an hour.

Tomlinson's eyes went from the generating station to that of
the Atlantis defense. Five hundred crack troops were spread out
in positions from which it would take a week for any attacking
force to remove them, and at a cost that would be devastating.
They were spread in the lava dome below the crystal structure
that had protected the capital. Ruins of the great city were now
teaming with machine-gun emplacements and mortar pits.

"We're ready," Engvall said as he removed his headphones.

Tomlinson saw the titanium enclosure where the diamond
was spinning at twice the speed of sound; the air passing over
it would be the only stylus needed to create the ancient tones.
The amplification lines led outward from Atlantis to the amplification domes sitting off the coasts of the target cities. He
smiled, knowing that New York would be the first to feel the
Wave as the Coalition vied to end the old world quickly.

"Dame Lilith, since you are the one lamenting the drastic
changes that have come about in your life, please do us the

honor of beginning the new life we have chosen. Start the Wave, please."

Lilith really did not care to touch anything on the platform. Her nerves at this last moment had tuned to jelly and her blood ran cold. Still, as she looked into the eyes of Tomlinson, she knew that she would do as he'd asked. Even Caretaker was standing by, as if he were one of the many stone statues lying in ruins in the city below them.

"Why . . . yes, of course," she replied.

Engvall rose from his chair and gestured for Lilith to sit, momentarily relieved that the responsibility for destroying so much of the planet would not be his. He replaced his headphones and adjusted the mike to his lips.

"Stations one and two, one hundred percent power on generators. The first tone will be a pulse to acclimate the tone amplifiers to their new computer settings."

Engvall turned to Tomlinson and slowly nodded.

"Dame Lilith, if you would raise the protective cover and push the ignition button, please."

"This one?" she asked as she saw a red flashing light underneath a clear glass cover.

"Yes."

Lilith lifted the cover and closed her eyes, then with two fingers she pushed down on the flashing button.

Immediately, everyone inside the city closed their eyes as the soundless tones started their long run for the Long Island Sound.

The first ripple of the Wave triggered Thor's Hammer.

Five thousand miles away, the Hammer fell, and Manhattan started to crumble.

LONG ISLAND SOUND
ONE MILE NORTH OF
PORT JEFFERSON STATION
LONG ISLAND, NEW YORK

The amplification domes had been laid down the year before by a local chartered workboat whose captain thought he was laying lobster-monitoring stations. That same year there had been a massive kill-off of the lobster beds, blamed on the toxicity of the Sound; little did anyone realize it was from the tuning forks inside the domes, which would sometimes chime in their deadly and soundless vibration that killed the lobsters on the bottom.

As the tones passed through the power lines to the amplifiers, every living aquatic creature shook and became still, and then died, for six miles around. The invisible Wave of Thor's Hammer slammed into the muddy bottom and reached out for the Davidson fault line and the distant continental plate.

NEW YORK CITY

At 4:00 PM on this Saturday, many of the workers who normally filed through the massive canyons of midtown Manhattan were at home. However, those who were out to catch the warmth of the sun saw the strangest sight they had ever before witnessed. Every bird in the city as one launched itself into the air, as if a magical switch had been thrown. People covered their heads and turned away from the billions of flapping wings. In Central Park, numerous New Yorkers were hurt as panicked pigeons sprang into the sky. Dogs across the city started barking and tried to break free of their owners. Several slammed through plate-glass windows in an instinctive effort to escape.

The first reaction to Thor's Hammer started in the East River as a barely perceptible wave struck the Brooklyn Bridge. Cars traveled across, never realizing that the bridge had sunk more than half an inch into the mud. That first ripple traveled into the lower reaches of the subway access tunnel far below the mass-transit line. As one shocked electrician looked on, a surface fracture in the old cement at first widened and then cracked through to the river itself. Within minutes, panicked calls were being made topside for assistance.

In Central Park, couples lying on the grass felt it through their backsides. The ground rippled like a wave, not so much as to actually lift a person from the ground, but more of a tickling sensation that people in California would have recognized instantly.

The first of the high-impact tones left the amplification domes and slammed hard into the seabed. The invisible Wave this second time slammed into the Davidson fault line and sent a tremendous jolt through the crust of the earth until it met the plate upon which the eastern United States sat.

Then the Hammer really went to work. As the Wave bounced back like a sonar ping, it hit once more the already damaged fault. The walls of the fault started to crumble only miles from the Verrazano-Narrows Bridge. As one of the world's longest cable-expansion structures, its pilings were sunk deep into the bedrock of the harbor. At the time of its construction, no one could possibly have seen or known of the minute cracking that had been sent through the rock strata. These small fissures and cracks were the first to let go, and the flowing water did the rest. Passengers on the upper and lower decks in the direct center of the great span felt it first—the sensation of sliding, though they knew that they were not. Then the first real jolt hit the bridge and the movement was perceptible to all. Cars involuntarily change lanes, causing many accidents and pileups up and down the entire span.

Suddenly, eight hundred feet beneath the lowest pilings, the bedrock gave way. As the eastern side of the bridge began to collapse into the mud, sinking forty feet, cars were smashed into the broken roadway on the onramp and others slammed into them. The giant cables held firm, keeping the entire east side from collapsing. Later, engineers would say that the collapsing bedrock actually saved the bridge from total collapse because the loose east end gave the bridge enough give to sustain itself against the onslaught of the earthquake.

The same could not be said as the ground shook in Brooklyn, Queens, the Bronx, and Manhattan. Older buildings first started losing their façades, then glass started breaking throughout the city. As displacement waves hit the air, the people on the streets became disoriented, and most could not keep their feet. The Empire State Building received the first real jolt of an earthquake in its long history, but the old girl stood firm.

Then the third swing of Thor's Hammer hit, only this time it traveled east, toward the suburbs of Nassau and Suffolk counties. Long Island was under attack.

For fifty miles up and down the Long Island coastline, older houses started to collapse. The seas were rising into the streets; the surf table was up by 50 percent of normal. The streets of the coastal towns were flooding, hampering police and fire-department responses.

The five boroughs of New York, along with Long Island, started to crumble and burn.

THE WHITE HOUSE
WASHINGTON, D.C.

Niles listened to the reports that were coming in from New York. Then they heard that the Wave had started in both China and Russia. The two countries were now saying that Crete had to be destroyed no matter the cost.

With the evacuation of the civilian population still far from complete, they were all in a tight spot. Which population was worth more than any other? they wondered.

"Give Colonel Collins time, Mr. President; he doesn't know how to quit!" Niles said, gritting his teeth.

The president just looked at his friend without saying anything. Then he nodded in affirmation that he would give Collins this one chance.

However, as Niles felt the relief hit him, the first tremble was felt through the flooring of the Oval Office.

CHAPTER

NINETEEN

ATLANTIS

The giant staircase had been chipped out of the surrounding stone by the hands of thousands of slaves. It was the grandest staircase, the likes of which the world had never seen. The entire company could traverse the stairs side by side and still have room on both sides.

"What do you think, Colonel?" the SEAL lieutenant asked.

"If it goes up, we go with it," he said as he looked at Sarah. "You sure you think we're below the main city?"

"Positive, Colonel. This is the Wave chamber that used to sit below the capital, and up there is the Coalition and the Wave equipment. I would bet my life on it."

"You just did, Lieutenant, yours and about half the population of the planet." Collins looked around. "Mr. Everett, you and the SEALs take the lead, and don't bump into anything blindly until we know what we have to face. The taking out of the Wave hardware is priority one." He looked from face to face. "Repeat: *priority one*. This is where I give you the old speech about we are all expendable to that one goal. Well, after you, navy boys."

The SEALs and Carl started out first at a brisk pace. Collins watched them disappear into the steam that escaped from the walls and then looked at the young faces of the marines around him.

"Lock and load; we may not have any time when we arrive on-site. I don't have to tell you what's at stake here. You are marines, you know the story and the drill, and this is one army-type asshole that's glad you're here. Let's go, Major. I'll take the first platoon and the rest of my people; you bring up the rear with the other three and heavy stuff."

"Yes, sir. Gunny, saddle up, and let's do something about this place, I hear they don't like marines," he shouted, making Jack cringe just a bit. But he let them cheer themselves. *After all*, he thought, *if they succeed or don't succeed, no one will ever even know they were here.*

Tomlinson smiled as the generators were holding up far better than anticipated. After the initial assault on everyone's senses, the effects had calmed and allowed everyone on the large platform to enjoy the moment. The diamond chamber was being cooled by a steady flow of liquid nitrogen to keep the titanium-reinforced module from melting because of the tremendous friction of the spinning Atlantean Key. One of the by-products of the tone grooves cut into the diamond was the fact that no one could get closer than ten feet because of the miniwave produced by the tremendous amount of air that passed over and around the diamond. It felt as if your head would explode if you attempted it.

Little did they know that with every revolution of the diamond, excess energy wasn't being bled off; instead it was absorbed by the blue diamond. The earth's rarest mineral was now acting as a battery, only it was now the most efficient storage element in the history of the world.

"We are receiving firsthand reports that New York is experiencing distress from the Wave," Engvall said above the noise and piercing scream of the large centrifuge that spun the giant diamond.

"'Distress'? Must we be so formal, Professor? You may say what it really is. Thor's Hammer has struck and the world is feeling it!"

"The Wave will travel east at five times the speed of sound and strike our old enemies, with Russia feeling it first, then China, to the east."

"Very good. Inform your technicians they have nothing to fear from above; the Americans have failed in their attempts to reopen the excavation. Soon, with practice, we can send the Wave directly at their offshore efforts and warships, and we need not fear reprisal."

Engvall looked from the confident face of Tomlinson to the rock-hard and emotionless face of Caretaker, and then to the scared countenances of Dame Lilith and the eighteen other Coalition board members. He walked away, hoping that this surreal nightmare would soon be at an end.

THE ATLANTEAN TUNNEL

The giant passageway and staircase were immense. Giant stalactites grew unchecked in the thousands of years of darkness, dampness, and disrepair. Huge fissures rent throughout the broken stairs. Thousands of feet below, the flowing lava that the Ancients had used for power generation ran free in a never-ending ribbon of hell's water.

Everett and the SEALs had been fifteen minutes ahead as Jack and the marine contingent followed. The climb was arduous in the extreme heat, but they all felt the pressure and the mugginess sliding away the closer to the top they got.

"Jack, we've reached a dead end here," Carl said as he backtracked to the main group.

Collins doubled his speed and caught up with the SEALs. Sure enough, as he looked around all he could see were the rough-hewn rock strata around them. The staircase dwindled to only fifteen feet across and abruptly ended.

"There's a loose panel of marble flooring above," the SEAL lieutenant said as he stepped up to Jack and Carl. "The sounds of machinery, engine noises, are easily coming through. Thought I would wait until you came back to open the door."

Jack walked past the SEAL team and looked at the section

of flooring above him. He looked at Carl and they both crouched to get as low as possible and used their legs and hands to push up on the panel. It moved easily, and as it did so, bright light poured into the shaft from above. This startled the two men and they lowered it back down momentarily until just a few inches were left open. Collins ventured a look around and saw that it was a large chamber of some kind. Marble pillars lay everywhere, and there was a general look of destruction, which was becoming a common site for the Backdoor team. As Jack looked out, a pair of boots stepped directly into his line of sight and he froze.

As Jack watched, he pointed up at Carl, who nodded. Collins held up one finger and then sliced that finger over his throat. Normally they would have waited this person out, but they were preciously low on time; they had to get above this subterranean level. Jack braced himself and looked at Carl. The ex-SEAL had his combat knife out and had the large blade clamped between his teeth and was looking directly at the marble flooring.

Five steps below, the marine major and SEAL lieutenant exchanged questioning looks.

Jack nodded and pushed up with all his might and in that split second of bright light Everett reached through and grabbed the unseen person's boots and pulled his feet out from under him, making the person fall flat on his face with just the sound of a thud in return. Then Everett used all his weight and dragged the person through the opening just as Jack let the floor marble fall easily back into place. It was if a trapdoor spider had plucked an insect from the surface.

As the SEAL lieutenant jumped in to help hold the shocked and stunned person in place, Everett brought the knife to his throat and then was shocked to see that it was a woman guard. Her eyes were wide and staring.

"Speak English?" Everett asked easily and slowly.

The blond woman's head bobbed up and down. The SEAL's hand was still placed hard over her mouth, and then he slowly removed it after placing a 9-millimeter to her temple.

"Nationality?" Everett asked.

"A . . . A . . . American," the woman said, looking around at the three faces staring down at her.

"What's above us?"

Jack just watched from his perch on the highest step.

The woman just shook her head.

"One time, and one time only: what is directly above us?" Everett persisted, his cold eyes staring a hole through the mercenary.

As she watched with wide eyes, she saw Everett reach out and take the 9-millimeter from the lieutenant's hand and then reach out again and take something from the man who had opened the piece of flooring she had been pulled through. Then her eyes went to the pistol as the large blond man attached the silencer. Then he quickly pointed it at her knee. The SEAL and the marine major were shocked when he didn't hesitate a split second before loosing a round into her kneecap. The SEAL clamped his hand down hard onto her mouth to cut off her scream.

"Knee number two goes when the question isn't answered the second time," Everett said as he shifted the silenced pistol to her undamaged leg.

The woman shook her head from side to side again and Everett nodded at the lieutenant, who eased his hold on her mouth.

"The Empirium Chamber," she groaned.

"Guards?" Jack asked from above them.

"All . . . out at . . . their . . . posts," she moaned in pain.

"Bring up Lieutenant McIntire," Carl said, anticipating Jack.

Sarah came forward and saw the woman, but her eyes held no sympathy.

"What surrounds this Empirium Chamber?"

"It's the central government building; all other buildings radiate out from this one."

"Not much help," Jack said. "Mr. Everett, assist our guest with her pain."

Everett nodded and then moved the pistol to her forehead.

The woman was in a panic as she moved her head vigorously until the SEAL's hand was shaken free.

"No. There's a lava mount directly behind the Empirium. It rises above the emplaced gun positions, and you can at least observe the city unseen from there. Please don't kill me. There's also an old aqueduct that rises three hundred feet above all the buildings."

"Mercenaries have changed somewhat," Everett said as he moved the pistol from her forehead.

"I was a part of the Fourth Infantry Division. I—"

Everett cut off her sob story before it could begin. He slugged her with his fist, knocking her unconscious.

"Yeah, and I bet they're real proud at how you turned out," he said as he stood and looked at Jack. "I guess we better have a look-see, huh, Jack?"

"After you, swabby," Collins said as he once again eased up the flooring.

As Jack moved the flooring aside, Everett slid through the opening and followed, and Sarah was right on their heels.

"Who are those guys? Do you know them?" the marine major asked the SEAL lieutenant once more.

"They're a little unorthodox, but they sure do know how to treat a lady, don't they, Major?"

The chamber was a mess. The klieg lights cast long shadows across the devastation. The great circular table, where thousands of years before the fate of the world had been decided by fools who wouldn't be around to see that fate, was broken in many places by fallen pillars of marble. A giant headless statue was at the center of the room as the team of Jack, Sarah, Carl, and the SEAL leader and the marine major advanced through with their MP-5s raised in readiness.

Collins paused and listened as the sound of the generators penetrated the chamber. Shouting voices and loudspeakers signaled a large contingent around them. As he listened, he verified that all the noise was coming from his far right, nothing to the left. He headed in that direction.

Slowly, one and two at a time, the marines followed.

Collins saw a large opening in the back and saw beyond that the black and gray rise of lava rock. He poked his head the opening and looked up. What he saw was an amazing sight. A wall of lava rose a thousand feet into the air. Sarah joined him and her mouth was open as she saw the curvature of the great Crystal Dome above them.

"Jesus, Jack, how that dome withstood the forces of a trillion tons of earth and water is beyond our engineering. This lava wall erupted from beneath and cooled as the island sank. The seafloor and landmass must have covered the dome as the strata beneath the island collapsed."

"I have to hand it to you, shorty, you have an eye for detail. But for right now, take a mental picture for one of your classes, and I'll be sure to take it in. For now, let's get above this mess and see what we can do to stop these madmen."

As Jack started using the large ripples of the ancient lava flow for cover, the entire marine company followed, not knowing they were outnumbered ten to one.

Something was wrong and Tomlinson could see it. Professor Engvall was running from technician to technician, throwing switches and yelling something. The other Coalition members were watching the same frightening scene below them on the bottom of the ancient dry lake. Tomlinson picked up a bullhorn.

"What is the problem down there?" he asked.

Engvall did not answer at first. Then Tomlinson heard the generators start to power down.

"What do you think you're doing?"

"We have problems!" the professor shouted back. "Shut down the centrifuge immediately!"

As men and women started to move, the pitch of the Atlantean Key became shrill-sounding as the diamond began to spin even faster. There was near panic as several men ran to the large steel carriage where the blue diamond was housed. As they drew near, their legs weakened and they went to their knees, and then as one, the three men collapsed.

"The centrifuge is being fed by stored energy from the

diamond and it's attacking faults and plates that aren't targeted!"

"What in the bloody hell is he talking about?" Dame Lilith asked as she grabbed Tomlinson's arm.

He roughly shrugged off her grip and used the bullhorn again.

"Explain yourself!"

Engvall stopped running for a moment and looked up at the raised platform.

"The damn Key is far too powerful; it's increasing the power to the amplifiers. The tones are out of control. Somehow the fault lines of every sector must be connected. It's not just the power of the diamond or the accuracy of the tone grooves. The fault and plate diagram of the Ancients was inaccurate, and now our monitors are picking up seismic stresses as far away as Africa, the Middle East, and Europe!"

Tomlinson still did not grasp what was happening.

"Are the tones working against our main targets?"

"Yes, they are! But they're also attacking the plates of every continent on the planet! The strata information on the chart was incorrect: the Key with its increased power output is tearing apart less dense rock and stone that make up the tectonic plates. The Ancients made mistakes in their calculations of density; that, coupled with the diamond storing and increasing power, is shattering the crust of the planet!"

As if for added emphasis, the stone flooring beneath them started to vibrate, and then rumbling sounds fed upward from below Atlantis.

"This cursed science was never meant to be used!" Engvall screamed.

Tomlinson just stared at him.

Jack and Everett, along with the two other marine team leaders, watched the activity below them. The ground was starting to move in small jerks and the remaining buildings of Atlantis were starting to move almost imperceptibly.

Jack and the others used their night-vision goggles in the

semidarkness around them. Arrayed around the city were machine-gun teams and what looked like mortar positions. There were even four artillery pieces, all aimed at the excavation opening that was now sealed.

"Well, we have the element of surprise, and, boys and girls, that's all we have," Jack said as he lowered his goggles.

"That's something, at least. Maybe we could—"

Everett's words were cut off as the porous rock around them started to shake.

"Do you get the feeling that something may have screwed up down there?" Sarah asked.

Jack looked around hurriedly. "We have to move now. I want the two mortar positions set up, with priority on their counterparts below. Then I need those howitzers taken out. Major, they're your men, get them into place. I'll need the three assault platoons for hitting that lake bed below. The third will assist with the mortar teams. Mr. Everett, you and the SEALs take out that platform and shut that equipment down; follow our lead, we'll make room. It's a plan on the fly, but as you can feel, things are starting to get a little dicey around here. I'm taking a fire team up the slope and getting on top of that aqueduct; we can cover everyone from there."

Everett looked at his watch. "I suggest we give the two mortar teams five minutes and then we go in exactly five minutes and thirty seconds."

"Check. Okay, Major, get your element ready. And remember, the first rounds you send out there have to be accurate as hell, that's your job. If they turn those mortars and artillery pieces against our men, we'll be cut to ribbons."

"Yes, sir, the corps won't let you down."

"Well, it won't be me as much as the entire world, son. Good luck."

"Sir, what about this dome structure? One stray round looks like it would do it in."

Collins looked around him and didn't have an answer for the major.

"Let's look at it this way: if that happens, we win."

As Collins moved off, the major mumbled to himself so that only Sarah caught his words: "I was hoping for something a little more inspirational than that."

THE BLACK SEA

Twelve thousand years before, the Black Sea was nothing more than a freshwater lake, a large lake to be sure, that supported a medium-size pre–Bronze Age civilization. This civilization of fishermen and hunter-gatherers was crushed by the Atlantean Wave when the waters of the Mediterranean rolled into the basin that is now the Black Sea. The beaches of pure white sand and the ruins of stone walls now lay at the bottom, over a thousand feet down. The Wave that had destroyed these long-dead people was rising again, this time from the very seafloor where they had once struggled to survive.

The next link in the chain was Russia. The attack was coming from the south, the closest the Coalition could get into that closed country. The fault line that the amplifiers lay over was one of the oldest in the world and had lain dormant since the last great quake of the area, in 1939. These were known to science as the most dangerous faults and plates in the entire world, capable of triggering earthquakes on other continents.

The amplifiers at the bottom of the sea started to vibrate and then the tone was sent out with the force of a nuclear weapon. The sound struck the first of the shallowest faults and started the chain reaction as that smaller fault led into a larger one and so on. The stresses involved and the cracking wide open of the faults started a continental shift of earth-changing dimensions.

The Black Sea lurched in its bed. When the waters retreated and then started their return, like a child dropping recklessly into a bathtub, the separated sea met in the middle and a plume of water shot straight up over a half a mile into the air. As the seabed continued to crack, a crazy zigzag pattern emerged outward from the sea toward Turkey and the Ukraine. The Urals actually started to crumble; their rocky strata were the first to succumb to the enormous movement.

The cities of Sevastopol and Odessa were the first to die. The mass populations were crushed in their homes without warning as the earth flew up six feet, moving as if a blanket had been shaken out. The next was the Romanian city of Bucharest. As one of the oldest cities in Europe, she didn't stand a chance; buildings shook once and then their foundations gave way after centuries of water rot. The rivers that flowed into and past the city changed course in a matter of moments and drowned those who had escaped the falling stone. The fires would burn out of control for two weeks due to a lack of water and men to fight them.

In Turkey's largest city, Istanbul, spires and ancient walls started to rock and fall. Two thousand people were lost in the first few minutes as they panicked and ran.

A thousand-mile-long strip of the richest soil in the Ukraine, the European breadbasket, split and rolled over to reveal a bloody-looking new landscape of molten rock as it was forced to the surface. It would leave a long and ugly scar for many thousands of years.

The last to feel the movement was Moscow. The cobbled roadways split and the air was filled with the smell of sulfur as long-dormant volcanoes erupted under the city. Mounds and vents that had been dead for a million years suddenly sprang to life as the forces of the Wave made for the paths of least resistance. Air-raid warnings sounded for the first time since the practiced drills in October 1963. Only this time it was no drill.

OVAL OFFICE
THE WHITE HOUSE
WASHINGTON, D.C.

The president held on to his large desk as the Secret Service made to assist him out of the White House and into the underground shelter. He shrugged them off angrily. He knew there was no place to hide.

Niles closed his eyes and tried to think about the tectonic structure in Washington, but he found that for the first time in years, his mind was blank. The only thing he could think of was his request to allow Jack the time to end this, and that was what was hurting him.

"Sir, Moscow is being hit hard. The Ukraine is a ruin and Turkey is flying to pieces. The effects are now starting to be felt in the lake region outside of Beijing," the national security adviser said as he read from the latest NSA dispatch. "The Black Sea was the focal point of the Wave. It's now gone!"

Suddenly the shaking stopped. They heard a picture fall off the wall not far from the office and a woman scream, then all was silent.

"What in the hell is happening, Niles?" the president asked, his body still shaking even though the room was still.

Niles picked up the phone in front of him and called the Event Center.

"Pollock."

"Virginia, what are our people saying?"

"This is to be expected. We have maybe twenty minutes to a half hour. The initial forces have been spent, but, Niles, the worst is yet to come."

The president was staring at the speaker box as if it were a person, until the chairman of the Joint Chiefs handed him a phone. "The Russian president."

"The buildup will continue with fresh materials from deeper in the earth that will replace those sent upward in the first forced strike. In laymen's terms, Niles, the earth is getting itself ready for a fight-ending punch and we don't know what's going to happen. We're still picking up the audio wave from the Long Island Sound, the navy is depth-charging the area in hopes of smashing their amplifiers, but our geology people are saying it may be too late."

"Thank you. Keep monitoring."

"Nothing from Jack and our ground team?" Virginia asked.

"Nothing."

The president and Niles hung up their phones simultaneously and looked at the fifteen faces in the Oval Office.

"The Russian president has just informed me that they have an attack submarine in the Med and he has ordered her to assist us."

"Inform the captain onboard the *Cheyenne* that a Russian attack boat is nearby and to allow it to stand by with them."

ATLANTIS

After the long climb up the lava wall, Collins and his eight-man fire team reached the aqueduct without being seen. The vantage point gave them a clear view of the entire area below. They set up two M-60 machine guns and the rest took up stations to fire down into the Coalition forces below.

Jack looked at his wristwatch. One minute. He raised his night-vision glasses and looked around. The marines were spread out and had made it to the assigned assault positions he had picked out for them, and he hoped that with a lot of luck, they wouldn't be noticed until it was too late. The darkness of the city hid them well. He shifted his view and saw Everett and his SEAL team right where they needed to be. Their outlines, due to their Nomex clothing, were far harder to see than were the marines.

Jack raised his radio. "Thirty seconds," he said softly. The transmission required no response.

Down below, he had assigned Mendenhall, Sarah, Ryan, and ten marines the job of stopping that centrifuge when the marines made their attack. He roamed the area where they were supposed to be but failed to pick them up. "Damn," he said under his breath. There was nothing he could do. If they had found difficulty in their route through the lava field to the center of the city, he knew he couldn't wait for them to do so.

"Sir, this position is starting to make me a little nervous," a young lance corporal said. "The shaking is getting stronger, and look at this," he said as he pointed to his right.

Collins looked over and saw what the corporal was talking about. A small waterfall had developed in the last few minutes, meaning that the Crystal Dome above them had started to fracture somewhere above. The ancient aqueduct was starting to run with seawater.

He turned and looked at the nineteen-year-old and held out his hand. "We don't have a lot of time here, so make 'em count, son," he said as he slapped the boy on the shoulder. With that, Collins aimed his MP-5 at the closest group of mercenaries firing from the side of one of the pyramids two hundred yards from the aqueduct.

Everett heard the thirty-second call and then looked out over the city. He saw the three massive electrical lines coming out of the dry lake at the center of the city. They were exposed for only ten feet before some paranoid engineer had sent them down through a crack in the cobbled roadway and then had covered them with cement. As he looked on, he knew that they would have precious little time to lay the explosives on the leads that led to thousands of miles of cable and ended at the sound-amplification modules in three different parts of the world.

Suddenly there was a loud crack and rumble as one of the remaining upright pillars of marble fell from its base. Carl winced as the twenty-five-ton pillar crashed into the center of the city, making a hundred or so Coalition troops run for cover. He looked over at the SEAL lieutenant.

"I don't know if that's good or bad. It cleared out part of our sector of responsibility, but this whole damn place could start coming down around our ears, and I don't think our little tiny skulls could handle the pressure this deep in the Med if that shaky-ass dome suddenly collapses."

Everett looked at his watch and waited. Three, two, one. Off in the distance Everett thought he heard the soft *thump-thump-thump* of the marines' mortar pits opening up. He turned and trained his glasses on the dry lake bed and the huge tower rising from its center. As he zeroed in on the tower's occupants, he saw one man in heavy clothing turn at the strange sound to his rear. He stood stock-still for a moment and then suddenly turned and ran for the scaffolding.

"Damn, that son of a bitch has a survival instinct to end all instincts."

Suddenly, flame and debris erupted out of the dry lake bed. One mortar round caught the tower and destroyed half of it and killed most of the observers there.

"Damn, that's good shootin'," Everett said as more 40-millimeter mortars fell into the dry lake bed. He ventured another look up and saw four more people run from the tower, one of whom he could swear was a well-dressed woman.

More rounds started targeting the heavy machine-gun emplacements throughout the destroyed city. Here and there eruptions of flame and shrapnel tore through men and old marble. But added to the fierceness of the marines' mortar attack was the power of the Wave as it started to add its weight to the fight. In a hundred different places the dome started to leak all at once. The already cracked and damaged ruins around them started to move in a frighteningly furious way. But still, Everett heard the shrill whistle coming from halfway around the ancient city.

The U.S. Marines came storming out of the natural darkness around Atlantis, screaming and firing their weapons at anything that moved to their front.

The assault was on, and the marines had just added one more verse to the corps hymn: the continent of Atlantis.

CHAPTER
TWENTY

Sarah, Mendenhall, Ryan, and the ten marines were caught between the lava mound and the dry lake bed. Mortar rounds were still going off, but their allotted number intended for the equipment in the dry lake bed had been expended. Now, the mortar teams concentrated on the Coalition positions; after their initial shock, the Coalition troops started to return fire in an amazing response time.

As they ran, tracers found them just before they ducked behind an ancient lava flow that had frozen in time. One marine cried out and hit the broken roadway. Machine-gun fire concentrated on the spot where they had vanished, and the soft stone didn't absorb the concussion all that well.

As they ducked and took stock, another of the stone-and-marble buildings leaned, and then it rolled over as easily as an animal in death.

Suddenly they heard machine-gun fire coming from somewhere above them, and he knew that Jack and his team had opened up from the aqueduct. They started laying a large volume of fire in the direction of their unseen attackers.

"Well, it looks like someone's paying attention up there," Ryan said as he started forward again and the others quickly followed.

* * *

Everett and the SEALs were having a much harder time of it. They faced about a hundred heavily armed Coalition mercenaries. As he ventured a peek up above a fallen pillar, Everett saw the three power lines; they were shaking with the earthquake but were still very much intact. He lowered his head and checked the magazine in his MP-5, then he straightened and fired ten rounds into the mass of soldiers hidden behind a solid stone covering.

"Come on, Jack, now's not the time to dawdle," he said to himself.

With that, Everett stood and fired again, and this time he heard a satisfying yelp from a hundred yards away.

"One down, about ninety-nine to go."

Collins ordered one machine gun to continue firing into the area of the lake bed to cover Sarah and her team, while splitting his firepower and opening up against the mercenaries penning Everett and his men down. All the while the aqueduct was filling with water from above. The volume was increasing every second and he and his men had to hold on to keep from being washed away to the broken end, where it fell off three hundred feet straight down.

Collins pulled the pins on three hand grenades and tossed them as far as he could into the Coalition lines. Ten of the men never heard their death knell as the grenades exploded behind them.

Suddenly, the sound hit Jack's ears. The crack came from above as a large section of the dome caved in. Thousands of tons of seabed and water cascaded and struck the aqueduct a hundred feet behind Jack and his men. It tore through the old stone, tearing their section away from the rest. The men felt the waterway beneath start to tremble, but it still held firm.

Sarah was the first to reach the side of the lake. She looked up at the mangled corpses of the people who had been on the high platform. She had no sympathy for them as she looked into the devastation of the lake. Equipment lay shattered; even the generators had been hit. But she saw and heard the centrifuge as it was spinning out of control.

"Carl hasn't cut the power lines yet—that damn thing's still broadcasting!"

Ryan and Mendenhall didn't hesitate. With five of the marines, they started down into the lake bed. Enemy fire increased a hundredfold and Mendenhall was singed by a round that knocked his Mylar helmet off his head. Sarah picked it up and tossed it to him.

"A little hot down here!"

"You can say that again," Will said as he turned and started to follow Ryan down the scaffold.

Sarah heard a loud crack somewhere to their rear and then felt the stone through her boots as the floor above them split in two. Then a rush of water started cascading from a crack in the great dome. The water from the Mediterranean struck one of the superhot generators and it exploded, sending out a thick wave of steel and sparks. As she traversed the scaffold, the crack in the floor reached them and she had to jump a five-foot crevasse, barely making it over to the far side. The platform above them started to wobble as the stabilizing cables started snapping like overtaxed guitar strings. It fell over, twisting as it did so. Ryan and the others ran quickly as the tower crashed into the scaffolding and tore it free from the rock, then both crashed into the lake bed.

All around the city, water was penetrating the dome at an alarming rate as the world started shaking once again, and this time it was like the death throes of a wounded beast, as the groan and bark of solid stone announced that Atlantis had started to crack apart.

The ancient city was dying for the second time.

USS *IWO JIMA*

The sudden rise of the sea ripped two U.S. Marine Sea Harriers from their moorings and tossed them into the churning ocean. All hands had been ordered belowdecks as the attack carrier's bow sank below the water as she slowly moved way away from the quay. She had taken on four thousand civilians, who huddled inside her hangar decks and screamed every time the carrier rolled one way or the other. Three miles away, the attack carrier *Nassau,* with a full load of refugees, had taken a massive wave strike that ripped all her antennas and close-in weapons from her superstructure. She was taking on water as she headed for Greece at all possible speed.

The surface waves were breeching at twenty-five feet as the *Iwo* was sent headlong into a giant trough. She dipped below the water once more as her superstructure and stern were the only visible portion of the ship above water. The admiral feared that they might not make it clear this time. But, as he held on to his chair tightly, the massive warship slowly started to rise out of the sea.

The last report had the seafloor erupting for five hundred miles from the now plotted epicenter, directly in the middle of the Mediterranean. Satellite photos had the Eurasian and American eastern coastlines sustaining heavy damage after the hour's lull. Detectors had picked up the Wave once more growing in intensity.

The world was coming apart.

ATLANTIS

Sarah was feeling sick to her stomach and as she looked at the faces of the men in her group, she realized that wasn't the only one. The invisible wave struck them as soon as they gained the floor of the dry lake bed. Several of the marines and Mendenhall had already vomited, and she herself was having a hard time keeping her feet as her inner ear started to give her problems.

From their location, they had pumped everything they had into the protective titanium shielding of the centrifuge. Three grenades had gone off right under the raised module, and they were stunned when the shrapnel had just bounced off. Ryan had emptied a full magazine into the large round chamber, with no effect whatsoever other than causing a spectacular light show with the bounding tracers. Now they were under heavy fire once again from above. The Coalition forces nearest the pyramids had them in their sights.

"Everett must be having trouble getting his team to the cables," Ryan said as he fell next to Sarah. "Is there something we've overlooked here?"

Sarah sat back against the stone pedestal of the statue of Poseidon and thought. They couldn't break the connection from there. The lines were too thick to cut through. They couldn't knock out the reinforced centrifuge and they couldn't shut down the power. The diamond was drawing self-sustaining electricity from the earth's magnetic field somehow, and there was nothing they could do to shut that off.

"We have to interfere with the Wave signal somehow, defuse it. Inject something that will break it up and make the tones meaningless," she thought out loud as a line of machine-gun bullets stitched the pedestal that covered them.

"What?" Ryan asked as Mendenhall edged around to the side of the stone bulwark and emptied the magazine of his MP-5 toward the upper edge of the lake bed.

"Your radio, give it to me," she ordered Ryan.

Ryan reached for the radio at his belt and pulled it out. Both of their hopes deflated immediately when they saw the bullet hole in the casing. Ryan tried it anyway but nothing happened.

"Well, at least the damn thing saved you from taking a bullet."

"What else can you use?"

"What have you got in that bag you're carrying?" she asked, eyeing Ryan's satchel.

"Well, nothing but a few of the colonel's old CDs and a Walkman. That's about—"

Mendenhall tumbled at their feet. "I don't mean to be a pest here, but we have Coalition forces lining up to take pot shots at us and we don't have the best defensive position here."

Just as Will's words were out of his mouth, the giant stone pedestal cracked and the forward half sank into the earth.

"Give me the Walkman and the headphones," Sarah shouted.

Ryan was about to hand over the satchel when a round from

above caught Sarah in the shoulder and spun her around. Mendenhall reacted quickly, reaching out and pulling her back to the cover of the remaining piece of stone.

Above, the Coalition troops had found the range and cut loose with a withering fire. Then, all at once, the wall of the lake bed cracked and the men at the top came tumbling down with a thousand tons of stone. The rocks and debris smashed into the centrifuge and knocked it askew of its mountings, but still the Wave continued to build.

Sarah was clenching her eyes closed with the pain of the bullet wound. She had been hit in the same shoulder the year before, in Brazil, and she couldn't believe that it had happened again.

"You've got to learn to duck, goddammit!" Mendenhall admonished.

"Jason," Sarah said as she tried to sit up. "Take the headphones and rip the wires out. Hurry!"

Ryan did as he was told.

"You've got to somehow connect the wires to the casing of the centrifuge and . . . and turn on . . . the . . ."

"What will that do?"

"Anything will break up the Wave, any . . . interference at all will destroy the tone."

Ryan reacted quickly, deciding to place his bet on her knowledge. He looked at Mendenhall as he laid Sarah's head onto the lap of the nearest marine.

"I'll need cover, Will. My ass is going to be hangin' in the wind out there."

Mendenhall inserted a fresh magazine into his MP-5 and nodded. He gestured for the eight remaining marines to take up firing positions to his left and right.

Ryan swallowed and tried to keep his stomach in check as the Wave effect was getting stronger.

"Damn thing is making me feel like a rough night in Singapore," he said as he blindly reached into the bag, pulled out a CD, and ripped it from its case.

"When you're ready," Mendenhall said, looking at Ryan.

"Most of the assholes tumbled down when that ledge broke free, but we'll pick off what we can."

"Okay," Ryan said. "Don't miss, buddy."

Ryan stood and on wobbly legs broke for the center of the lake bed. Mendenhall and the marines rose as one and placed a withering fire onto the ledge above, the first few rounds catching the first five Coalition men and dropping them.

Ryan had gone only ten feet when another large quake shook the ground. As the floor around him erupted in steam and gas, Ryan vomited and tried to get to his knees, but he fell over onto his back. As he looked up, another rush of cascading stone rolled free of the top, and he had to force himself to roll and keep rolling. As the stones crashed by him, he swallowed and came to his knees. Taking a deep breath, he ran the forty yards to the centrifuge. His head felt like it was going to explode out of his ears as he approached. Blood started trickling down from the eruption of his eardrums as the Wave penetrated his skull. He stumbled forward and fell flat on his face. He shook his head, the pain almost unbearable as he crawled the remaining few feet to the screaming centrifuge. As he rolled over and rested his head on a stanchion, he removed the small Walkman and just stared at it. His mind was fuzzy and he had to think hard on the instructions Sarah had given him. He tried to focus all his concentration on her words as they flooded into his mind:

"Attach the wires to the casing."

Ryan looked at his right hand and saw the portable CD player and the dangling wires and he had a quick flashback to the Blue Nile and what he had done there to attract the bad guys. Now he remembered, and he sucked up the pain and leaned toward the red-hot centrifuge. Then he realized that he didn't have anything with which to attach the wires to the titanium casing. He rolled over again as nausea hit him so hard that his stomach cramped and he felt bile rising in his throat.

Medenhall looked over and grimaced as he saw Ryan flat on his back. The ground shook and he heard a large crack from far above his head and he looked up just in time to see a large panel of the Crystal Dome separate from its frame. The

eight-foot-thick piece of crystal was followed by a torrent of
seawater and sand, mud, and rock, which struck the ruins a
thousand feet away. As he looked on, steam shot up as the cold
water came in contact with the hot ground of the dead city.

The earth around them shook again and a crack appeared
not far from Ryan's supine position. Steam rose as if shot out
of a fire hose and magma bubbled to the surface. The very
sick Ryan rolled away quickly but not before his pant leg
caught fire. He slapped at it until the flames were snuffed and
then he looked at Mendenhall's position and shook his head
again. Now he remembered what Sarah had told him to do. He
reached the centrifuge once more and raised the Walkman to
the carriage. He pulled his knife from its scabbard, reached
down, and plucked up a knife tip full of magma. The blade
started to melt as another convulsion shook the ground. Ryan
steadied himself and placed the knife blade against the two
wires and then against the titanium shield. He pressed as hard
as he was able and then released the melting knife and saw
that his makeshift weld had held.

Mendenhall watched as Ryan stupidly looked his way and
smiled. Will shook his head as the wobbling naval pilot
swayed and almost fell over, but he managed to reach out and
push the Play button on the small device.

Collins and his men were almost out of ammunition, but it no
longer mattered. The sea was falling as if ten Niagara Falls had
opened up above them. The remains of the aqueduct rocked and
spun with the weight of the water striking it. The men could no
longer sustain their precarious hold on the high walls. The water washed them away.

Jack was under water for a hundred feet before he managed
to bob above the torrent. He knew that soon they would fly off
the broken end and smash into the ruins below.

The fall of seawater increased as more of the Crystal Dome
gave way and slammed into the trembling remains of the aqueduct. The pressure was so great that it spun the waterway on its
columns of stone. It rotated to the left and fell.

*   *   *

Everett and his SEALs were no closer to the Wave lines than they had been when he had started shooting. He jumped as men came screaming from their rear as he fed his last belt of ammunition into the M-60. He turned and saw that it was the fifteen marines of the mortar crew.

"Glad you boys could make it," he said.

"We're out of rounds, sir; thought you could use a hand."

Everett heard a tremendous stone-on-stone crack. He looked up in time to see the aqueduct turn to the left and collapse. Water was streaming from its broken end as it fell toward the centermost pyramid. He cursed, knowing that Jack had had it.

Collins and his fire team slid down the moss-covered stone as the aqueduct impacted with the largest of the three pyramids. The water that was carrying Jack and his men ran so fast that it spilled them down slippery sides As luck would have it, the aqueduct had collapsed and tilted just enough to slam against the pyramid, saving the team from a fall that would have crushed them all to death.

Collins found himself on a waterslide from hell as he careened down the stone pyramid. Water hit the bottom and splashed up so high that it covered Jack again as he hit the growing lake of water below. The Coalition men who had used the pyramids for cover were drowned and crushed.

Jack tried to fight his way to the surface as he was hit with the waterfall from high above. Giant stone blocks hit and narrowly missed him as he finally broke the surface of the building sea that covered the ruins.

Everett fired a few rounds and then ducked as return fire drove him backward. His team was down to twelve men. Ten were dead and the others had been wounded either by enemy fire or falling debris. The water was rising at an alarming rate, covering their legs.

Suddenly, Everett felt his head lighten, and he grabbed for the rock wall to steady himself. The feeling of lightness filled his head and he looked around him. The SEALs were as confused as he was. The sickness they had been feeling because of the Wave effect was now gone. The headache that Carl thought was robbing him of any sense he had to take control of the battle before him was also dwindling, and what had taken its place was something he couldn't begin to believe.

"What the hell?" he said.

" 'Sweet home Alabama,' " one of the SEALs said.

Suddenly, overpowering the sound of music in their heads was a scream from above, and Everett looked up. Coming down the lava hill in a headlong charge were fifteen marines.

"This has got to be the strangest day of my life," Carl said as he yelled for the SEALs to follow him. "Let's go blow something the fuck up!"

The SEALs charged in tandem with the marine assault.

Suddenly, from behind, the marine lieutenant and fifty other marines saw what was happening and followed suit. At once, the Coalition forces arrayed against them were caught off guard and a professional fighting force was coming at them screaming for blood, and the defenders panicked and started to break apart.

To the sounds of Lynyard Skynyrd's "Sweet Home Alabama" thumping in their ears, the U.S. Marine Corps, led by a navy captain from a department of the government no one had ever heard about, the Atlantis expeditionary force made their fanatical charge.

NEW YORK CITY

A million and a half people had fled to Central Park in the hope of dodging tons of falling glass and masonry. The ground was shaking so violently that most could not stand and were sitting and looking at the panicked people around them. The ground had split open in several areas and steam was rising from the wounded earth. In the distance, the buildings were caught in a warbling wave of displacement that made them appear to snake back and forth.

Without warning, the shaking stopped and the world became silent. People shook their heads in disbelief as the strains of the rock-and-roll song from the 1970s filled their ears. Those who were closest to the splits in the Central Park grass could have sworn that it was coming from the ground.

MEDITERRANEAN SEA
USS *CHEYENNE* (SSN 773)

The USS *Cheyenne* broke the surface of the reeling Mediterranean at the same time as the Russian Akula-class *Gephard* did. The waves washed over the two vessels and rocked them left to right. The captain didn't believe they would ever be able to see, much less rescue, any survivors. But he had his orders.

CHAPTER
TWENTY-ONE

ATLANTIS

Sarah lay on her back as Will Mendenhall and two of the marines tended to her wound. Will halfheartedly smiled as he pressed a bandage down hard onto her shoulder. The wound was far worse than he had first thought and he was kicking himself for having left her unattended for so long.

"Owwww," Sarah cried when Mendenhall placed most of his weight on her small body.

"Sorry, I—"

"Listen," Sarah said, almost in a dreamlike state. "Ryan did it . . . he did it, Will."

Mendenhall hadn't been paying attention because he had been dodging bullets and tending to her, but now he noticed that he did feel better physically. Gone were the nausea and headache. In their places was something he tried to ignore because he could swear it was coming from his dental fillings.

"Ah . . . I love this song," Sarah said as her eyelids fluttered.

Suddenly, Ryan thumped over the broken pedestal and landed against one of the marines after dodging machine-gun fire as he ran back to cover.

"God damn! I guess those assholes don't appreciate good

music," he said, smiling, and then he saw Sarah and her condition.

"Dammit, I didn't think it was that bad," he said as he took in the serious way Will was treating her.

"Listen, I know I'm not . . . doing too . . . good, and before Will caves in my chest . . . something is wrong—"

"Yeah, well, tell us about it later. I need you to—"

"Shut up! Remember, I outrank you by fourteen months," Sarah said as she tried to sit up. "Now listen . . . the ground is still shaking here. . . . The Wave must have destabilized the island's foundation. . . . or whatever Atlantis . . . landed on when it . . . sank. . . ."

Sarah closed her eyes as if she had fallen asleep.

"Oh, shit!" Will cried as he felt for her pulse. He finally found one on her neck but it was slow and weak. "Damn, she's losing too much blood. We need that marine medic over here," he said, trying to look around. Then he saw tracers fly over their position and he ducked back.

"I'll go. Stay put and keep her alive, buddy. I'll be back as soon as I find the medic."

Before Mendenhall could say anything, Ryan was gone. He heard the shift of Coalition fire as it found a new target.

He looked down at Sarah and saw her shallow breathing and the soaked-through pressure bandage covering her wound.

"Dammit, hang in there, girl!"

The surprise charge, coupled with the fact that before the attackers reached the floor of the city they felt a 100 percent better, caught the remaining Coalition forces off guard. They attempted to hold off the crazy charge, but one by one, and then in a flood, they ran for the Empirium Chamber, where they had seen Tomlinson and the few remaining board members take shelter. Buildings toppled around them and other debris took its toll, and by the time they arrived at the great bronze doors, there were only about five of the five hundred Coalition defenders remaining.

Everett waved the SEALs forward, where they finally had a clear a path to the power lines. The three two-foot-thick cables were clamped side by side and looked like small tree trunks. He stood guard over three SEALs as they laid the charges. As he did so, he saw a familiar face emerge from the gas and steam, followed by four marines. He watched as Jack steadied himself against the increasing movement of the city.

"How in the hell did you survive that little ride, Colonel?"

Collins had to bend at the waist and catch his breath. "I was just in a hurry to get down here and kill Ryan for stealing my Lynyard Skynyrd CD."

"I have a feeling that Sarah may have had something to do with that. Now let's hope that severing these power lines will get this place to stop shaking."

As the words were said, another loud crack was heard from high above as more of the Crystal Dome gave way, allowing more Niagara-size waterfalls to strike the western edge of the city.

"I don't think we have too much longer at this wonderful resort spot," Jack said as he straightened up. That was when he saw Ryan stumbling toward them.

"Colonel," he started to say.

"Good job over there. What made you—"

"Jack, it's Sarah; she took one in the shoulder. It's bad."

Collins kept his face neutral, but inside, his blood chilled.

Carl reacted first. "Medic!"

"Will's with her, but she's lost a lot of blood," Ryan said, out of breath.

"Go on, Jack, we've got this covered," Everett said as he placed his hand on Collins's shoulder and pushed a little.

"No. I saw some of the Coalition run into that Empirium Chamber—I want them."

"Jack—"

Collins turned and left the area at a run.

Everett knew that Jack didn't want to be there if Sarah died. After all the men under his command who had been lost through all the conflicts of his career, this was one casualty he knew would break him for good. Ryan grabbed the medic when he arrived and looked at Everett, who just closed his eyes

and nodded for him to go. Then he turned and saw the figure of
Jack Collins disappearing into the rising smoke and steam.

"Fire in the hole!"

Everett was grabbed by the SEAL lieutenant and pushed
behind a large piece of broken roadway just as the detonator
ignited twenty pounds of C-4. When the smoke and rubble
cleared away, they saw that the three power cables were shredded and dead.

But, as Everett watched, more water started cascading
from the high dome and the ground movement was increasing
in its intensity.

"We've had it," he said to himself. "Major, Lieutenant,
round up our men and meet at the edge of the dry lake bed—"

At that moment, a three-hundred-foot section of framework
holding the triangular crystal panels in place gave way to the
moving and crushing seabed above it, and the Mediterranean
started pouring in as the floodgates were now truly opened.

Atlantis lurched and shook as the tectonic plate could not
withstand any more, even though the Black Sea Wave had
been halted. The domino theory of the plates was close to becoming a fact that was about to destroy a city that it had failed
to crush fifteen thousand years before.

The final death throes of Atlantis had begun.

Tomlinson would not argue with Dame Lilith and Caretaker.
He knew that the only way out was the way in which the American assault force had come in to strike them unseen.

"They came through here someplace, they had to," he said
as he examined the flooring.

"Enough," Caretaker said.

Tomlinson heard the finality in the old man's tone and
looked up. He smiled when he saw the small .32-caliber pistol
pointed at him as part of the marble ceiling fell from high up.
It joined the debris of the ancient quake, and Tomlinson saw
that Caretaker couldn't have cared less about the danger of the
shaking earth.

"You have cost the Coalition everything. We shall never recover from this, no matter how much of the world's assets we

have arranged to hide. We will not attempt to survive this debacle. You will remain here with the rest of the Juliai Coalition."

Tomlinson stood stock-still and smiled more broadly than before. "Very noble; spoken like Caesar himself. But, old man, you and those cowards behind you may be defeated, but I am most assuredly not," he said as he looked beyond Caretaker's shoulder.

The old man's expression never changed as the knife caught him at the base of the skull and was twisted. His brain was immediately rendered useless and the pistol fell from his grip.

Dame Lilith finally saw the mercenary in the darkened chamber as he allowed Caretaker's body to slide from his hands to the broken marble floor.

"You may as well murder me, too," she shouted above the noise of the quake, and with all the dignity she could muster.

Tomlinson didn't even grace her with a response. He just nodded at the man who held the knife. The big merc, who had so elegantly slaughtered Special Agent William Monroe and his young wife in their home on Long Island, stepped forward and pushed the large knife into the center of Dame Lilith's chest until he felt the blade strike her backbone, and then he slowly withdrew it, watching as the life drained from her eyes. The three other Coalition members backed away from Lilith's assailant but were cut down with machine-gun fire by five remaining mercenaries standing behind the knife wielder.

"You and your men have just become some of the wealthiest soldiers in the history of the world, but for now we must find the passageway out of here, and quickly."

Will and the medic had to use a stretcher to get Sarah out of the dry lake bed. The bowl had filled to overflowing with seawater as the torrent continued. The pressure was starting to crack the dome and the seabed above them at an alarming rate.

Everett assisted with Sarah the last few feet while in the background a few of the remaining statues and monuments creaked and tumbled to the broken roads beneath them. A geyser of molten rock erupted were the Coalition excavation

had weakened the strata of the ancient lava dome that had protected the sunken city for millennia.

Some of the klieg lights started to short out and sparks flew
to join the flames in a strobelike effect that added a surrealis-
tic air to the situation, one that Everett knew they would not
get out of. With a look toward the Empirium Chamber, Carl
knelt by Sarah's side.

"How are you doing, shorty?" he asked, trying his best to
smile.

"I don't think it'll hurt . . . much longer," she said as her
lips turned down in pain.

Mendenhall looked away.

"No, I don't think it will," Everett answered with a wink as
he watched the medic get an IV line started with a bag of
blood plasma. Carl met his eyes and the medic shrugged.

"Where is . . . Jack?"

"Where he always is—off playing hero."

"Ass . . . hole," she commented weakly.

"That was a pretty good idea you had, about the CD inter-
fering with the Wave tones."

Sarah looked like she had finally passed out, but she
smiled. "Ryan . . . managed to . . . leave Jack's CD in . . . the
lake bed. He's going . . . to be . . . pissed."

"He'll get over it." Everett looked at Mendenhall and then
at Ryan. Both stood protectively over Sarah, shielding her
from falling debris and sparks from the open lava vents that
were springing up all over Atlantis. "Sarah, what's your best
guess as to the rest of the targets on the Coalition wish list?"

Her eyes fluttered open and she looked at Carl. "The pressure . . . of the plates have more . . . than . . . likely . . . played
themselves out. This . . . this wasn't dictated by the natural . . .
forces of . . . the planet." Sarah grimaced in pain for a moment
as the medic leaned down and injected her with a styrette of
morphine. "The earth knows when to let off steam, so . . . there
was nothing pushing it forward . . . other than the Wave . . . but
here, the old scar is reacting . . . trying to finish what was started
thousands of . . ." Sarah looked straight at Carl. "Where's Jack?"
She tried to get up.

"He'll be along; you know him," Everett answered as he eased her back down.

"Jesus!" Ryan said as he looked skyward as a tremendous roar filled the dome.

Everett watched as the entire top third of the dome give way just as the earth lurched under them. A waterfall larger than anything on the face of the earth flowed through the breach, and before the men could react they were up to their knees in water. Twenty of the young marines and six of the SEALs were crushed by iron frames falling from above. Everett reached down and plucked Sarah from the water and, along with her dangling IV bag, started running for the high ground at the back.

Then suddenly a loud wrenching noise sounded and the city leaped from the subterranean caves that supported it. Everett fell as the city tilted thirty degrees and the last of the buildings around them started to tumble.

"Start looking for anything that floats!" he ordered the remaining fifty marines. The survival instinct kicked in as Everett ran for the wall of ancient lava and started to climb to higher ground.

"Here!" Tomlinson shouted.

As the six mercenaries stopped their search and started over to where Tomlinson stood, the broken chamber erupted in automatic gunfire. Four of the Coalition mercenaries went down with bullet holes stitching their backs.

Jack Collins crouched in the doorway but had to move when another marble slab and its supporting beams crashed down right next to him.

Tomlinson was on the ground, shaking, near the hole in the floor that Jack and the others had come through less than an hour before.

"William Tomlinson?"

He couldn't believe that someone was calling him by name. He looked at the man who had wielded his knife so well in his service and gestured with his hand for him to get out there and kill whoever it was.

"Leave me alone! It's over!" he called out.

"No . . . not yet," Collins answered back in a monotone as he slowly crawled to a new position. He checked his MP-5 and decided that he didn't want it. He laid it down and pulled his Beretta from its holster. Then he pulled his body armor off and silently set it down.

"Who are . . . you?" Thomlinson asked, to get a bearing on where the man was hiding in the shadowy chamber.

"I'm the guy sent here to kill you," Jack said. Then he saw what he wanted. A thin shadow was playing across the marbled wall about fifty feet away. He looked around and finally realized that it was one of the remaining mercs who was squatting behind the stub of a broken pillar, so he moved slowly around a crushed bust of a long-dead patron of Atlantis to get into a better position. Another chunk of stone fell and narrowly missed his lowered body, but still he crept forward.

"You are just one, we are—"

A gunshot sounded with a flash of light in the chamber and Tomlinson let out a yelp.

"Now just two," Jack said as he watched the second-to-last mercenary slide over onto his side with a bullet hole in the side of his head, which had come from Jack ricocheting a round off the pillar to hit his target.

"Who are you?" Tomlinson shouted, gesturing at the same time for his last man to find out where their assailant was.

"You ordered my people killed at our warehouse in New York, and now I'm here to kill you."

Tomlinson rolled over onto his back. Now he realized that this was the man of whom Dahlia had sent the video when he and three others had arrived at the warehouse and again at the law offices. *That strange Group that calls the desert in Nevada home. . . . Jesus, who are these people?* he thought.

Tomlinson saw his man crouch deep into shadow, but he wasn't going to wait for the outcome of their confrontation because he had the distinct feeling that the man from the Group in the desert would undoubtedly win. He crawled silently toward the hole in the floor, pushing aside the skeletal remains of the

Atlantean he had been looking at earlier, and then slid inside and disappeared.

Jack was moving slowly, keeping his dark profile as low as he could. The noise problem was moot due to the crumbling of the city around them and the constant eruptions of the earth.

Before Jack knew what was happening, water flooded the broken chamber, inundating him and pushing him headlong into a smashed marble table. Then, before he could recover, a dark shape leaped from the shadows and fell upon him. Just before the man could plunge his knife into him, Collins threw up his knee and arrested the large man's momentum, giving himself time to slide from the tabletop. He came up but realized that he didn't have his gun any longer. The killer had gotten to his feet as water splashed high onto his legs as he advanced toward Jack. The man lunged, but Collins dipped and let his momentum carry him back until water completely covered him. He turned and tried to swim around the debris-strewn floor of the chamber.

The mercenary started forward. He could barely see his target as he came closer to the one remaining light stand in the chamber.

Collins knew that he was closing in on the subterranean entryway because he felt the rush of water increasing as it, too, fought to escape. As he pulled his way along, knowing that any second might be his last, his hand brushed up against a skeletal arm. Unknown to Jack, this was the body of the ancient Androlicus, the man who had let the once-powerful civilization of Atlantis slide away into myth and legend; he lay where he had fallen many thousands of years before. Clutched in his hand was the knife he had wished to use upon himself, but the cruel gods of his people had not allowed him that one last dignity. Jack snatched the up bronze weapon and rolled onto his back just as the shadow of the mercenary fell upon his submerged form.

As the man raised his hand to strike, Collins thrust his own hand out of the water and caught the large man in the crotch. He doubled over, and then Jack pulled the knife free and struck again, this time catching the man in the throat.

Collins surfaced, spiting salt water from his mouth, and found the man just staring at him. Then slowly he fell face-first into the water, dead. Collins kicked at the body and then stood. The sea had risen five feet in the two minutes he had been under the water. He looked around, knowing that his main target had gone through the tunnel entrance. The water was a swirling vortex where it filled the hole in the floor. As he watched, the suction it created tugged at his body, and that was when he let out a primal scream of rage, knowing that he could not pursue William Tomlinson.

As Jack turned and angrily made his way out of the chamber, the remainder of the Empirium started coming down around him. He ducked and ran as fast as the rough waters allowed, and then finally he dived through the broken bronze-covered doorway and into the nightmare of Atlantis.

Tomlinson was pushed down the stairs with the torrent of water. He had dislocated his left shoulder as he landed forty feet down on the winding stone staircase. The complete and utter darkness was terrifying to him; he had never before known the want of light or the touch of filth. He buried his hand in his shirt to support the shoulder and took two tentative steps down, where he saw a torrent of water exploding from its mix with lava. Tomlinson screamed and made his way back up the steps. He knew he would have to fight his way past the opening and that he would more than likely drown. He thought that anything was better than dying like this.

The water was fast rising to the crumbled tops of the marble and stone buildings. The earth cracked open and pushed up ancient material that had been buried underneath the domed section of the city when Atlantis had exploded long ago. A giant bronze statue of Venus rose from a gorge, spitting flame and lava. The magnificent moss- and mold-covered beauty rose until her original base was pushed through the surface by molten rock, and then like a tired old woman she slowly rolled onto her face and sank beneath the water, creating a tidal surge that rushed up to the lone lava wall.

As Jack swam toward the temporary safety of the rising lava bed, he felt the water becoming warmer by the stroke. The earthquake was a constant shaking that sent larger and larger pieces of the dome and the seabed that covered it tumbling down. He only hoped that they had stopped the same from happening to the entire world.

Out of the red-tinted darkness, hands reached out and dragged him onto the shaking but for the most part solid rock.

"Glad to see you, Jack," Everett said as he yanked Collins up by the collar.

Jack didn't respond as he tried to catch his breath.

"Come on, Sarah's over here."

Jack nodded and followed Everett up the incline to join the other survivors of Operation Backdoor, who were waiting for the inevitable end. The medic was sitting by Sarah as Mendenhall and Ryan knelt nearby. They stood as Collins approached.

Below them, the last of the light towers went under the water and Atlantis dimmed to an unearthly yellow-and-red glow. Lava bursts were erupting out of the fast-rising water and steam was clouding their view of the second destruction of the city.

Collins went to his knee and looked at Sarah, placing his hand on her cheek. Ryan, Mendenhall, and Everett made a semicircle as the medic moved off to the fifty-six others who awaited their fate.

"I ordered you to keep your ass down, Lieutenant."

Sarah's eyes remained closed as she was in the full embrace of the morphine injection. Her lips parted and she barely moved them, but Collins saw that she had said his name. Then she tried to smile but failed.

Collins leaned in close and for the first time wasn't self-conscious for doing so in front of others.

"I love you, little girl," he said into her ear.

She remained still, but he saw her lips moving again.

"I knew that . . . ass."

Collins swallowed and was about to say something when the entire city jumped on the seabed. Men were tossed like rag dolls onto the hard lava rise that was quickly becoming a beach.

"This is it," Everett said as the seabed above the dome

cracked and the crystal panes with it. The Mediterranean came in full force and they were all caught in the torrent.

Jack held on to Sarah as they were washed away into the tumult that was now like a glass bowl being filled with water. He was holding her up as he tried desperately to tread water, but he knew that her weight and his own would drag them down. He held her tight and kissed her cheek as an eruption of gas and water created a giant air bubble and they fell underneath the tumult, Jack holding Sarah for the last time.

Twenty of the marines and two of the remaining SEALs surfaced and were immediately crushed by the collapsing lava mount that had initially saved them. The rest tried to swim away from the now-exposed Crystal Dome, which the lava mount had been covering. Outside the crystal structure of the dome, the Mediterranean bubbled and boiled as the long-extinct volcano erupted with its original fury. The explosion was so massive that the seabed for three hundred miles broke free of the crust of the earth and trillions of tons of molten material started edging the ancient seabed toward the surface of the sea, two and a half miles up.

Everett pulled Ryan up, and he, Medenhall, and the SEAL lieutenant started to help marines stay afloat as the agitated waters swirled around them just as the final building sank below them.

Carl anxiously looked for Jack and Sarah, but they were nowhere to be seen. As he turned and looked through the dome's wall, he saw boiling lava rising up its side and then cooling to a solid mass before being overtaken by fresh material from the crust of the earth. He knew that the dome would totally collapse soon, and he hoped that their deaths would be as quick as Jack's and Sarah's.

USS *CHEYENNE* (SSN 773)

Captain Burgess had ordered his watch team below. The way the boat was rolling, he knew that some of his crew would go over the side and they would never stand a chance of recovering them. The admiral had finally broken through the extreme radio interference caused by the static electricity in the air and had ordered him to secure his boat below the surface. But he knew that he couldn't do that now, after the admiral had let it slip that the carrier was standing by to go back to Crete for survivors. He would not run while a surface ship stayed.

Captain Burgess scanned the roiling sea around the *Cheyenne* and smiled when his glasses picked up the rolling Russian submarine *Gephard*. He could see that her captain was the only one on the ship's sail, just as he himself was. Burgess raised his hand and was surprised when his Russian counterpart waved back.

"Son of a bitch, I guess he's just as crazy as me."

As a large wave crashed over the *Cheyenne*'s tall sail, Burgess ducked for cover. When he stood back up, he saw giant whirlpools around his boat. He saw steam vents rise like the towers of a great city, and the heated water was creating a fog system of its own. All he could think of was that the Mediterranean was getting ready to die and was giving out its last warning.

"Captain, conn."

Burgess held on to the tower with one hand and pressed the headphone into his ear and listened.

"Go ahead, conn," he said as another wave hit the *Cheyenne* and she shook and rolled hard to port, almost dislodging him and throwing him into the sea.

"Captain, sonar says they're picking up some very strange readings here."

"What in the hell are you talking about, Billy?"

"Sir, the operators say it's almost as if we are bottoming. The seafloor is rising, Captain."

Burgess had heard what his first officer said, but it took a moment to sink in.

"Goddammit, man, contact the *Gephard* and the *Iwo,* tell them to get the hell out of the area!"

"Captain?"

"Take her down to a hundred feet, order all ahead flank, make *Cheyenne* fly, Billy, fly! The damn seafloor is rising and we're right in the way!"

As Burgess made it to the hatch, the large Los Angeles–class attack boat started to sink beneath the large waves. At her stern, her single-scimitar-shaped propeller threw up a torrent of water as her hull came free of the sea. Then, in a matter of ten seconds, the *Cheyenne* was running for her life.

CHAPTER
TWENTY-TWO

Everett fought to stay afloat. The violence of the shaking had subsided and an unnatural rolling sensation hit them. They were only a hundred feet from the damaged top of the Crystal Dome and the whitewater foam was drawing near as the sea continued to flood the interior. The water was close to 150 degrees and Carl knew that if they didn't drown soon, they would be cooked, and he preferred drowning far and away over that.

"Stay together!" he shouted, but he knew they couldn't hear him any longer. Even if they floated through the giant hole in the dome, assuming that they could get past a trillion gallons of water flooding through, the pressure of the surrounding sea would crush them as if they were made of glass. But even that was preferable to being cooked to death.

"I really thought I would die flying," Ryan said as he and Mendenhall held on to each other as they kicked at the water to stay afloat.

"What, did you think we would get out of this mess?" Everett shouted back.

A curious look crossed Ryan's face as he spit out sulfur-tasting water.

"Well, yeah, I thought I would. Maybe not you and Will here, but I was thinking—"

"Thanks, buddy," Mendenhall said at his side.

Suddenly a dull light began filtering up from beneath the

water. Everett looked around and then ducked his head below the surface. He saw nothing but darkness and was at a loss as to where the light was coming from. He brought his head back to the surface and looked around. The water was only eight feet below the damaged top of the dome and the rushing water was starting to rip men apart, sending them in every direction. That was when he saw Jack and Sarah. Jack wasn't struggling like the others, just floating in the tossed waters with Sarah held tightly in his arms. Carl reached out and pulled him toward him and the others.

"Jack . . . Jack—"

Everett stopped when he saw that Collins's face was blank as he held Sarah close to his chest.

"Sarah?"

"She's dead," Jack said as he maintained his tight hold on her.

Instead of talking, Everett pulled both Jack and Sarah closer to him. Then he felt Mendenhall and Ryan helping to support the two. Carl looked into the serene face of Sarah McIntire and felt his own pain and loss return, and for a moment the specter of imminent death didn't seem so unjust. He looked from Sarah to Jack, and then he placed his arms around Will and Ryan as they were thrust under the floodgates of the broken dome.

An eruption the size of which the world had not seen for thousands of years blew out the recently formed lava mount that had taken the remains of Atlantis up with it. The volcano blowout made the eruption of Mount St. Helen's pale in comparison. Seismographs and Richter scales all around the world went crazy, casting a solid line across the numbers 18.9.

The explosion that was the final spasm of the Atlantean Wave, which had begun its devastating work over several millennia earlier. It shook the rising waters around the drowning men and they saw bubbling lava rising against the sides of the dome.

Everett knew that whatever the light was that was being cast in the dark waters around them, it wouldn't matter, because the end for them was only seconds away.

USS *CHEYENNE* (SSN 773)

The boat was shallowing and Burgess knew that if he didn't come to a stop he would rip the bottom out of her.

"Emergency stop! Sound the collision alarm!"

Throughout the *Cheyenne,* a loud squawking was heard as every man and woman reached for something substantial to hold on to. Around them they heard *Cheyenne* throw her engine into reverse to halt their forward momentum. The crew struggled to hang on, but many were thrown forward off their feet and onto the deck. As they tried to stand, they felt a powerful crunch from below the keel, and then suddenly the submarine rolled violently over onto her starboard beam. The lights blinked and then went out, soon to be replaced by the red-tinted emergency lighting.

"Captain, we've bottomed, but we're rising to the surface at sixty feet a second!" the first officer called out from sonar. "We're surfacing, Captain!"

USS *IWO JIMA*
FORTY-TWO MILES
WEST OF EPICENTER

The admiral couldn't believe what he was seeing through his binoculars. As the carrier's bow sank into a giant trough, the upper section of the great dome breached the surface of the Mediterranean. The sun, though partially obscured by the massive storm clouds that had formed, allowed in enough light to reveal the most amazing sight in the history of the planet.

Atlantis was rising from the sea.

As all the leaders in the world watched the live feed provided by the American KH-11 satellites, they couldn't believe what they were seeing. The great Crystal Dome had breached the surface of the sea and was rising at a rate that was unfathomable. They saw great statues that had survived the original destruction fifteen thousand years before rise beside the protective dome. The entire broken city was coming up after its long absence from the sunlight to a world that had never believed in its myth and legend.

Several statues lost their fight with gravity and fell into the churning sea. Large buildings that had remained upright caved in after their long submergence in the Mediterranean, and a giant pyramid next to the dome crumbled as if knocked over by the foot of an angry god.

Still the rising lava bubble beneath them continued to spread and grow, now encompassing sixteen square miles. The parts of Atlantis that hadn't been protected by the great dome but had once sat close-by rose with the new island. The great pressure of the sea had caved in the sides of the structure and it was now leaking huge torrents of pressurized water two and three hundred feet out from the dome as it continued to rise.

In Washington, Niles and the president watched with fascination as the great city rose once again, this time into the light of the modern world. From its vantage point high in space, the orbiting KH-11 Blackbird picked out the great center island that had once sat in the middle of the great ringed continent just as a giant pressure wave parted the clouds and allowed bright sunshine to strike the crystal for the first time, making it seem as though a diamond were surfacing in the middle of the Mediterranean.

Both submarines were caught on the lower edges of the crust. Three hundred feet above the stranded boats the dome rose.

The *Cheyenne* and the *Gephard* were but a mile apart and both found themselves in the middle of a cracked and damaged thoroughfare that had once upon a time been used for chariots and vendors of every sort. Around them, damaged buildings fell.

Captain Burgess opened the sail hatch and stared skyward at the great city. Atlantis rose above the *Cheyenne* like a magical kingdom that had suddenly sprung to life and come forth to breathe air for the first time in thousands of years.

* * *

Inside the dome, Everett couldn't believe what was happening. Bright sunlight had filled the interior and the water was slowly going down.

"Jack! Jack! The damn thing was pushed out of the sea by the eruptions!"

Collins shook his head as he still held Sarah and then looked up. His instincts came back with a sudden flash.

"Get the men up through the opening, Captain. Hurry! The water is leaking out of this thing—get them out!" he said as he pulled Sarah's body toward the sunlight coming through the torn opening at the top of the dome.

Around them the water was calming but still increasing in heat. On the sides of the now-exposed dome, great chunks of ancient seabed and lava rock from the original eruption were peeling away like the scabs off an old wound, and with it they were taking large plates of the thick crystal, and the water was starting to cascade from the interior at a rate that was drawing the water farther and farther from the top.

Three SEALS reached the breach first and climbed out onto the support frame of the crystal lenses. They immediately and hurriedly started hauling marines out one and two at a time as the water was falling away from them. Luckily, one of the SEALS had managed to hang on to fifty feet of nylon rope and was using that to haul the men out. Eventually Jack tied a rope to Sarah's body and it was lifted free of the water. Then he looked around and nodded for Ryan and Mendenhall to go.

"Feel that, Jack?" Everett asked.

"Yeah. Atlantis isn't destined to stay up; she's going back down, the new seabed can't support her weight."

Below them, large voids in the cooling lava started to explode like miniature nuclear weapons. Each one disintegrated thousands of yards of new land, the very base upon which Atlantis had risen. With a jerking reaction the new seafloor started to give way, and the City of Legend started to slip back into the sea.

Everett went up the rope that was now dangling thirty-five feet below the dome top. He hurriedly threw the rope back down for Jack, but instead of tying it around himself he tied it to the body of Major Esterbrook. Jack just couldn't leave the marine's body behind.

Far above, Everett wanted to scream at Collins, but he understood what he was doing. He was just afraid that if any more bodies floated by, Jack would try to get them, too.

Finally, the rope was lowered and Jack tied himself off. As he rose he saw another figure struggling in the falling level of the water. He couldn't believe his own eyes. William Tomlinson was fighting against the death that surrounded him as he stared up at Collins as he was pulled up. Jack felt no emotion as he was pulled out of the dome.

"I hope you can hold your breath, you bastard," he said to no one but himself.

USS *CHEYENNE* (SSN 773)

Burgess was just getting ready to abandon the sail when he got a call from the conn.

"Captain, we just received a flash message from National Command Authority, direct from the president."

"Jesus Christ, does he know we have a situation going on here?" he said into the squawk box.

"Yes, sir, they're watching it live. Sir, we have survivors being monitored from the satellite imagery; they're on the top of the dome."

"What?"

"National Command was wondering if we have room for some marines. *Gephard* is asking to stand by to assist after they get under way."

Suddenly the *Cheyenne* rocked as Atlantis started to sink at a faster rate. Giant waterspouts rose into the air as supporting air pockets beneath the newly formed lava bed exploded outward.

The crust beneath the ancient continent began to heal itself and was shrugging the weight of the city from it, taking it down as the crust collapsed into its new depth and position.

As the captain watched around him, the sea rushed back into the broken ruins of the city and rocked the submarine again in a violent rolling motion as water began to lift her keel from the rocky shoreline.

"Stand by to get under way. Headway only; we'll have to wait for the elevator to come to us."

Giant air bubbles, most the size of Manhattan, rose to the surface of the Mediterranean as the island began its descent to the bottom, almost four miles down. The survivors on the top of the dome were just happy to die outside instead of encased in a dead city at the bottom of the sea.

Everett knelt by Jack as he held Sarah in his arms. Her head rested on his chest as they slowly began their fall to the roiling ocean below.

"Hey, look at that!" Ryan yelled out.

As Everett and Jack turned their heads, four red flares rose into the sky, two from the southeast and two from the west. Then one of the SEALS who had ventured close to the extreme curvature of the dome called back to them.

"We have two subs down there, and boy do they look great!"

As huge explosions of sea and steam rose around them, every man, with the exception of Jack rose, to his feet and tried to balance himself on the rocking dome. The sea was getting closer and closer as Atlantis started to fall to the bottom as the lava and seabed beneath gave way hundreds of feet at time.

"Come on, Jack, time to get up. Let me have Sarah for a while," Everett said as he leaned over.

"No. I . . . I'll take her." Everett looked into Jack's eyes and saw an emptiness there that would haunt him forever. He knew then that Jack had never really cared for anyone as he had for Sarah.

"You got it, buddy." Everett helped Jack to his feet as water was now rushing at them from the interior of the dome and as it came over the curvature.

"There she is, Jack. We have to jump and swim for it."

At that moment, as if the great ghosts of the once-proud civilization had pulled one more magic trick out of their ancient bag of wonders, Atlantis stopped moving. It was as if a giant hand had reached out and held it in place for just enough time for the men to slide off and swim for the submarine that slowly made its way closer until its sonar dome struck the last of the crystal panes above the sea.

The *Cheyenne* crewmen were tossing ropes to the swimming men and even the *Gephard* had taken three from the sea already.

Collins watched as Sarah's body was placed on a stretcher and taken in through the divers trunk in the sail. Then a horn sounded.

"All stations, prepare to dive."

"Come on, Jack, let's go get some coffee and get the hell out of here."

"Look at that son of a bitch!" Mendenhall shouted.

As they all turned, several sailors shouted out that there was one more man in the water.

Jack's eyes widened and the fire that burned in them took the others by surprise as he stared at the flailing arm of William Tomlinson.

"Is that who I think it is?" Ryan asked as he was being pushed toward the hatch.

Collins immediately reached down for the rope. Everett tried to stop him, but Jack elbowed him as hard as he could and sent him sprawling.

"Sorry, swabby, this fish is mine," he said as he tossed Everett one end of the rope.

Collins dived into the water, narrowly escaping Mendenhall's last-second leap to try to stop him.

Jack swam out toward the dome as it suddenly started sliding beneath the surface; it was as if the gods of Atlantis had just pulled their reprieve of a moment before.

Captain Burgess appeared on the sail and ordered everyone below.

"Move it, damit! You think a ship creates suction when it goes down? Just think what this fucking thing is going to do!"

Everett angrily shook off the hands of the seamen trying to pull him into the hatch, and Mendenhall and Ryan went to his side. They were all watching as Jack caught up to Tomlinson, punched him once in the face to stop his struggling, and then started tying the rope around his waist, just under his arms.

"Now tie it on to yourself, damn you!" Everett screamed, swearing beneath his breath that he was going to kick Collins's ass as soon as they pulled him up.

The dome was close to going under when Jack pushed Tomlinson toward the *Cheyenne*. Then suddenly a great underwater eruption exploded out of the sea, covering Jack, Tomlinson, and the *Cheyenne* in a waterspout. Everett felt the bow of the sub being pulled down by the incalculable suction of Atlantis as it was pulled under the sea. When Carl looked, he couldn't see Collins or Tomlinson on the roiling surface.

"Damn you, Jack!" he screamed as he started pulling on the rope. Both Mendenhall and Ryan started pulling, too. Three seamen ran forward and waited for the two men to surface.

Captain Burgess watched as his sub was beginning to be pulled under. The water was washing around the deck and covering the remaining men outside up to their knees.

"Captain, we have a strange contact at two hundred feet and rising, coming on slow," the squawk box reported.

Burgess looked around and saw that the Russian sub *Gephard* had already submerged. "It must be the Russians, the only smart bastards around here today," he said as he anxiously turned back to the rescue.

"But, Captain, this contact is over seven hundred feet in length; we believe it to be a submarine."

"We can't deal with that now!"

"Captain, the submerged contact has now departed the area at . . . Jesus! At over seventy knots!"

Burgess ignored the obvious mistake from down in the conn and watched the effort below as they continued to be pulled under by the sinking island.

Everett and the others strained as they wrestled with the deadweight that was being pulled away from them by the sinking island. Finally, with one last tug, Tomlinson surfaced, screaming and spitting water. Blood coursed down from his fractured nose as he was pulled to the sub. As they pulled him up, Everett realized that Collins hadn't tied himself to the rope.

"Where's the colonel?" Ryan asked in near panic.

Mendenhall pushed past the sputtering Tomlinson and through the three seamen and had to be restrained by Everett.

"No," was all Will could utter as Everett pulled him away and then tuned him toward the hatch that was now flooding with water.

"Come on, Will," was all he could say as the younger man held on to him and went through the hatchway without a last look back.

Ryan did look back. "God, not both of them," he said as he slowly turned away and followed the last of his friends through the diving trunk and pulled the hatch closed and dogged it down tightly. Ryan leaned against the cold steel and placed his head in the crook of his arm until he thought he could control himself.

The *Cheyenne* slowly slipped under the rough seas and all that was left on the surface was emptiness.

The earth had stopped its convulsions and Thor's Hammer would never sound again.

The Ancients would forever lie quiet in their deep and dark abyss.

Everett was in the officers' wardroom, staring blankly at the cup of coffee the mess steward had brought in. Will was sitting across from him and Ryan was pacing. The SEAL lieutenant had excused himself, having detected the closeness of these people, and gone to for check on his men. What was left of them.

"I . . . I . . ." Everett started to say something and then couldn't finish.

The door to the officers' mess opened and the *Cheyenne's* pharmacist's mate knocked on the frame.

"Colonel Collins?"

Everett looked up and saw the man, but he was really looking right through him.

"He's . . . he's not here," Ryan said as he patted Will on the back and stepped up to the door.

"Well, uh, the lieutenant was asking for him," the young seaman said, looking at the three solemn men.

"Lieutenant? He just left here to check on his men," Everett said from his chair.

"Uh, no, sir, the woman officer—she was asking for a Colonel Collins."

"What in the hell are you talking about?" Everett said as he slowly stood up.

Will straightened at the long table and with moist eyes stared questioningly at the young sailor.

"The casualty that was brought aboard, sir—she's awake and asking for Colonel Collins."

Everett was through the door before the pharmacist's mate could move out of the way. He was unceremoniously shoved aside and watched in shock as Ryan and Mendenhall quickly followed.

Everett, Mendenhall, and Ryan stood over the small figure on the bed. The lights had been lowered and they could see the IV that was pumping O-negative blood into her tiny arm. There was an oxygen line running into her nose, held in place by a piece of tape. Her shoulder wound wasn't covered; the bullet hole was held open by four stainless steel clips. Her bleeding had stopped. Her hair was still damp but had been brushed back. She looked as weak as any person Everett or the others could remember ever having seen before.

The men were quiet as they watched the rise and fall of her chest. Everett turned to the senior hospital corpsman.

"She was dead. I . . . I felt no pulse at all," he whispered.

"Well, sir, that's what happens when you don't have any blood. No blood, no blood pressure. She was damn near bled out and that's why you felt no pulse." The corpsman wrote something down on her chart and then looked at Everett.

"She's a strong young lady. She'll make it. As soon as we can get her transferred to the *Iwo,* a doctor can take that bullet out of her shoulder."

"God," Mendenhall said as he stared down at Sarah, one of his only friends.

Everett waited until the corpsman had walked over and sat at his desk, then he leaned over and touched Sarah's cheek.

He pulled back when her eyes fluttered open. They stayed that way for a moment and then slowly closed.

"Where's . . . Jack? Did he . . . save the . . . world?" she asked weakly, her words slow and full of cotton.

"Yeah, Sarah, he did." Everett leaned over and whispered into her ear as Sarah slowly went back out. "Go back to sleep, we'll be here for you."

Mendenhall and Ryan lowered their heads, dreading the time when Sarah would have to be told about Jack.

"Yeah," Everett said as he straightened. "He saved the world."

EPILOGUE
The Last of the Ancients

EVENT GROUP CENTER
NELLIS AIR FORCE BASE, NEVADA

Niles Compton walked slowly beside the president of the United States. The commander in chief looked far older than his fifty-two years. He walked with his hands behind his back. His Secret Service detail was nowhere to be seen, having been left behind in Niles's outer office. The president had decided that if he couldn't be safe here, he wouldn't be anywhere.

"I'll always have doubts about the moves I made. How many lives did I cost in the end by not acting decisively?"

Niles didn't answer at first; he just looked straight ahead at the long and curving corridor of level seventeen. Alice Hamilton and Virginia Pollock were ten steps behind and didn't hear the president's concern.

"I think you have to judge yourself just how many people you saved. To look at these things any other way is nonconstructive."

"Not exactly a ringing endorsement."

Niles shrugged and then looked at his old friend. "The world has changed, but we get no wiser. We always expect our enemies to be easily identifiable and never, ever one of our own kind. The most dangerous enemy is the one who thinks like we do, has the same dreams of controlling those people who we think are below us, when in fact . . ." Niles paused. "You did the best anyone could have done, and I now believe the world is a more trusting place today because you took the time to prove an innocence when others wouldn't listen. Now you have a leg up in the area of credibility, and in this world, Jim, that counts for a lot."

Niles came to a door with a marine corporal standing guard outside. The back letters on the door read CONTAINMENT.

"And now your opinion on these two," the president asked.

Niles nodded for the guard to unlock the door.

"My opinion is that we can learn a lot from them. But I also believe they are traitors to their country, traitors to the peace they claimed to embrace. They and their kind knew all there was to know about the Juliai Coalition for over two thousand years, and yet they remained silent through their arrogance. You and I lost a lot of good people because this group was allowed to flourish, and they were a part of that. No matter how noble their intentions."

The door opened and Niles stepped across the threshold and froze. The president saw the director's shoulders sag he looked into the simply furnished two-room containment apartment.

"What is the—"

The words froze in the president's mouth as he saw what Niles was staring at. Carmichael Rothman and Martha Laughlin sat peacefully on the small couch. Her head rested on his left shoulder and they looked as if they were sleeping. On the small table before them was Carmichael's medication for his cancer. The bottle was on its side and the morphine was gone.

Niles walked into the room and felt the wrists of both Ancients and found no pulse on either. He picked up the note that lay beside the empty bottle and read it and then handed it to the president.

"*Guilty,*" it said.

Niles walked to a small chair and sat down and rubbed his hands over his face.

The president looked at the old couple with a curious look

on his face. Then he put the note back down beside the bottle and shook his head.

"All their knowledge and wisdom . . . they couldn't have found a better way to atone for their silence?"

Niles looked up. "People of their intelligence have a terminal disease. It's called lack of imagination. No," he said, standing and walking to the door. "In their minds, they had no other way to go, and that's why their kind is now extinct."

The president watched Niles turn at the door.

"The way it was always meant to be."

PACIFIC OCEAN
200 MILES EAST OF JAPAN

Major General Ton Shi Quang, former commander of the People's Army, was dressed appropriately in a white silk shirt and white muslin pants as he drank ice tea on the fantail of a two-hundred-foot yacht owned by one of William Tomlinson's corporations. The crew members had orders to take it slow and easy during their trip to Taiwan, where Shi Quang would receive his reward for loyal service to the Juliai Coalition.

His escape from Korea had been planned well in advance of his treasonous actions and he had left the coastal waters on a fishing boat for his rendezvous in the Sea of Japan. He knew that at this very moment he was one of the most hunted men in the world; but with what he earned, he would find no difficulty at all in vanishing into a broken world still reeling from the Coalition's strike. The reward offered by America for his capture was insulting for a man of his stature and very much a useless gesture on their part.

A waiter brought him a fresh glass of ice tea and then walked to the galley entrance of the luxurious yacht. After placing the tray just inside the doorway, he suddenly turned and walked briskly to the streamlined bow of the ship, where he met members of the crew.

The waiter placed a small, portable beacon on the bow of the ship and then gestured for the men to get over the side of the yacht.

The captain stepped from the well-appointed bridge and yelled down, asking what in the hell they thought they were doing. It was too late; the fifteen crew members had started the small outboard and were already fifty feet away. That was when the captain heard the roar of aircraft overhead.

The general squinted into the sun-filled sky. He never saw death as it struck seconds later. Two American-made AMM-RAM missiles smashed into the $22 million yacht and blew it to pieces.

Pulling up and out of their attack run, two U.S. Navy Super Hornets from the carrier USS *Roosevelt* screamed back into the skies.

The judge and jury, consisting of five hundred dead U.S. sailors, had rendered their verdict against Major General Ton Shi Quang.

FBI BUILDING
WASHINGTON, D.C.

William Tomlinson and the woman code-named Dahlia sat in the small room. Tomlinson was wide-eyed and had not said a word since being placed in the room next to his former assassin.

Carl Everett walked into the room, followed by Mendenhall and Ryan. They stood with the door open but did not move, with the exception of Everett, who pulled something from his pocket and placed it on the table in front of the two handcuffed prisoners. Then he stood stock-still and waited.

Thirty seconds later, the president of the United States entered the room and sat across from the two Coalitionists. He stared at them for a full fifteen seconds.

"I believe you signed a document that pardoned me from any crime I may have committed in return for the cooperation I gave your people," Dahlia said when she realized that Tomlinson was content just to sit and stare.

The president did not say a word in response. He just pulled out a set of notes he had written. He adjusted the cell phone that Everett had placed on the table to make sure every word was heard.

"William Tomlinson and Loraine Matheson, AKA Dahlia, you are being charged with treason and crimes against humanity. As president of the United States, acting at a time of war, you are hereby sentenced to death. Said sentence will be carried out in two days at Leavenworth Federal Penitentiary."

The president started to rise, but stopped when Dahlia shook her head.

"You can't do this. We . . . I demand a trial under the laws of the Constitution!"

The president looked closely at the woman, then his eyes darted to Tomlinson, who was now aware of where he was and looking at Dahlia. Tomlinson shook his head.

"Power is the ability to be ruthless," he mumbled.

"Correct, Mr. Tomlinson. If the world finds out that I broke the law by hanging you, so be it, I can live with that."

The president stood and left the room.

"The man that saved your worthless life died. He would not have favored the actions of the president, because he was the most just man I ever knew. I know this because in a very short time he became my best friend," Everett said as he leaned on the table. "But one thing my friend never understood—that sometimes bad people need to end badly. You will, at the end of a rope."

Everett straightened, retrieved the cell phone, and started from the room, but then he stopped and faced the two Coalitionists one last time.

"I am not like my best friend, as much as I want to be. As much as I strive to be just like him. I know that I will sleep well with the knowledge you two will burn in hell for the millions you have killed."

Everett stopped outside in the hallway with Will and Ryan watching him. He raised the cell phone to his ear and spoke.

"You get some rest. It's all over. We'll be home soon."

Carl closed the cell phone and tossed it to Ryan, who

caught it and then followed Everett and Mendenhall down the hallway.

Three thousand miles away, Niles Compton easily removed the phone from Sarah McIntire's weak grip, then he slowly closed it and placed it on her nightstand.

Then Sarah rolled over onto her right side and cried for the first time over the loss of Jack Collins.

Outside the closed door of Sarah's room, the Event Group went on.

Read on for an excerpt
from David Lynn Golemon's next book

LEVIATHAN

Now available from St. Martin's Paperbacks

SEVENTY-FIVE MILES OFF THE COAST OF VENEZUELA

The aged supertanker *Goliath* made her way slowly along the Venezuelan coast, her empty oil bunkers allowing the VLCC (Very Large Crude Carrier) to ride high, well above her loaded waterline. The newly constructed crude depot at Caracas waited to load her with its inaugural shipment of refined oil from the controversial facility. The many construction short-cuts and current unrest of union oil workers allowed a pall of contention and outright anger to hover over the plant's ceremonial opening.

The Panamanian-flagged *Goliath* was no stranger to controversy herself as she plied her way toward port. The old and decrepit tanker was a constant thorn in the side of most nations and oil companies, as her deteriorating double-hulled design was continually leaking her wares into the open sea. It was only the recently rogue nation of Venezuela that kept the supertanker viable and in business, as the other exporting nations shunned her almost to the scrap heap.

A mile to her stern was her ever-present Greenpeace escort, *Atlantic Avenger*, out of Perth, Australia. She shadowed *Goliath*, taking water samples and harassing the great vessel whenever she could. The Chinese diesel-powered attack submarine *Red*

Banner shadowed both vessels at one kilometer away, far beneath the sea. The communist Chinese government was taking massive, and some would say illegal, steps to ensure *Goliath* made her delivery date in the next few weeks as the oil-poor superpower sought desperately to feed her ever-expanding industrial might.

On the bridge of *Goliath*, Captain Lars Petersen scanned the waters just to the south. The tell-tale wake of a submarine periscope was cutting a wide and intentionally arrogant path through the Atlantic as the Chinese made their presence known to the activist ship shadowing them. He smiled and then walked out onto the bridge wing and scanned his binoculars to the south and west.

The *Atlantic Avenger* was starting to make her hourly run toward the stern of the giant ship. They would pass close to the supertanker, filming the leakage of her bunkers and holding up their protest banners, stating his vessel was the scourge of the sea.

"We have surface contact bearing 1-3-8 degrees. Contact is possible Venezuelan Navy escort vessel."

Captain Petersen took one last look at the one-hundred-foot Greenpeace ship and then turned to his first officer.

"Our friends are starting their harassment run. Watch them and make sure they keep the proper safety distance."

"Aye, Captain."

Petersen stepped into the giant bridge of the *Goliath* and scanned the horizon. He finally spied the vessel in question, and he could see by her silhouette it was their old friend, the *General Santiago*, a small missile frigate formerly belonging to the French navy and then sold to Venezuela five years before.

"I have visual contact—send to *General Santiago*, welcome and to please take up station to our starboard beam. Inform them we have a friendly submerged contact bearing one kilometer astern."

"Aye, sir."

Petersen was about to walk out onto the bridge wing and view the Greenpeace run on his ship when a sudden, piercingly loud alarm warning sounded.

"We have a submerged contact bearing 0-1-9 at two thousand yards. This is a hard contact, we wouldn't have heard it, but—oh, my God—someone is opening torpedo tubes to the sea!"

"What?" Petersen was taken aback by the sudden, stunning announcement.

"We have high speed noises, possible torpedoes in the water!"

The captain froze in abject horror. His first officer called out he had a visual on the spot of contact, but Petersen just stood frozen to the deck.

"Torpedoes?" was all he could get out of his frozen throat.

PEOPLE'S REPUBLIC OF CHINA
SUBMARINE RED BANNER

"What do you mean torpedoes?" Captain Xian Jiang asked loudly as he picked up a set of headphones at the sonar station and listened.

The high-pitched sound was nothing like the turning propellers of any high-speed torpedo he had ever heard. His sonar man was saying something about the new quieter airjet–powered weapons the Americans had been working on, instead of listening; he slammed his fist down on the operator's shoulder to quiet him. He heard the sound of the approaching weapons when a loud pop sounded in the headphones.

"More torpedoes in the water!" the operator called out. "They are actively seeking and are bearing right on us!"

"Distance?" Xian shouted.

"Three hundred yards—closing fast!"

"Impossible, nothing could have gotten that close without being detected."

"Sir, nonetheless, we are under attack. The weapons went active as soon as they hit the water—torpedoes have acquired!"

"All-ahead flank, hard left rudder! Weapons officer, match bearing on the attack line and fire! Countermeasures launch a full spread!"

The torpedoes struck almost simultaneously at the stern

and under her keel amidships. The immense pressure wave cracked the Chinese hull like an eggshell and crushed all aboard in a microsecond.

SUPERTANKER *GOLIATH*

Petersen finally caught sight of the two fast-approaching torpedoes that had suddenly popped toward the surface. As he watched in absolute horror, he saw in surreal slow motion the Greenpeace vessel *Atlantic Avenger* innocently and unknowingly swing her razor-sharp bow into the oncoming path of the outside weapon. The torpedo struck, blowing her beautifully painted bow off in a violent explosion that shook the giant oil tanker.

Petersen now had a slim hope that the remaining weapon would not be enough to hurt his massive ship. As he grasped on to that lone shred of hope, a sudden explosion to the south sent water upward in to a plume of white foam and violence that announced that two subsurface-to-surface missiles were launched just as the errant torpedo had been sent into the wrong ship. First one, then the other missile arched into the blue sky. As one missile kept climbing, the other turned down and to the north as it streaked far ahead of the water-bound torpedo. The missile slammed into *Goliath* at her stern, ripping free her rudder and sending men sprawling to her elongated deck.

Petersen tried to pick himself up off the deck as the ship was rocked again, this time from a distance as the second missile found its mark and slammed into the afterdeck of the guided missile frigate, *General Santiago,* two miles away.

Who could be doing this? His mind raged as he reached for the sill lining the front windows of the bridge. Could it be the Americans, the Russians? They were the only two nations capable of such stealth and weaponry. The captain finally managed to gain his feet and look out onto the expanding horror that was *Goliath*'s foredeck. Fires were raging and he could see the giant ship was starting to list severely to starboard.

"Mr. Jansen, counter flood, goddamn it, counter flood the port bunkers!"

"More missiles in the air!" someone screamed.

As Petersen looked on in shock, six separate trails of fire exited the sea. Four streaked to the west and gained altitude, and two came directly at them. He managed a quick glance down at *Atlantic Avenger* just as she started to slide bow-first into the green sea as crew and protesters were sliding and jumping from her decks. He closed his eyes in a silent prayer for them as the next two missiles found their mark, driving deep into the superstructure of the tanker.

CITGO CRUDE OIL FACILITY
CARACAS, VENEZUELA

The newly constructed crude oil facility, owned and operated by the Citgo Oil concern, was a monstrosity that had displaced seventy-five thousand impoverished inhabitants in the suburbs of Caracas. Outside of her main gates, six hundred of these citizens stood side by side with five hundred union workers protesting the Venezuelan government's recent treatment of them and for nationalizing the oil industry, thus tossing the unions into oblivion.

The CEO of Citgo Oil and the National Interior Minister of Venezuela shook hands, smiling broadly. The latter was there in place of President-for-life Hugo Chavez, a sworn enemy of the very democracies that had helped them in their national oil exploration treaties a decade before. Even after the threat that had been passed on by the president of the United States, Chavez still held firm that nothing, or no one, would stand in the way of his achieving an international power base and a strategic partner in China for his oil products. He even had announced plans for expanding into the Gulf of Mexico—an area that was quickly becoming a hot spot for environmentalists.

The interior minister was about to take the microphone to denounce the unpatriotic actions of the protesters outside the gates, when air raid sirens began to blare loudly around the new facility. The Venezuelan minister looked around in confusion, the smile still stretched across his dark features, when three security men jumped upon the stage, took him by the arm, and then moved him off the raised platform. The Chinese representative looked on in confusion, as did his Cuban counterpart. Then another set of military police appeared and harshly pulled the two diplomats to their feet.

"What is the meaning of this?" the Cuban minister cried out in Spanish as he was pulled unceremoniously from the dais.

"We have an air force warning of incoming cruise missiles, please come with us, we have to—"

That was as far as the military security guard explanation got, as the sound of four shrieking missiles froze everyone inside and outside the oil facility.

"Look," the Chinese minister shouted as he pointed skyward.

As they turned, they saw the distinctive vapor trails of four missiles as they crossed over dry ground on their trek inland from the sea. The first missile dipped and came apart just over the crude-oil loading facility. A nuclear airburst set to detonate at three hundred feet vaporized the docks and pipeline that carried crude from the plant to the ocean-side loading facility. The next three missiles traveled one, two, and three miles inland and then detonated over the two-mile-wide plant itself. The fireball created by the simultaneous detonations in the yield range of 5.5 megatons each, a relatively light package by military standards, that melted steel and flash-fried human flesh as the brand-new and controversial facility along with everyone present ceased to exist in the blink of an eye. The weapons did not differentiate protester from government lackey, as all were instantly vaporized in a microsecond of heat and wind.

EVENT GROUP COMPLEX
NELLIS AIR FORCE BASE, NEVADA

Director Niles Compton sat with the sixteen departmental heads of the Event Group and silently watched a briefing delivered to the president of the United States by his national security team from the White House. The council there did not know the Event Group was listening in.

Admiral Fuqua, the naval chief of staff, opened a file folder and cleared his throat as if he were uncomfortable with what he was about to say.

"The detonations at sea against the oil tanker, the Greenpeace vessel, and the Chinese attack submarine were nuclear in nature. The yield of each weapon was estimated at only 5.6 kilotons. As with the warheads detonated over Caracas, the radiation yield was almost non-existent. These were the cleanest weapons we have ever come across. Dissipation occurred only hours after the attacks, and there are no lingering effects to air, ground, or sea."

"That's impossible," ventured the president's National Security Adviser. "No one has weapons that clean, we would have—"

"Andy, what have the boys across the river come up with as far as where this nuclear material originated?" the president asked of CIA Director Andrew Cummings.

"Well, sir, the samples we received from our naval asset in the area and sent to us by courier supports no conclusions as to where this material was bred; it only raises more questions."

"Come on, Andy, I'm not going to hold you to it, give me what your people are thinking."

"We have nothing on record as far as a nuclear fingerprint goes. This material may have been spawned by a breeder reactor that has not been identified."

"Again, that's impossible; the Nuclear Regulatory Commission has—"

"Damn it," the president slammed his palm down on the tabletop, cutting his security adviser short once more. "I think everyone in this room better have learned by now that there are people out there we know nothing about. The Atlantis incident should have taught you that. Assume we have someone out there that can toss clean nukes around. Let's concentrate on finding out who and why, not the impossibility of it," the president said angrily. "General Caulfield, Admiral Fuqua, best guess, who could have done this?"

"Ladies and gentlemen, with the exception of the directors

of CIA, FBI, NSA, the Secretary of Defense, and the National Security Advisor, and the Joint Chiefs, would you please excuse us? Mr. President, I don't know who's on the other end of that camera, but I advise shutting it down," General Caulfield said, suspecting that the answer lay in the strange little man who had assisted in the Atlantis operation a few weeks before and was part of the president's private think-tank.

"I'll leave it on for now, Ken. With the exception of those named, please excuse us."

The rest of the cabinet and council filed quickly from the room.

When the room cleared, Caulfield nodded toward Admiral Fuqua who stood and pulled down a viewing screen as the lights dimmed.

"Mr. President, we have information we received from the attack boat USS *Columbia*, one of our newest Los Angeles Class subs. She is the asset I spoke of earlier. She may have picked up a glimmer of something else, maybe the attacking force, we're not sure. As you see, this is a tape of her sonar."

On the screen was the waterfall display from the BQQ passive sonar display on *Columbia*. It was a series of lines running downward on the screen, and those lines represented the water around the sub. As they watched, there was nothing out of the ordinary on the display screen. Then a shadow of darkness presented itself for a split second and vanished.

"This object was thought at first to be a glitch in the sonar, but we have learned the object was solid, and we caught it only because of the burst of speed it displayed when it started diving away from the attack area. It's three and a half miles off *Columbia*'s bow. The estimate of its size is close to a thousand feet in length, and it went from a static, or zero buoyancy, position to over seventy knots."

Several men started speaking at once while the president sat in his chair looking at the sonar display.

"This object was verified by a depth chart graph that showed the keel of *Columbia* raised eight feet in depth as whatever this thing is passed beneath her—and that is substantiated. So with this strange blip on sonar, coupled with the massive water displacement, there's little doubt we have one hell of a problem out there."